SONIC™

THE HEDGEHOG

BATTLE FOR
THE EMPIRE

SEGA®

@IDWpublishing
IDWpublishing.com

Cover Art by
Nathalie Fourdraine

Series Edits by
David Mariotte
and **Riley Farmer**

Collection Edits by
Alonzo Simon

Collection Goup Editor
Kris Simon

Collection Design by
Shawn Lee

ISBN: 978-1-68405-953-9
26 25 24 23
1 2 3 4

Originally published as SONIC THE HEDGEHOG issues
#50–51, SONIC THE HEDGEHOG FREE COMIC BOOK DAY
2022, and SONIC THE HEDGEHOG ANNUAL 2022.

Nachie Marsham, Publisher
Blake Kobashigawa, SVP Sales, Marketing & Strategy
Mark Doyle, VP Editorial & Creative Strategy
Tara McCrillis, VP Publishing Operations
Anna Morrow, VP Marketing & Publicity
Alex Hargett, VP Sales
Jamie S. Rich, Executive Editorial Director
Scott Dunbier, Director, Special Projects
Greg Gustin, Sr. Director, Content Strategy
Kevin Schwoer, Sr. Director of Talent Relations
Lauren LePera, Sr. Managing Editor
Keith Davidsen, Director, Marketing & PR
Topher Alford, Sr. Digital Marketing Manager
Patrick O'Connell, Sr. Manager, Direct Market Sales
Shauna Monteforte, Sr. Director of Manufacturing Operations
Greg Foreman, Director DTC Sales & Operations
Nathan Widick, Director of Design
Neil Uyetake, Sr. Art Director, Design & Production
Shawn Lee, Art Director, Design & Production
Jack Rivera, Art Director, Marketing

Ted Adams and Robbie Robbins, IDW Founders

Special thanks to Mai Kiyotaki, Michael Cisneros, Sandra Jo, Sonic Team,
and everyone at Sega for their invaluable assistance.

For international rights, contact licensing@idwpublishing.com

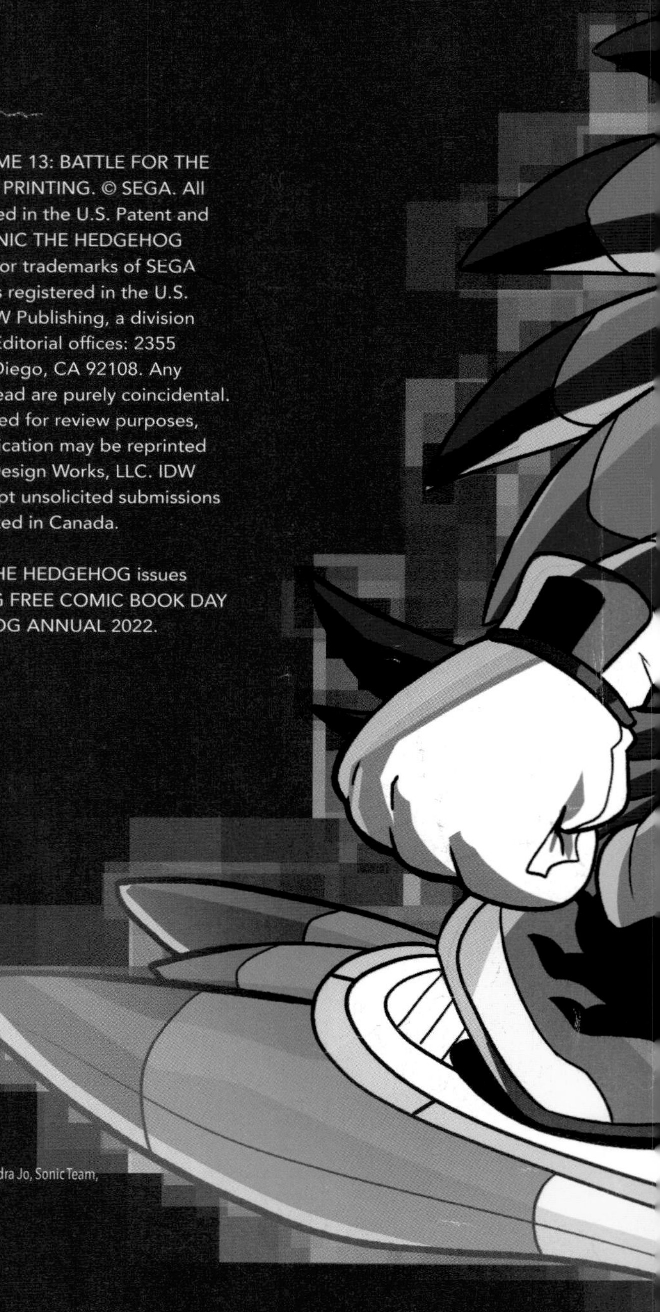

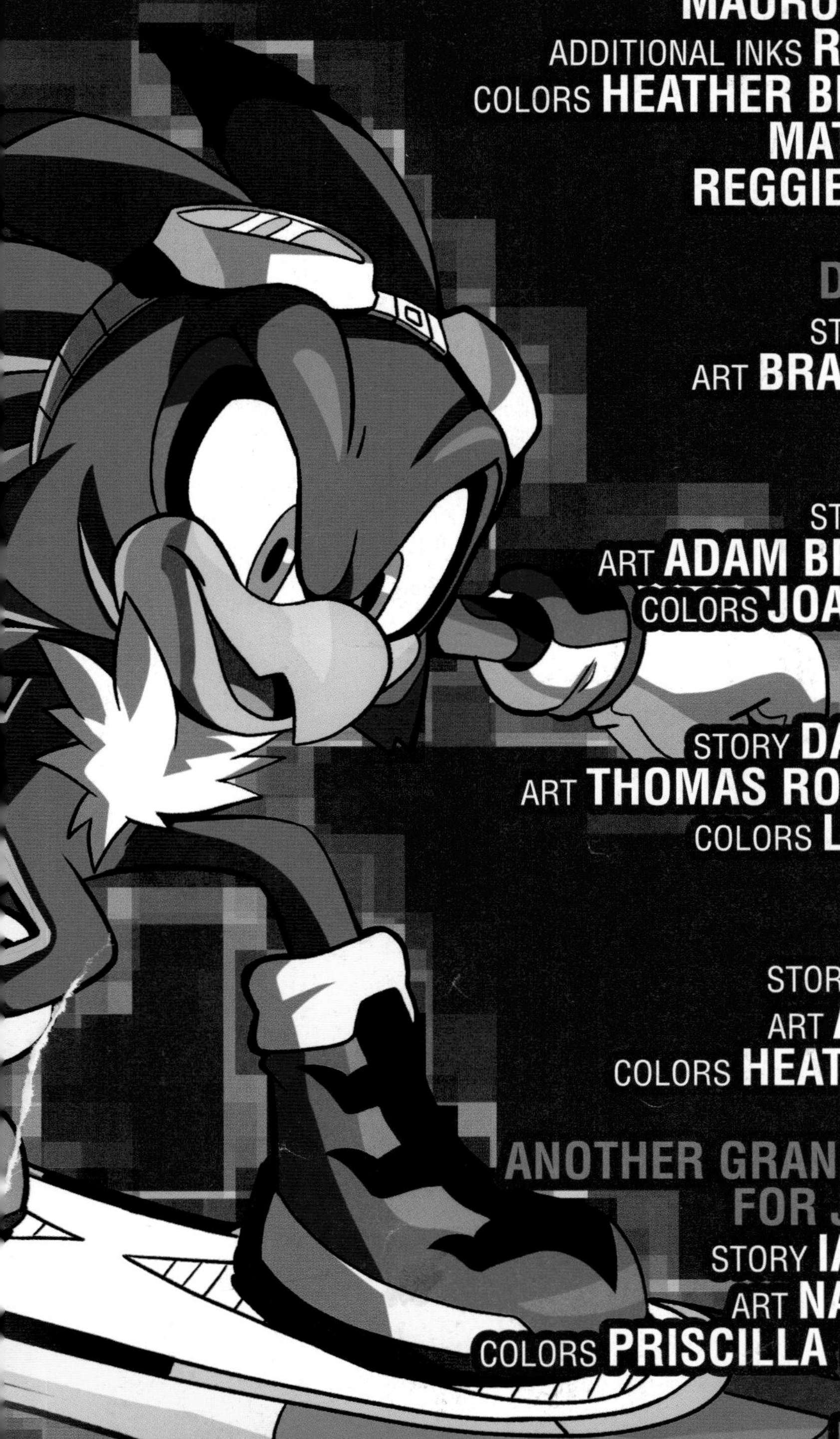

#50–51
STORY **IAN FLYNN**
ART **ADAM BRYCE THOMAS** (#50–51)
MAURO FONSECA (#51)
ADDITIONAL INKS **RICK MACK** (#51)
COLORS **HEATHER BRECKEL** (#50–51)
MATT HERMS (#50)
REGGIE GRAHAM (#50)

DEEP TROUBLE
STORY **IAN FLYNN**
ART **BRACARDI CURRY**

GUARDIANS
STORY **IAN FLYNN**
ART **ADAM BRYCE THOMAS**
COLORS **JOANA LAFUENTE**

WEAPONS
STORY **DANIEL BARNES**
ART **THOMAS ROTHLISBERGER**
COLORS **LEONARDO ITO**

HERO CAMP
STORY **INDIA SWIFT**
ART **ABBY BULMER**
COLORS **HEATHER BRECKEL**

ANOTHER GRAND ADVENTURE FOR JET THE HAWK
STORY **IAN MUTCHLER**
ART **NATALIE HAINES**
COLORS **PRISCILLA TRAMONTANO**

ROUGH PATCH
STORY & ART **AARON HAMMERSTROM**
COLORS **VALENTINA PINTO**

LETTERS **SHAWN LEE**

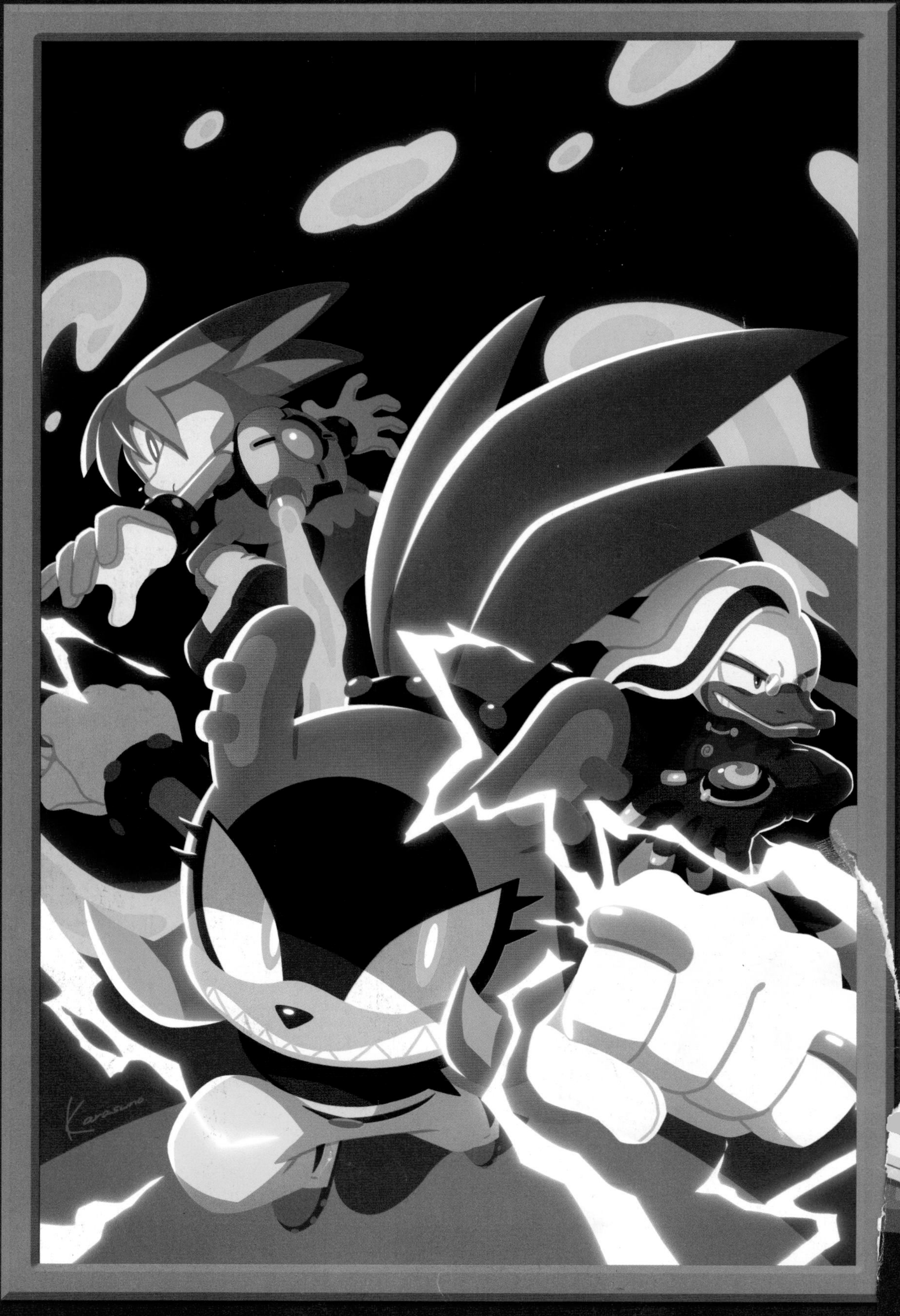
Karasuno

ART BY **YUI KARASUNO** OF SONIC TEAM

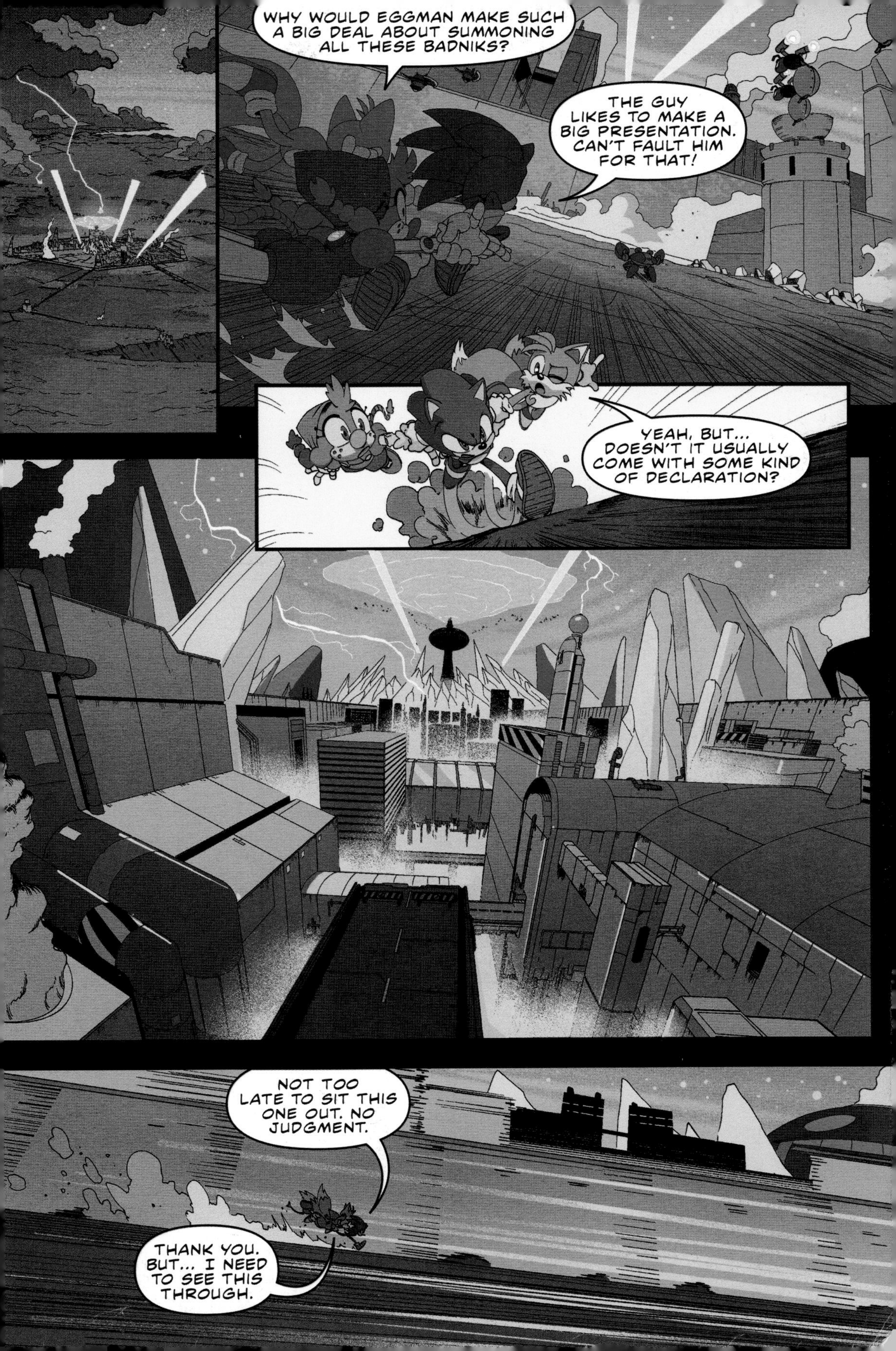

WHY WOULD EGGMAN MAKE SUCH A BIG DEAL ABOUT SUMMONING ALL THESE BADNIKS?
THE GUY LIKES TO MAKE A BIG PRESENTATION. CAN'T FAULT HIM FOR THAT!
YEAH, BUT... DOESN'T IT USUALLY COME WITH SOME KIND OF DECLARATION?
NOT TOO LATE TO SIT THIS ONE OUT. NO JUDGMENT.
THANK YOU. BUT... I NEED TO SEE THIS THROUGH.

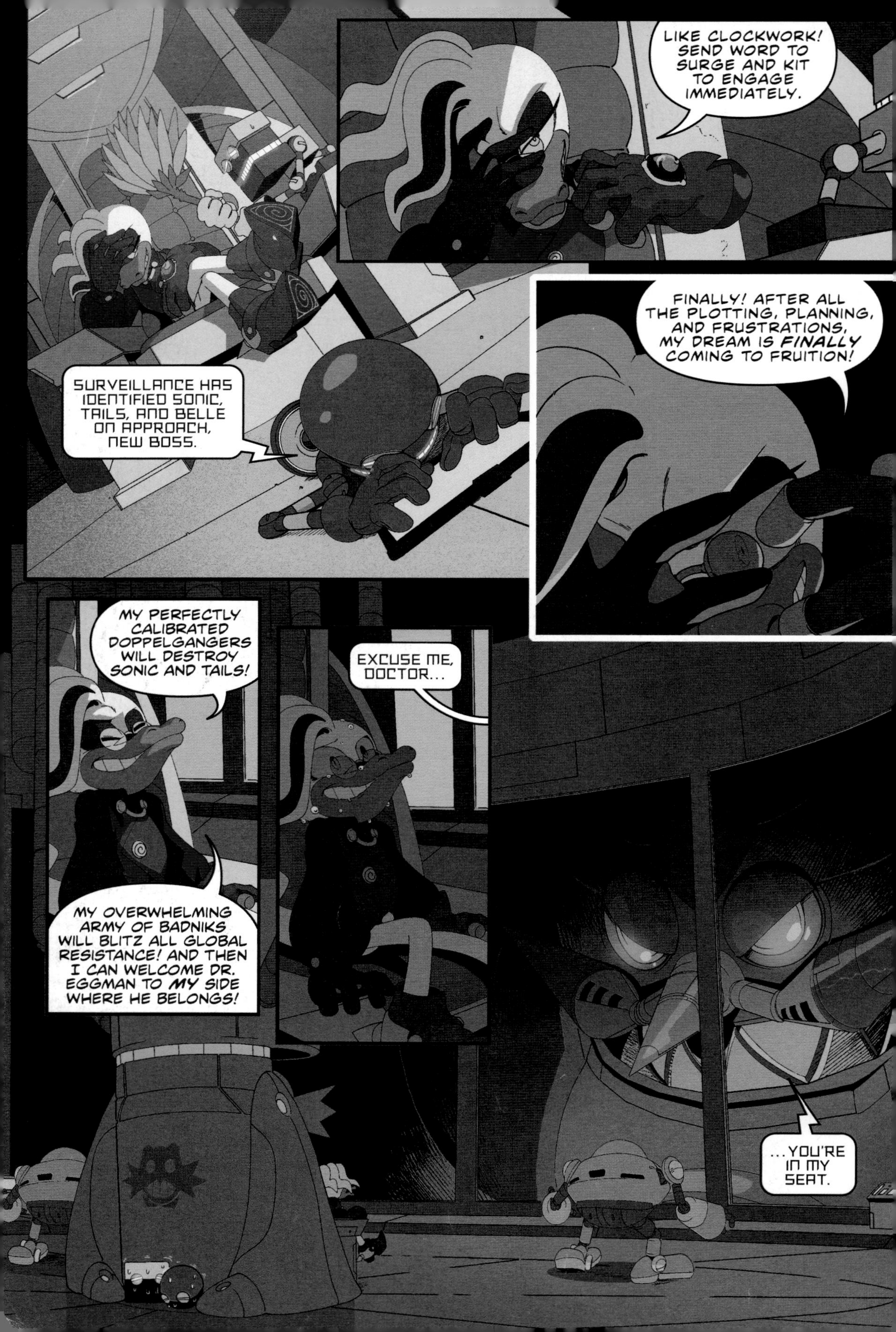
LIKE CLOCKWORK! SEND WORD TO SURGE AND KIT TO ENGAGE IMMEDIATELY.
SURVEILLANCE HAS IDENTIFIED SONIC, TAILS, AND BELLE ON APPROACH, NEW BOSS.
FINALLY! AFTER ALL THE PLOTTING, PLANNING, AND FRUSTRATIONS, MY DREAM IS FINALLY COMING TO FRUITION!
MY PERFECTLY CALIBRATED DOPPELGANGERS WILL DESTROY SONIC AND TAILS!
MY OVERWHELMING ARMY OF BADNIKS WILL BLITZ ALL GLOBAL RESISTANCE! AND THEN I CAN WELCOME DR. EGGMAN TO MY SIDE WHERE HE BELONGS!
EXCUSE ME, DOCTOR...
...YOU'RE IN MY SEAT.

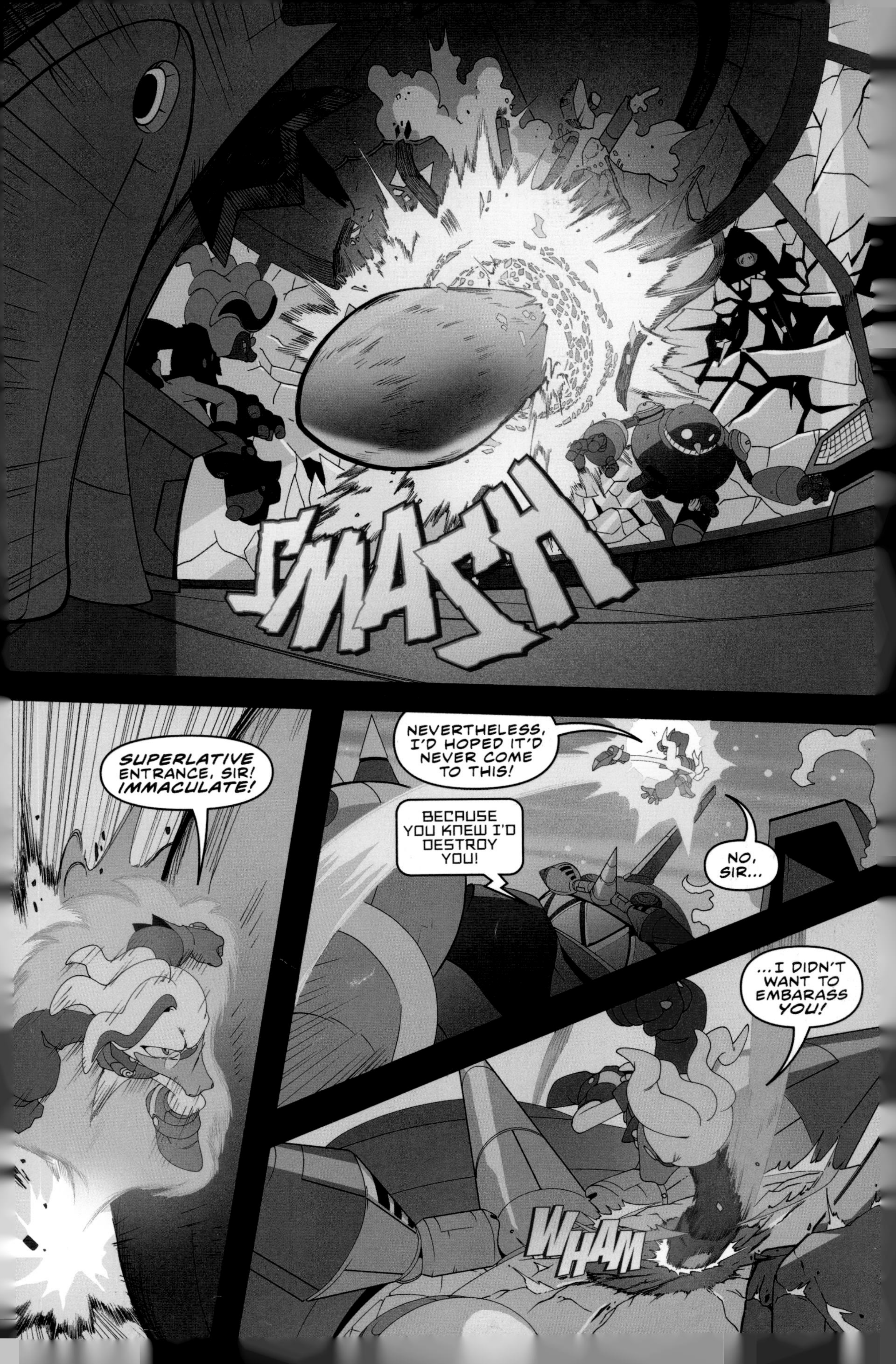
SMASH
SUPERLATIVE ENTRANCE, SIR! IMMACULATE!
NEVERTHELESS, I'D HOPED IT'D NEVER COME TO THIS!
BECAUSE YOU KNEW I'D DESTROY YOU!
NO, SIR...
...I DIDN'T WANT TO EMBARASS YOU!
WHAM

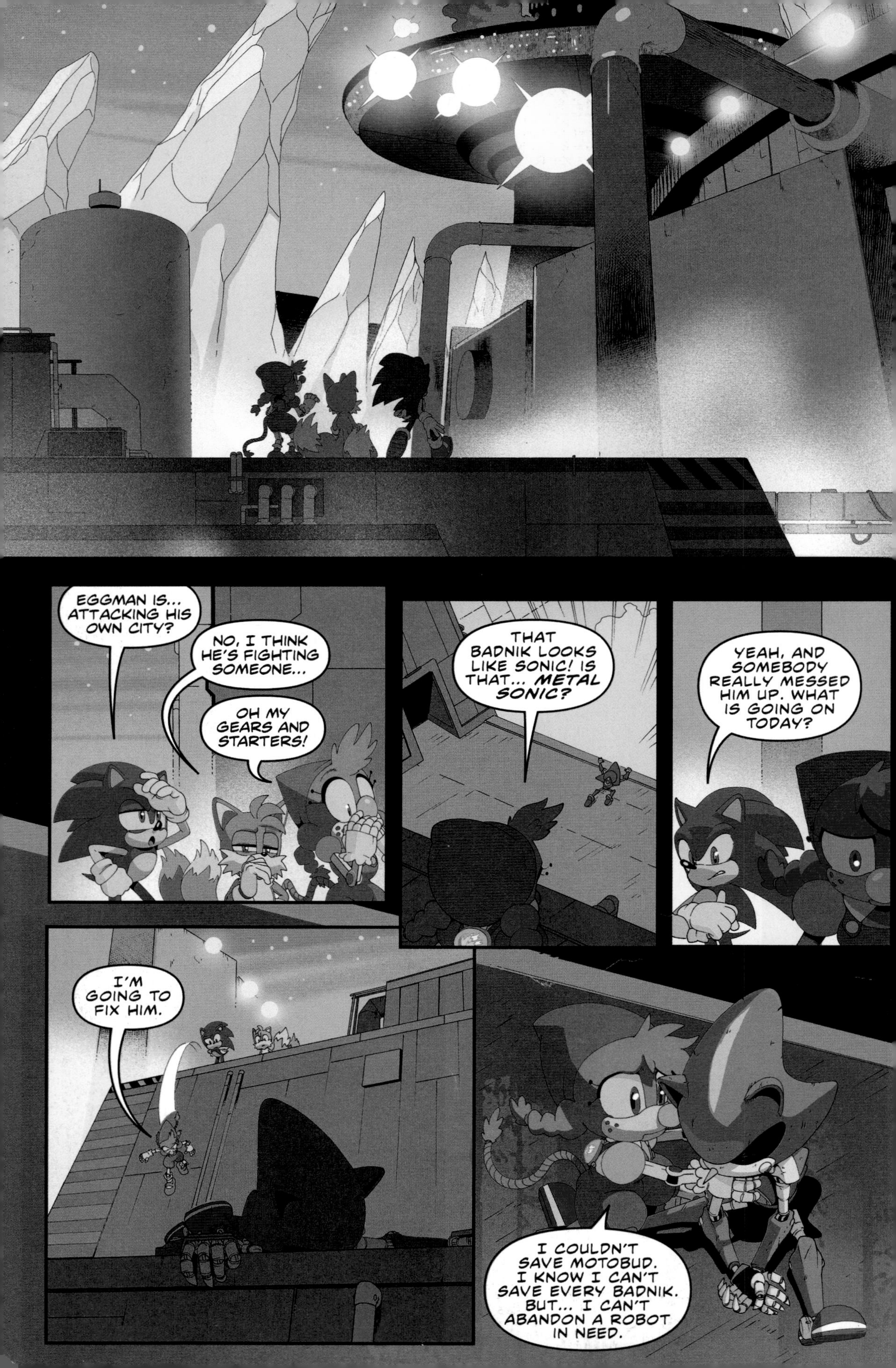
EGGMAN IS... ATTACKING HIS OWN CITY?
NO, I THINK HE'S FIGHTING SOMEONE...
OH MY GEARS AND STARTERS!
THAT BADNIK LOOKS LIKE SONIC! IS THAT... *METAL SONIC?*
YEAH, AND SOMEBODY REALLY MESSED HIM UP. WHAT IS GOING ON TODAY?
I'M GOING TO FIX HIM.
I COULDN'T SAVE MOTOBUD. I KNOW I CAN'T SAVE EVERY BADNIK. BUT... I CAN'T ABANDON A ROBOT IN NEED.

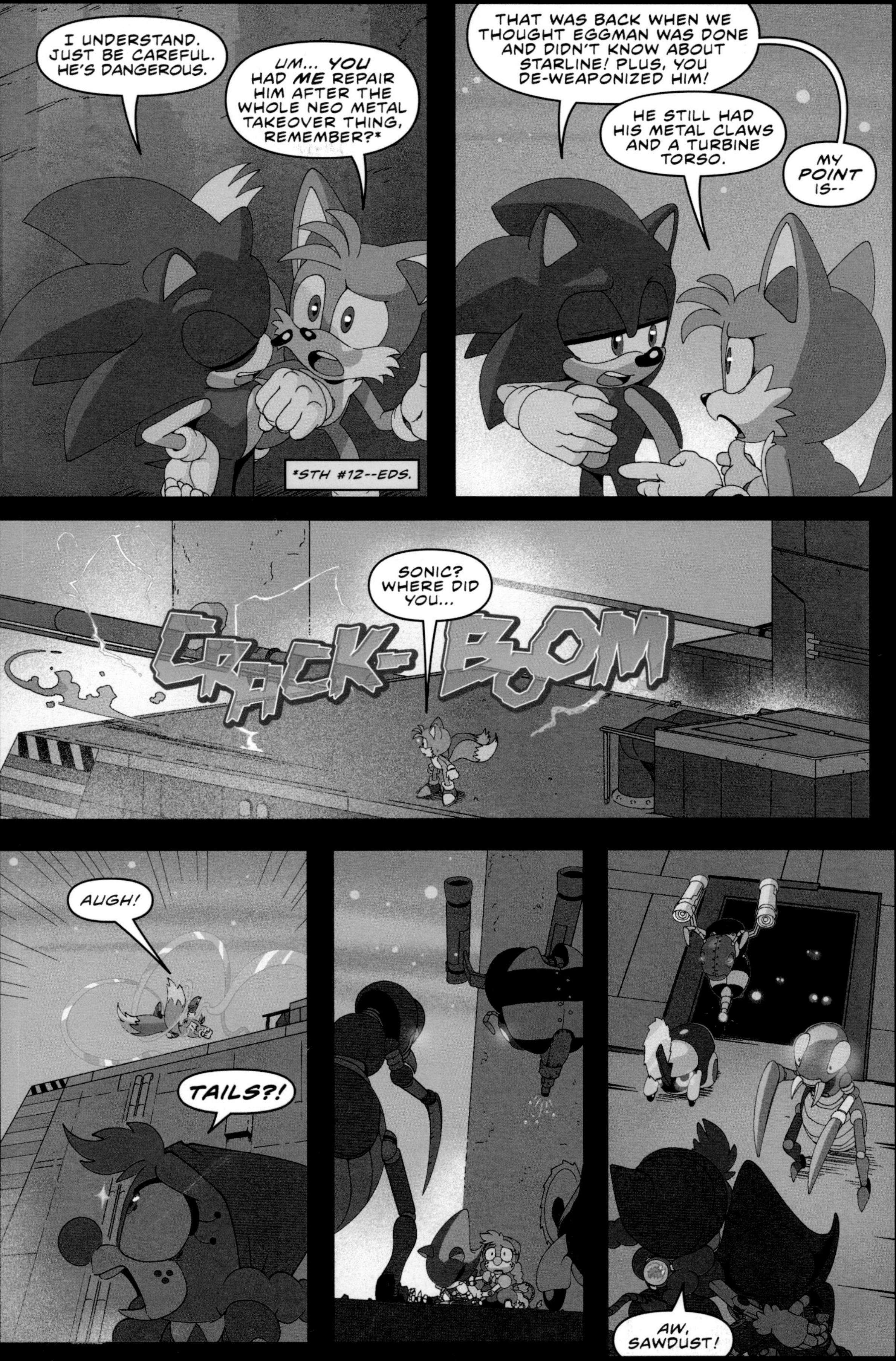
I UNDERSTAND. JUST BE CAREFUL. HE'S DANGEROUS.
UM... YOU HAD ME REPAIR HIM AFTER THE WHOLE NEO METAL TAKEOVER THING, REMEMBER?*
*STH #12--EDS.
THAT WAS BACK WHEN WE THOUGHT EGGMAN WAS DONE AND DIDN'T KNOW ABOUT STARLINE! PLUS, YOU DE-WEAPONIZED HIM!
HE STILL HAD HIS METAL CLAWS AND A TURBINE TORSO.
MY POINT IS--
SONIC? WHERE DID YOU...
CRACK-BOOM
AUGH!
TAILS?!
AW, SAWDUST!

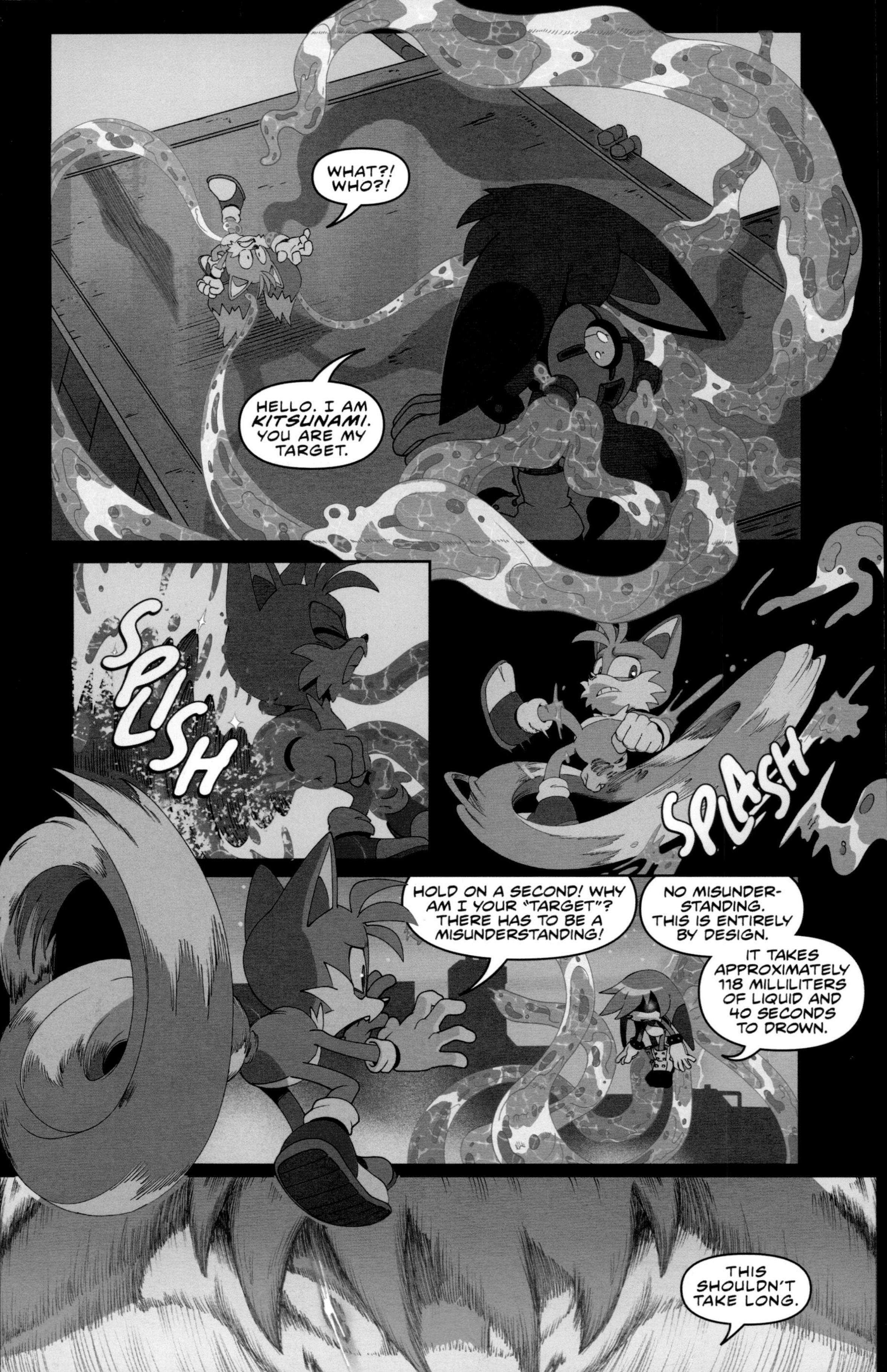
WHAT?! WHO?!
HELLO. I AM *KITSUNAMI*. YOU ARE MY TARGET.
SPLISH
SPLASH
HOLD ON A SECOND! WHY AM I YOUR "TARGET"? THERE HAS TO BE A MISUNDERSTANDING!
NO MISUNDER-STANDING. THIS IS ENTIRELY BY DESIGN.
IT TAKES APPROXIMATELY 118 MILLILITERS OF LIQUID AND 40 SECONDS TO DROWN.
THIS SHOULDN'T TAKE LONG.

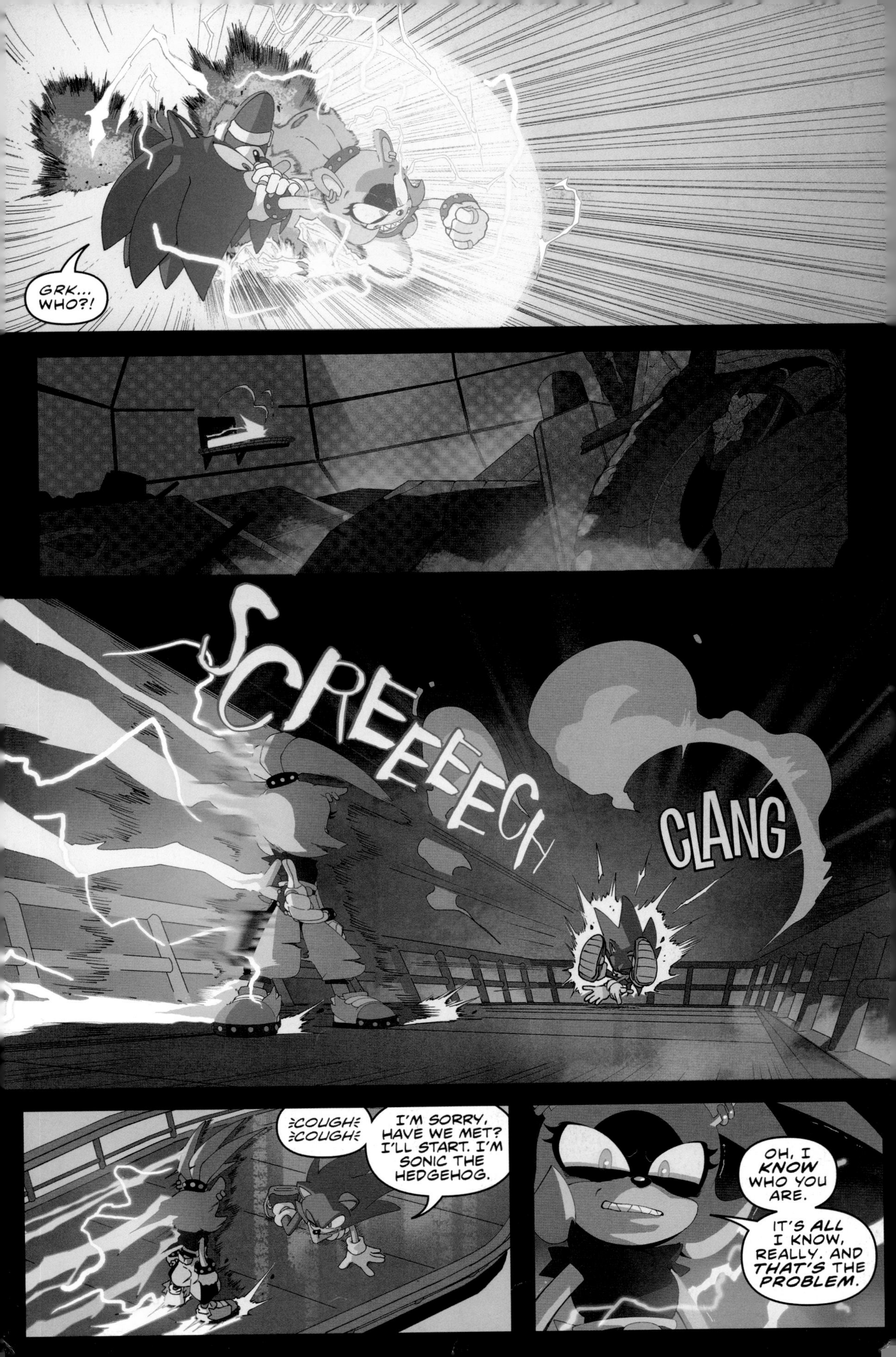

GRK... WHO?!
SCREEEECH
CLANG
COUGH *COUGH*
I'M SORRY, HAVE WE MET? I'LL START. I'M SONIC THE HEDGEHOG.
OH, I KNOW WHO YOU ARE.
IT'S ALL I KNOW, REALLY. AND THAT'S THE PROBLEM.

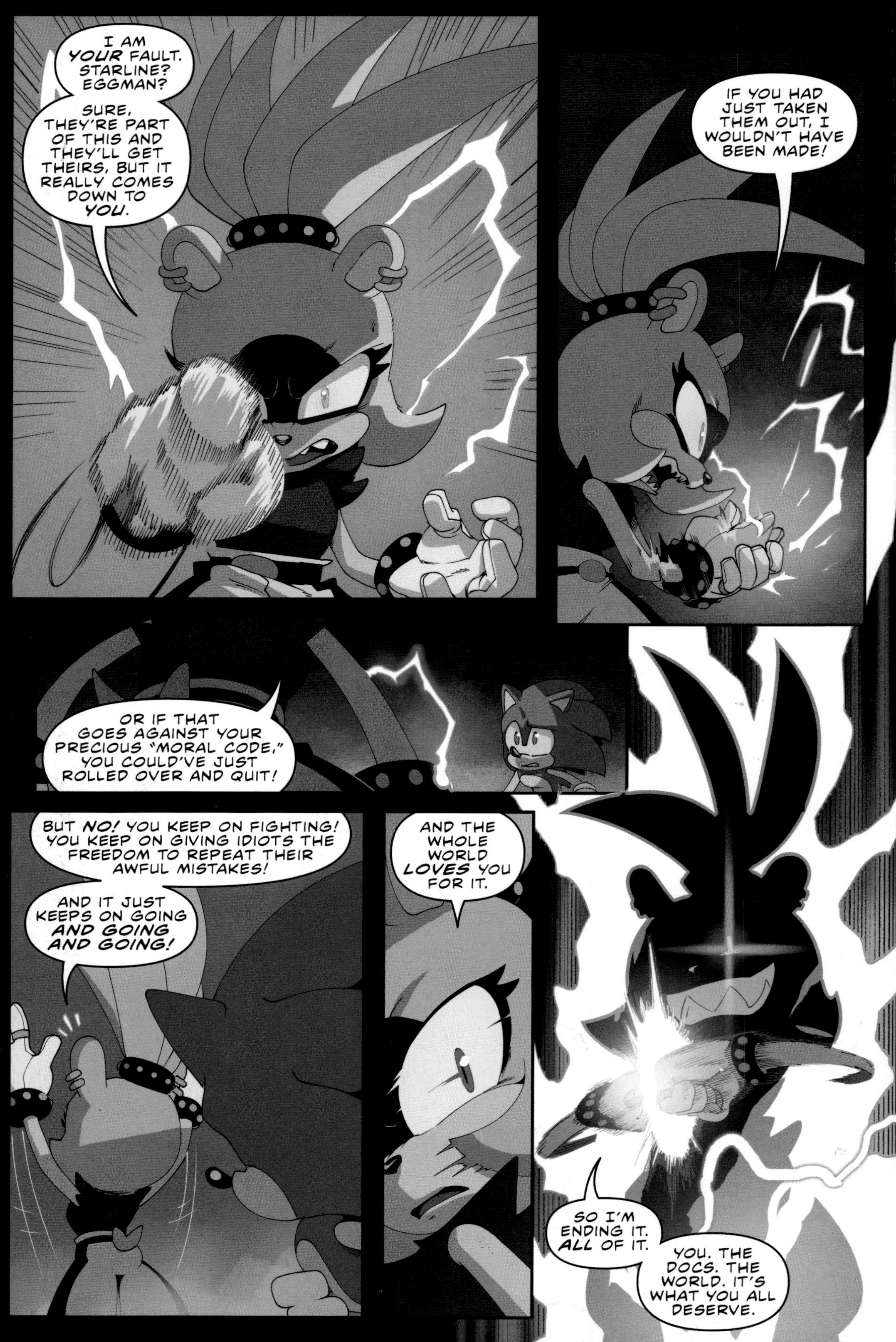
I AM YOUR FAULT. STARLINE? EGGMAN?
SURE, THEY'RE PART OF THIS AND THEY'LL GET THEIRS, BUT IT REALLY COMES DOWN TO YOU.
IF YOU HAD JUST TAKEN THEM OUT, I WOULDN'T HAVE BEEN MADE!
OR IF THAT GOES AGAINST YOUR PRECIOUS "MORAL CODE," YOU COULD'VE JUST ROLLED OVER AND QUIT!
BUT NO! YOU KEEP ON FIGHTING! YOU KEEP ON GIVING IDIOTS THE FREEDOM TO REPEAT THEIR AWFUL MISTAKES!
AND IT JUST KEEPS ON GOING AND GOING AND GOING!
AND THE WHOLE WORLD LOVES YOU FOR IT.
SO I'M ENDING IT. ALL OF IT.
YOU. THE DOCS. THE WORLD. IT'S WHAT YOU ALL DESERVE.

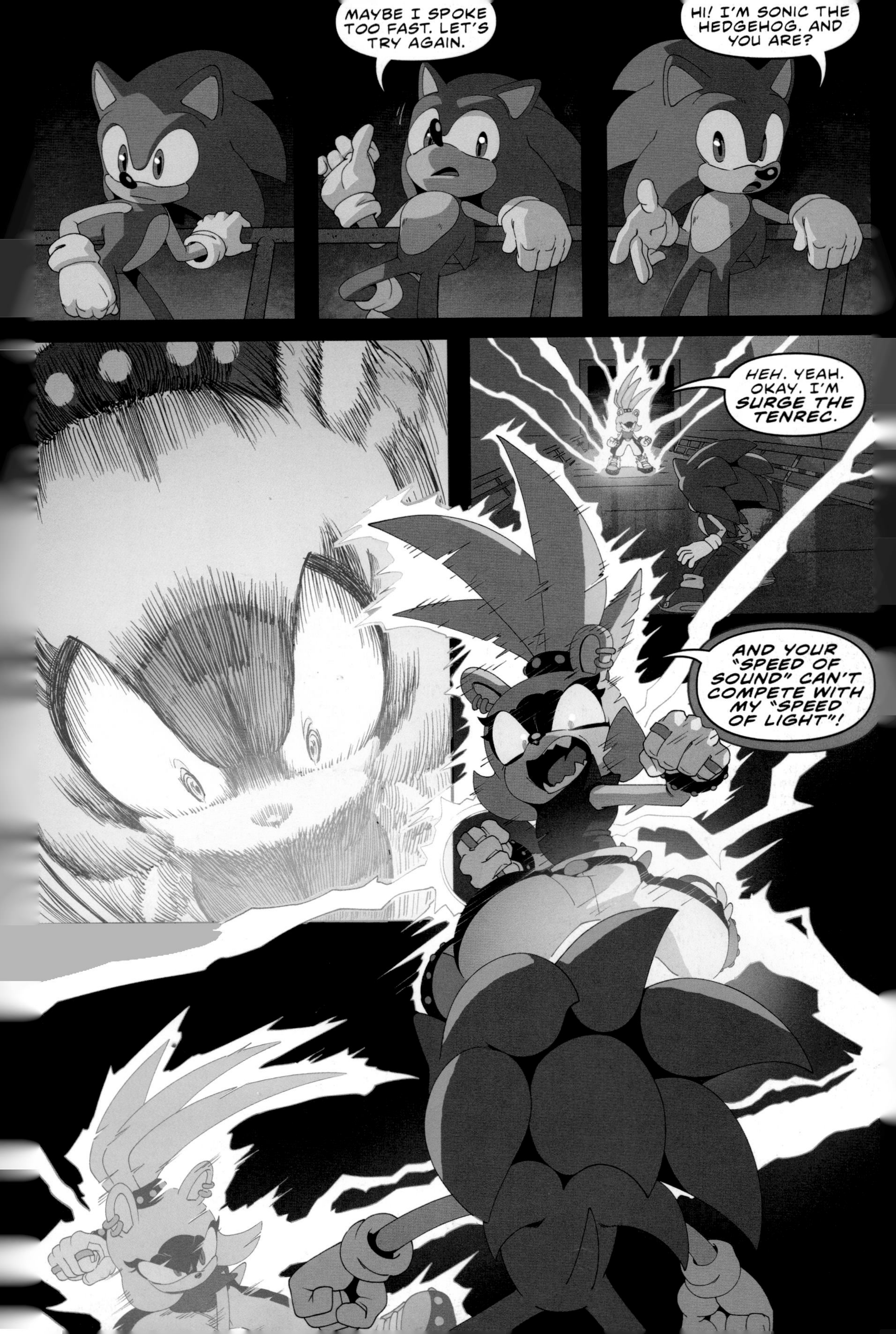
MAYBE I SPOKE TOO FAST. LET'S TRY AGAIN.
HI! I'M SONIC THE HEDGEHOG. AND YOU ARE?
HEH. YEAH. OKAY. I'M SURGE THE TENREC.
AND YOUR "SPEED OF SOUND" CAN'T COMPETE WITH MY "SPEED OF LIGHT"!

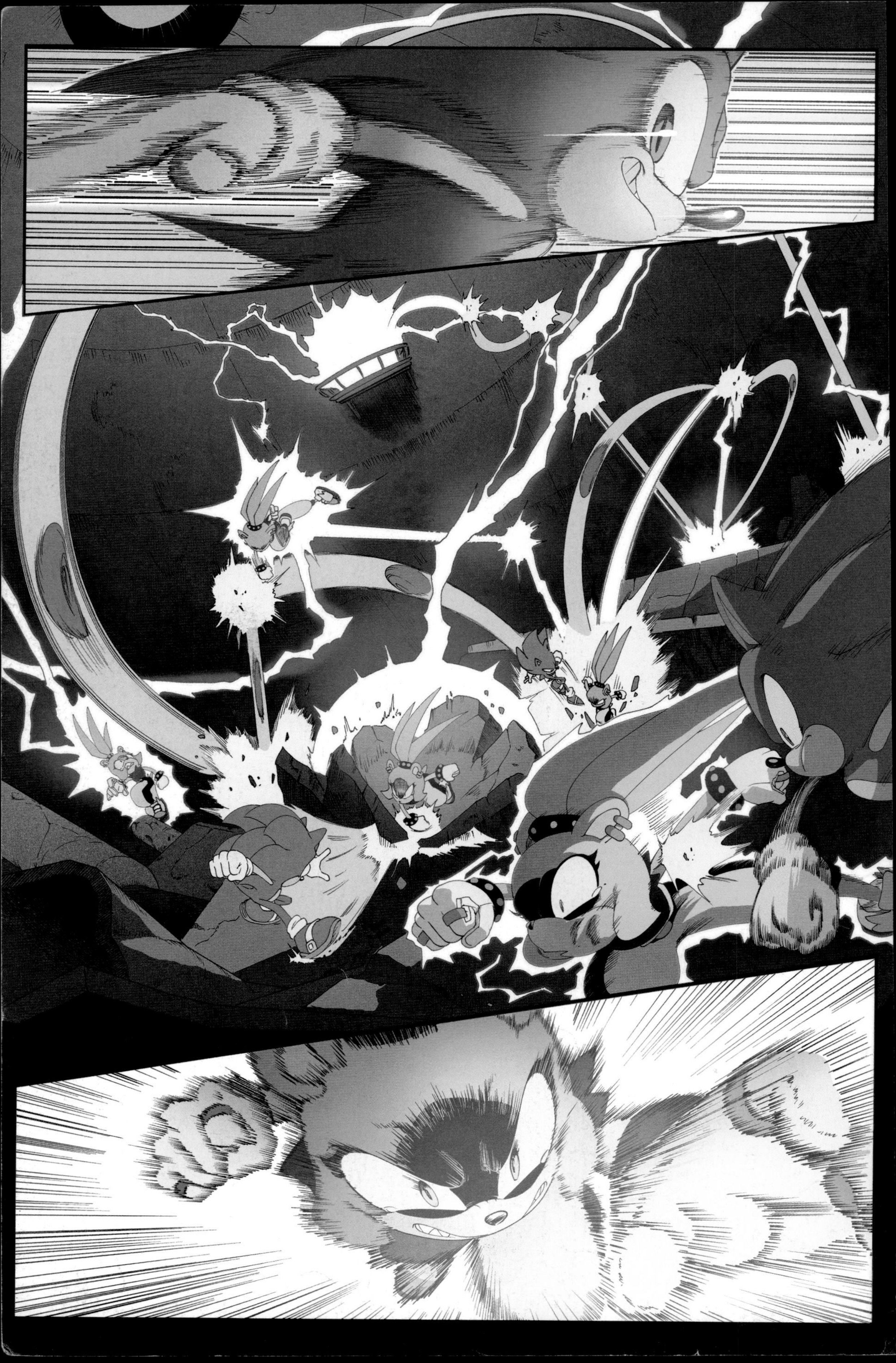

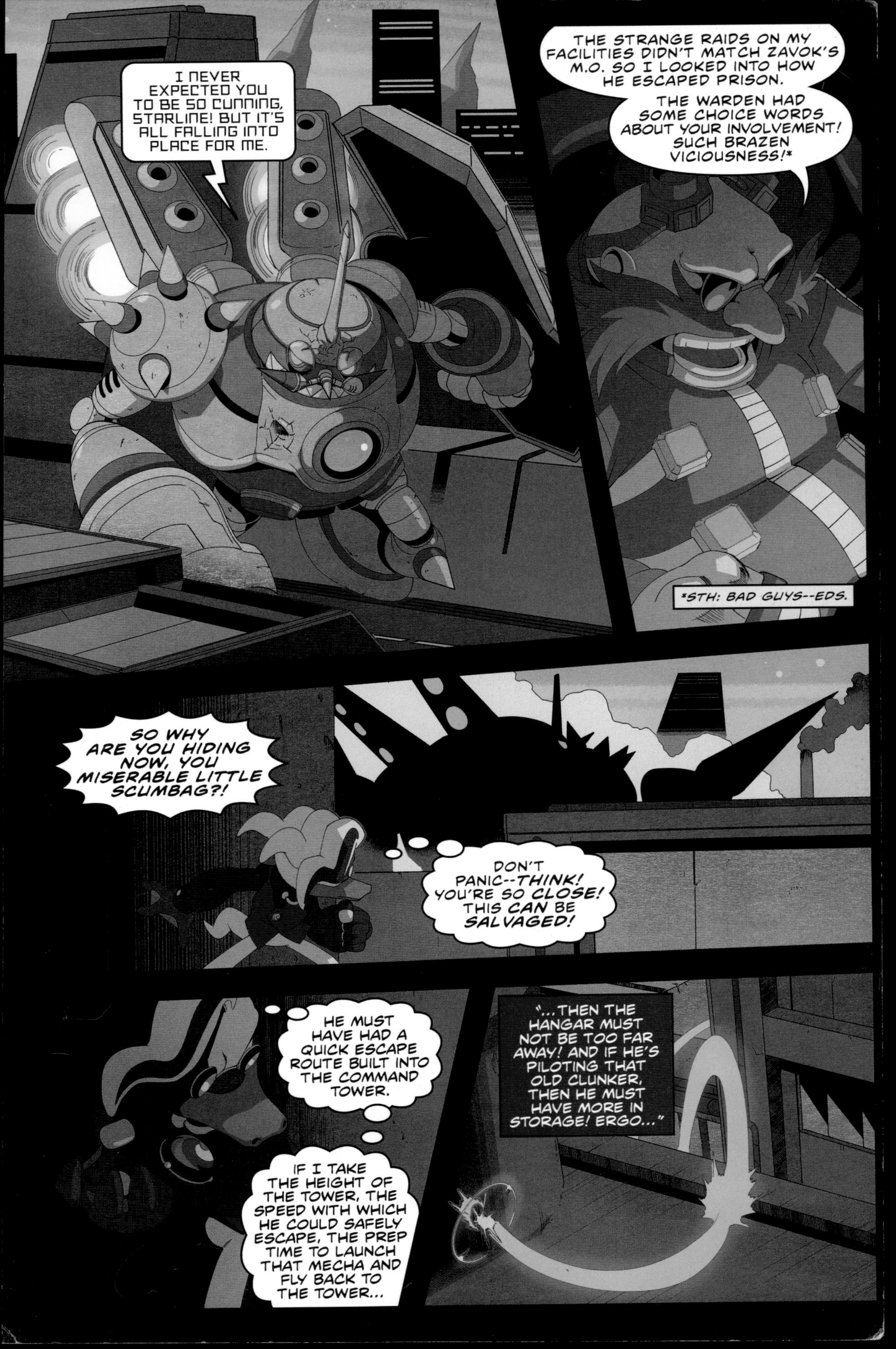
I NEVER EXPECTED YOU TO BE SO CUNNING, STARLINE! BUT IT'S ALL FALLING INTO PLACE FOR ME.
THE STRANGE RAIDS ON MY FACILITIES DIDN'T MATCH ZAVOK'S M.O. SO I LOOKED INTO HOW HE ESCAPED PRISON.
THE WARDEN HAD SOME CHOICE WORDS ABOUT YOUR INVOLVEMENT! SUCH BRAZEN VICIOUSNESS!*
*STH: BAD GUYS--EDS.
SO WHY ARE YOU HIDING NOW, YOU MISERABLE LITTLE SCUMBAG?!
DON'T PANIC--THINK! YOU'RE SO CLOSE! THIS CAN BE SALVAGED!
HE MUST HAVE HAD A QUICK ESCAPE ROUTE BUILT INTO THE COMMAND TOWER.
IF I TAKE THE HEIGHT OF THE TOWER, THE SPEED WITH WHICH HE COULD SAFELY ESCAPE, THE PREP TIME TO LAUNCH THAT MECHA AND FLY BACK TO THE TOWER...
"...THEN THE HANGAR MUST NOT BE TOO FAR AWAY! AND IF HE'S PILOTING THAT OLD CLUNKER, THEN HE MUST HAVE MORE IN STORAGE! ERGO..."

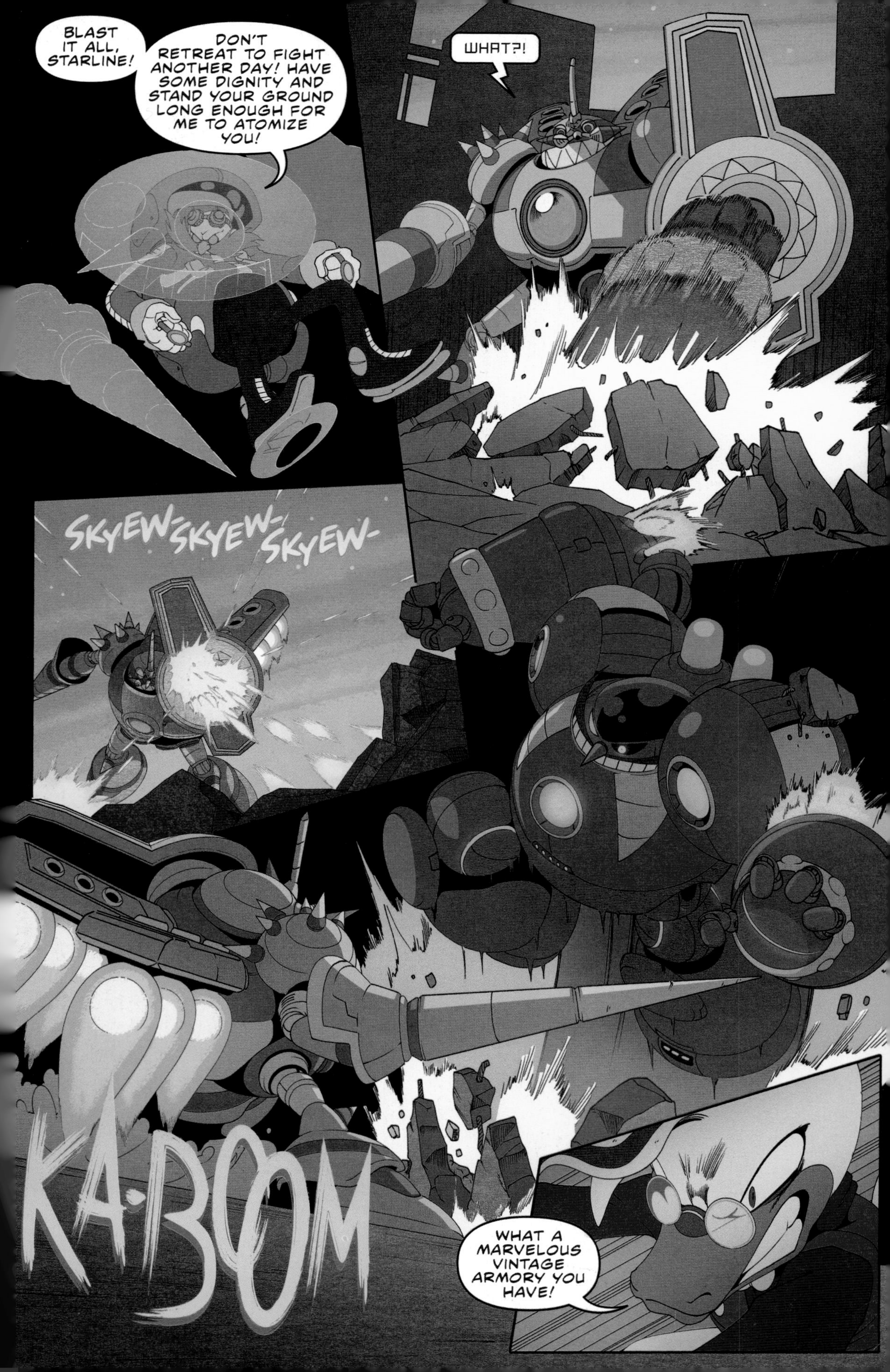
BLAST IT ALL, STARLINE!
DON'T RETREAT TO FIGHT ANOTHER DAY! HAVE SOME DIGNITY AND STAND YOUR GROUND LONG ENOUGH FOR ME TO ATOMIZE YOU!
WHAT?!
SKYEW-SKYEW-SKYEW-
KA-BOOM
WHAT A MARVELOUS VINTAGE ARMORY YOU HAVE!

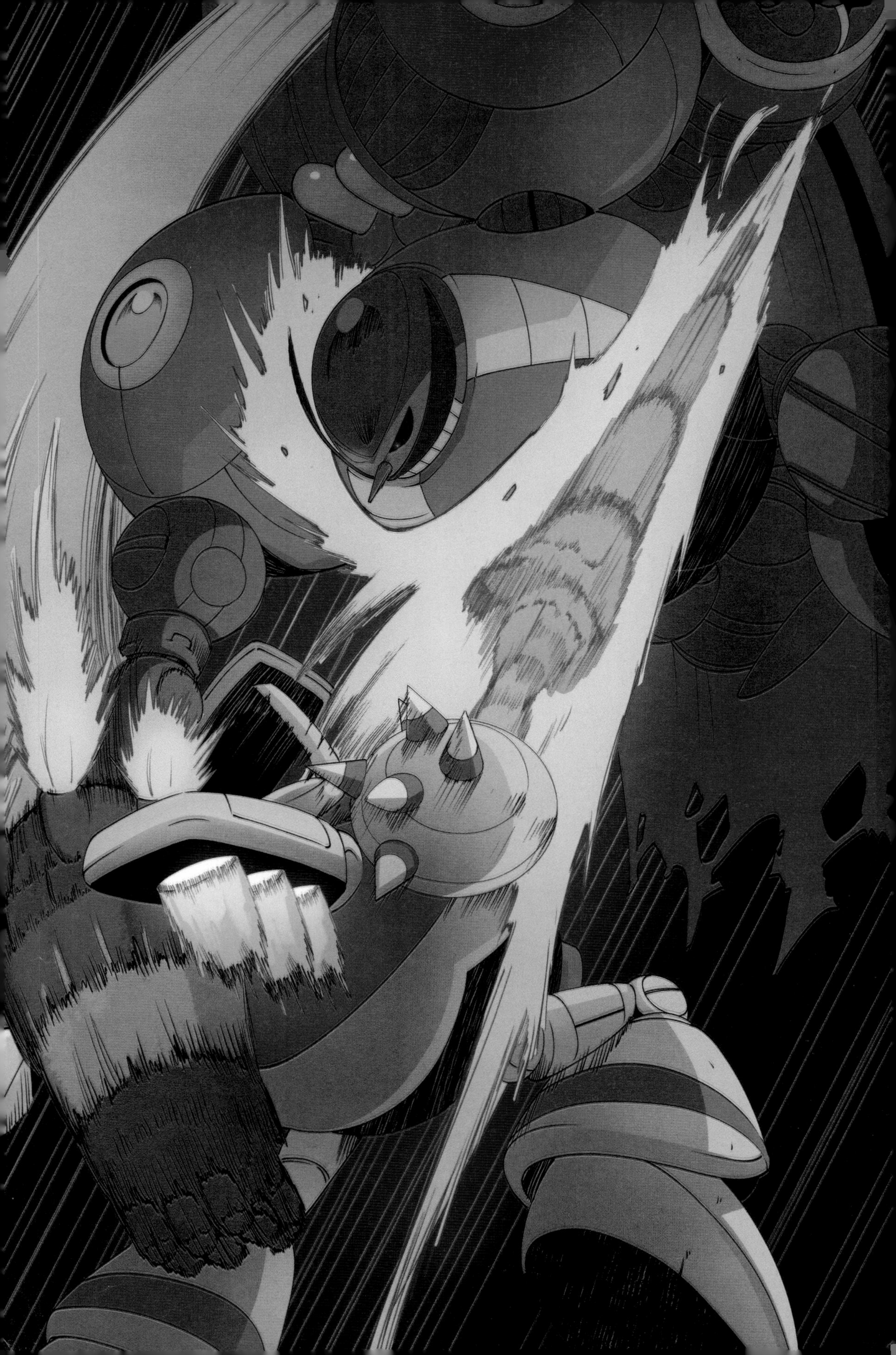

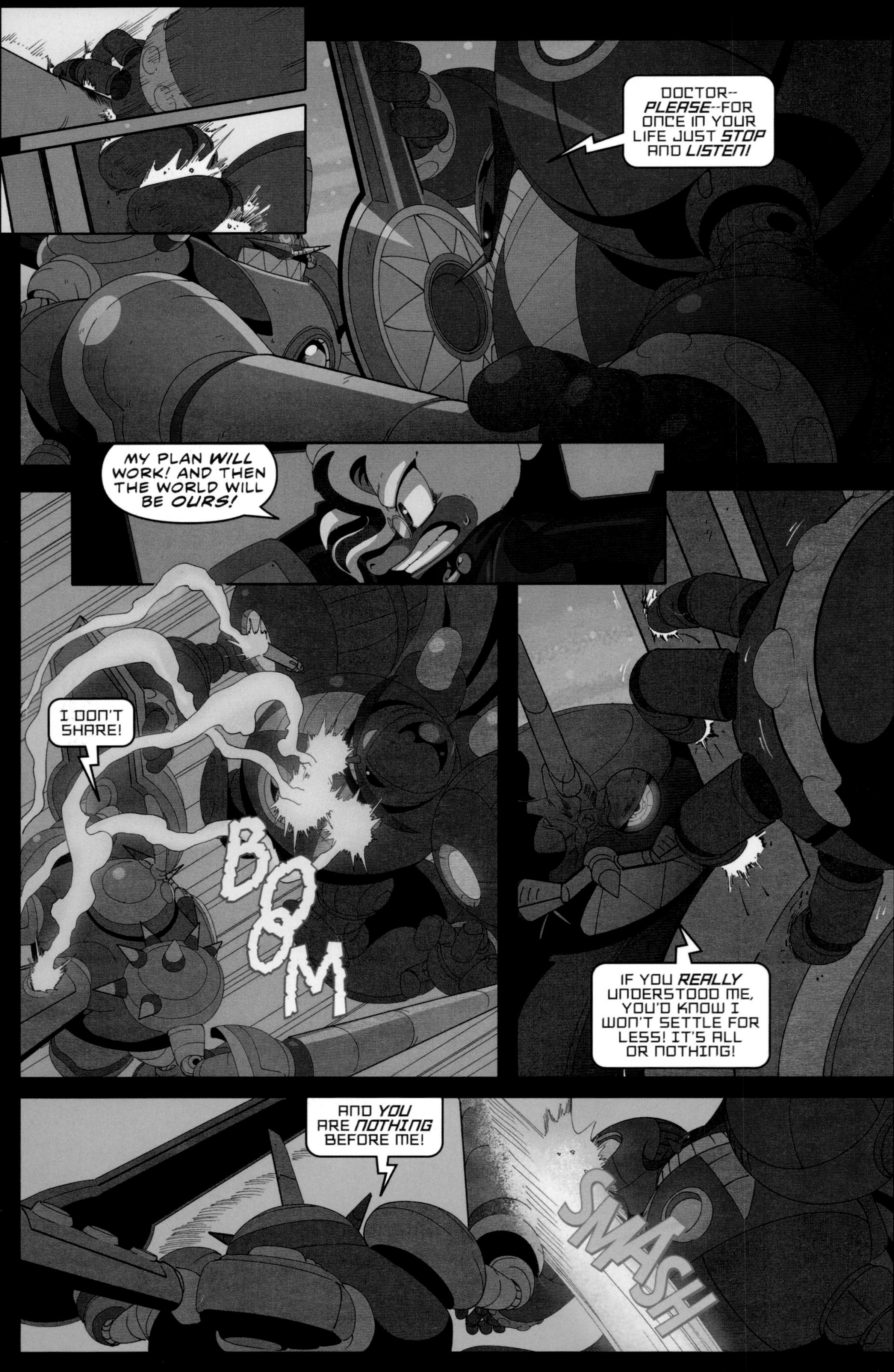
DOCTOR-- PLEASE--FOR ONCE IN YOUR LIFE JUST STOP AND LISTEN!
MY PLAN WILL WORK! AND THEN THE WORLD WILL BE OURS!
I DON'T SHARE!
BOOM
IF YOU REALLY UNDERSTOOD ME, YOU'D KNOW I WON'T SETTLE FOR LESS! IT'S ALL OR NOTHING!
AND YOU ARE NOTHING BEFORE ME!
SMASH

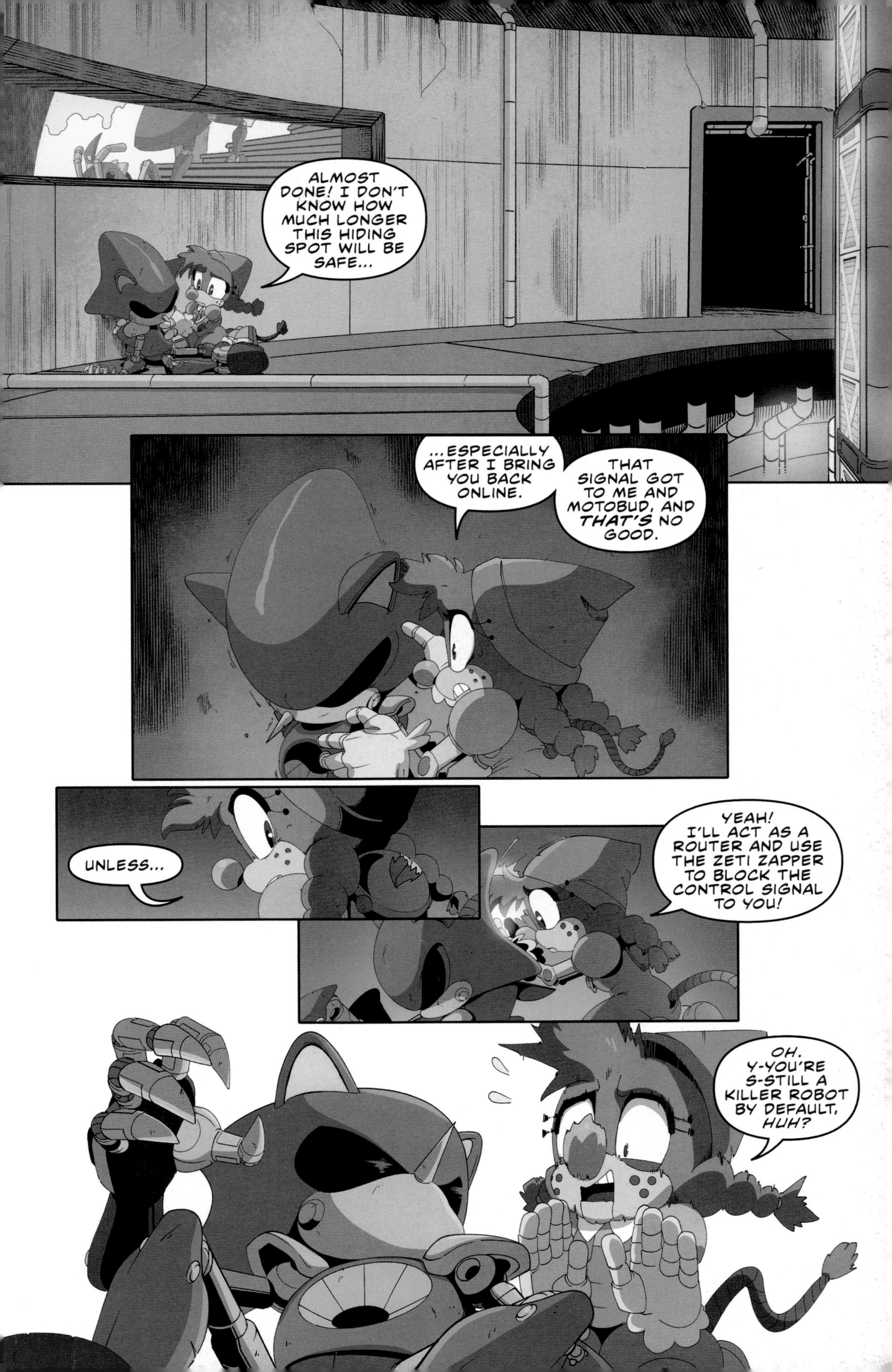
ALMOST DONE! I DON'T KNOW HOW MUCH LONGER THIS HIDING SPOT WILL BE SAFE...
...ESPECIALLY AFTER I BRING YOU BACK ONLINE.
THAT SIGNAL GOT TO ME AND MOTOBUD, AND *THAT'S* NO GOOD.
UNLESS...
YEAH! I'LL ACT AS A ROUTER AND USE THE ZETI ZAPPER TO BLOCK THE CONTROL SIGNAL TO YOU!
OH. Y-YOU'RE S-STILL A KILLER ROBOT BY DEFAULT, *HUH?*

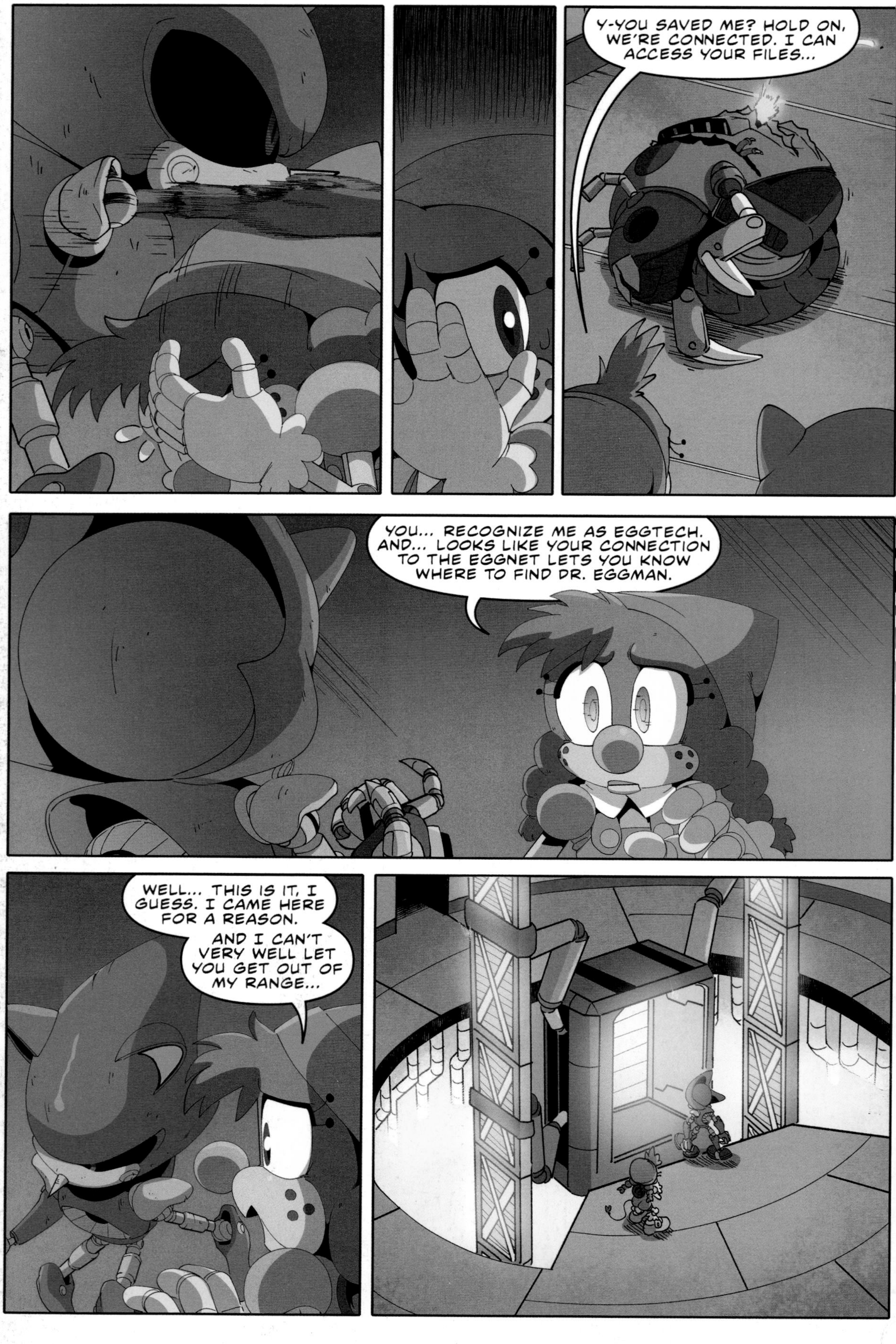
Y-YOU SAVED ME? HOLD ON, WE'RE CONNECTED. I CAN ACCESS YOUR FILES...
YOU... RECOGNIZE ME AS EGGTECH. AND... LOOKS LIKE YOUR CONNECTION TO THE EGGNET LETS YOU KNOW WHERE TO FIND DR. EGGMAN.
WELL... THIS IS IT, I GUESS. I CAME HERE FOR A REASON.
AND I CAN'T VERY WELL LET YOU GET OUT OF MY RANGE...

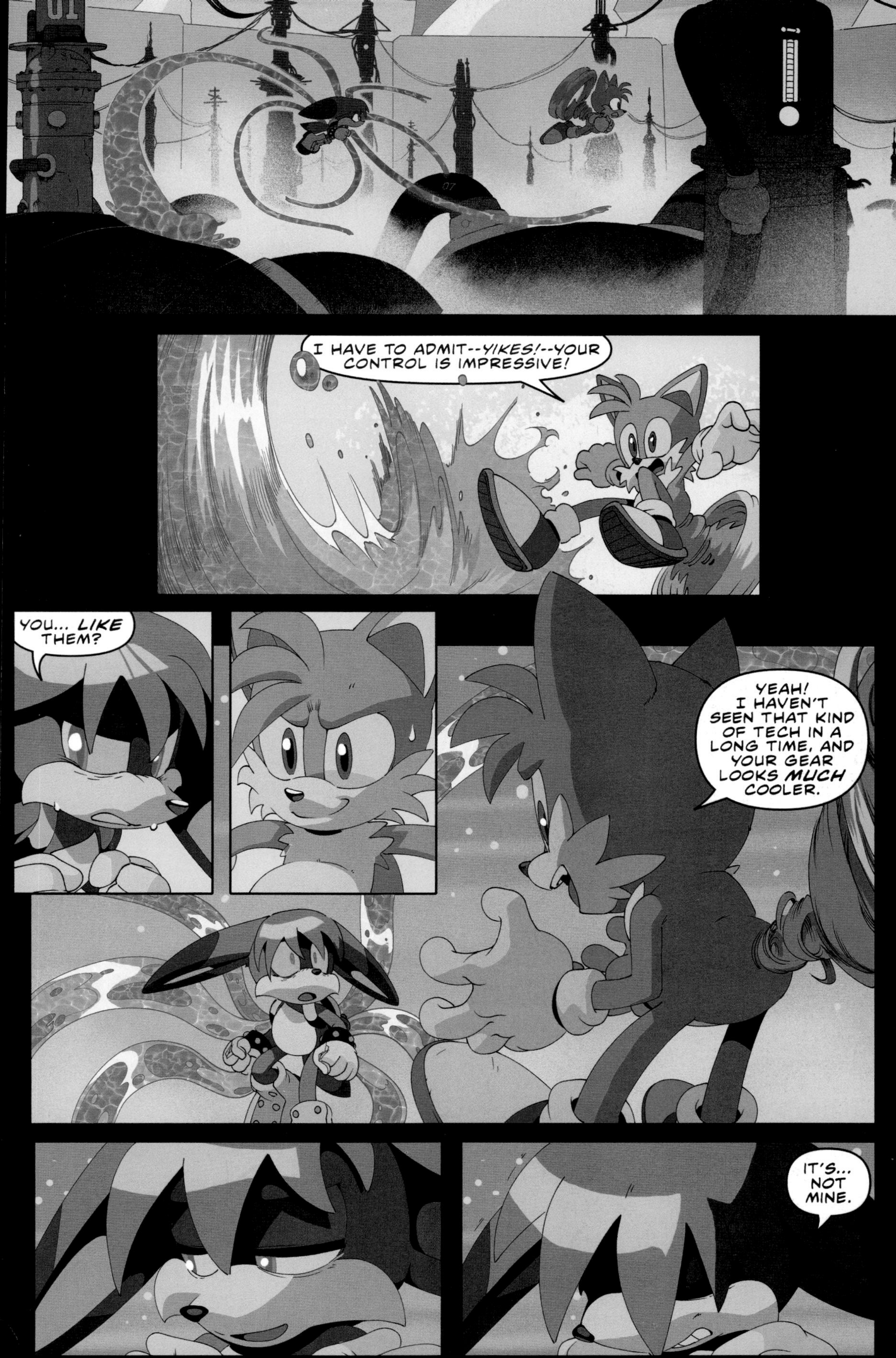
01
I HAVE TO ADMIT--YIKES!--YOUR CONTROL IS IMPRESSIVE!
YOU... LIKE THEM?
YEAH! I HAVEN'T SEEN THAT KIND OF TECH IN A LONG TIME, AND YOUR GEAR LOOKS MUCH COOLER.
IT'S... NOT MINE.

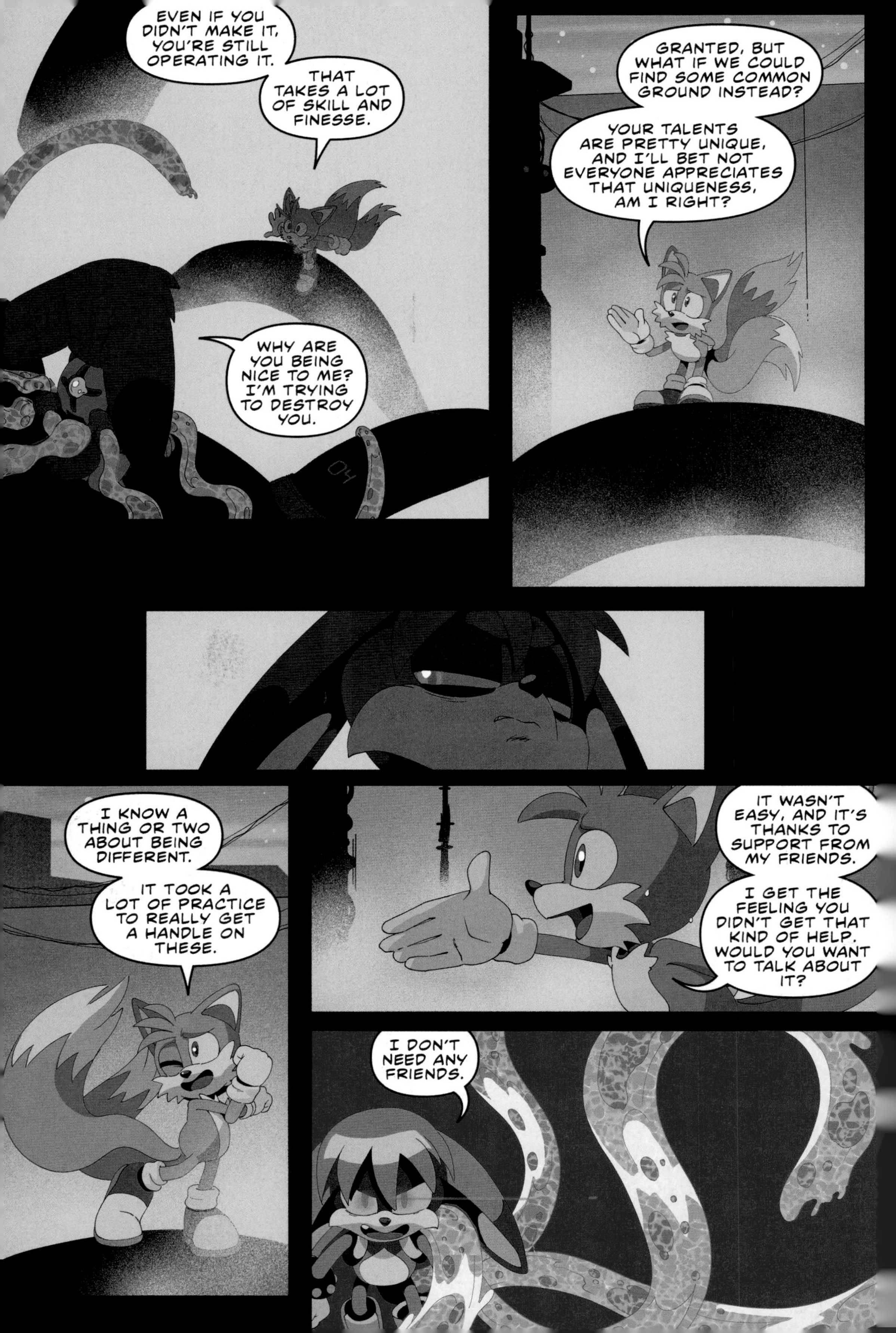
EVEN IF YOU DIDN'T MAKE IT, YOU'RE STILL OPERATING IT.
THAT TAKES A LOT OF SKILL AND FINESSE.
WHY ARE YOU BEING NICE TO ME? I'M TRYING TO DESTROY YOU.
04
GRANTED, BUT WHAT IF WE COULD FIND SOME COMMON GROUND INSTEAD?
YOUR TALENTS ARE PRETTY UNIQUE, AND I'LL BET NOT EVERYONE APPRECIATES THAT UNIQUENESS, AM I RIGHT?
I KNOW A THING OR TWO ABOUT BEING DIFFERENT.
IT TOOK A LOT OF PRACTICE TO REALLY GET A HANDLE ON THESE.
IT WASN'T EASY, AND IT'S THANKS TO SUPPORT FROM MY FRIENDS.
I GET THE FEELING YOU DIDN'T GET THAT KIND OF HELP. WOULD YOU WANT TO TALK ABOUT IT?
I DON'T NEED ANY FRIENDS.

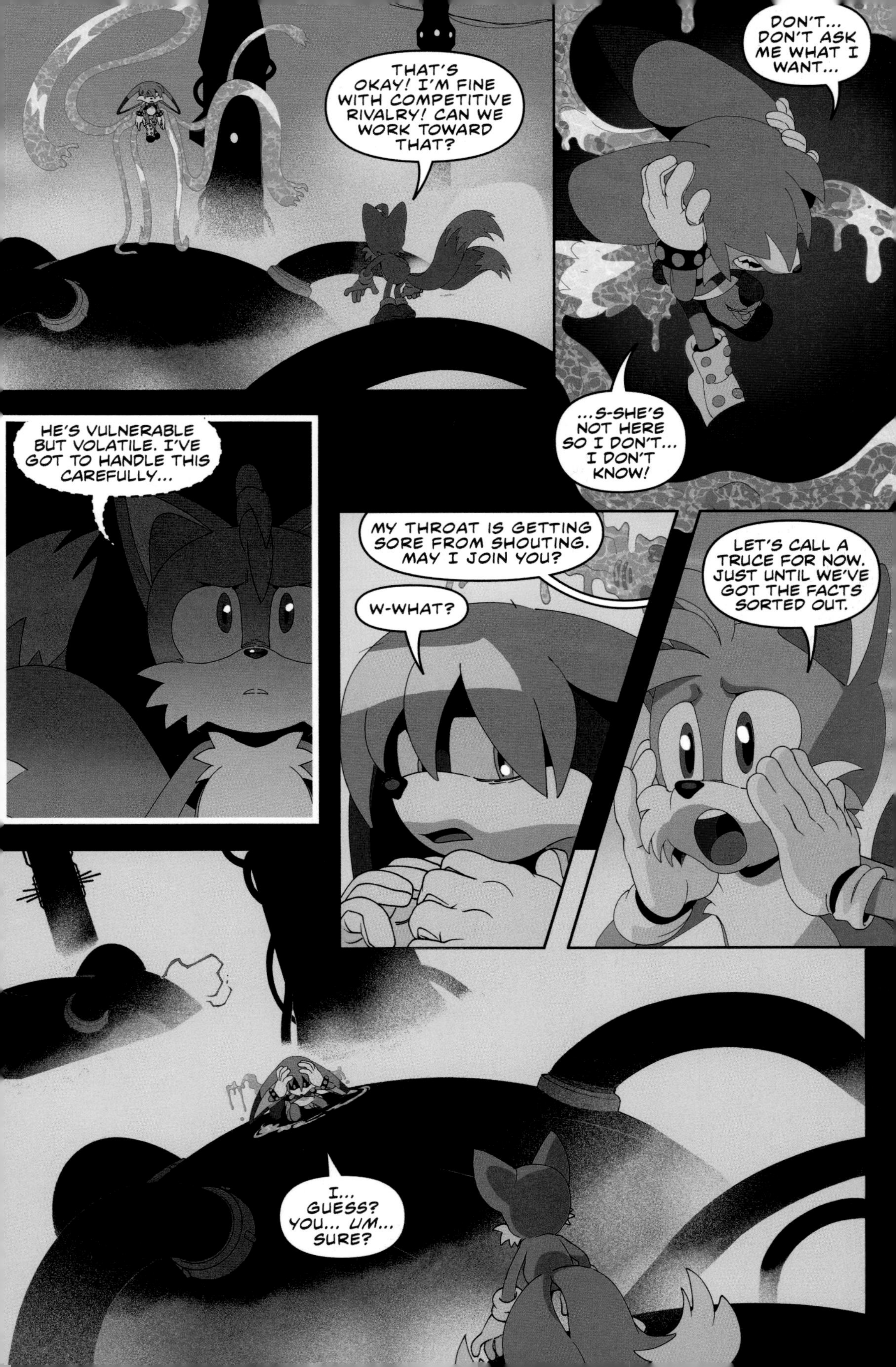
THAT'S OKAY! I'M FINE WITH COMPETITIVE RIVALRY! CAN WE WORK TOWARD THAT?
DON'T... DON'T ASK ME WHAT I WANT...
...S-SHE'S NOT HERE SO I DON'T... I DON'T KNOW!
HE'S VULNERABLE BUT VOLATILE. I'VE GOT TO HANDLE THIS CAREFULLY...
LET'S CALL A TRUCE FOR NOW. JUST UNTIL WE'VE GOT THE FACTS SORTED OUT.
MY THROAT IS GETTING SORE FROM SHOUTING. MAY I JOIN YOU?
W-WHAT?
I... GUESS? YOU... UM... SURE?

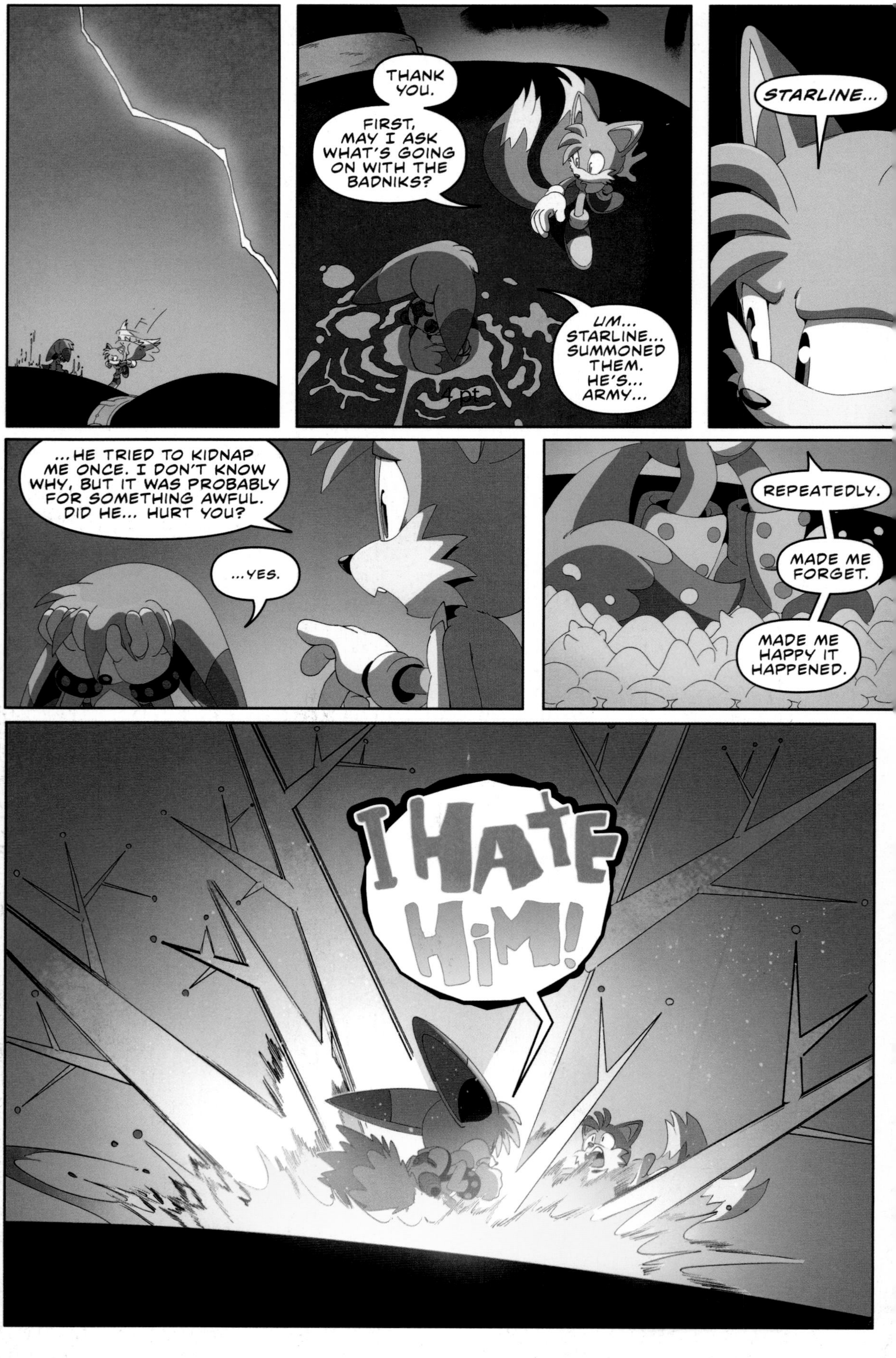
THANK YOU.
FIRST, MAY I ASK WHAT'S GOING ON WITH THE BADNIKS?
UM... STARLINE... SUMMONED THEM. HE'S... ARMY...
STARLINE...
...HE TRIED TO KIDNAP ME ONCE. I DON'T KNOW WHY, BUT IT WAS PROBABLY FOR SOMETHING AWFUL. DID HE... HURT YOU?
...YES.
REPEATEDLY.
MADE ME FORGET.
MADE ME HAPPY IT HAPPENED.
I HATE HIM!

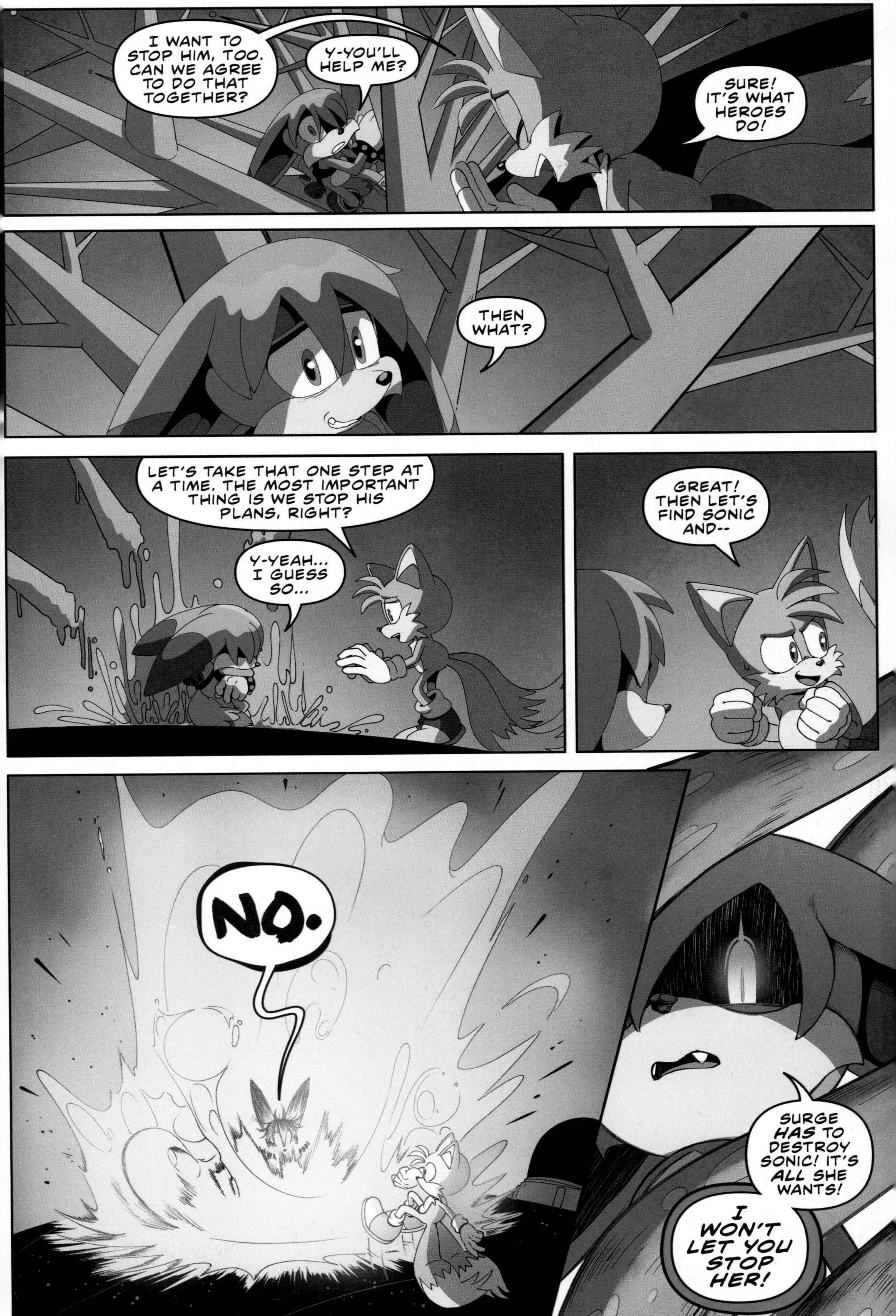
I WANT TO STOP HIM, TOO. CAN WE AGREE TO DO THAT TOGETHER?
Y-YOU'LL HELP ME?
SURE! IT'S WHAT HEROES DO!
THEN WHAT?
LET'S TAKE THAT ONE STEP AT A TIME. THE MOST IMPORTANT THING IS WE STOP HIS PLANS, RIGHT?
Y-YEAH... I GUESS SO...
GREAT! THEN LET'S FIND SONIC AND--
NO.
SURGE HAS TO DESTROY SONIC! IT'S ALL SHE WANTS!
I WON'T LET YOU STOP HER!

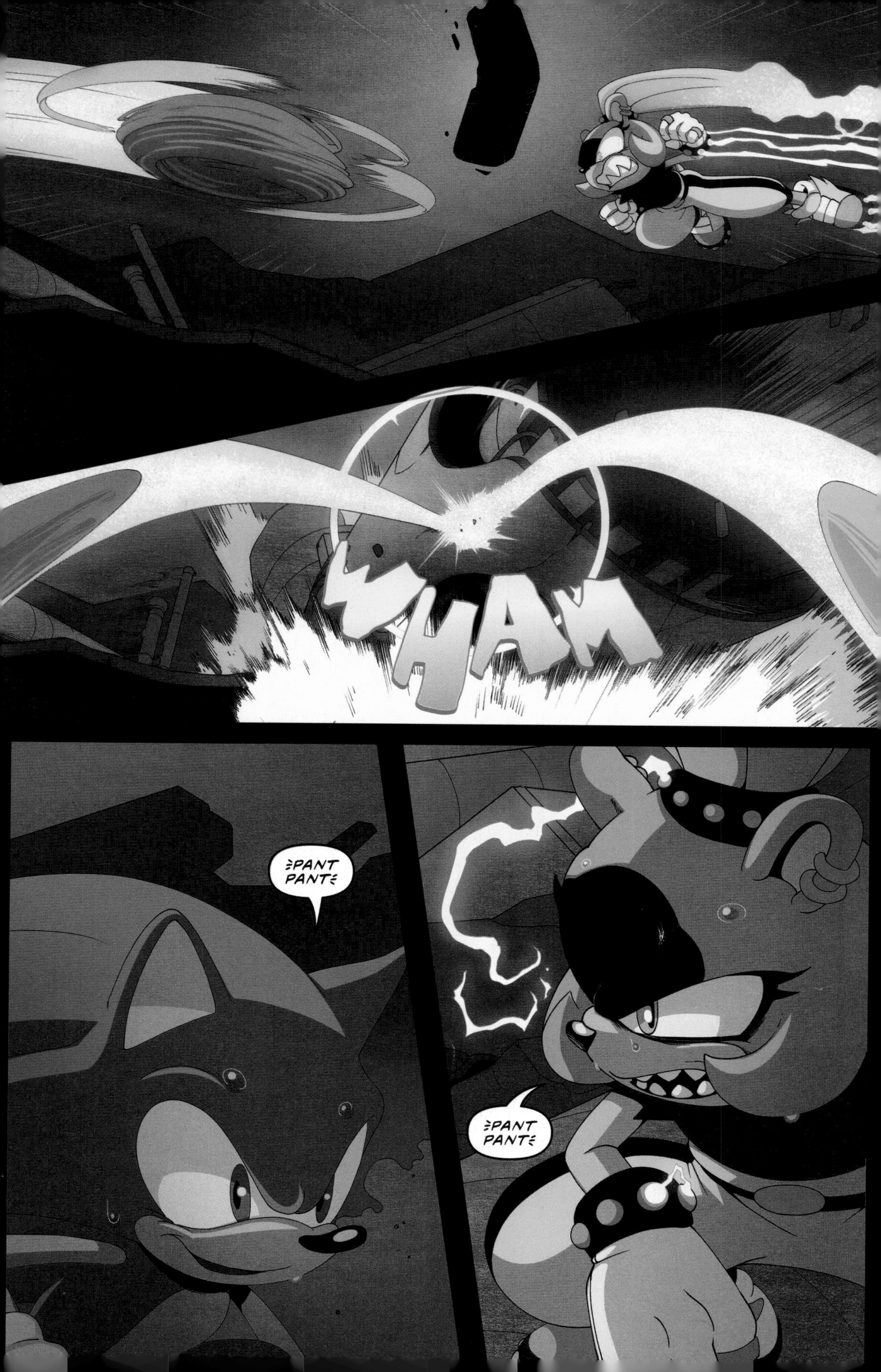
WHAM
PANT PANT
PANT PANT

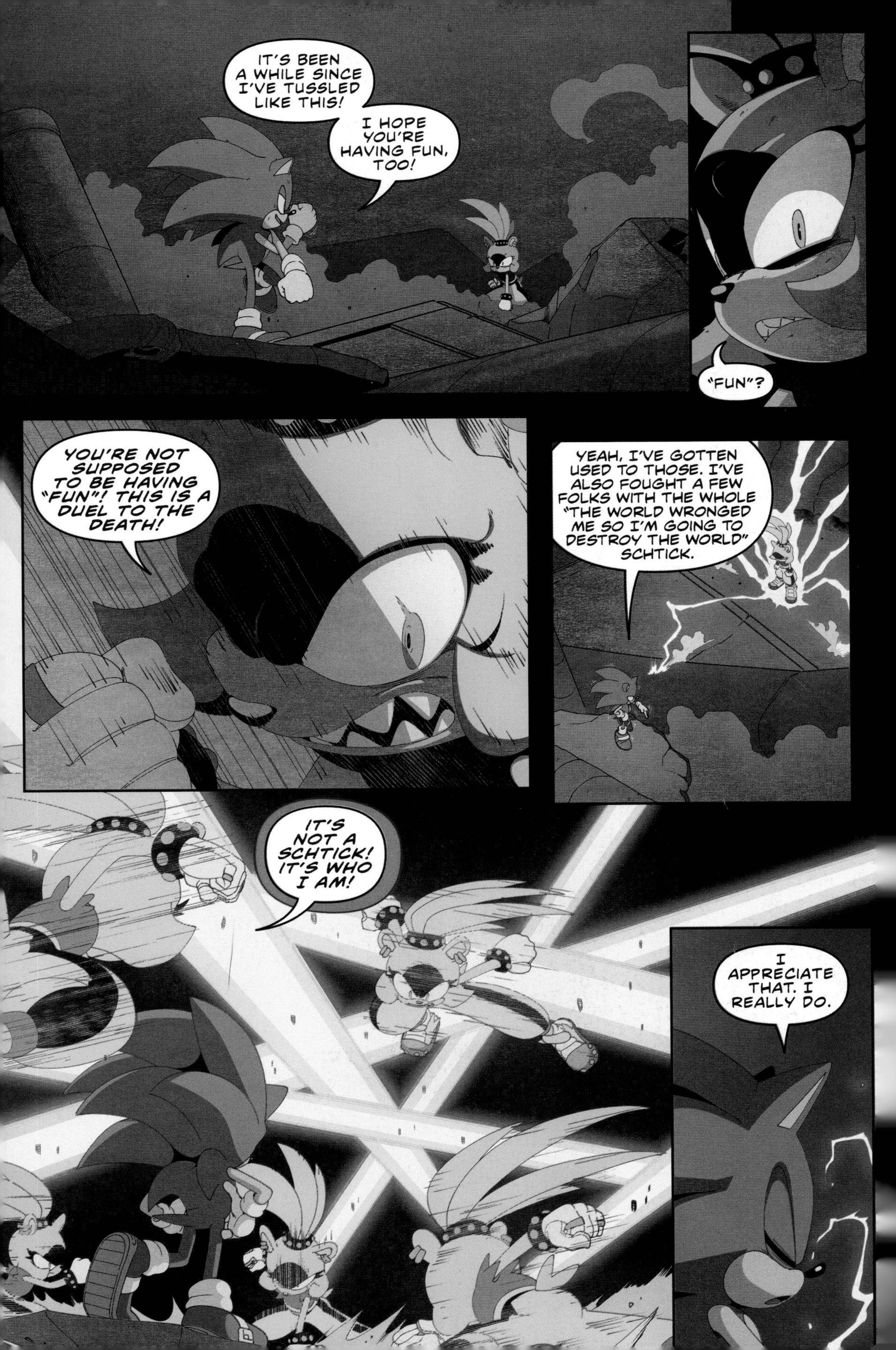
IT'S BEEN A WHILE SINCE I'VE TUSSLED LIKE THIS!
I HOPE YOU'RE HAVING FUN, TOO!
"FUN"?
YOU'RE NOT SUPPOSED TO BE HAVING "FUN"! THIS IS A DUEL TO THE DEATH!
YEAH, I'VE GOTTEN USED TO THOSE. I'VE ALSO FOUGHT A FEW FOLKS WITH THE WHOLE "THE WORLD WRONGED ME SO I'M GOING TO DESTROY THE WORLD" SCHTICK.
IT'S NOT A SCHTICK! IT'S WHO I AM!
I APPRECIATE THAT. I REALLY DO.

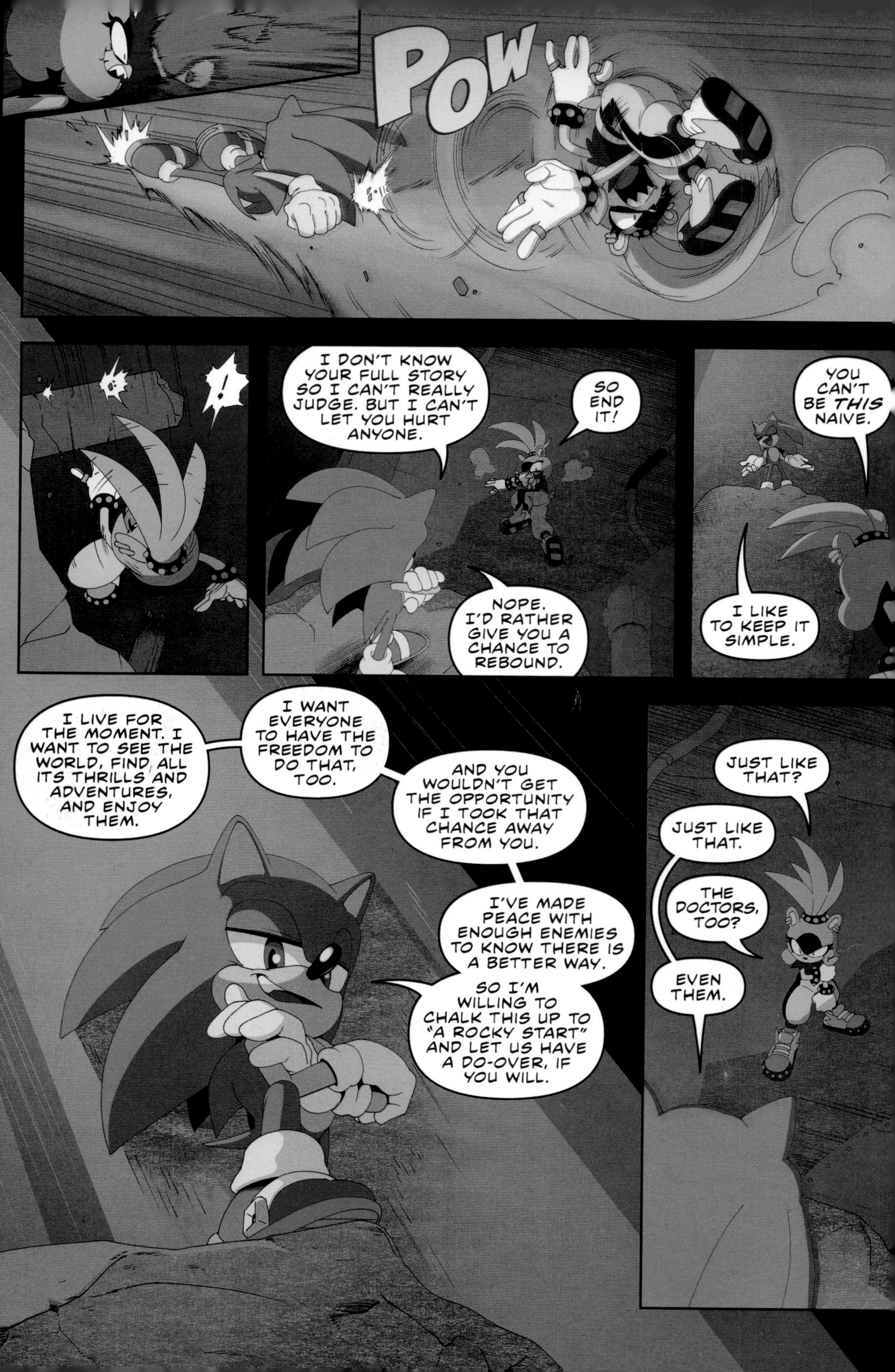
POW
I DON'T KNOW YOUR FULL STORY SO I CAN'T REALLY JUDGE. BUT I CAN'T LET YOU HURT ANYONE.
SO END IT!
NOPE. I'D RATHER GIVE YOU A CHANCE TO REBOUND.
YOU CAN'T BE *THIS* NAIVE.
I LIKE TO KEEP IT SIMPLE.
I LIVE FOR THE MOMENT. I WANT TO SEE THE WORLD, FIND ALL ITS THRILLS AND ADVENTURES, AND ENJOY THEM.
I WANT EVERYONE TO HAVE THE FREEDOM TO DO THAT, TOO.
AND YOU WOULDN'T GET THE OPPORTUNITY IF I TOOK THAT CHANCE AWAY FROM YOU.
I'VE MADE PEACE WITH ENOUGH ENEMIES TO KNOW THERE IS A BETTER WAY.
SO I'M WILLING TO CHALK THIS UP TO "A ROCKY START" AND LET US HAVE A DO-OVER, IF YOU WILL.
JUST LIKE THAT?
JUST LIKE THAT.
THE DOCTORS, TOO?
EVEN THEM.

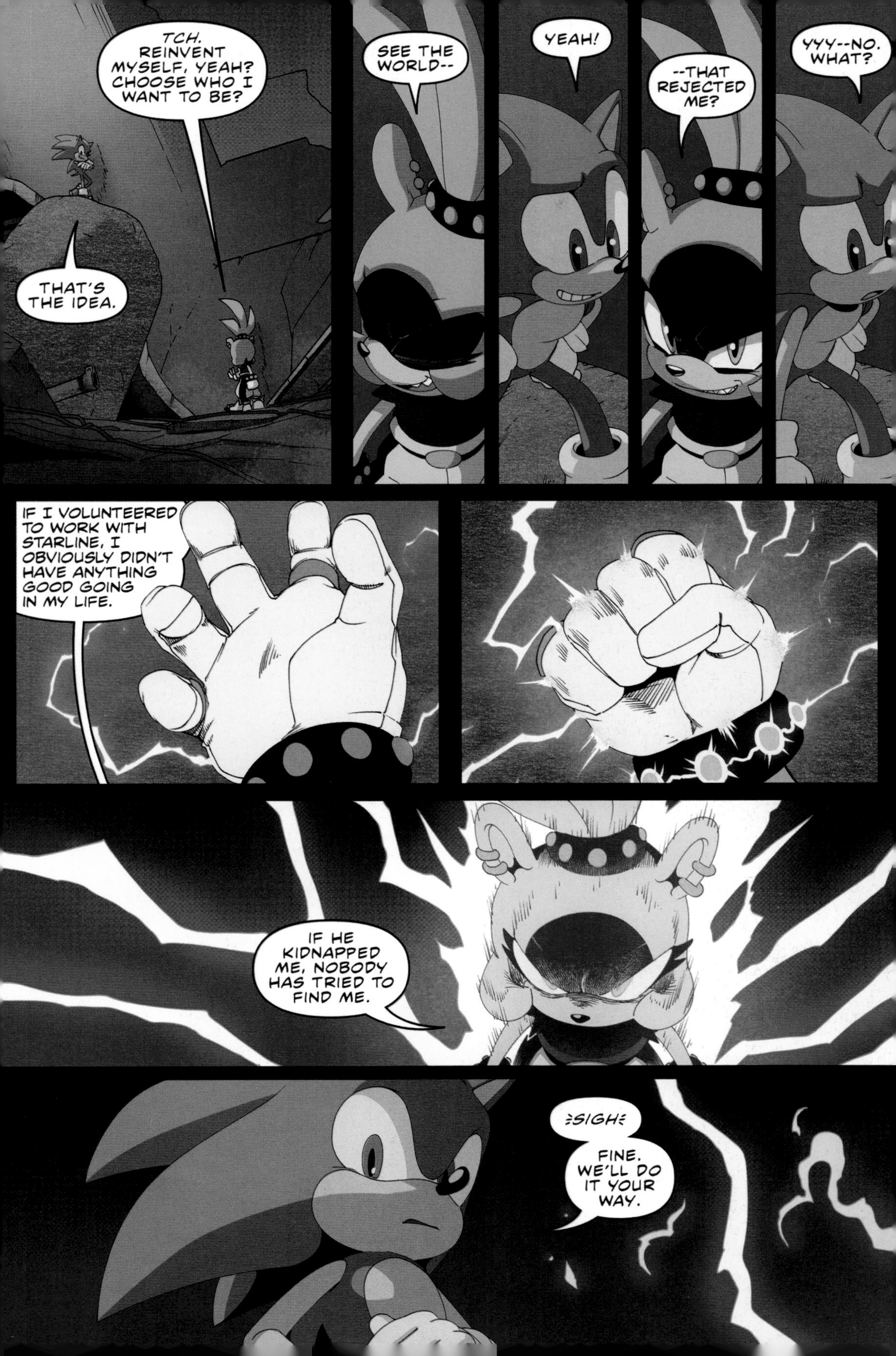
TCH. REINVENT MYSELF, YEAH? CHOOSE WHO I WANT TO BE?
THAT'S THE IDEA.
SEE THE WORLD--
YEAH!
--THAT REJECTED ME?
YYY--NO. WHAT?
IF I VOLUNTEERED TO WORK WITH STARLINE, I OBVIOUSLY DIDN'T HAVE ANYTHING GOOD GOING IN MY LIFE.
IF HE KIDNAPPED ME, NOBODY HAS TRIED TO FIND ME.
SIGH
FINE. WE'LL DO IT YOUR WAY.

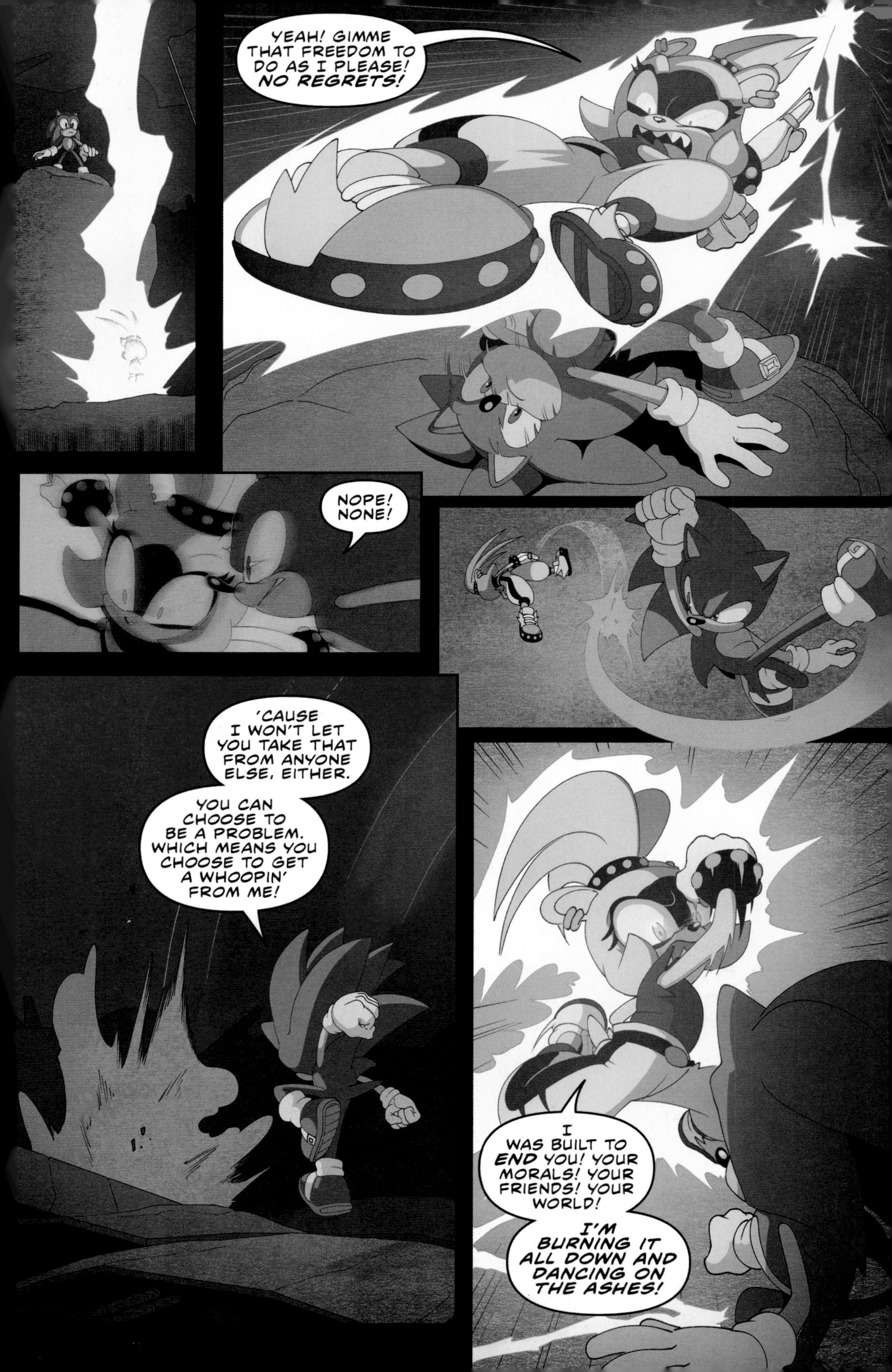
YEAH! GIMME THAT FREEDOM TO DO AS I PLEASE! NO REGRETS!
NOPE! NONE!
'CAUSE I WON'T LET YOU TAKE THAT FROM ANYONE ELSE, EITHER.
YOU CAN CHOOSE TO BE A PROBLEM. WHICH MEANS YOU CHOOSE TO GET A WHOOPIN' FROM ME!
I WAS BUILT TO END YOU! YOUR MORALS! YOUR FRIENDS! YOUR WORLD!
I'M BURNING IT ALL DOWN AND DANCING ON THE ASHES!

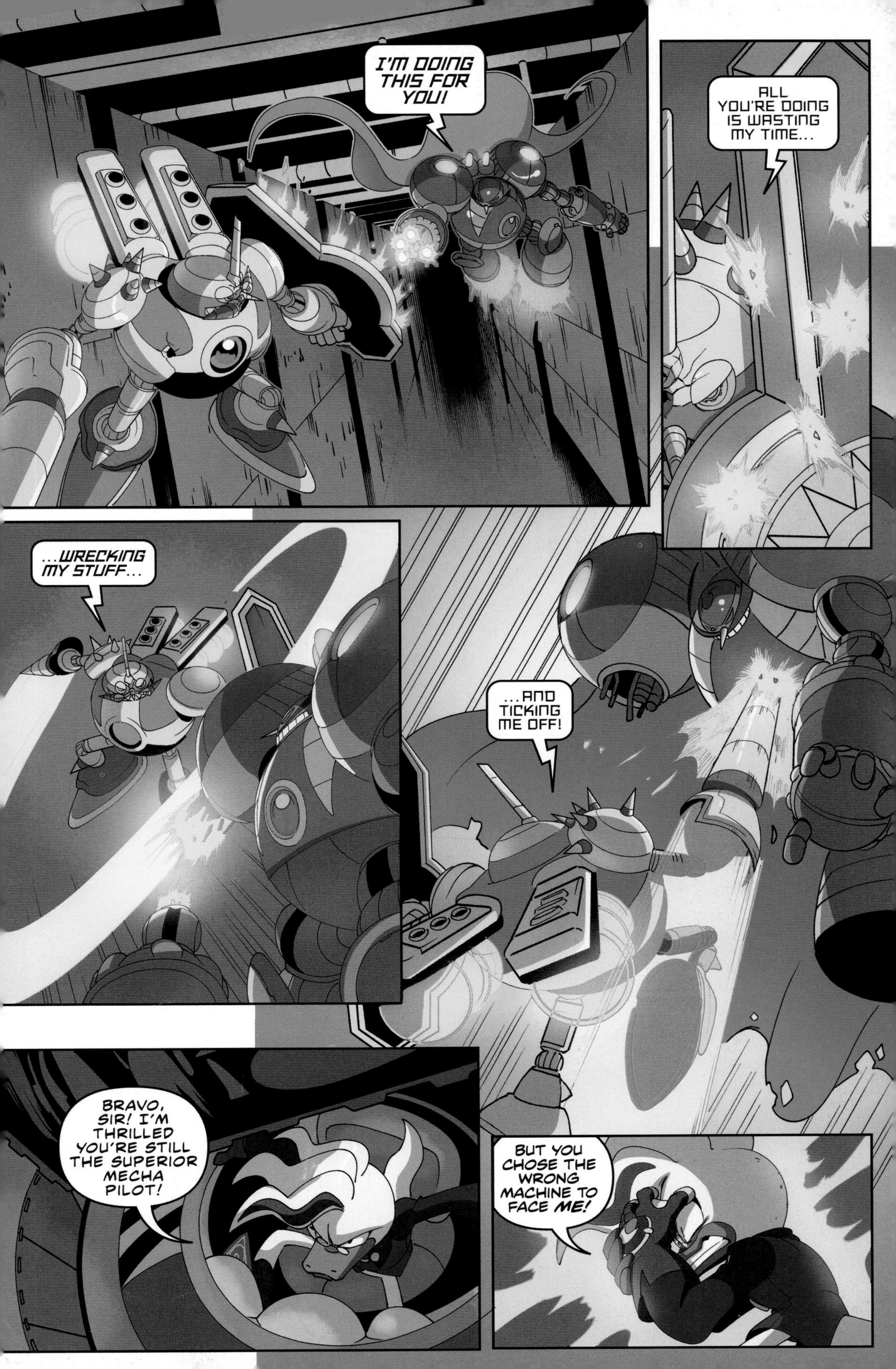
I'M DOING THIS FOR YOU!
ALL YOU'RE DOING IS WASTING MY TIME...
...WRECKING MY STUFF...
...AND TICKING ME OFF!
BRAVO, SIR! I'M THRILLED YOU'RE STILL THE SUPERIOR MECHA PILOT!
BUT YOU CHOSE THE WRONG MACHINE TO FACE ME!

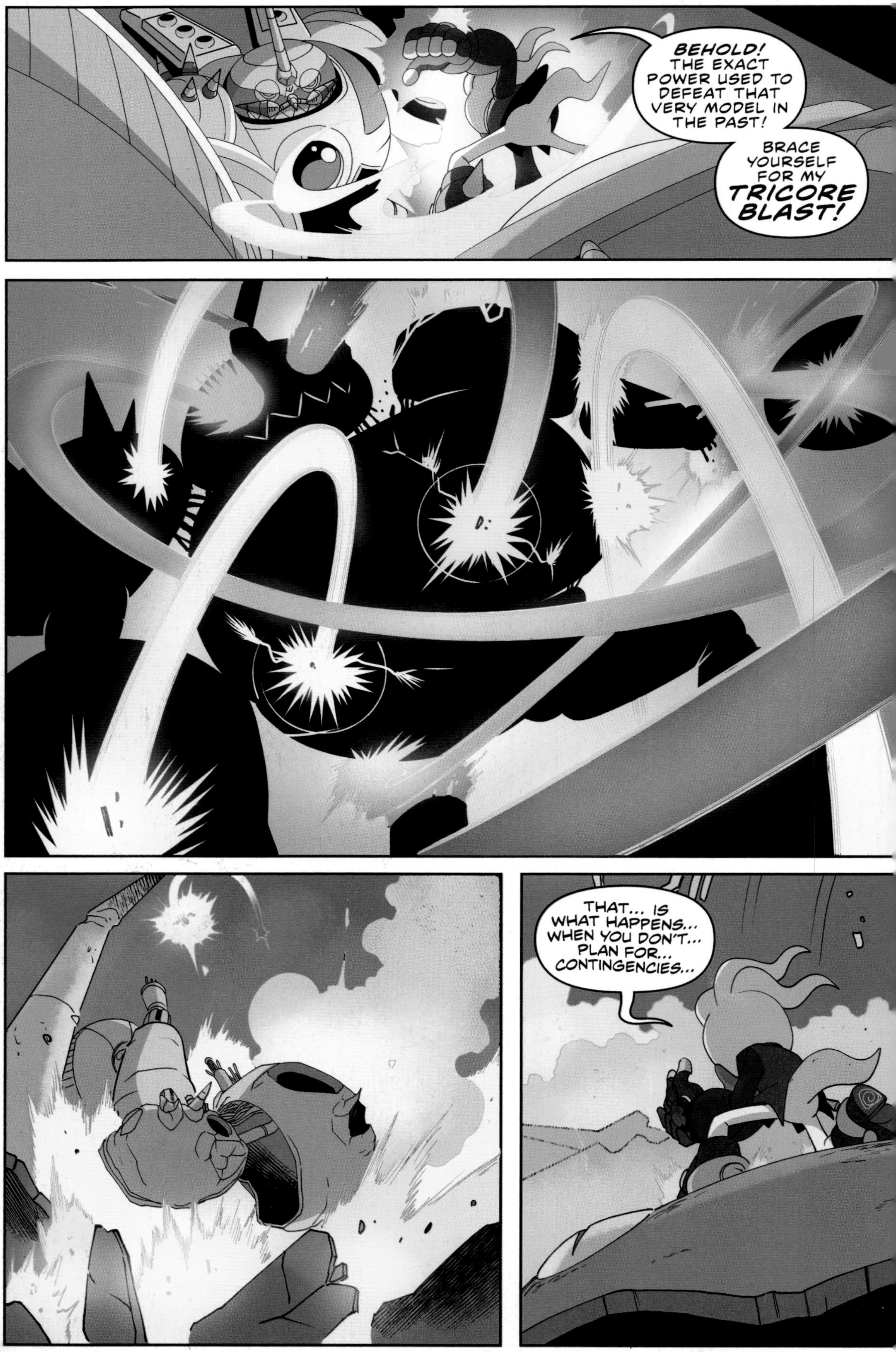
BEHOLD! THE EXACT POWER USED TO DEFEAT THAT VERY MODEL IN THE PAST!
BRACE YOURSELF FOR MY TRICORE BLAST!
THAT... IS WHAT HAPPENS... WHEN YOU DON'T... PLAN FOR... CONTINGENCIES...

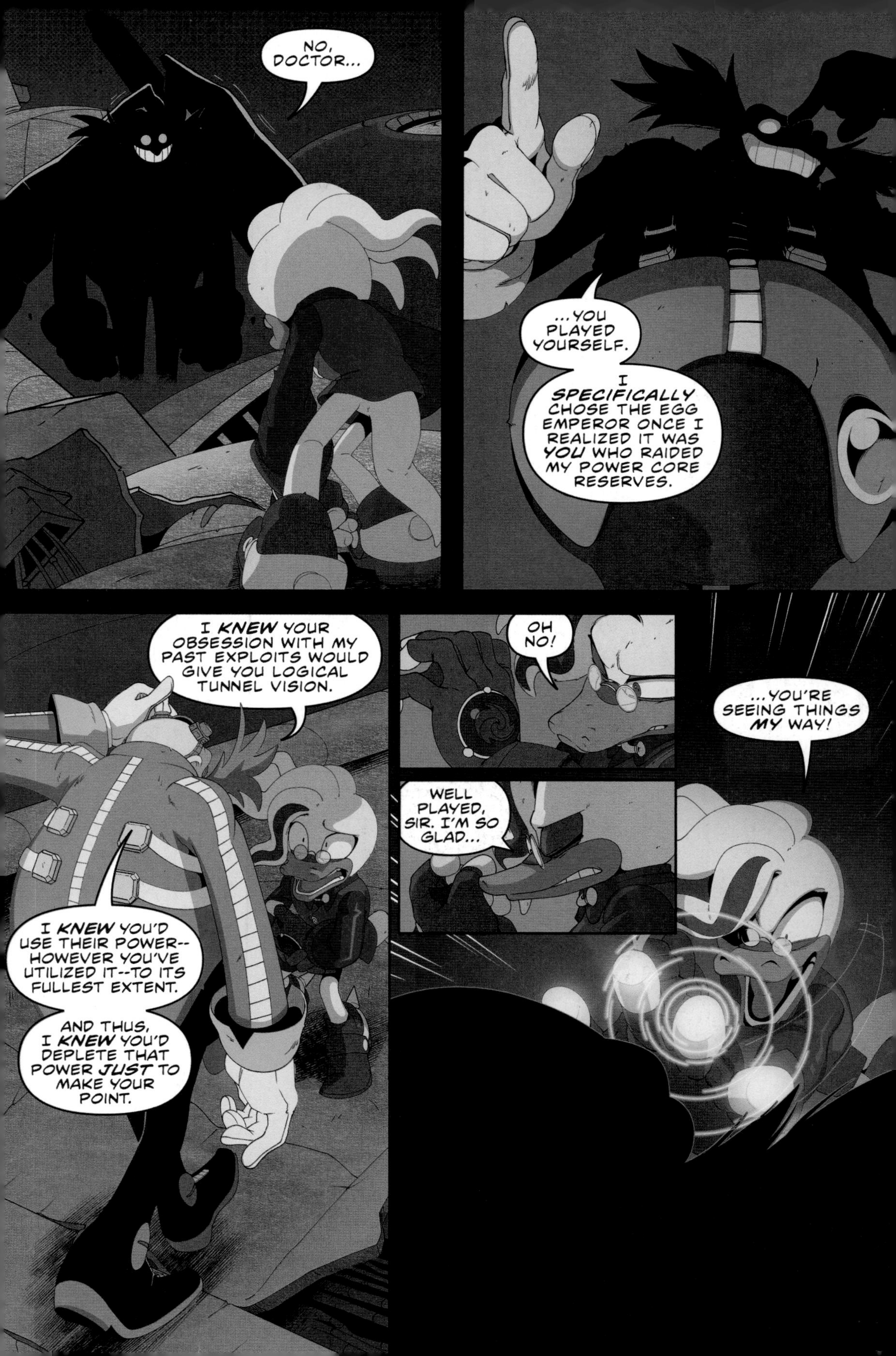
NO, DOCTOR...
...YOU PLAYED YOURSELF.
I SPECIFICALLY CHOSE THE EGG EMPEROR ONCE I REALIZED IT WAS YOU WHO RAIDED MY POWER CORE RESERVES.
I KNEW YOUR OBSESSION WITH MY PAST EXPLOITS WOULD GIVE YOU LOGICAL TUNNEL VISION.
I KNEW YOU'D USE THEIR POWER--HOWEVER YOU'VE UTILIZED IT--TO ITS FULLEST EXTENT.
AND THUS, I KNEW YOU'D DEPLETE THAT POWER JUST TO MAKE YOUR POINT.
OH NO!
WELL PLAYED, SIR. I'M SO GLAD...
...YOU'RE SEEING THINGS MY WAY!

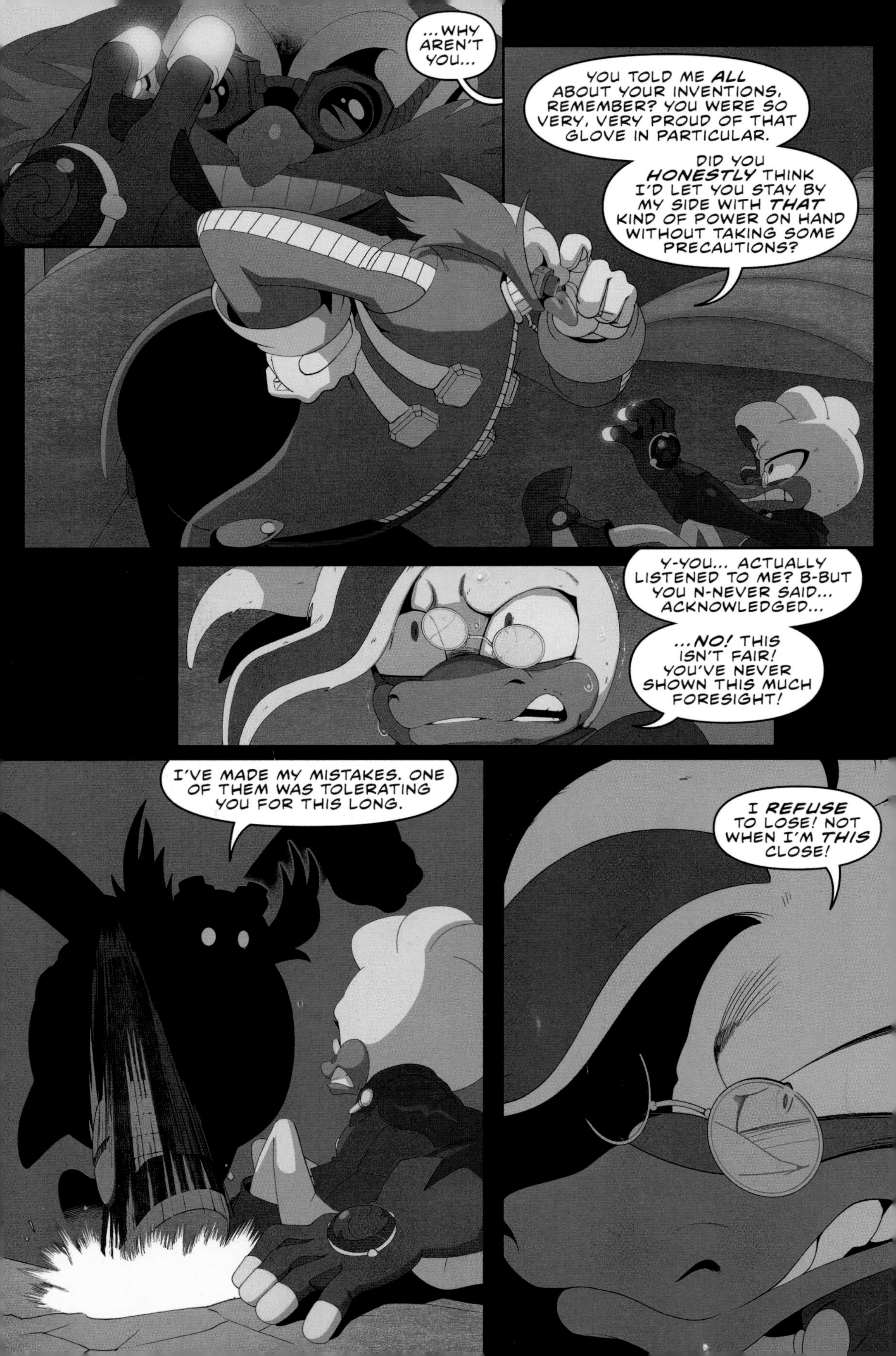
...WHY AREN'T YOU...
YOU TOLD ME ALL ABOUT YOUR INVENTIONS, REMEMBER? YOU WERE SO VERY, VERY PROUD OF THAT GLOVE IN PARTICULAR.
DID YOU HONESTLY THINK I'D LET YOU STAY BY MY SIDE WITH THAT KIND OF POWER ON HAND WITHOUT TAKING SOME PRECAUTIONS?
Y-YOU... ACTUALLY LISTENED TO ME? B-BUT YOU N-NEVER SAID... ACKNOWLEDGED...
...NO! THIS ISN'T FAIR! YOU'VE NEVER SHOWN THIS MUCH FORESIGHT!
I'VE MADE MY MISTAKES. ONE OF THEM WAS TOLERATING YOU FOR THIS LONG.
I REFUSE TO LOSE! NOT WHEN I'M THIS CLOSE!

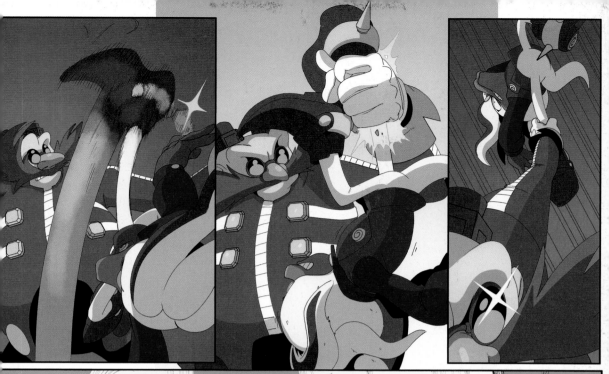

GLONK

LITTLE MAN, WHAT MAKES YOU THINK YOU HAVE ANY CHOICE IN THE MATTER?

FATHER!

EH?

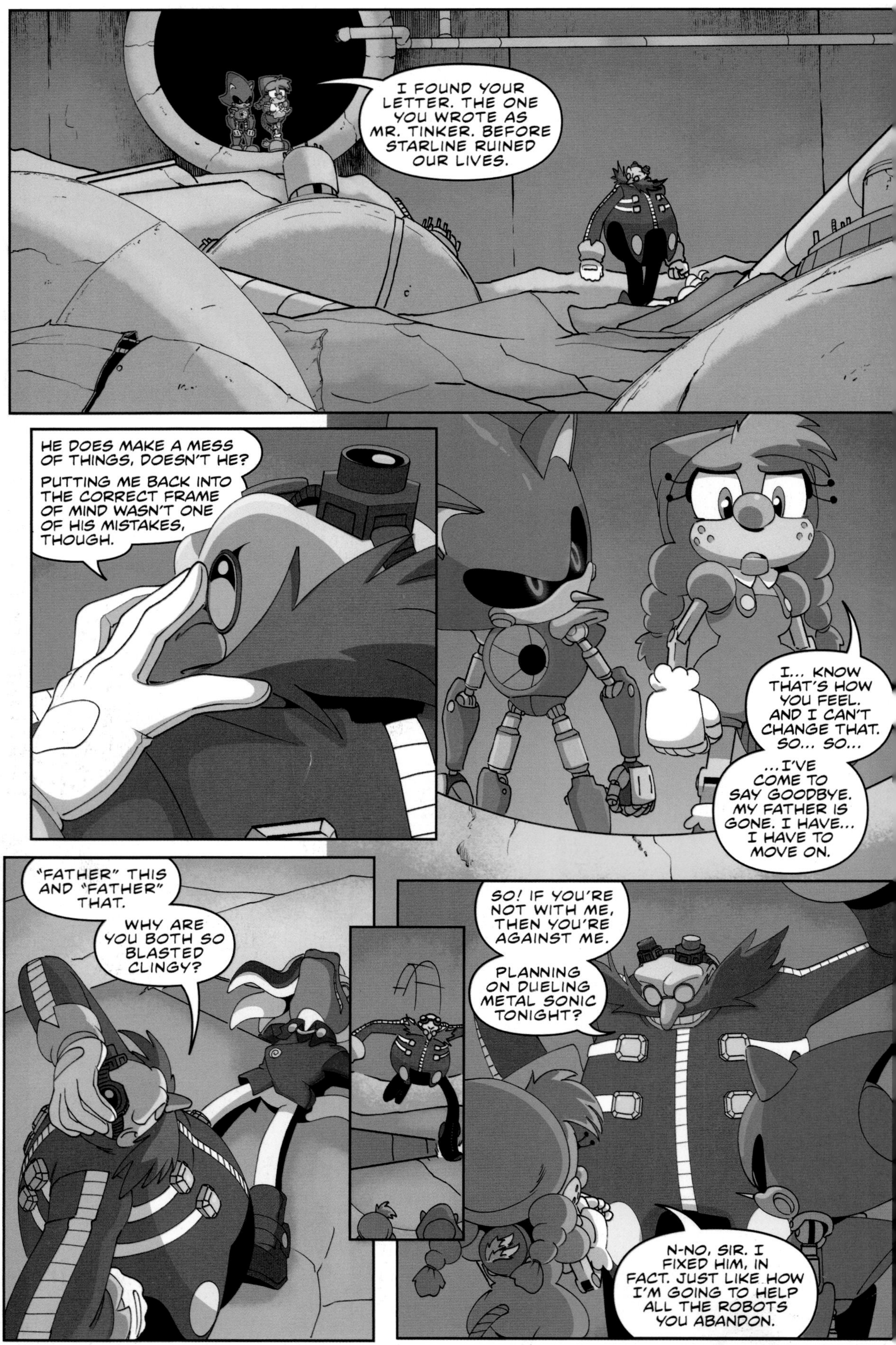
I FOUND YOUR LETTER. THE ONE YOU WROTE AS MR. TINKER. BEFORE STARLINE RUINED OUR LIVES.
HE DOES MAKE A MESS OF THINGS, DOESN'T HE?
PUTTING ME BACK INTO THE CORRECT FRAME OF MIND WASN'T ONE OF HIS MISTAKES, THOUGH.
I... KNOW THAT'S HOW YOU FEEL. AND I CAN'T CHANGE THAT. SO... SO...
...I'VE COME TO SAY GOODBYE. MY FATHER IS GONE. I HAVE... I HAVE TO MOVE ON.
"FATHER" THIS AND "FATHER" THAT.
WHY ARE YOU BOTH SO BLASTED CLINGY?
SO! IF YOU'RE NOT WITH ME, THEN YOU'RE AGAINST ME.
PLANNING ON DUELING METAL SONIC TONIGHT?
N-NO, SIR. I FIXED HIM, IN FACT. JUST LIKE HOW I'M GOING TO HELP ALL THE ROBOTS YOU ABANDON.

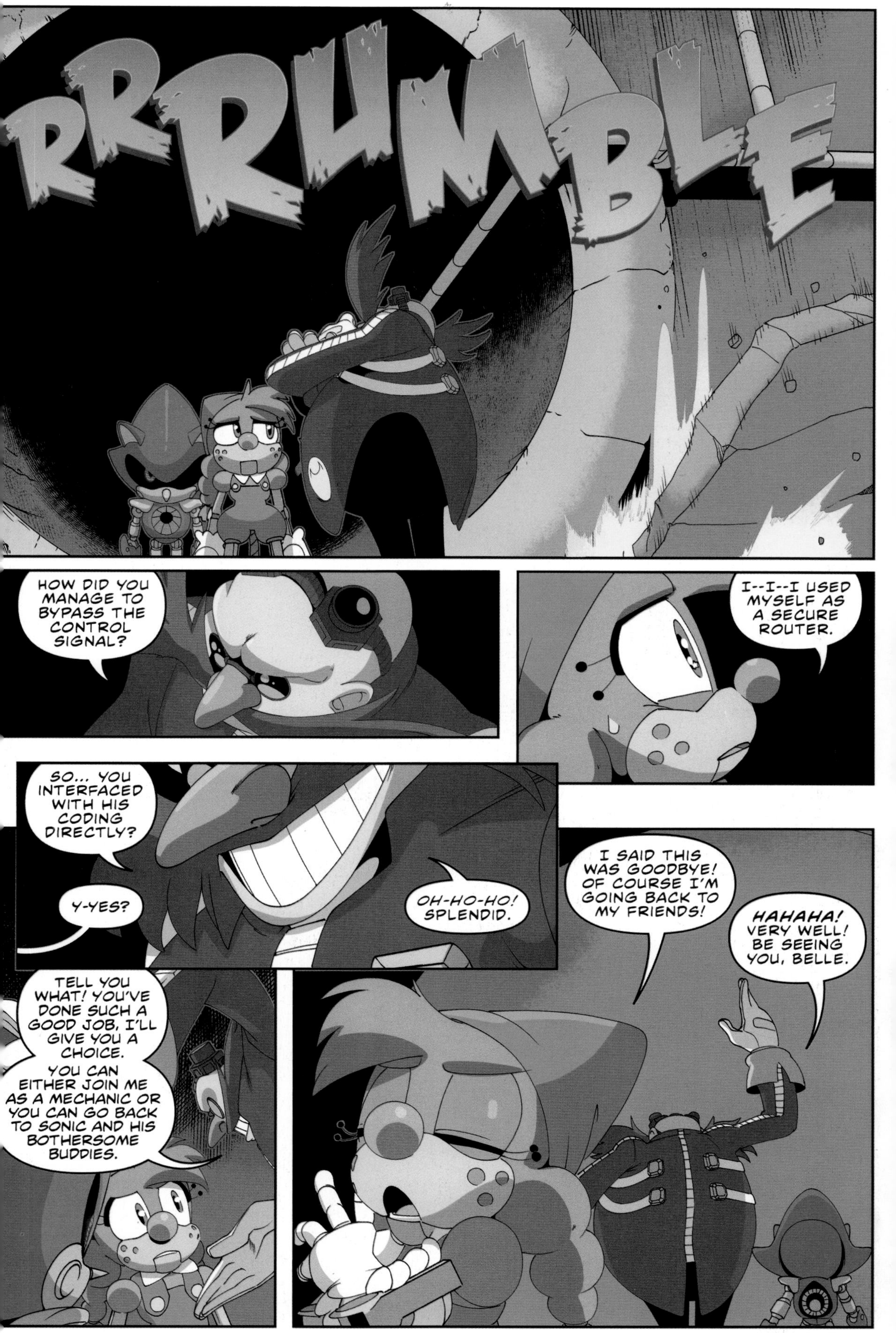
RRRUMBLE
HOW DID YOU MANAGE TO BYPASS THE CONTROL SIGNAL?
I--I--I USED MYSELF AS A SECURE ROUTER.
SO... YOU INTERFACED WITH HIS CODING DIRECTLY?
Y-YES?
OH-HO-HO! SPLENDID.
TELL YOU WHAT! YOU'VE DONE SUCH A GOOD JOB, I'LL GIVE YOU A CHOICE.
YOU CAN EITHER JOIN ME AS A MECHANIC OR YOU CAN GO BACK TO SONIC AND HIS BOTHERSOME BUDDIES.
I SAID THIS WAS GOODBYE! OF COURSE I'M GOING BACK TO MY FRIENDS!
HAHAHA! VERY WELL! BE SEEING YOU, BELLE.

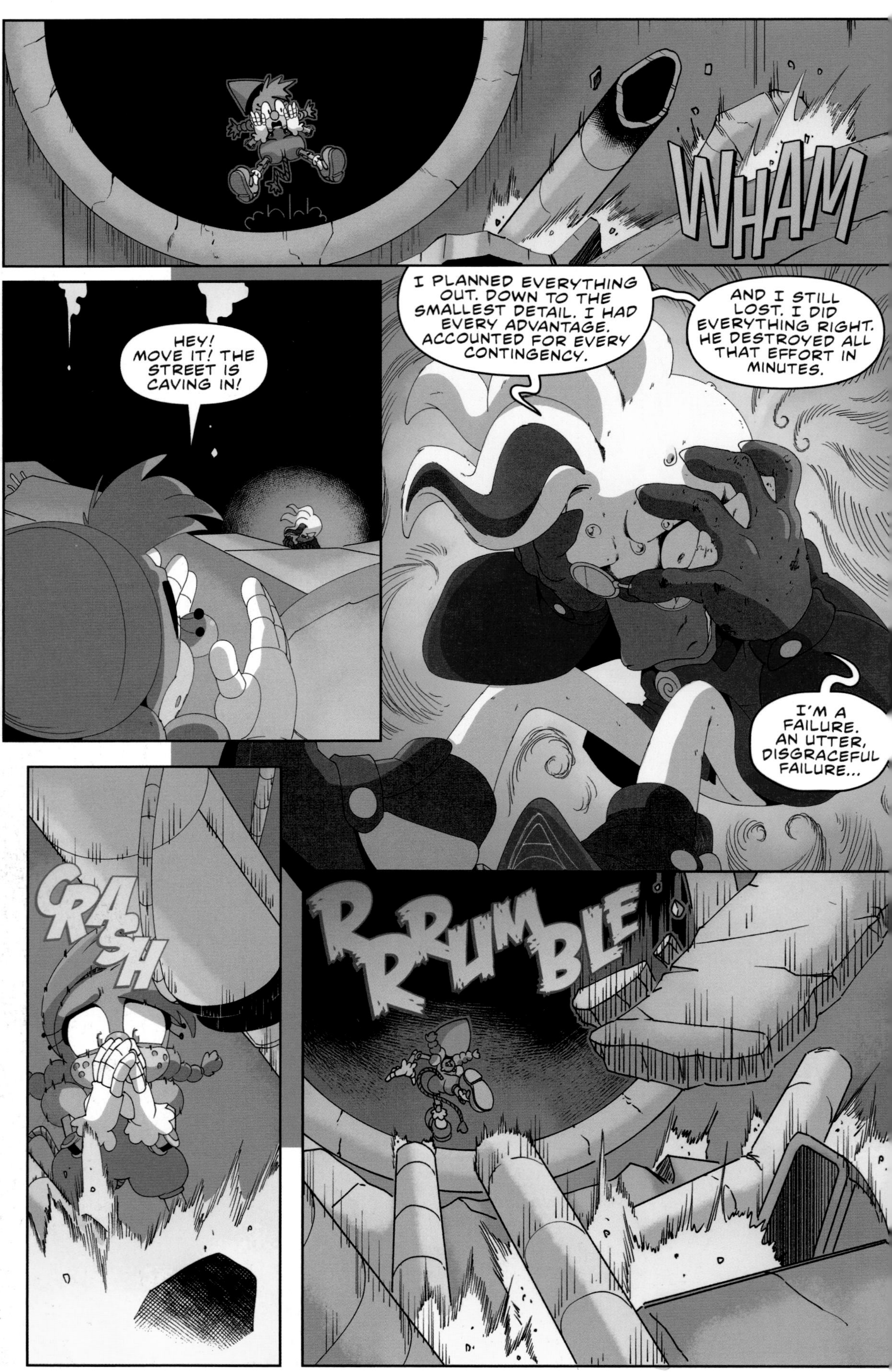
WHAM
HEY! MOVE IT! THE STREET IS CAVING IN!
I PLANNED EVERYTHING OUT. DOWN TO THE SMALLEST DETAIL. I HAD EVERY ADVANTAGE. ACCOUNTED FOR EVERY CONTINGENCY.
AND I STILL LOST. I DID EVERYTHING RIGHT. HE DESTROYED ALL THAT EFFORT IN MINUTES.
I'M A FAILURE. AN UTTER, DISGRACEFUL FAILURE...
CRASH
RRRUMBLE

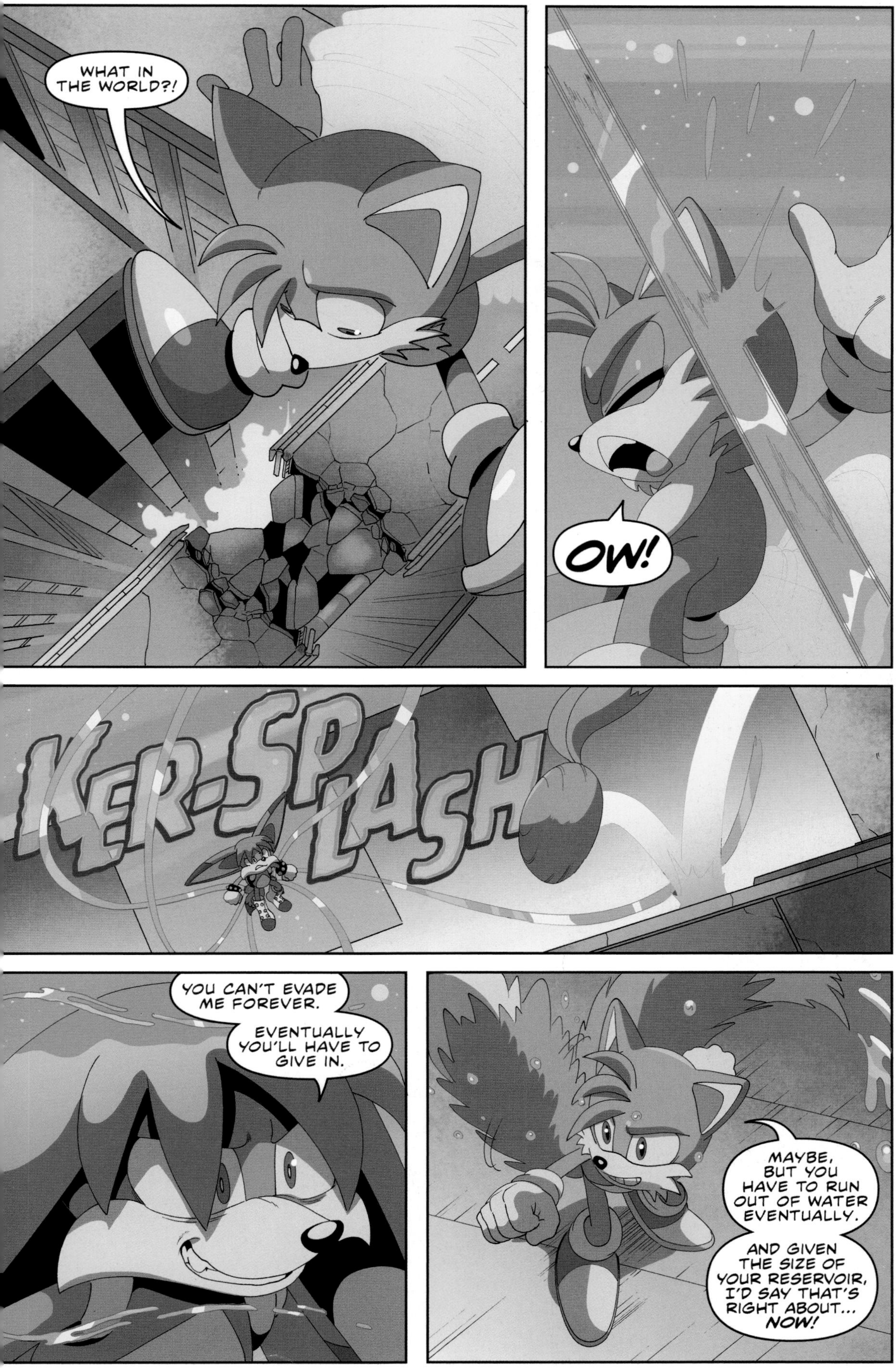
WHAT IN THE WORLD?!
OW!
KER-SPLASH
YOU CAN'T EVADE ME FOREVER.
EVENTUALLY YOU'LL HAVE TO GIVE IN.
MAYBE, BUT YOU HAVE TO RUN OUT OF WATER EVENTUALLY.
AND GIVEN THE SIZE OF YOUR RESERVOIR, I'D SAY THAT'S RIGHT ABOUT... NOW!

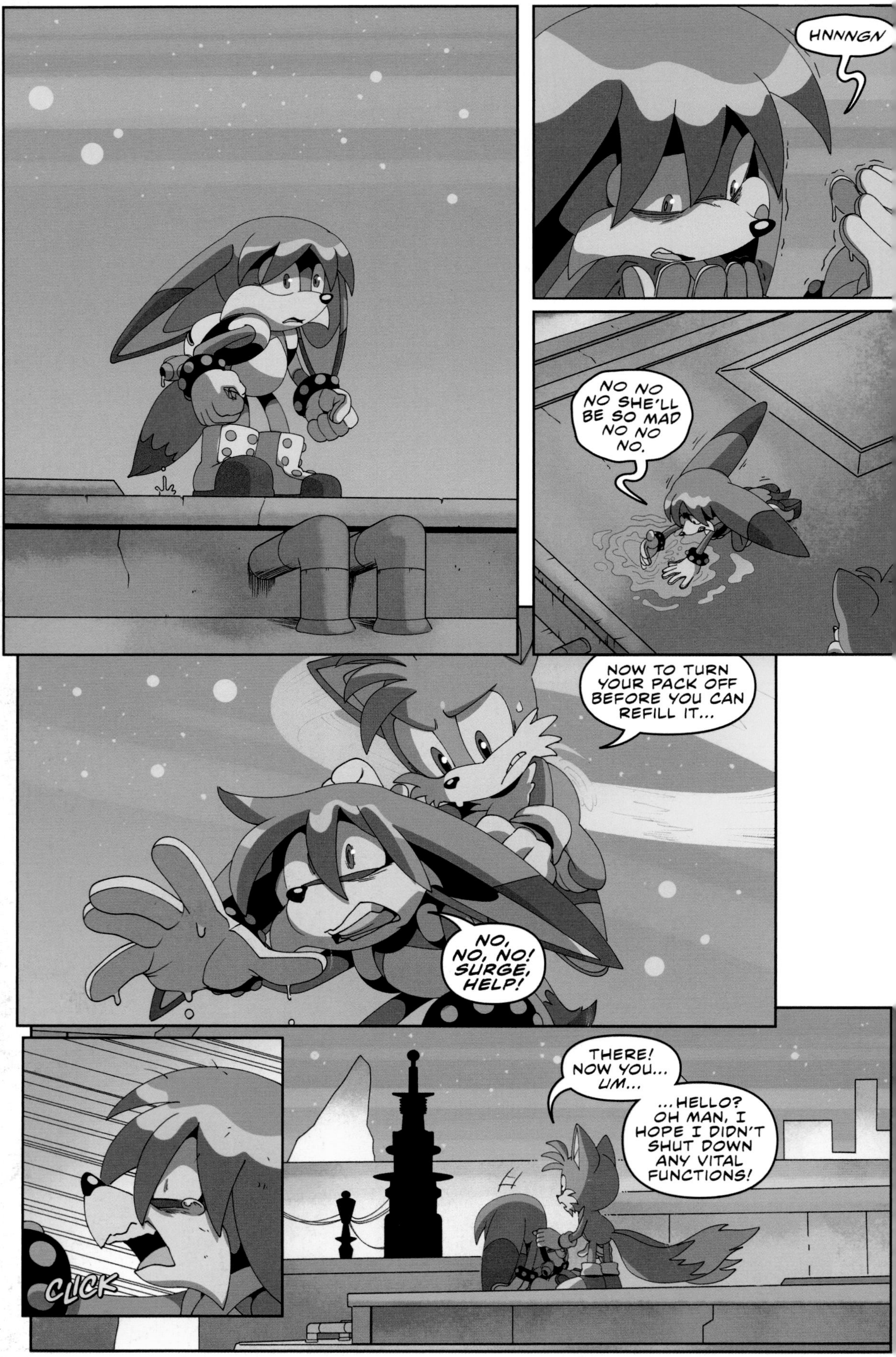
HNNNGN
NO NO NO SHE'LL BE SO MAD NO NO NO.
NOW TO TURN YOUR PACK OFF BEFORE YOU CAN REFILL IT...
NO, NO, NO! SURGE, HELP!
CLICK
THERE! NOW YOU... UM...
...HELLO? OH MAN, I HOPE I DIDN'T SHUT DOWN ANY VITAL FUNCTIONS!

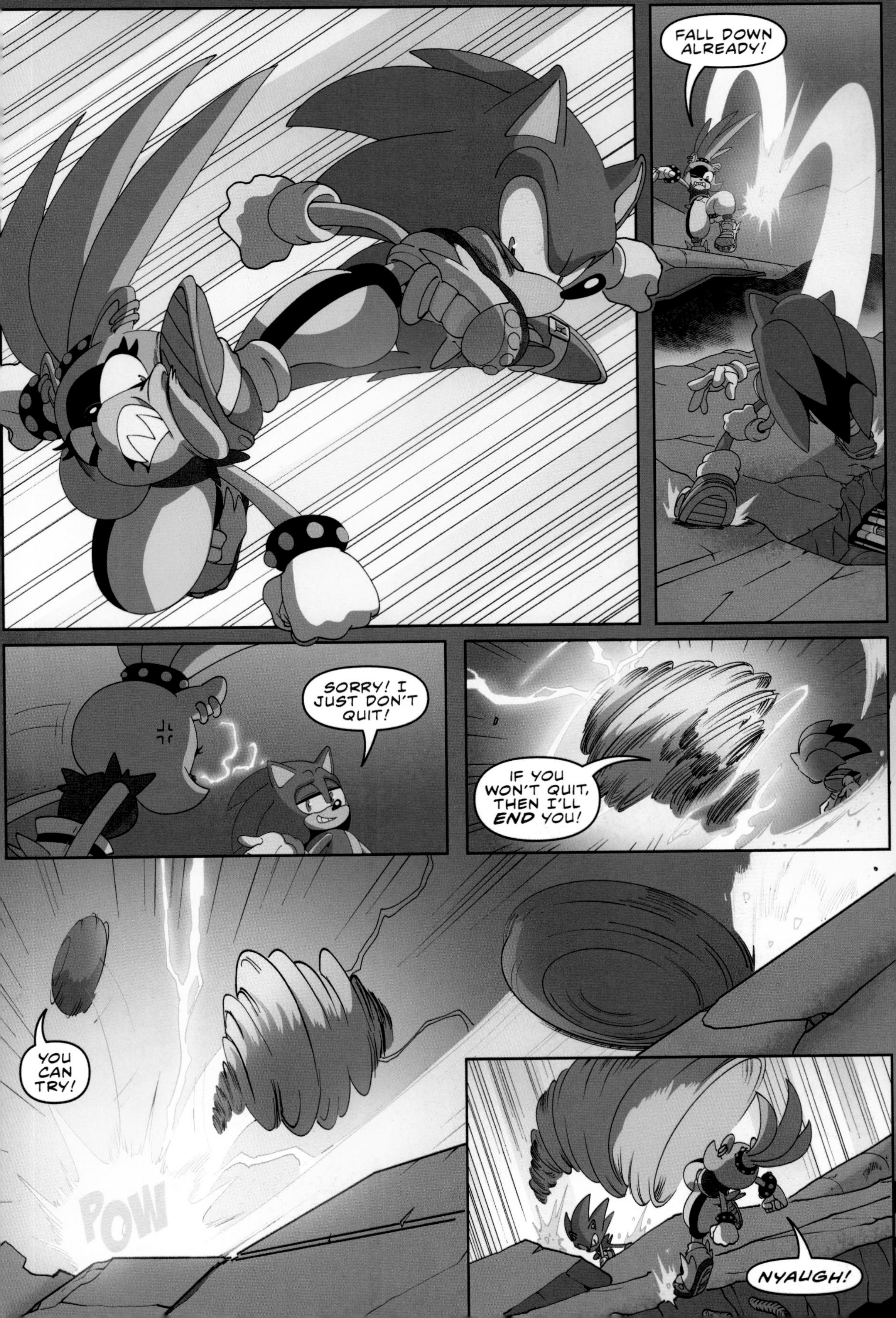
FALL DOWN ALREADY!
SORRY! I JUST DON'T QUIT!
IF YOU WON'T QUIT, THEN I'LL END YOU!
YOU CAN TRY!
POW
NYAUGH!

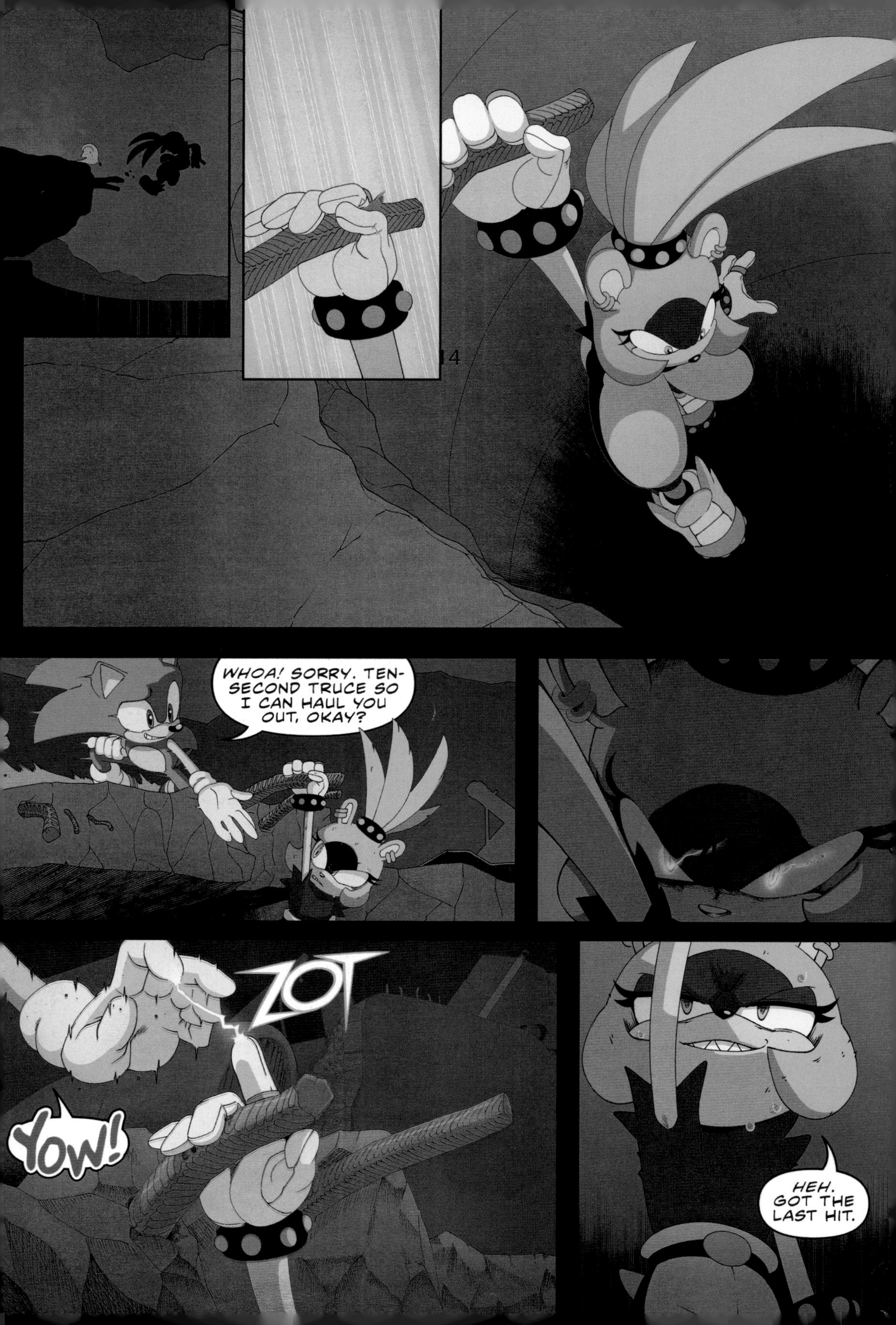

14
WHOA! SORRY. TEN-SECOND TRUCE SO I CAN HAUL YOU OUT, OKAY?
ZOT
YOW!
HEH. GOT THE LAST HIT.

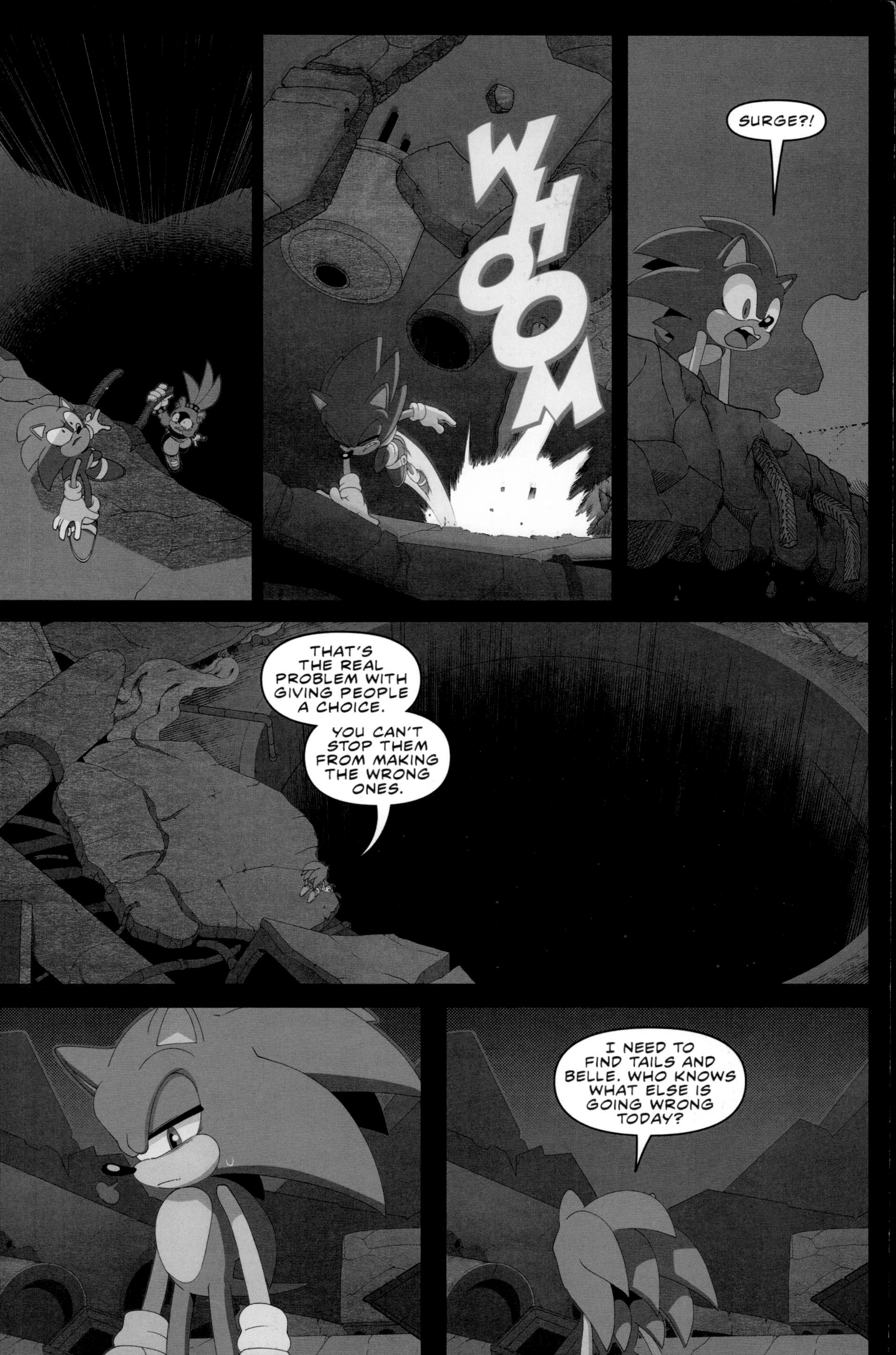
WHOOM
SURGE?!
THAT'S THE REAL PROBLEM WITH GIVING PEOPLE A CHOICE.
YOU CAN'T STOP THEM FROM MAKING THE WRONG ONES.
I NEED TO FIND TAILS AND BELLE. WHO KNOWS WHAT ELSE IS GOING WRONG TODAY?

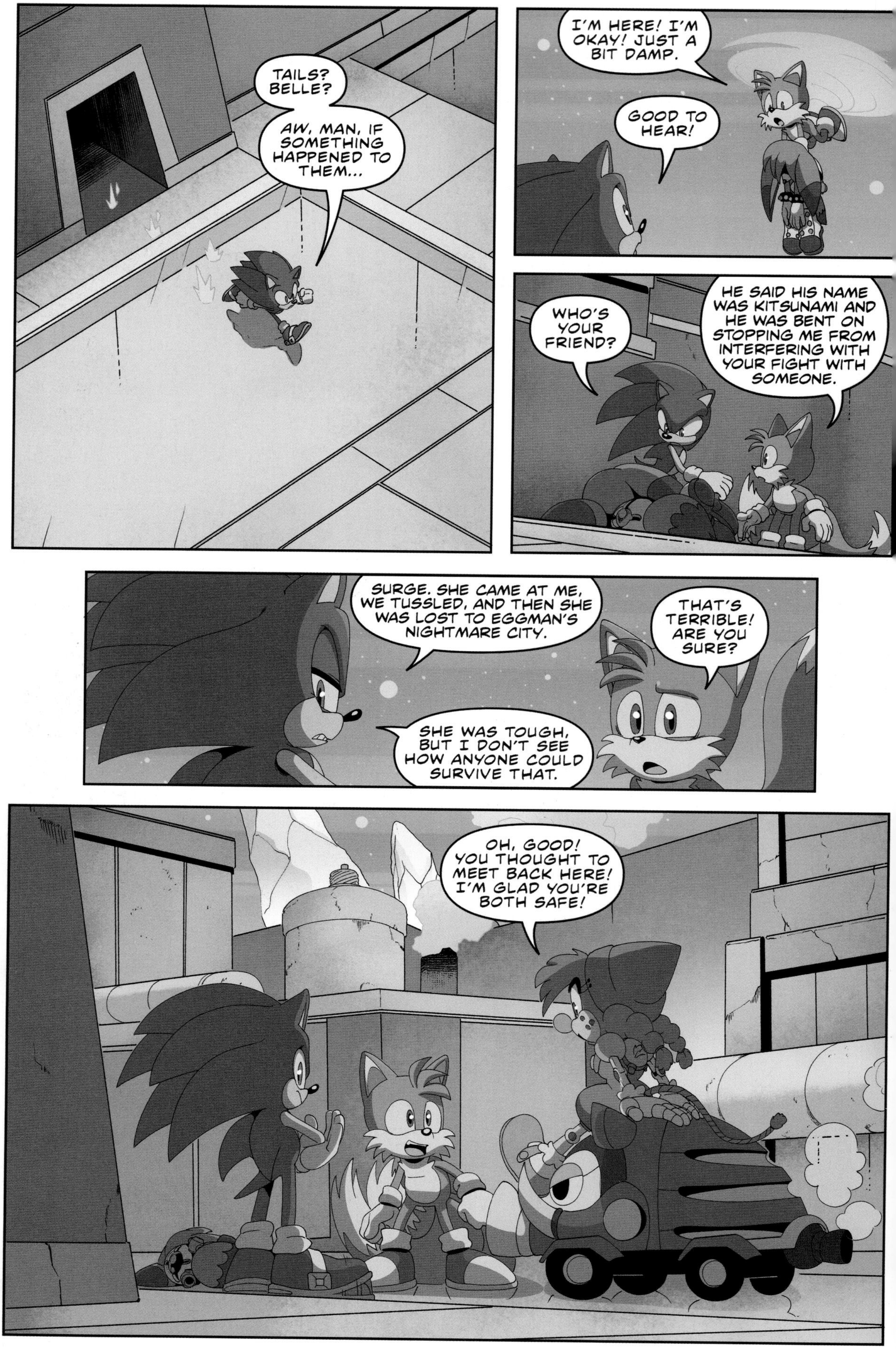
TAILS? BELLE?
AW, MAN, IF SOMETHING HAPPENED TO THEM...
I'M HERE! I'M OKAY! JUST A BIT DAMP.
GOOD TO HEAR!
WHO'S YOUR FRIEND?
HE SAID HIS NAME WAS KITSUNAMI AND HE WAS BENT ON STOPPING ME FROM INTERFERING WITH YOUR FIGHT WITH SOMEONE.
SURGE. SHE CAME AT ME, WE TUSSLED, AND THEN SHE WAS LOST TO EGGMAN'S NIGHTMARE CITY.
THAT'S TERRIBLE! ARE YOU SURE?
SHE WAS TOUGH, BUT I DON'T SEE HOW ANYONE COULD SURVIVE THAT.
OH, GOOD! YOU THOUGHT TO MEET BACK HERE! I'M GLAD YOU'RE BOTH SAFE!

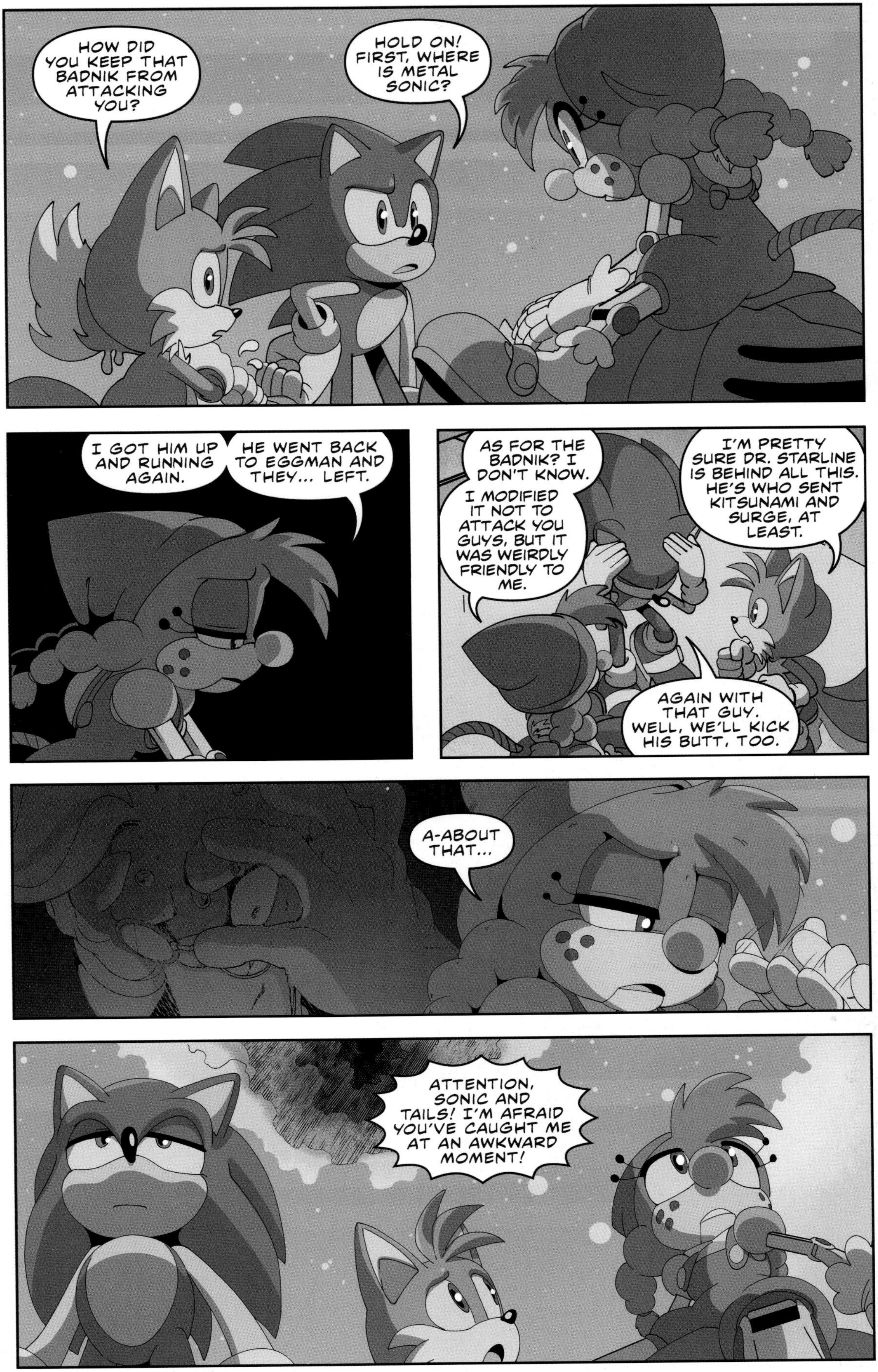
HOW DID YOU KEEP THAT BADNIK FROM ATTACKING YOU?
HOLD ON! FIRST, WHERE IS METAL SONIC?
I GOT HIM UP AND RUNNING AGAIN.
HE WENT BACK TO EGGMAN AND THEY... LEFT.
AS FOR THE BADNIK? I DON'T KNOW.
I MODIFIED IT NOT TO ATTACK YOU GUYS, BUT IT WAS WEIRDLY FRIENDLY TO ME.
I'M PRETTY SURE DR. STARLINE IS BEHIND ALL THIS. HE'S WHO SENT KITSUNAMI AND SURGE, AT LEAST.
AGAIN WITH THAT GUY. WELL, WE'LL KICK HIS BUTT, TOO.
A-ABOUT THAT...
ATTENTION, SONIC AND TAILS! I'M AFRAID YOU'VE CAUGHT ME AT AN AWKWARD MOMENT!

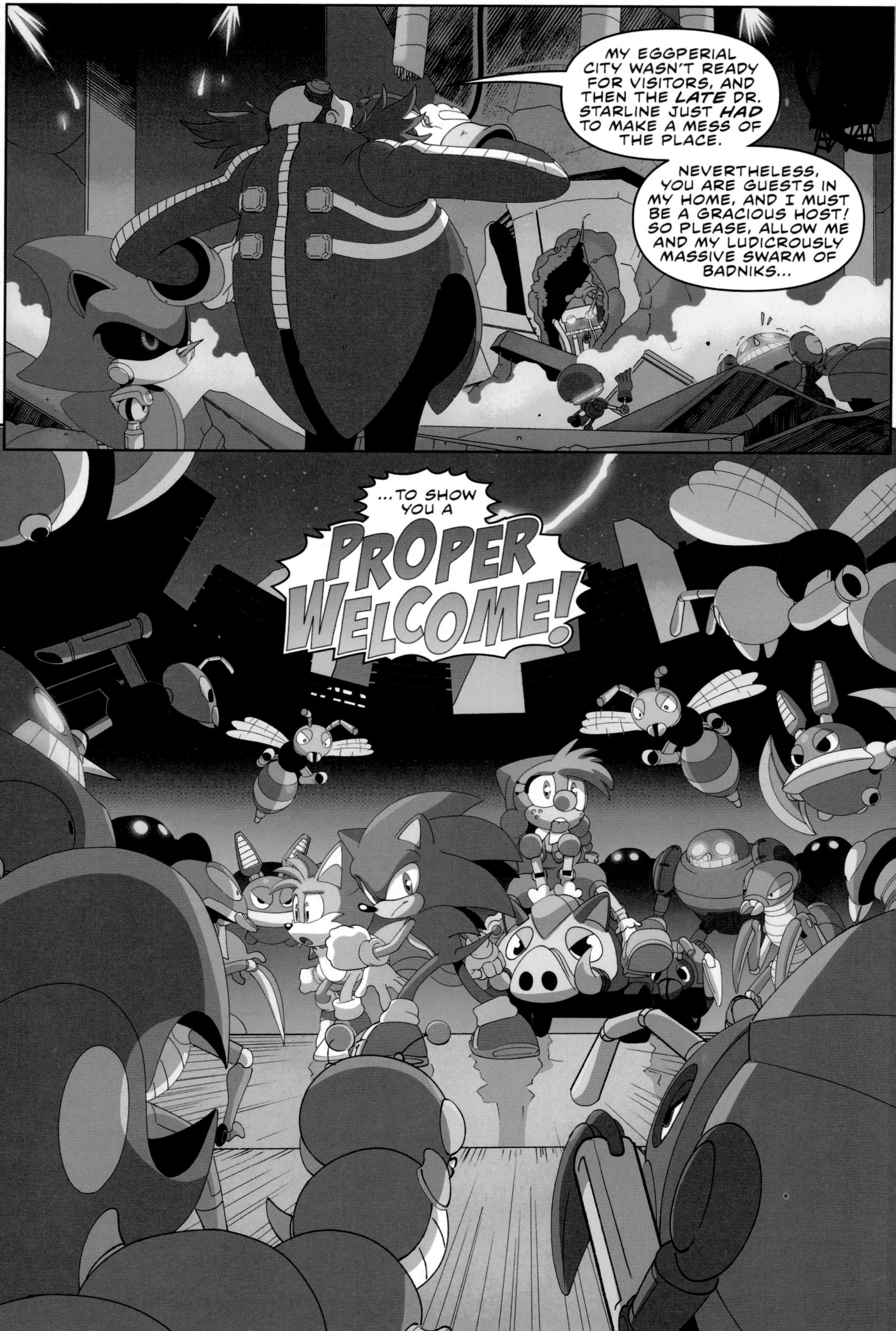
MY EGGPERIAL CITY WASN'T READY FOR VISITORS, AND THEN THE *LATE* DR. STARLINE JUST *HAD* TO MAKE A MESS OF THE PLACE.
NEVERTHELESS, YOU ARE GUESTS IN MY HOME, AND I MUST BE A GRACIOUS HOST! SO PLEASE, ALLOW ME AND MY LUDICROUSLY MASSIVE SWARM OF BADNIKS...
...TO SHOW YOU A
PROPER WELCOME!

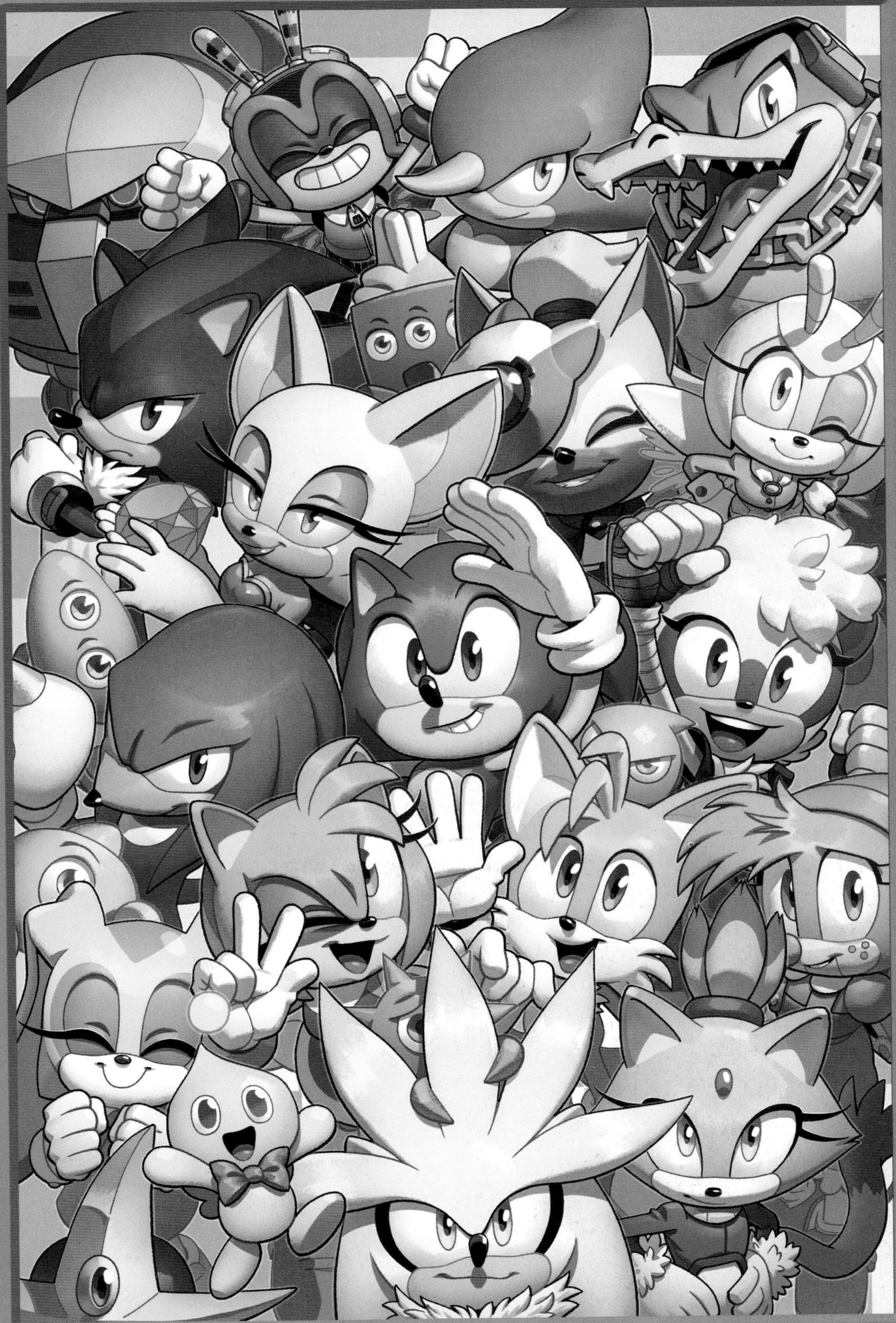

ART BY **EVAN STANLEY**

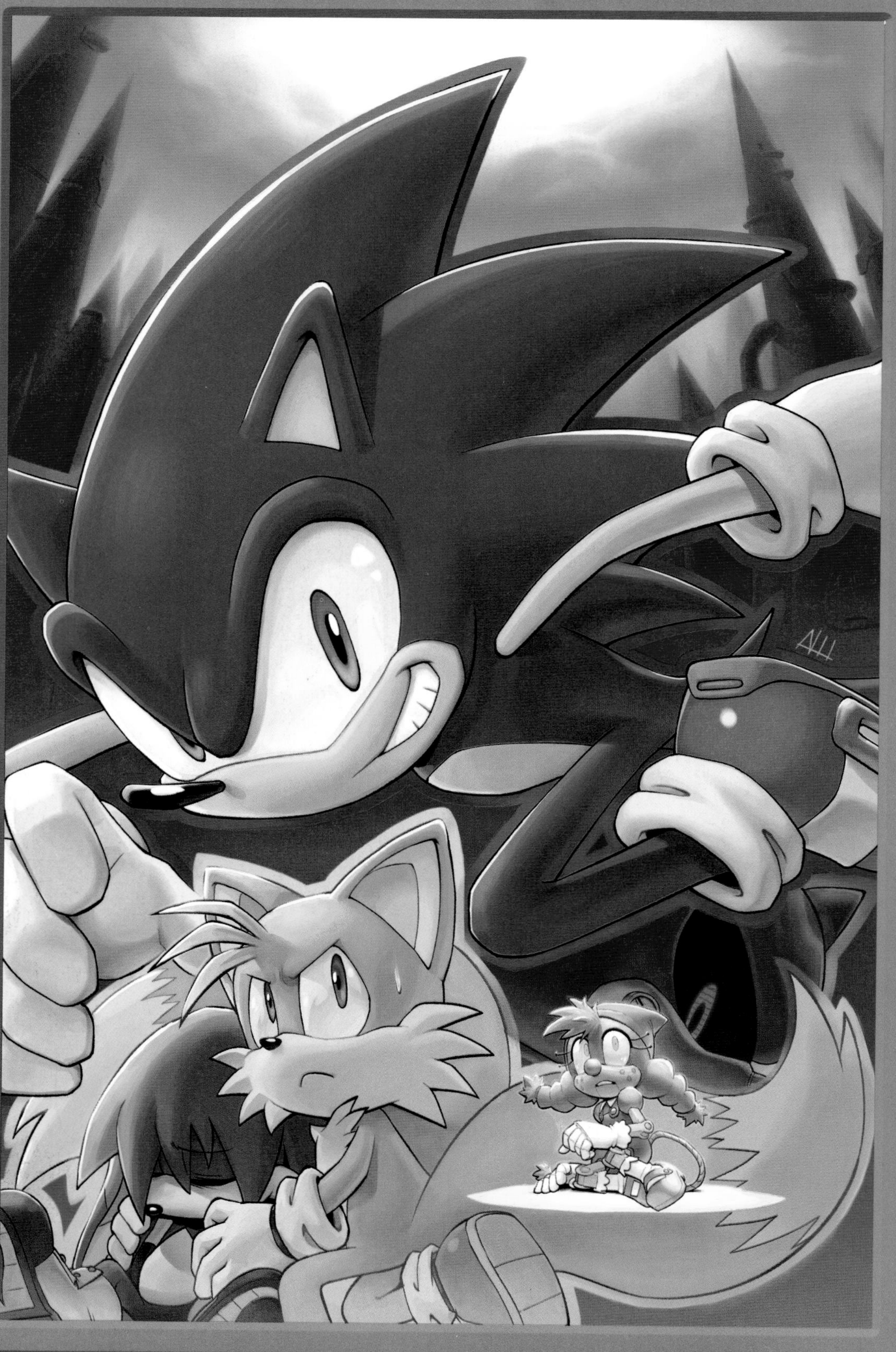

ART BY **AARON HAMMERSTROM**

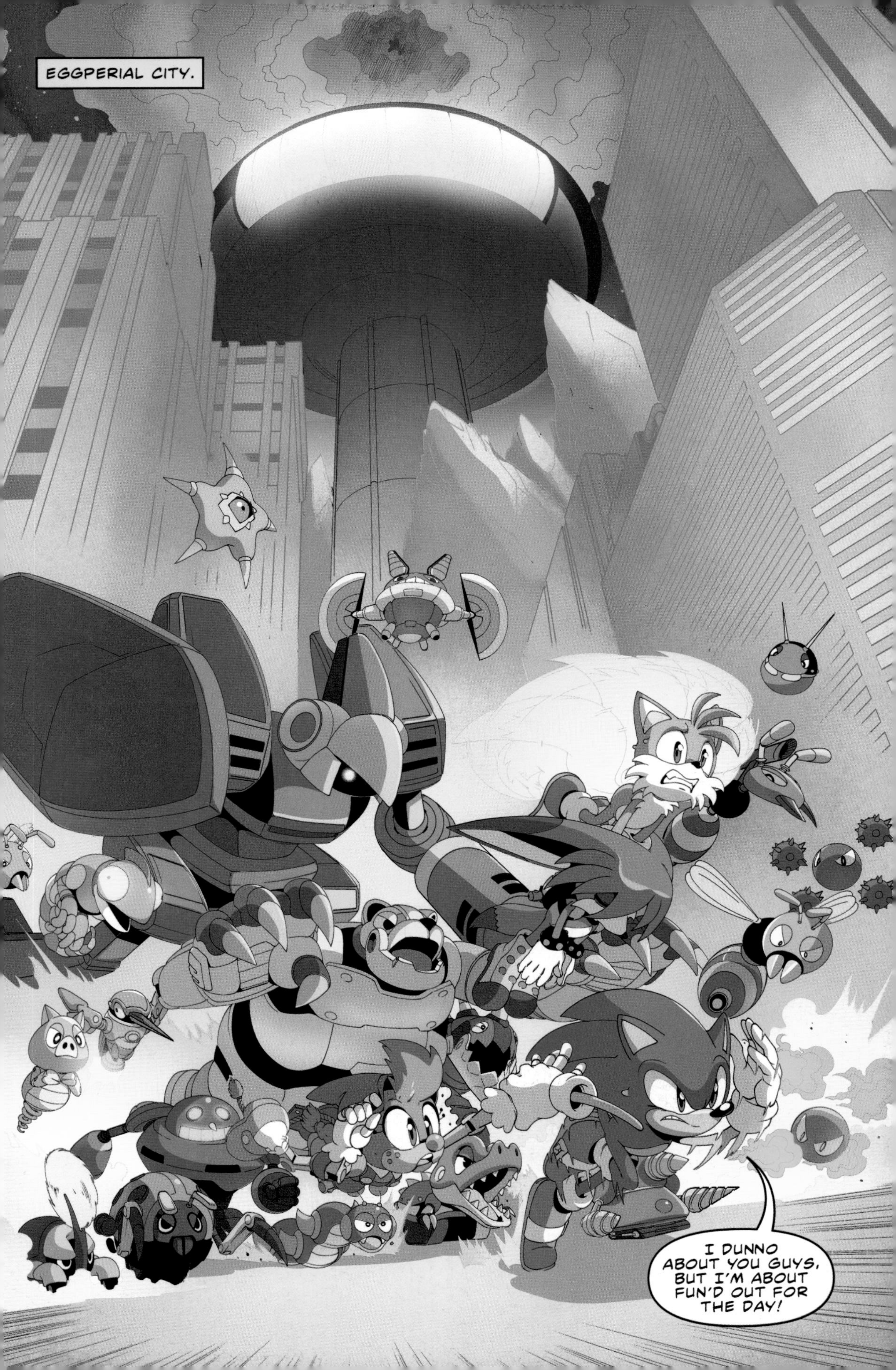
EGGPERIAL CITY.
I DUNNO ABOUT YOU GUYS, BUT I'M ABOUT FUN'D OUT FOR THE DAY!

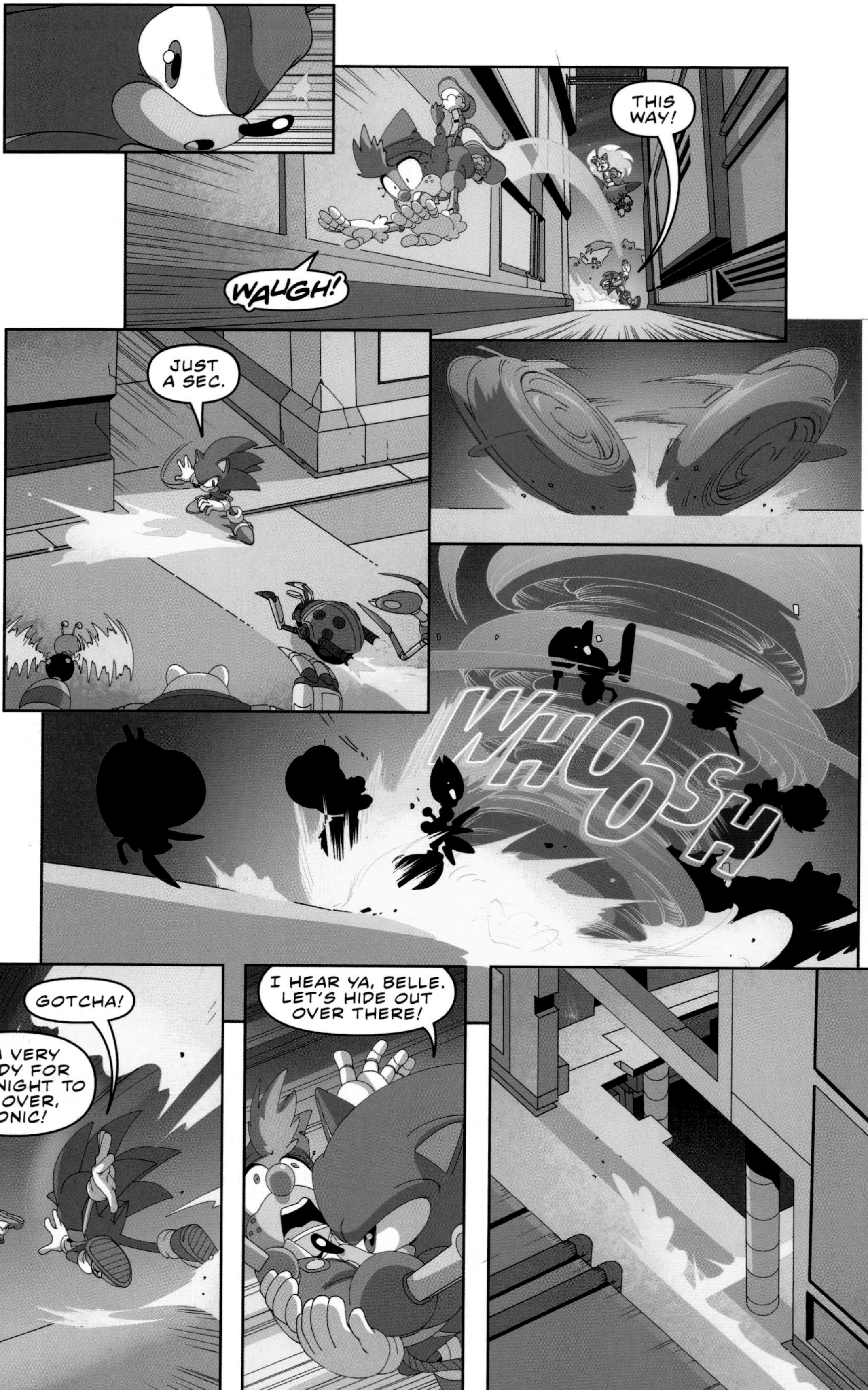
THIS WAY!
WAUGH!
JUST A SEC.
WHOOSH
GOTCHA!
I'M VERY READY FOR THIS NIGHT TO BE OVER, SONIC!
I HEAR YA, BELLE. LET'S HIDE OUT OVER THERE!

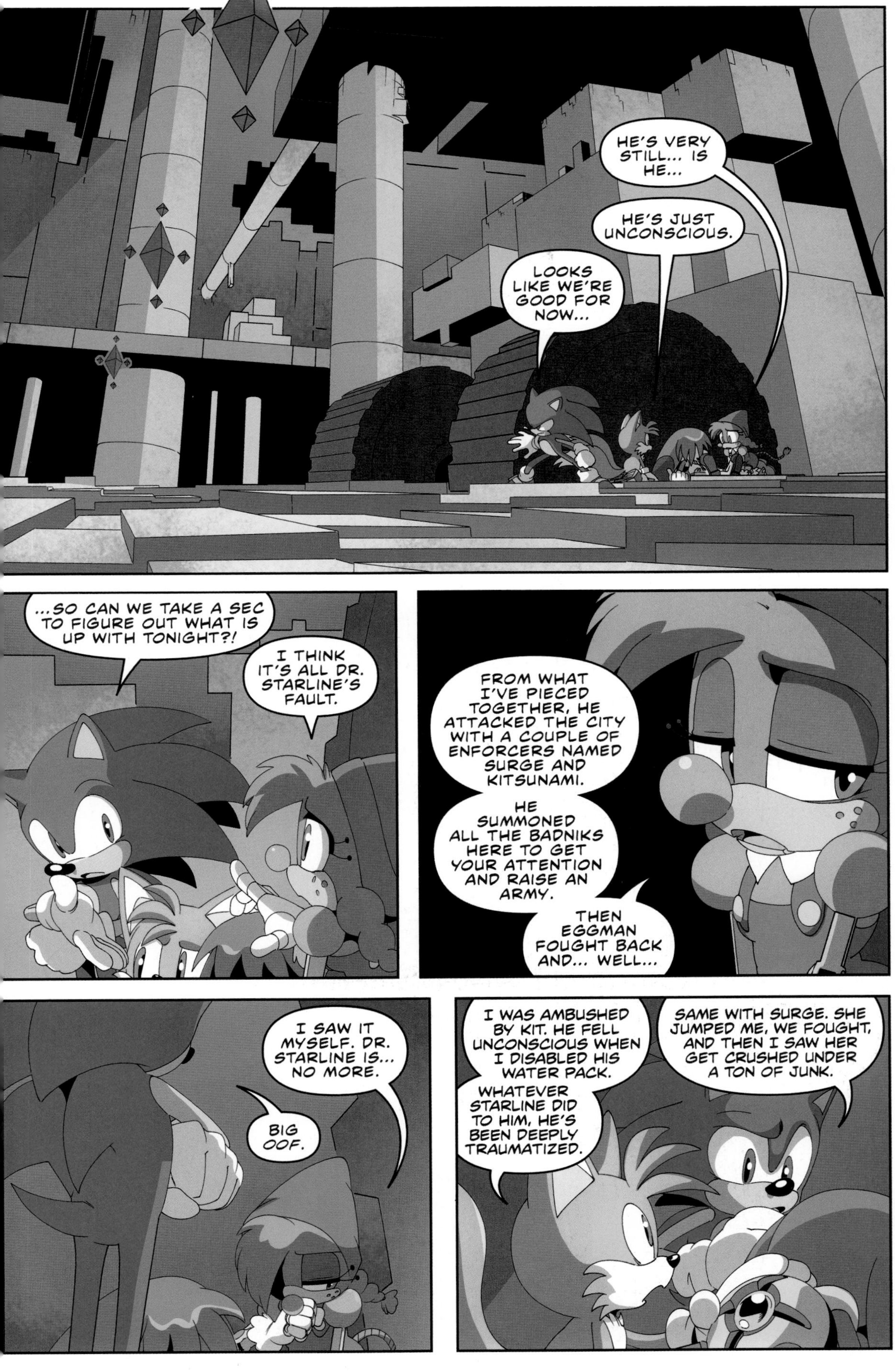
HE'S VERY STILL... IS HE...
HE'S JUST UNCONSCIOUS.
LOOKS LIKE WE'RE GOOD FOR NOW...
...SO CAN WE TAKE A SEC TO FIGURE OUT WHAT IS UP WITH TONIGHT?!
I THINK IT'S ALL DR. STARLINE'S FAULT.
FROM WHAT I'VE PIECED TOGETHER, HE ATTACKED THE CITY WITH A COUPLE OF ENFORCERS NAMED SURGE AND KITSUNAMI.
HE SUMMONED ALL THE BADNIKS HERE TO GET YOUR ATTENTION AND RAISE AN ARMY.
THEN EGGMAN FOUGHT BACK AND... WELL...
I SAW IT MYSELF. DR. STARLINE IS... NO MORE.
BIG OOF.
I WAS AMBUSHED BY KIT. HE FELL UNCONSCIOUS WHEN I DISABLED HIS WATER PACK.
WHATEVER STARLINE DID TO HIM, HE'S BEEN DEEPLY TRAUMATIZED.
SAME WITH SURGE. SHE JUMPED ME, WE FOUGHT, AND THEN I SAW HER GET CRUSHED UNDER A TON OF JUNK.

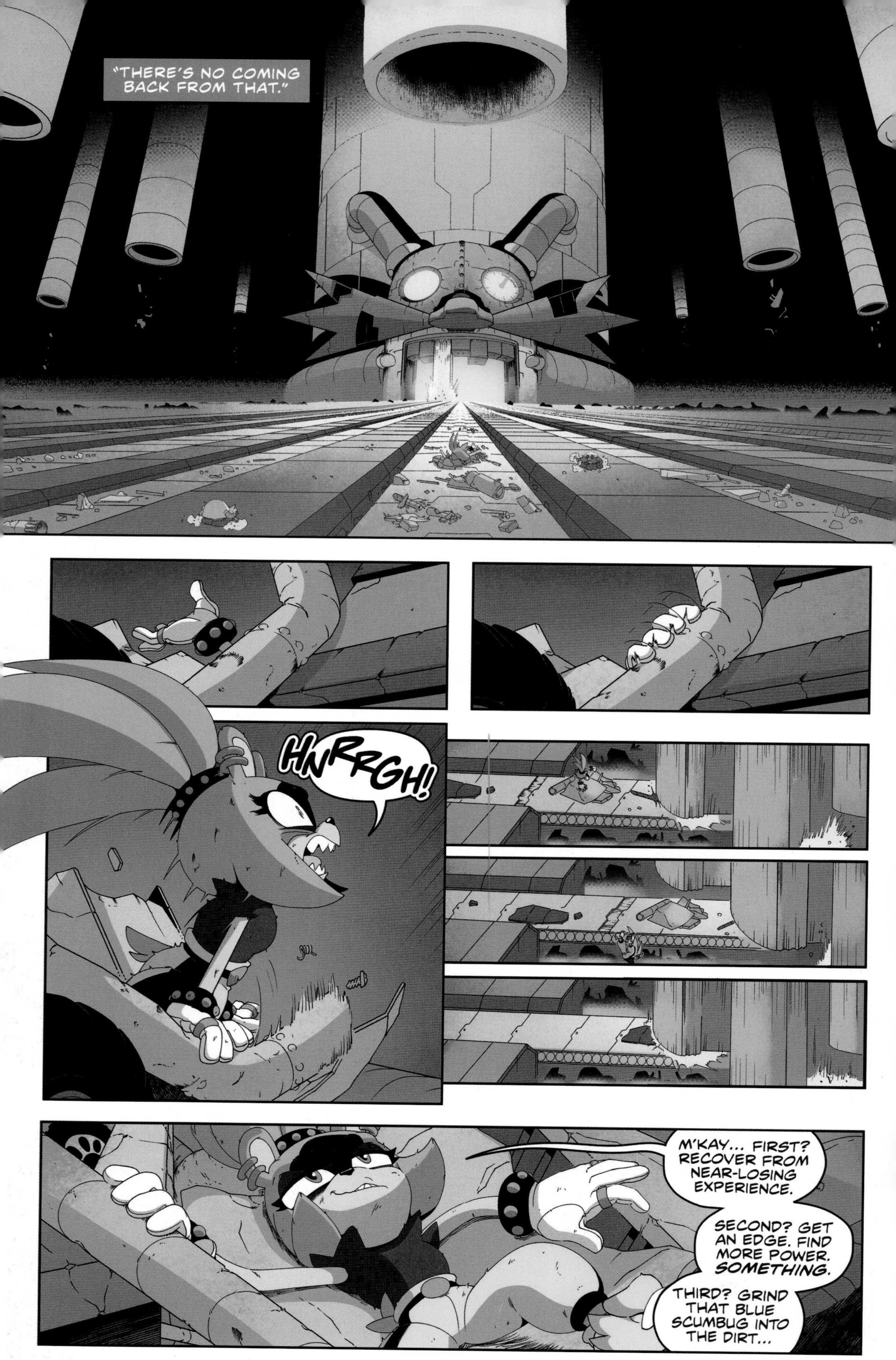
"THERE'S NO COMING BACK FROM THAT."
HNRRGH!
M'KAY... FIRST? RECOVER FROM NEAR-LOSING EXPERIENCE.
SECOND? GET AN EDGE. FIND MORE POWER. *SOMETHING.*
THIRD? GRIND THAT BLUE SCUMBUG INTO THE DIRT...

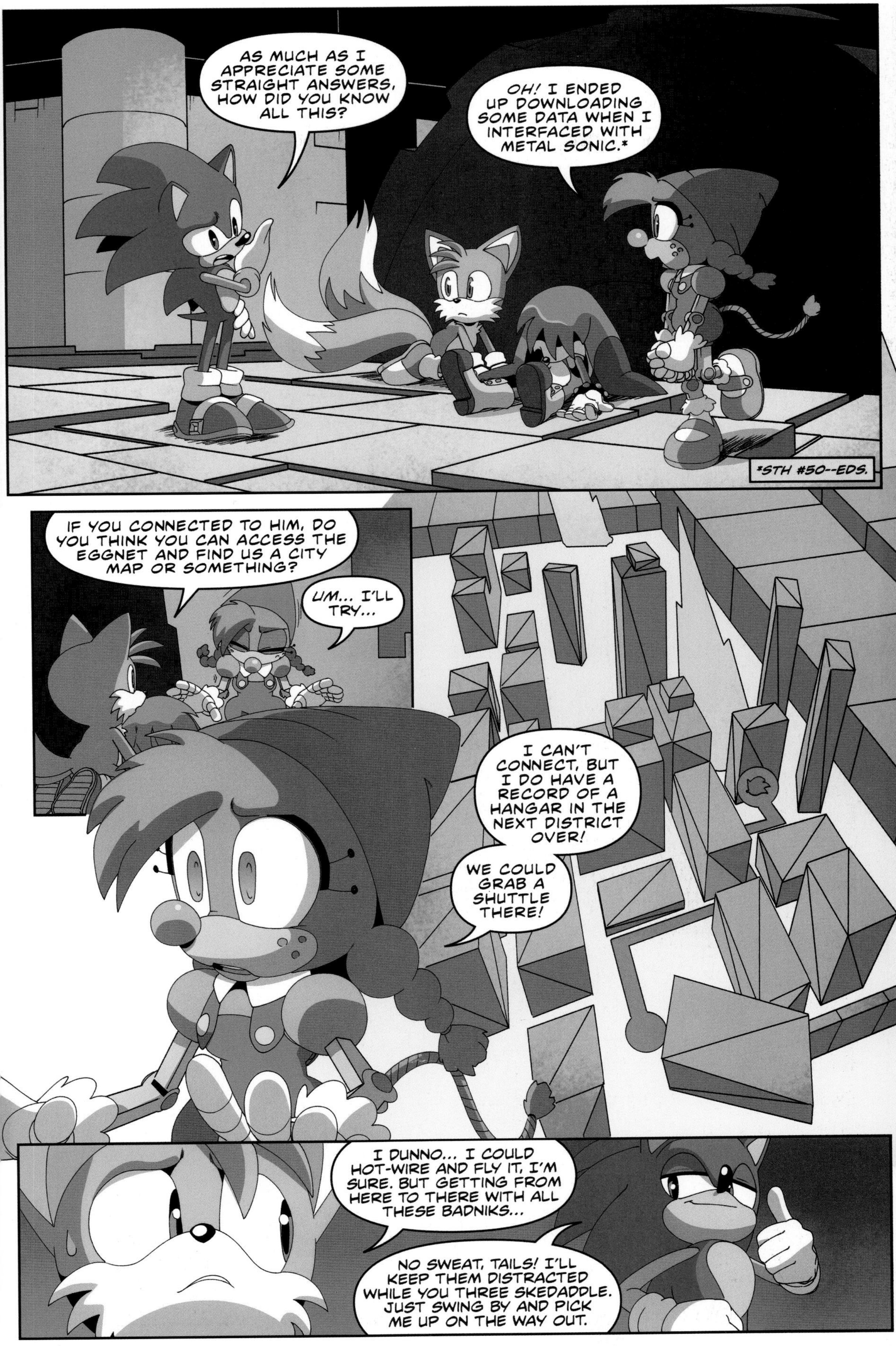
AS MUCH AS I APPRECIATE SOME STRAIGHT ANSWERS, HOW DID YOU KNOW ALL THIS?
OH! I ENDED UP DOWNLOADING SOME DATA WHEN I INTERFACED WITH METAL SONIC.*
*STH #50--EDS.
IF YOU CONNECTED TO HIM, DO YOU THINK YOU CAN ACCESS THE EGGNET AND FIND US A CITY MAP OR SOMETHING?
UM... I'LL TRY...
I CAN'T CONNECT, BUT I DO HAVE A RECORD OF A HANGAR IN THE NEXT DISTRICT OVER!
WE COULD GRAB A SHUTTLE THERE!
I DUNNO... I COULD HOT-WIRE AND FLY IT, I'M SURE. BUT GETTING FROM HERE TO THERE WITH ALL THESE BADNIKS...
NO SWEAT, TAILS! I'LL KEEP THEM DISTRACTED WHILE YOU THREE SKEDADDLE. JUST SWING BY AND PICK ME UP ON THE WAY OUT.

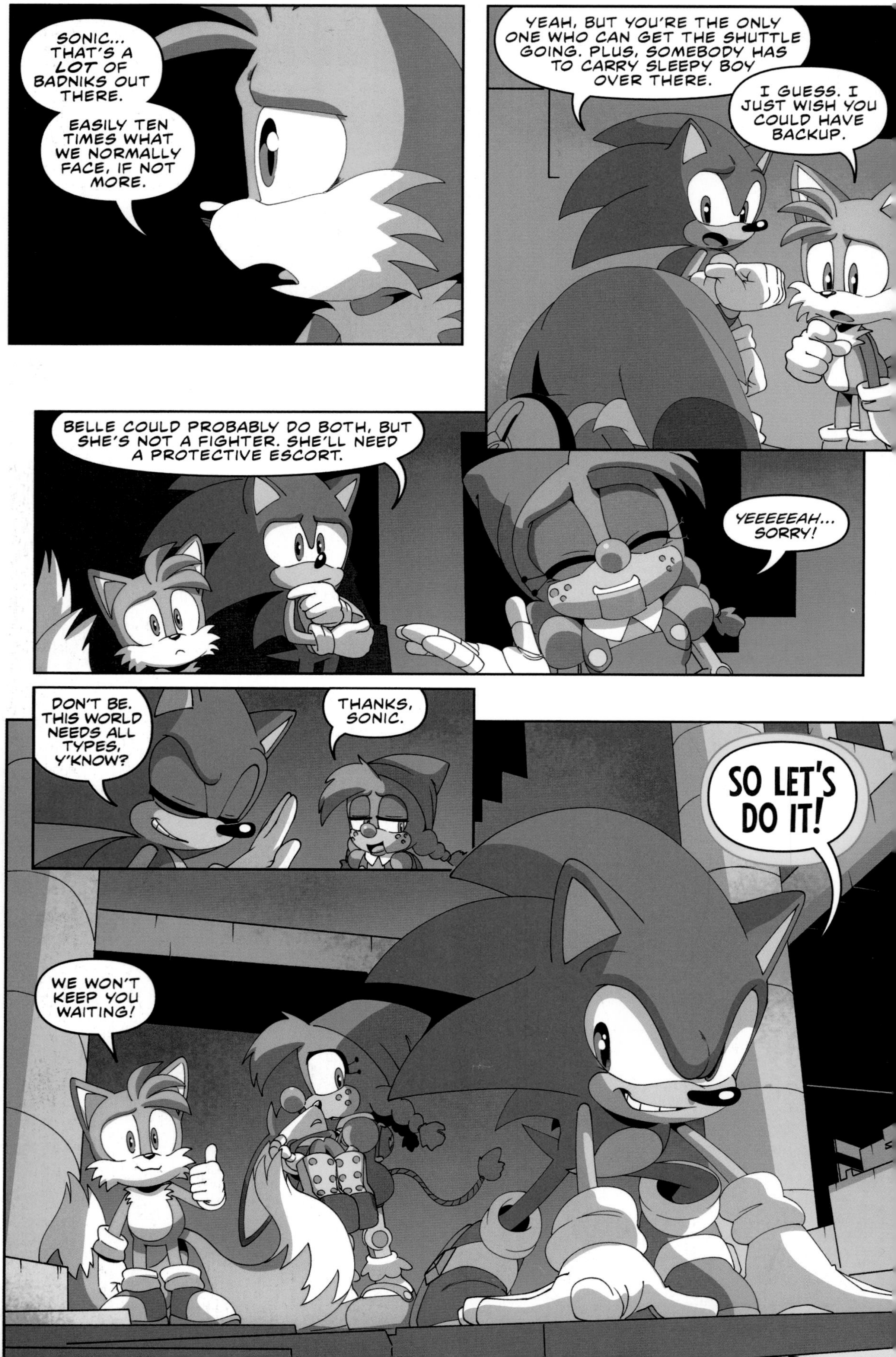
SONIC... THAT'S A *LOT* OF BADNIKS OUT THERE.
EASILY TEN TIMES WHAT WE NORMALLY FACE, IF NOT MORE.
YEAH, BUT YOU'RE THE ONLY ONE WHO CAN GET THE SHUTTLE GOING. PLUS, SOMEBODY HAS TO CARRY SLEEPY BOY OVER THERE.
I GUESS. I JUST WISH YOU COULD HAVE BACKUP.
BELLE COULD PROBABLY DO BOTH, BUT SHE'S NOT A FIGHTER. SHE'LL NEED A PROTECTIVE ESCORT.
YEEEEEAH... SORRY!
DON'T BE. THIS WORLD NEEDS ALL TYPES, Y'KNOW?
THANKS, SONIC.
SO LET'S DO IT!
WE WON'T KEEP YOU WAITING!

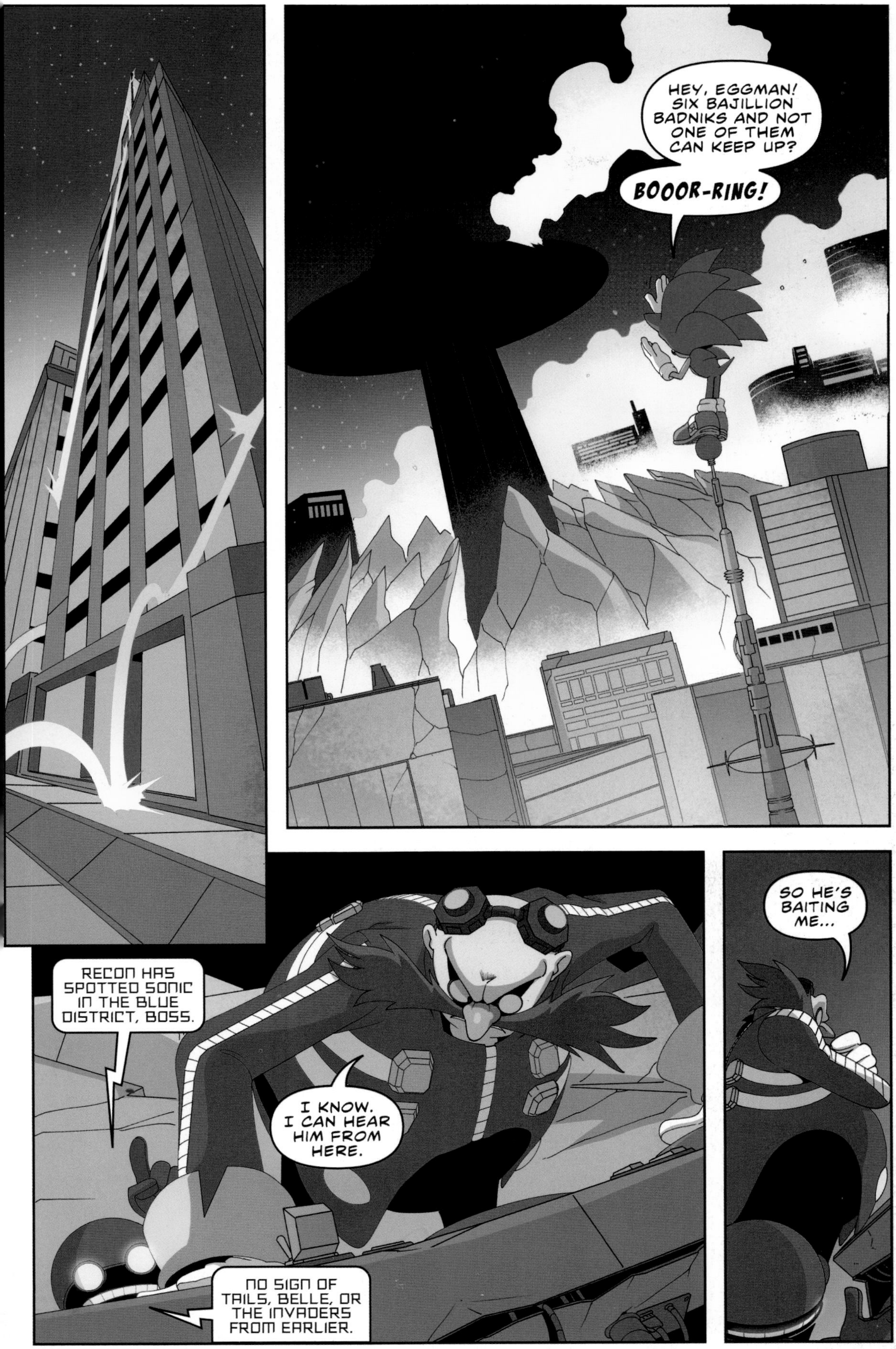
HEY, EGGMAN! SIX BAJILLION BADNIKS AND NOT ONE OF THEM CAN KEEP UP?
BOOOR-RING!
RECON HAS SPOTTED SONIC IN THE BLUE DISTRICT, BOSS.
I KNOW. I CAN HEAR HIM FROM HERE.
NO SIGN OF TAILS, BELLE, OR THE INVADERS FROM EARLIER.
SO HE'S BAITING ME...

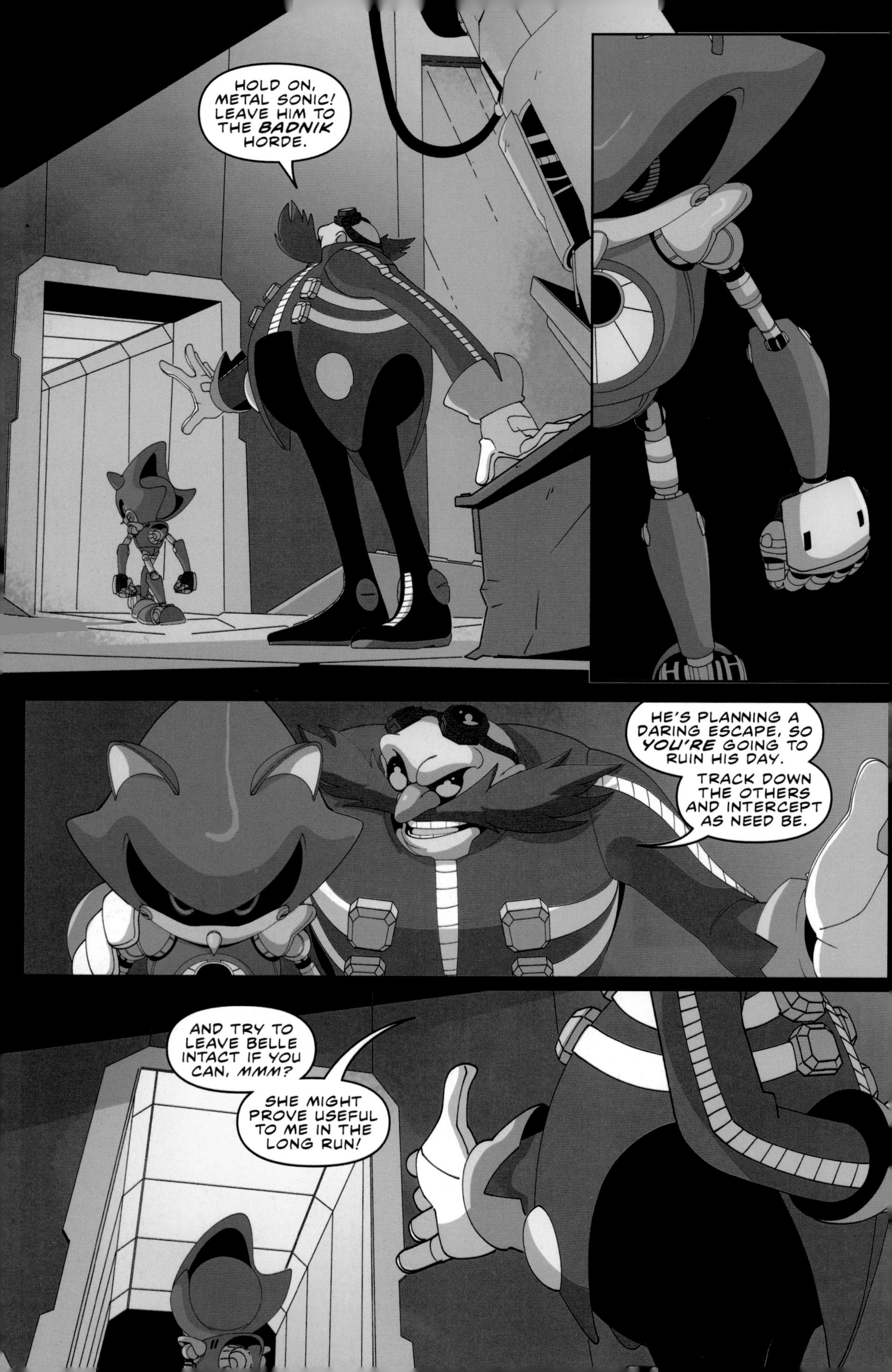
HOLD ON, METAL SONIC! LEAVE HIM TO THE *BADNIK* HORDE.
HE'S PLANNING A DARING ESCAPE, SO *YOU'RE* GOING TO RUIN HIS DAY.
TRACK DOWN THE OTHERS AND INTERCEPT AS NEED BE.
AND TRY TO LEAVE BELLE INTACT IF YOU CAN, *MMM?*
SHE MIGHT PROVE USEFUL TO ME IN THE LONG RUN!

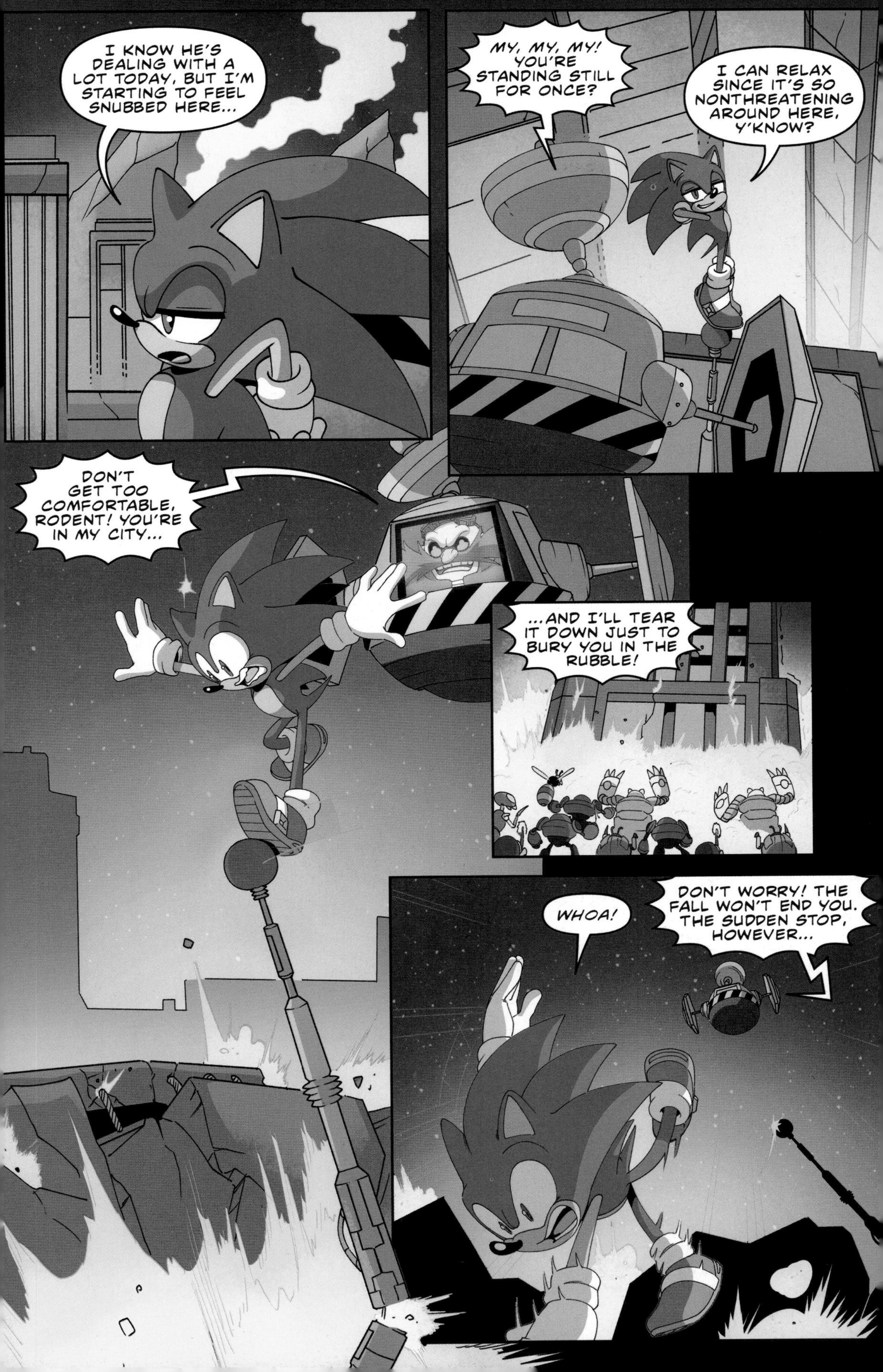
I KNOW HE'S DEALING WITH A LOT TODAY, BUT I'M STARTING TO FEEL SNUBBED HERE...
MY, MY, MY! YOU'RE STANDING STILL FOR ONCE?
I CAN RELAX SINCE IT'S SO NONTHREATENING AROUND HERE, Y'KNOW?
DON'T GET TOO COMFORTABLE, RODENT! YOU'RE IN MY CITY...
...AND I'LL TEAR IT DOWN JUST TO BURY YOU IN THE RUBBLE!
WHOA!
DON'T WORRY! THE FALL WON'T END YOU. THE SUDDEN STOP, HOWEVER...

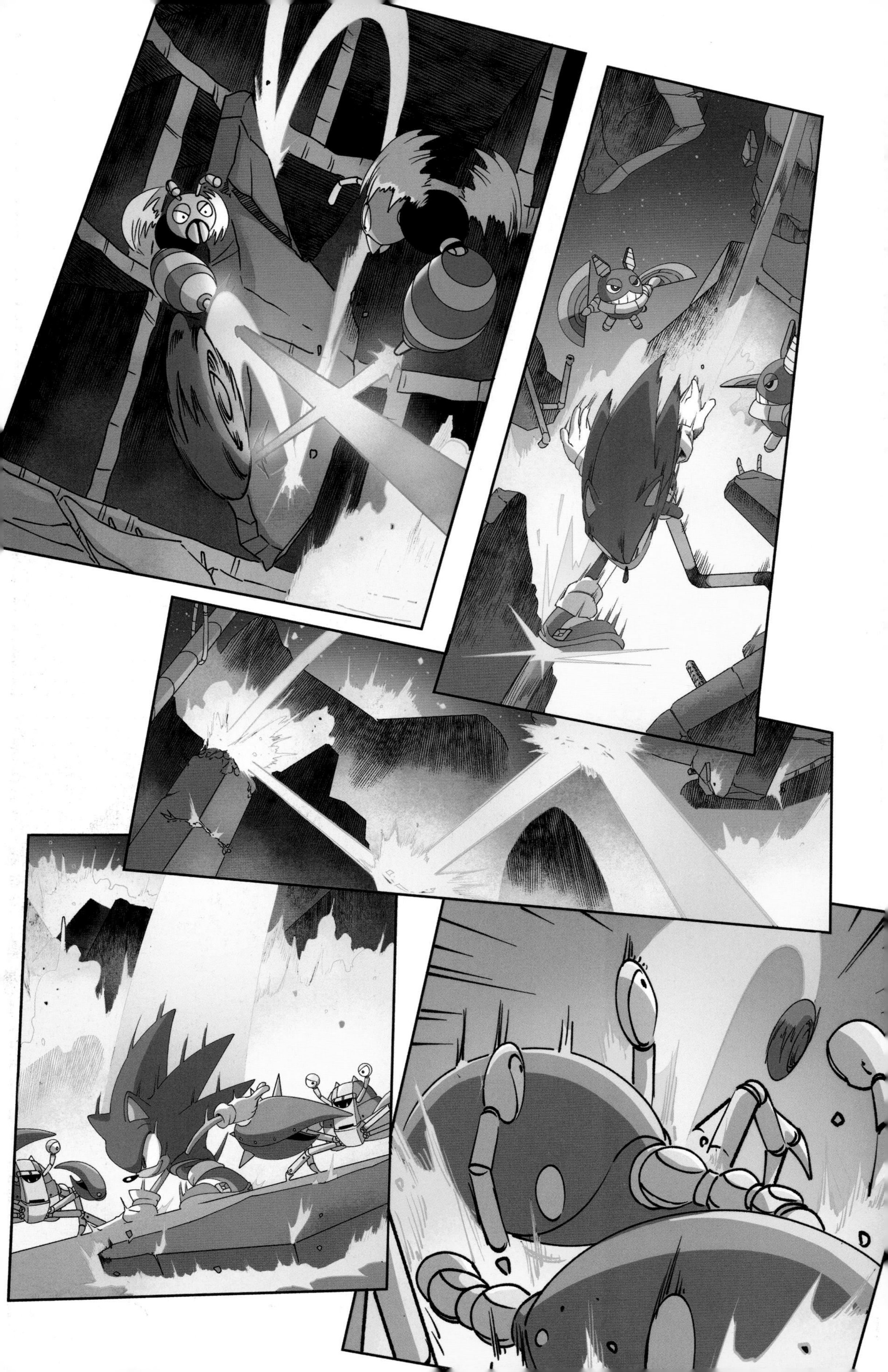

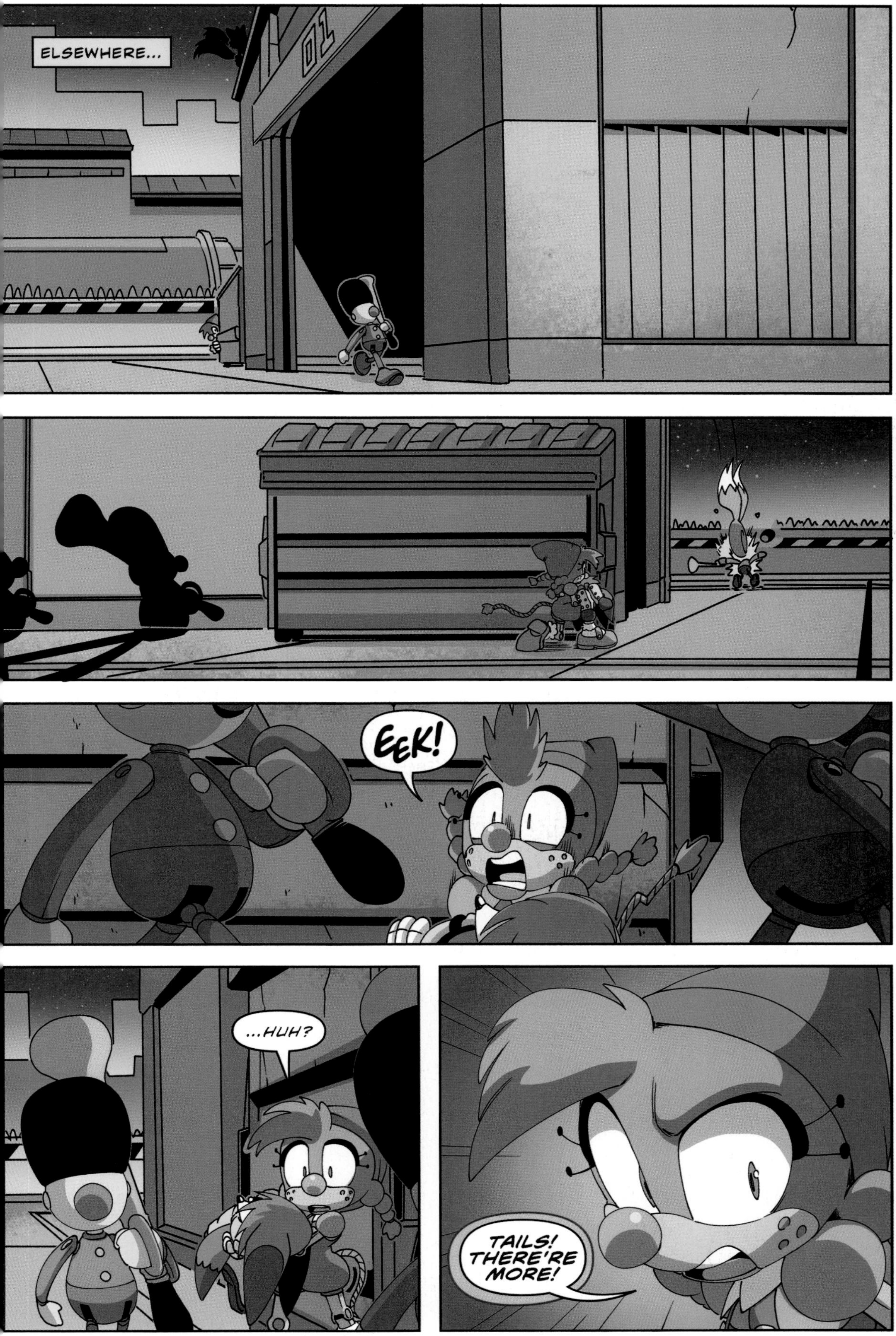
ELSEWHERE...
01
EEK!
...HUH?
TAILS! THERE'RE MORE!

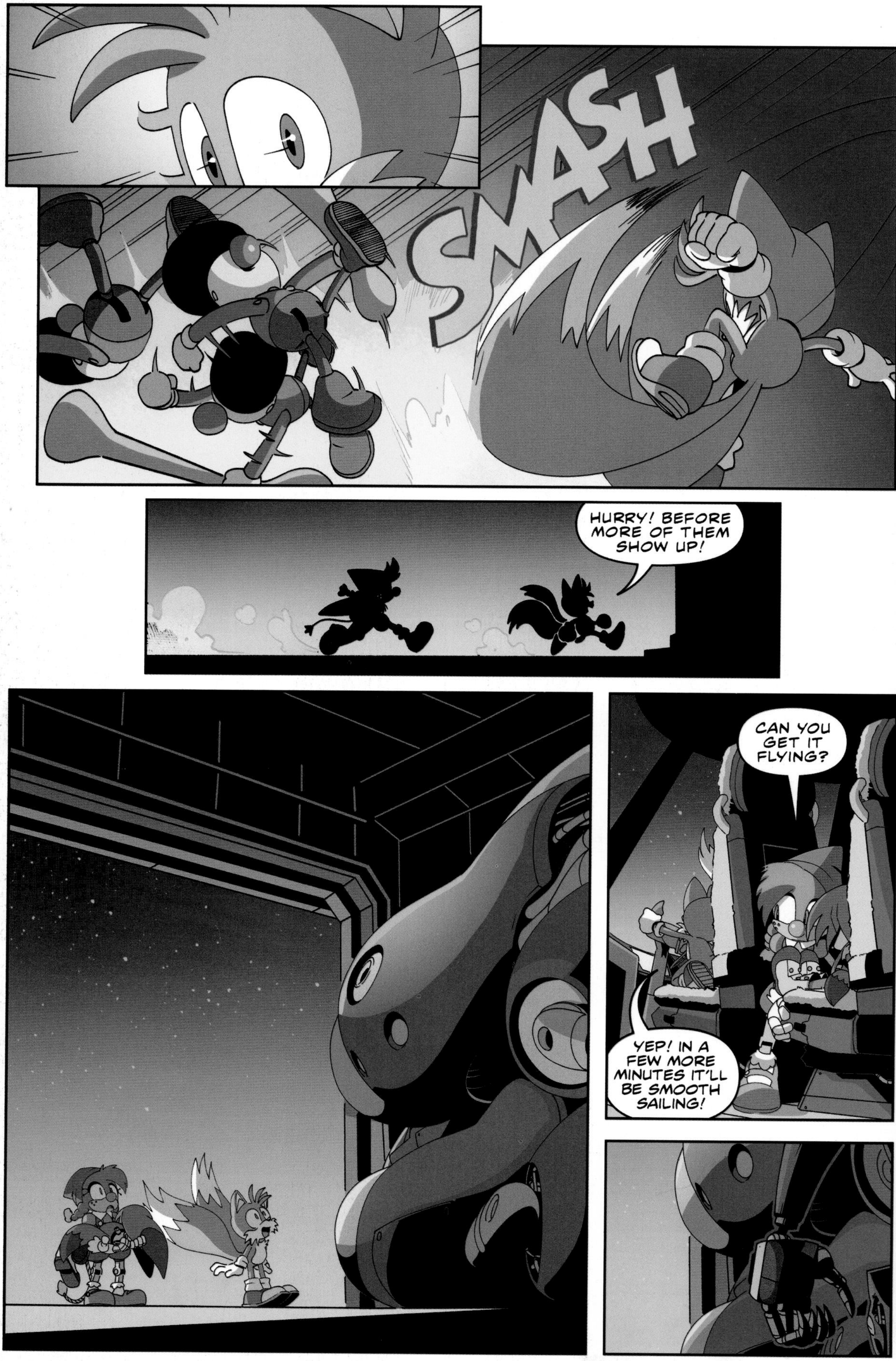
SMASH
HURRY! BEFORE MORE OF THEM SHOW UP!
CAN YOU GET IT FLYING?
YEP! IN A FEW MORE MINUTES IT'LL BE SMOOTH SAILING!

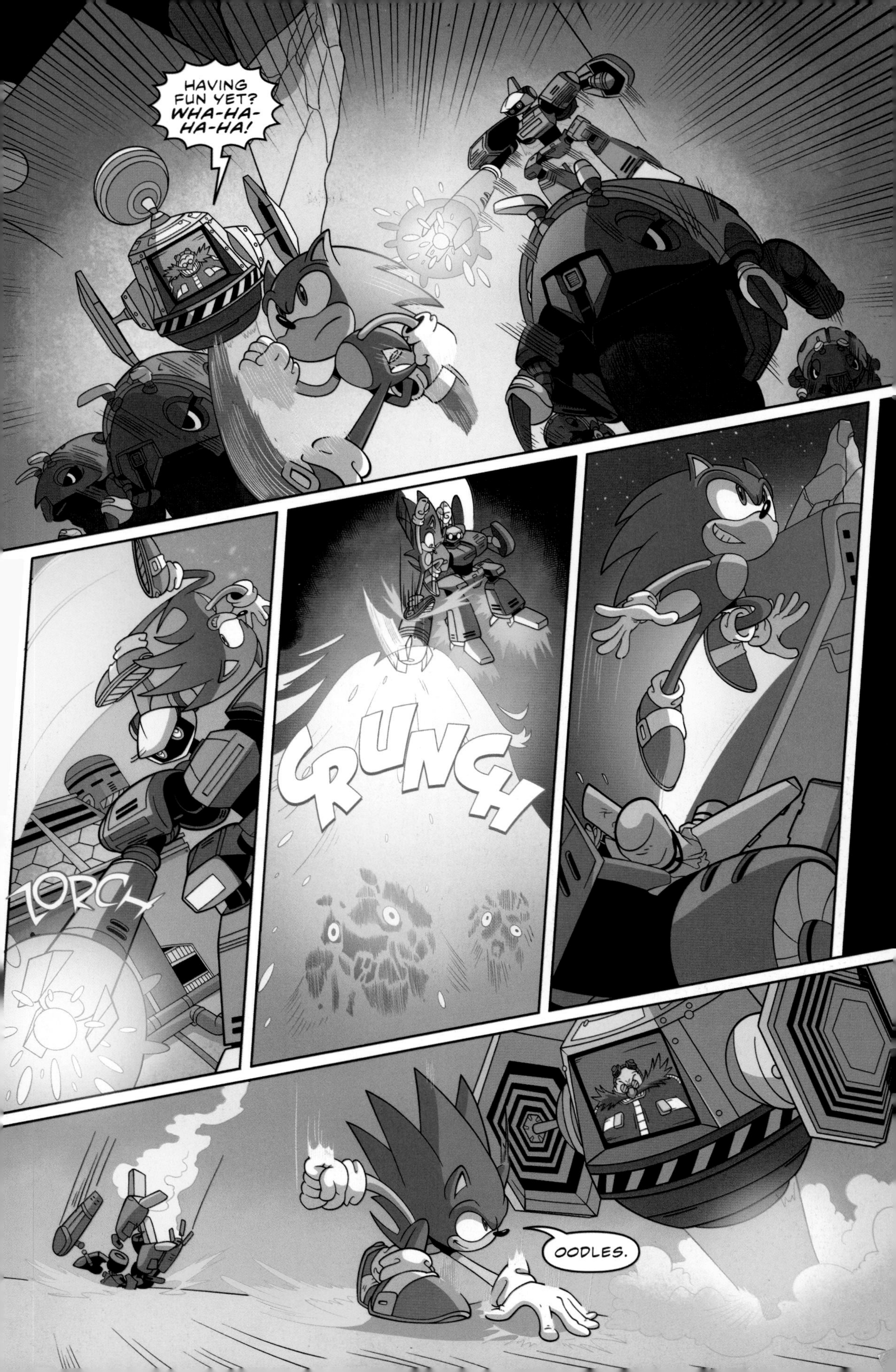
HAVING FUN YET? WHA-HA-HA-HA!
ZORCH
CRUNCH
OODLES.

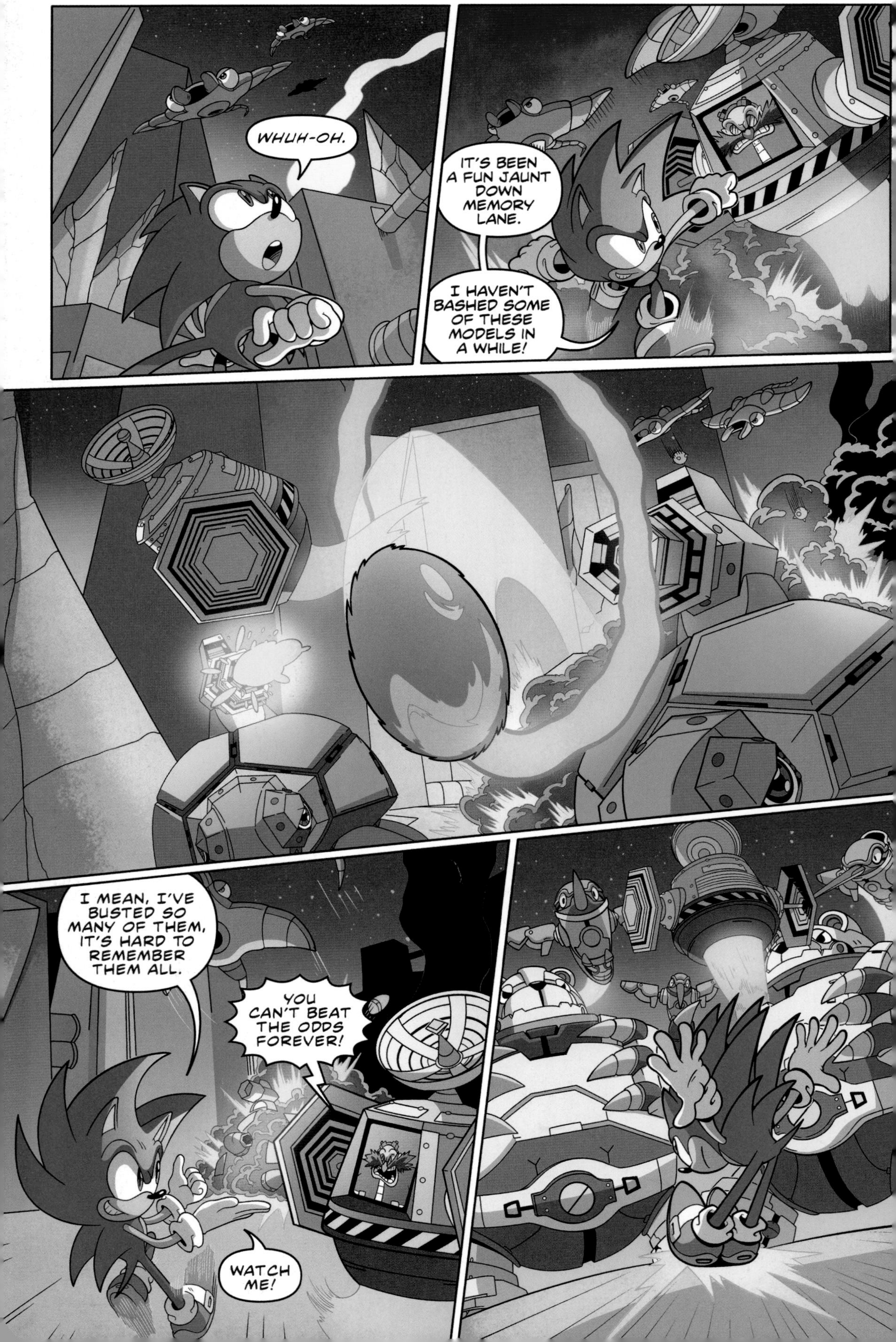
WHUH-OH.
IT'S BEEN A FUN JAUNT DOWN MEMORY LANE.
I HAVEN'T BASHED SOME OF THESE MODELS IN A WHILE!
I MEAN, I'VE BUSTED SO MANY OF THEM, IT'S HARD TO REMEMBER THEM ALL.
YOU CAN'T BEAT THE ODDS FOREVER!
WATCH ME!

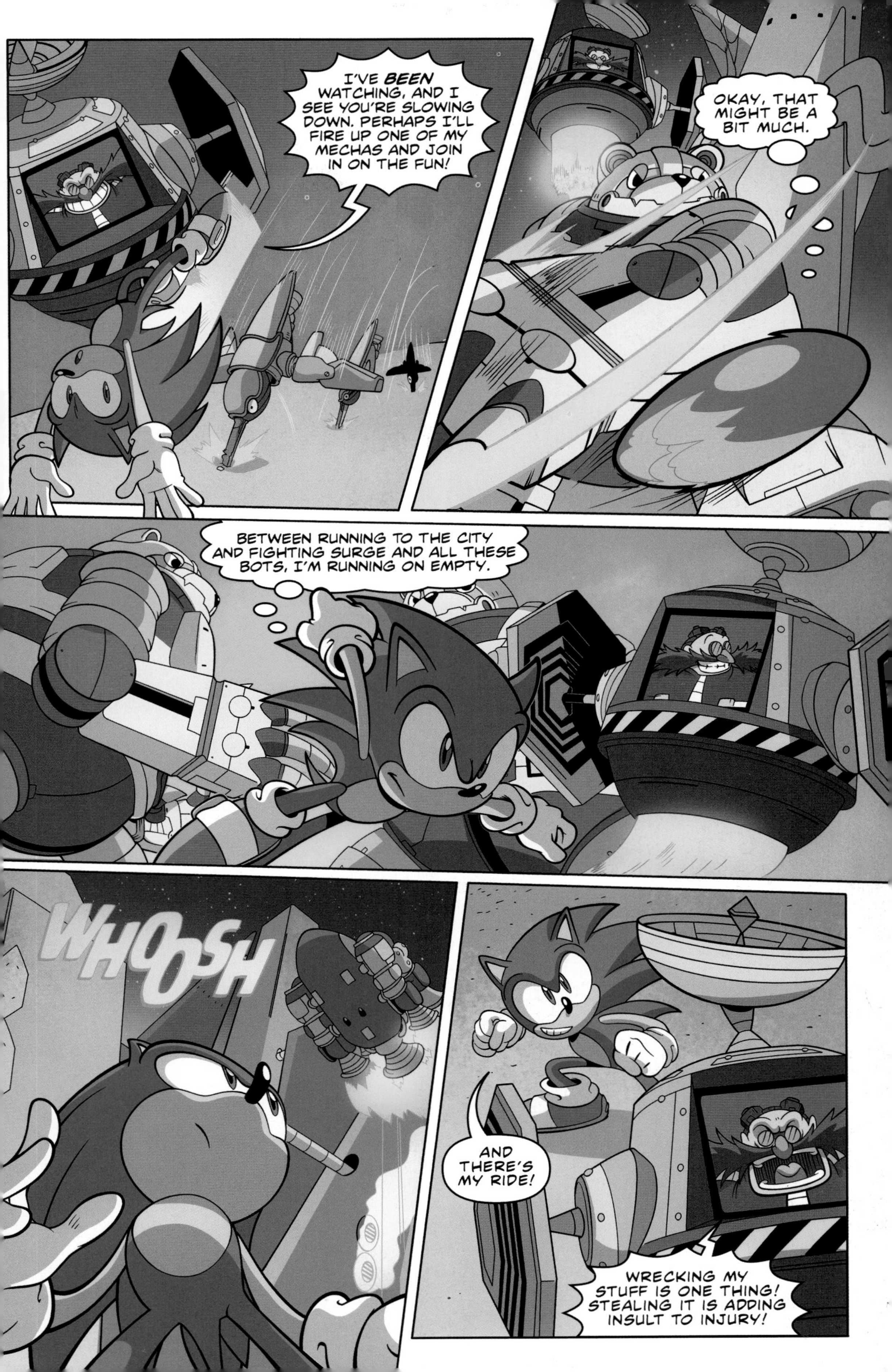
I'VE BEEN WATCHING, AND I SEE YOU'RE SLOWING DOWN. PERHAPS I'LL FIRE UP ONE OF MY MECHAS AND JOIN IN ON THE FUN!
OKAY, THAT MIGHT BE A BIT MUCH.
BETWEEN RUNNING TO THE CITY AND FIGHTING SURGE AND ALL THESE BOTS, I'M RUNNING ON EMPTY.
WHOOSH
AND THERE'S MY RIDE!
WRECKING MY STUFF IS ONE THING! STEALING IT IS ADDING INSULT TO INJURY!

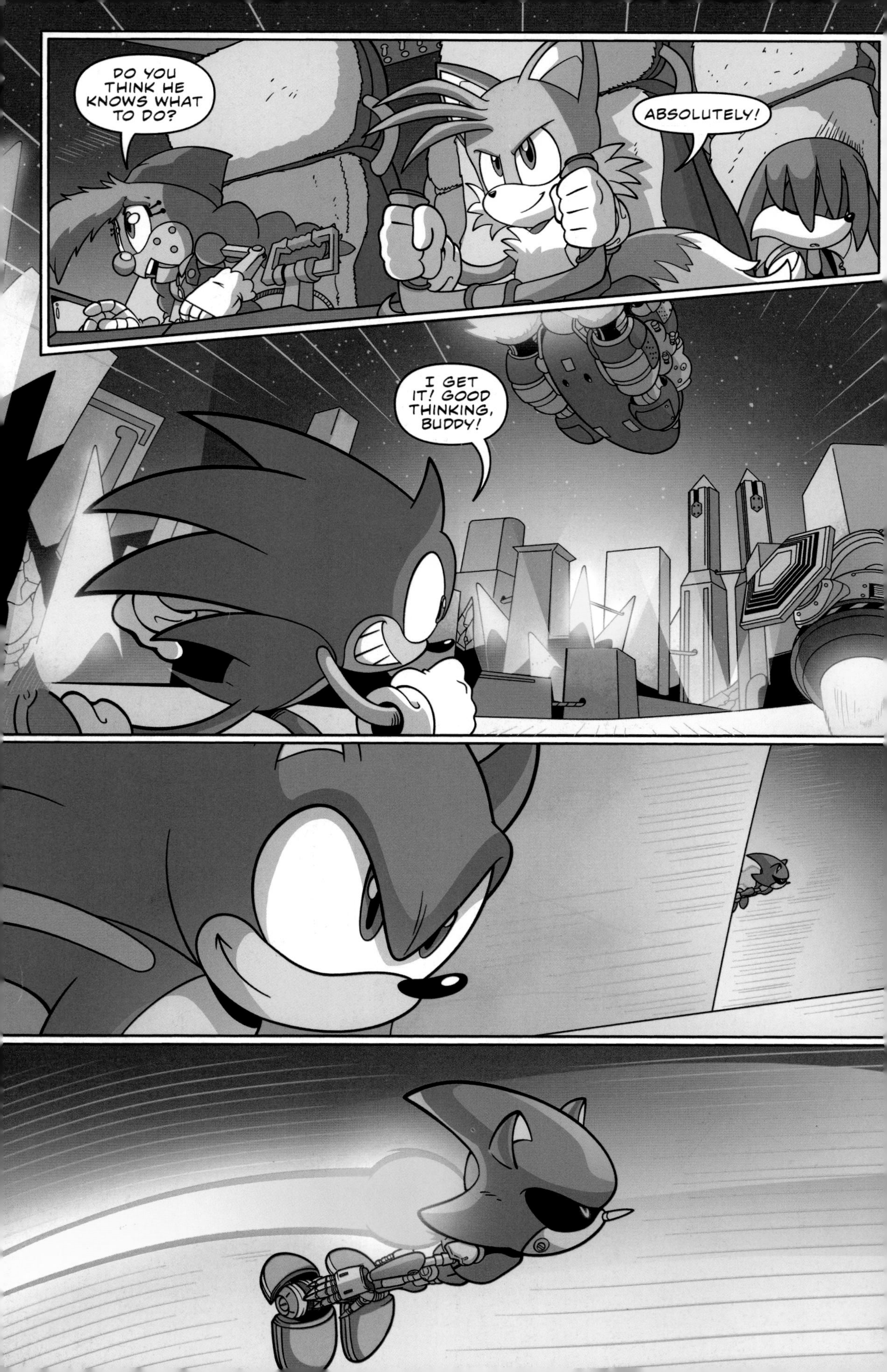
DO YOU THINK HE KNOWS WHAT TO DO?
ABSOLUTELY!
I GET IT! GOOD THINKING, BUDDY!

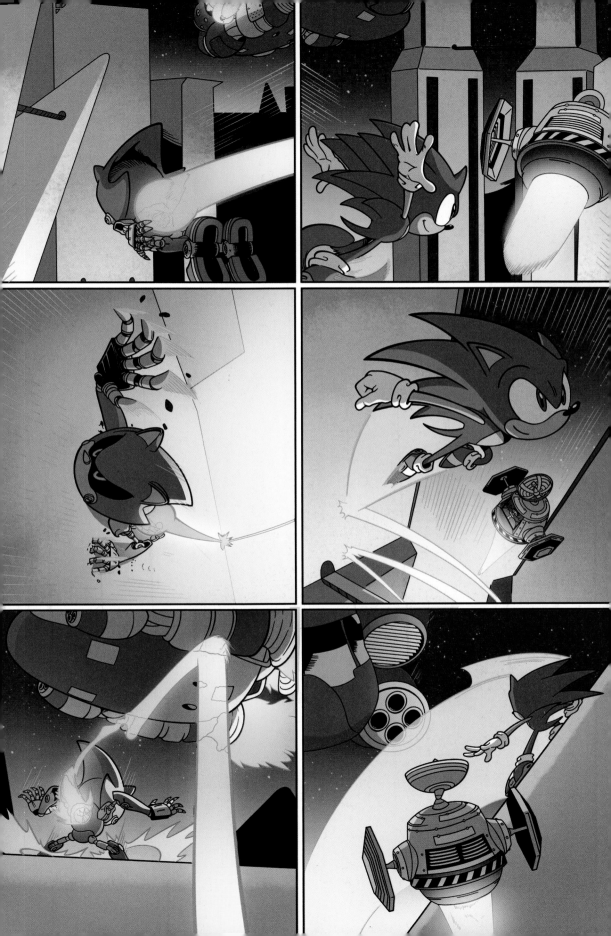

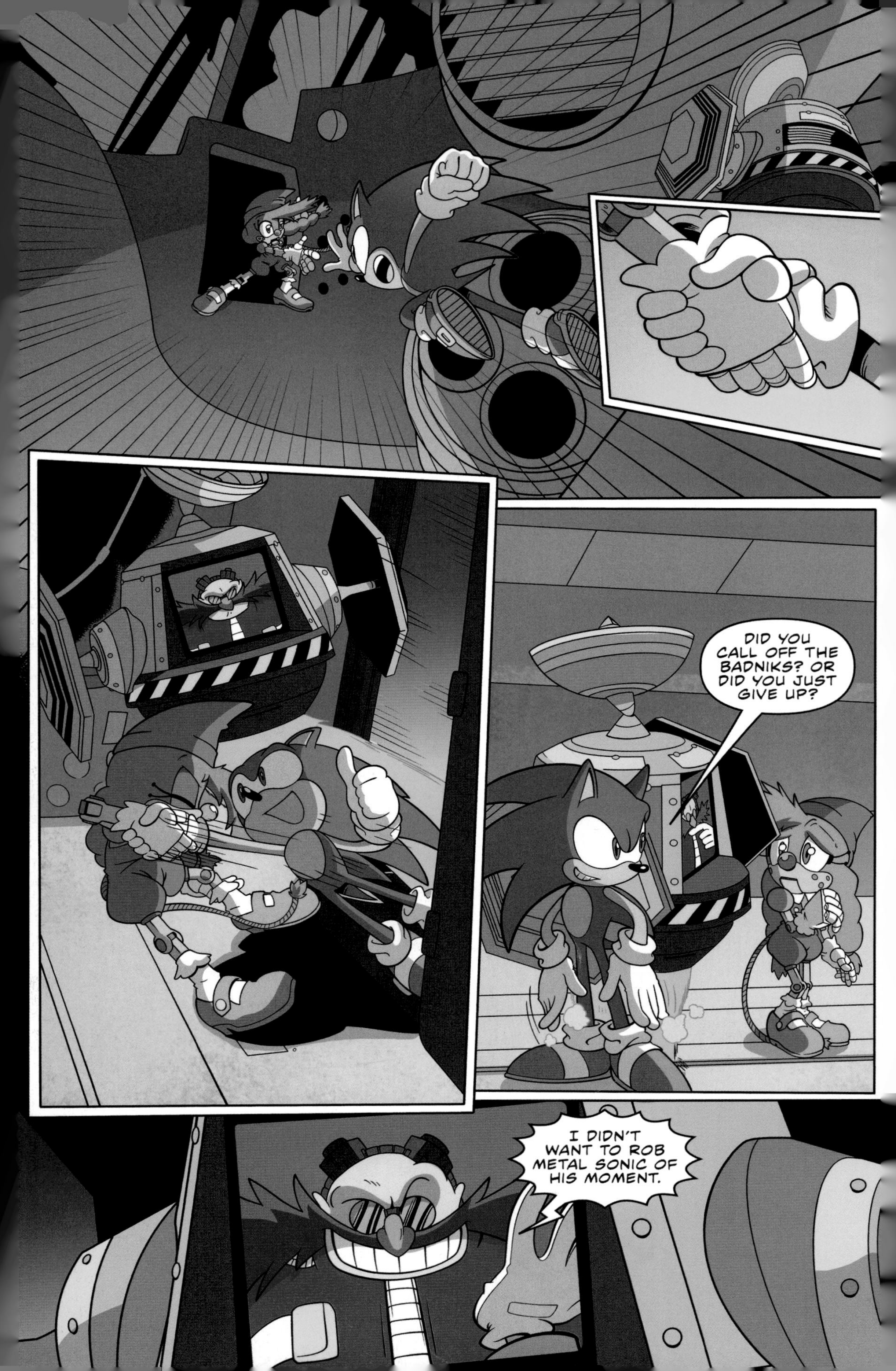
DID YOU CALL OFF THE BADNIKS? OR DID YOU JUST GIVE UP?
I DIDN'T WANT TO ROB METAL SONIC OF HIS MOMENT.

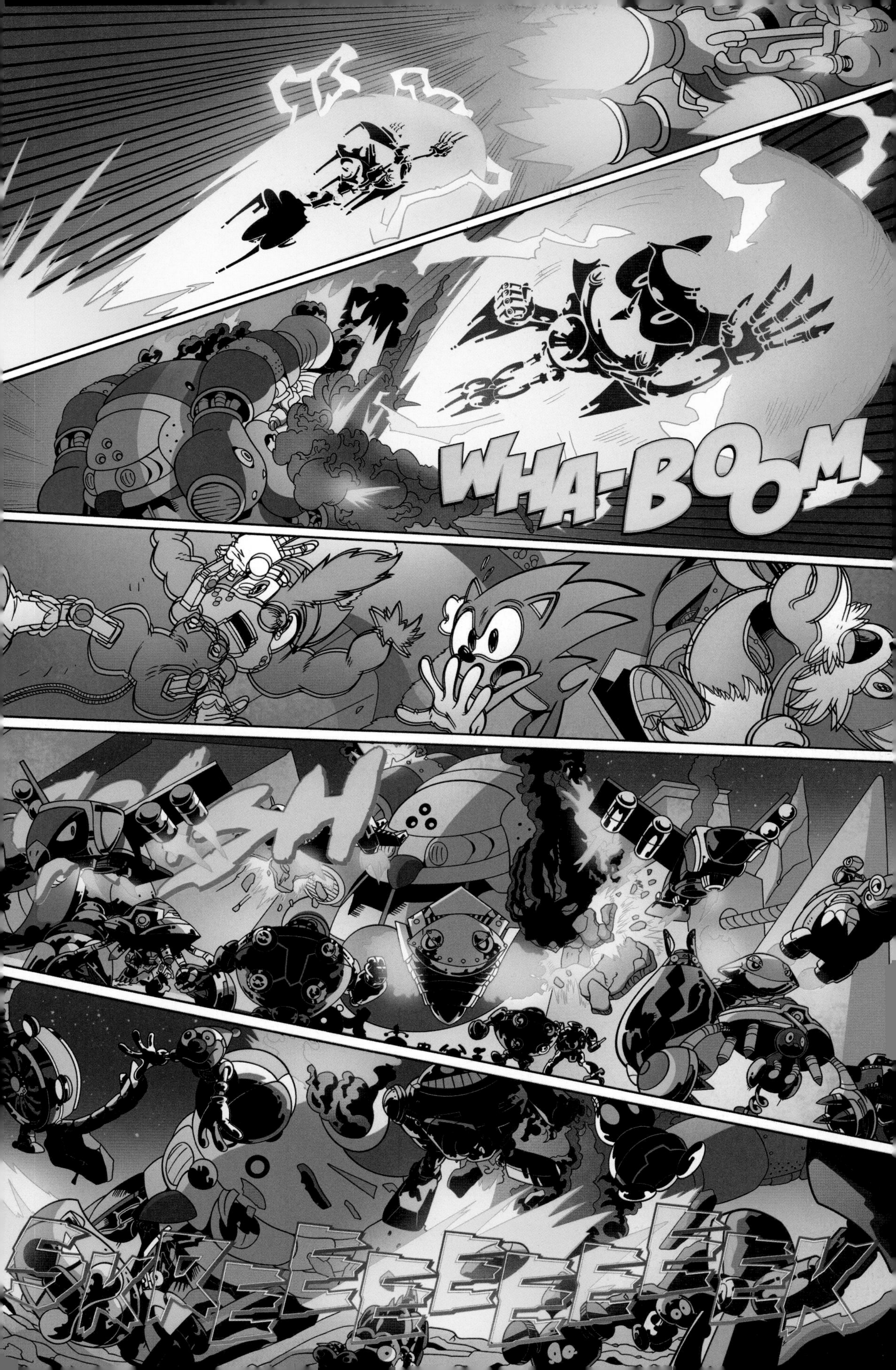
WHA-BOOM
SKREEEEEEEEK

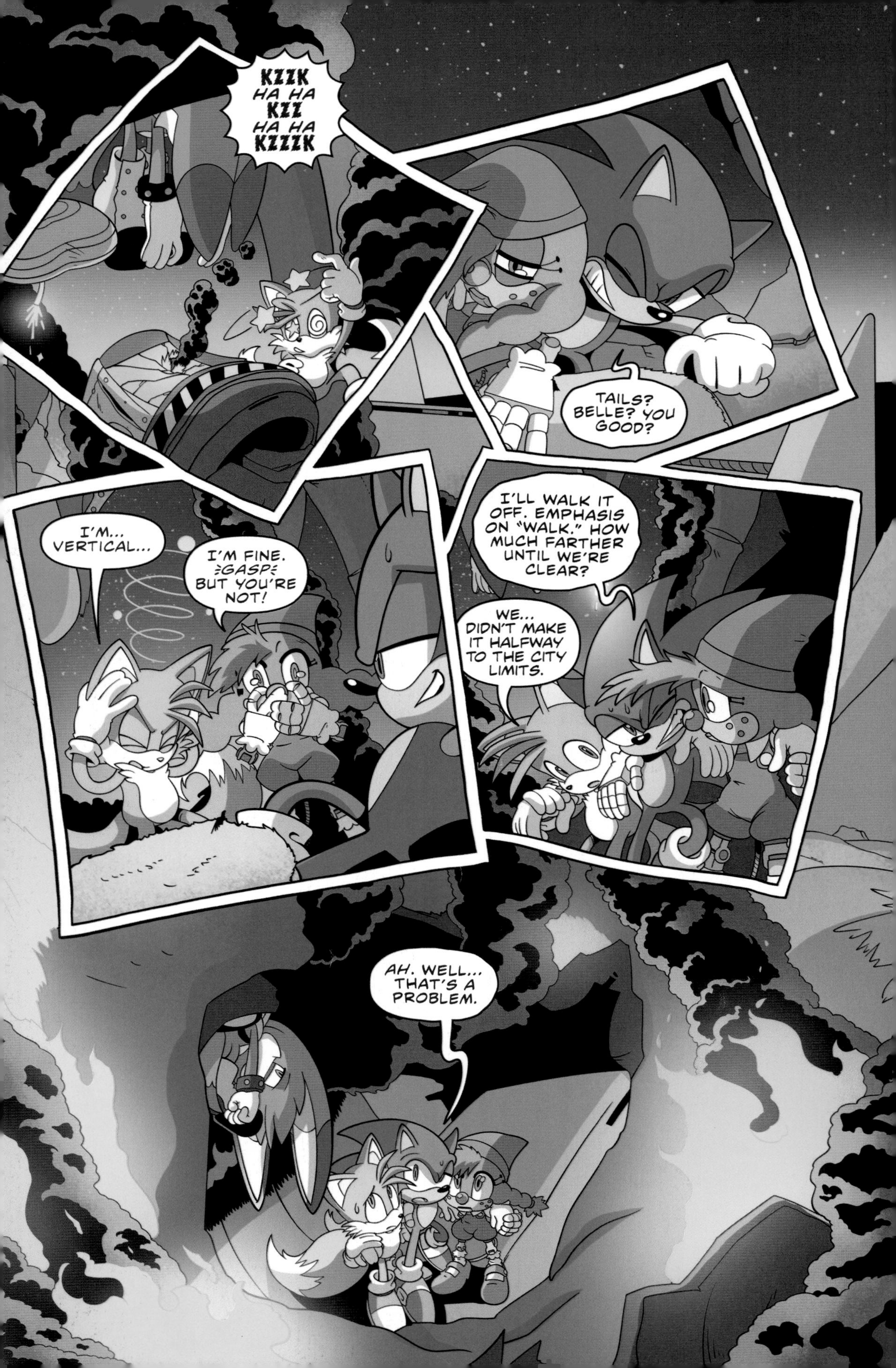
KZZK HA HA KZZ HA HA KZZZK
TAILS? BELLE? YOU GOOD?
I'M... VERTICAL...
I'M FINE. ≈GASP≈ BUT YOU'RE NOT!
I'LL WALK IT OFF. EMPHASIS ON "WALK." HOW MUCH FARTHER UNTIL WE'RE CLEAR?
WE... DIDN'T MAKE IT HALFWAY TO THE CITY LIMITS.
AH. WELL... THAT'S A PROBLEM.

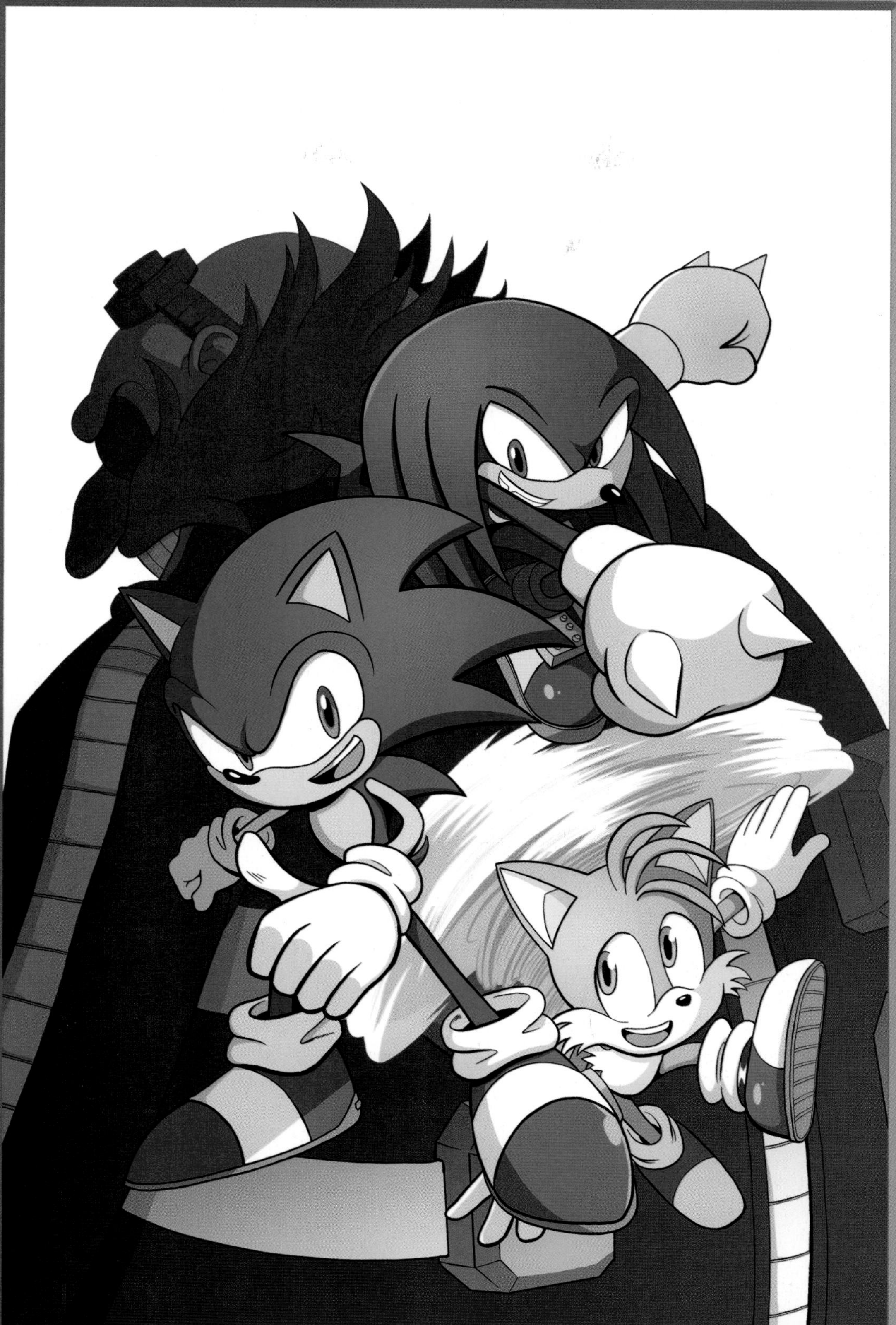

ART BY **ERIC LIDE**

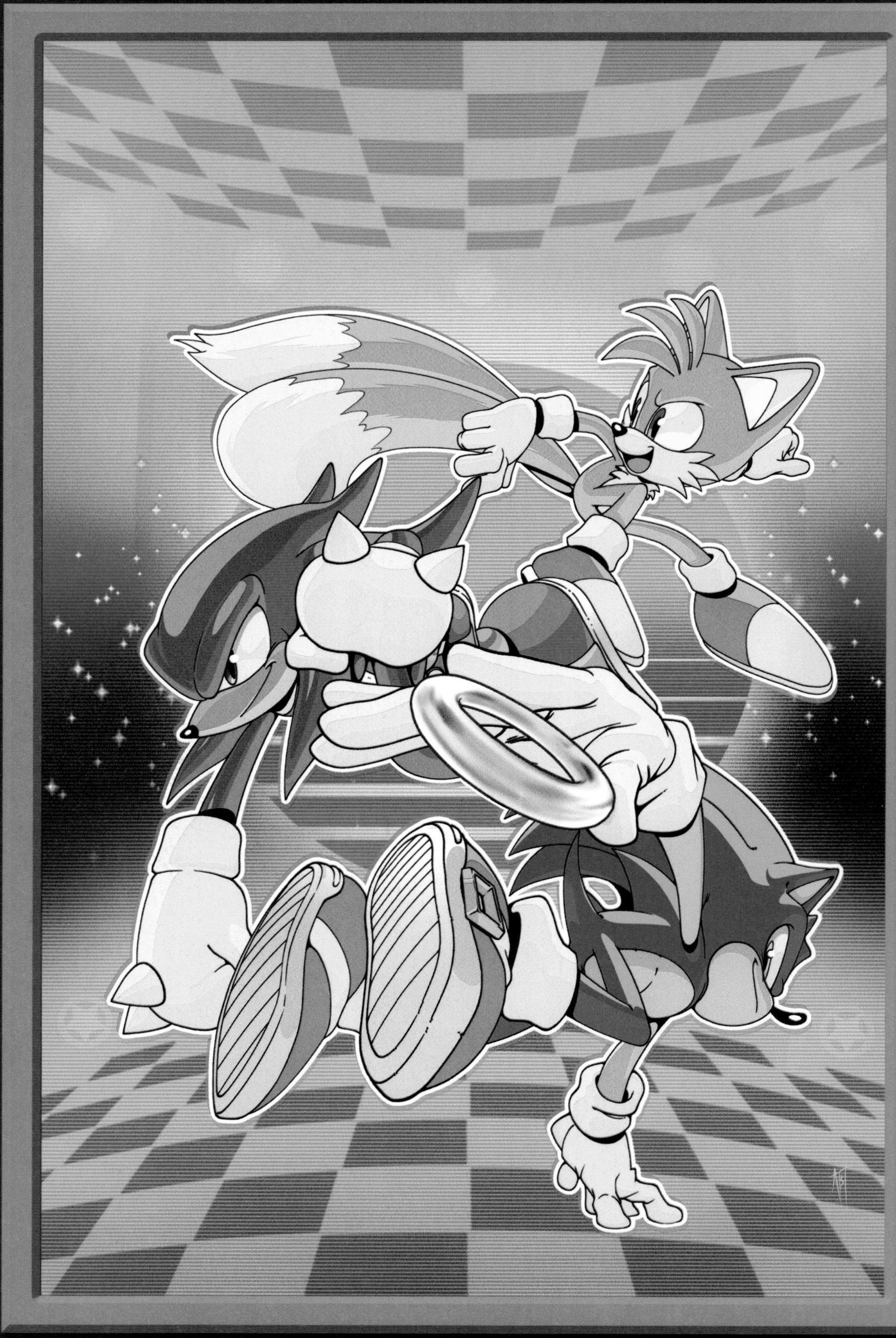

ART BY **ADAM BRYCE THOMAS**

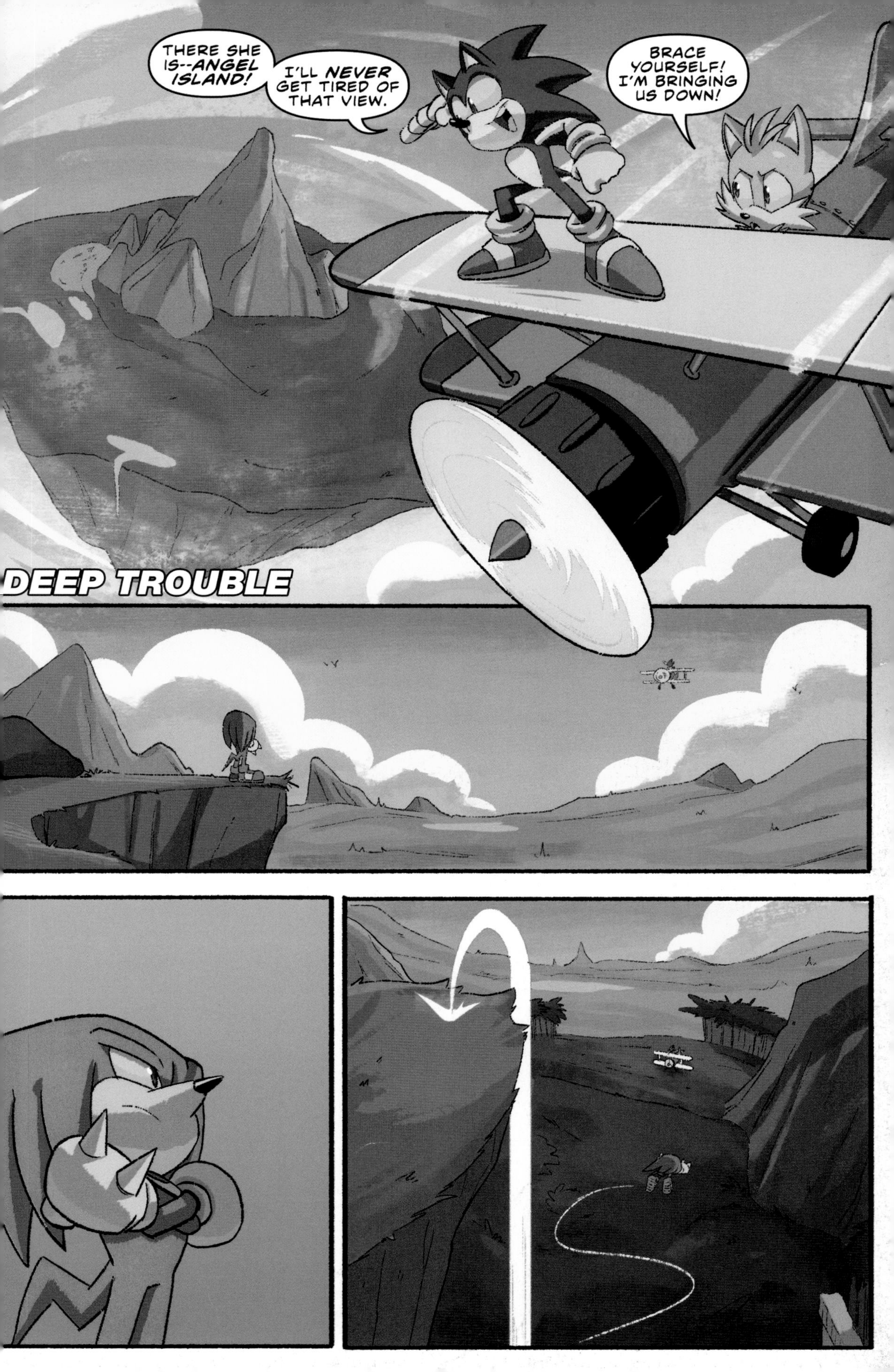
THERE SHE IS--ANGEL ISLAND!
I'LL NEVER GET TIRED OF THAT VIEW.
BRACE YOURSELF! I'M BRINGING US DOWN!
DEEP TROUBLE

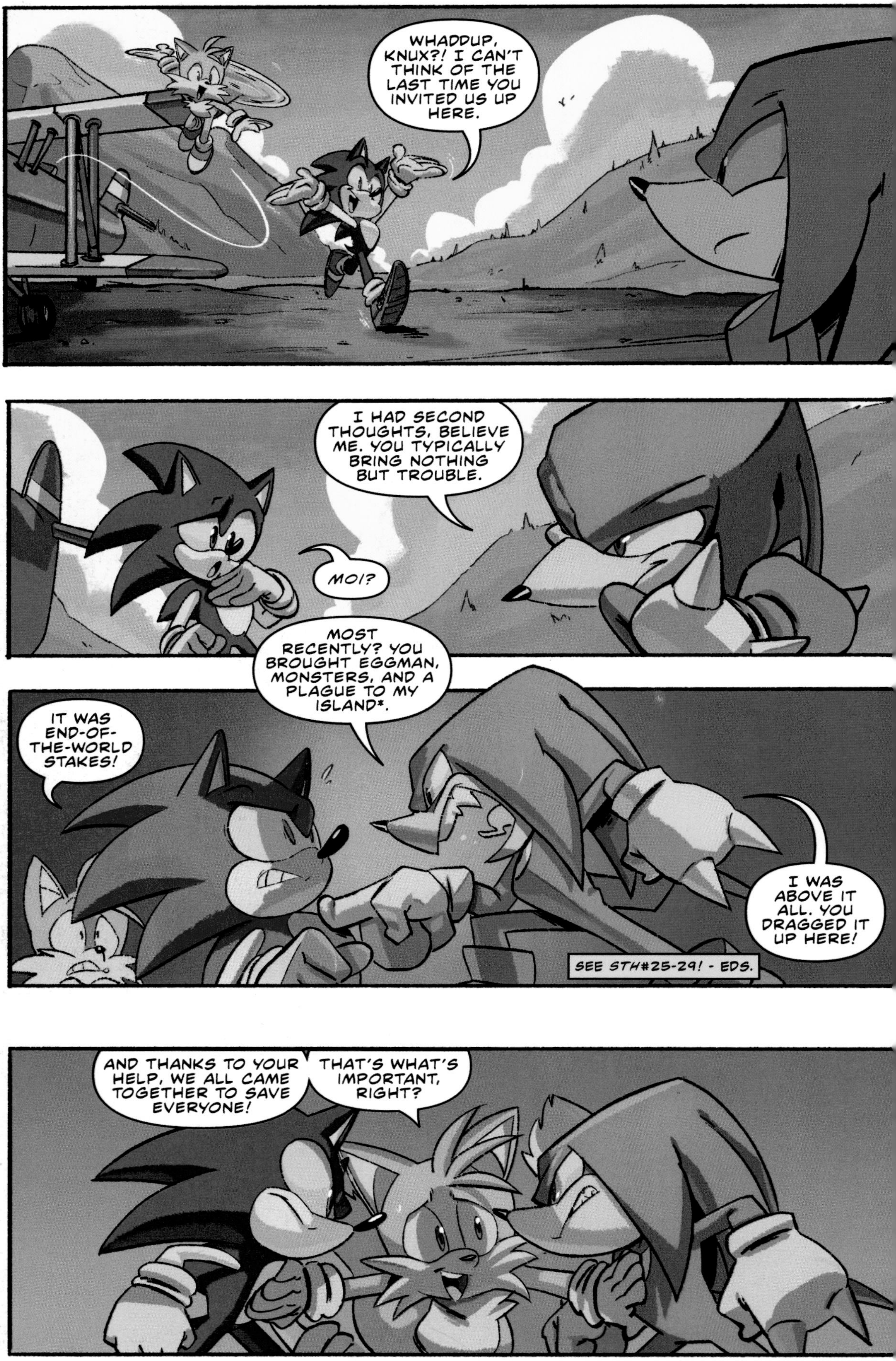
WHADDUP, KNUX?! I CAN'T THINK OF THE LAST TIME YOU INVITED US UP HERE.
I HAD SECOND THOUGHTS, BELIEVE ME. YOU TYPICALLY BRING NOTHING BUT TROUBLE.
MOI?
MOST RECENTLY? YOU BROUGHT EGGMAN, MONSTERS, AND A PLAGUE TO MY ISLAND*.
IT WAS END-OF-THE-WORLD STAKES!
I WAS ABOVE IT ALL. YOU DRAGGED IT UP HERE!
SEE STH#25-29! - EDS.
AND THANKS TO YOUR HELP, WE ALL CAME TOGETHER TO SAVE EVERYONE!
THAT'S WHAT'S IMPORTANT, RIGHT?

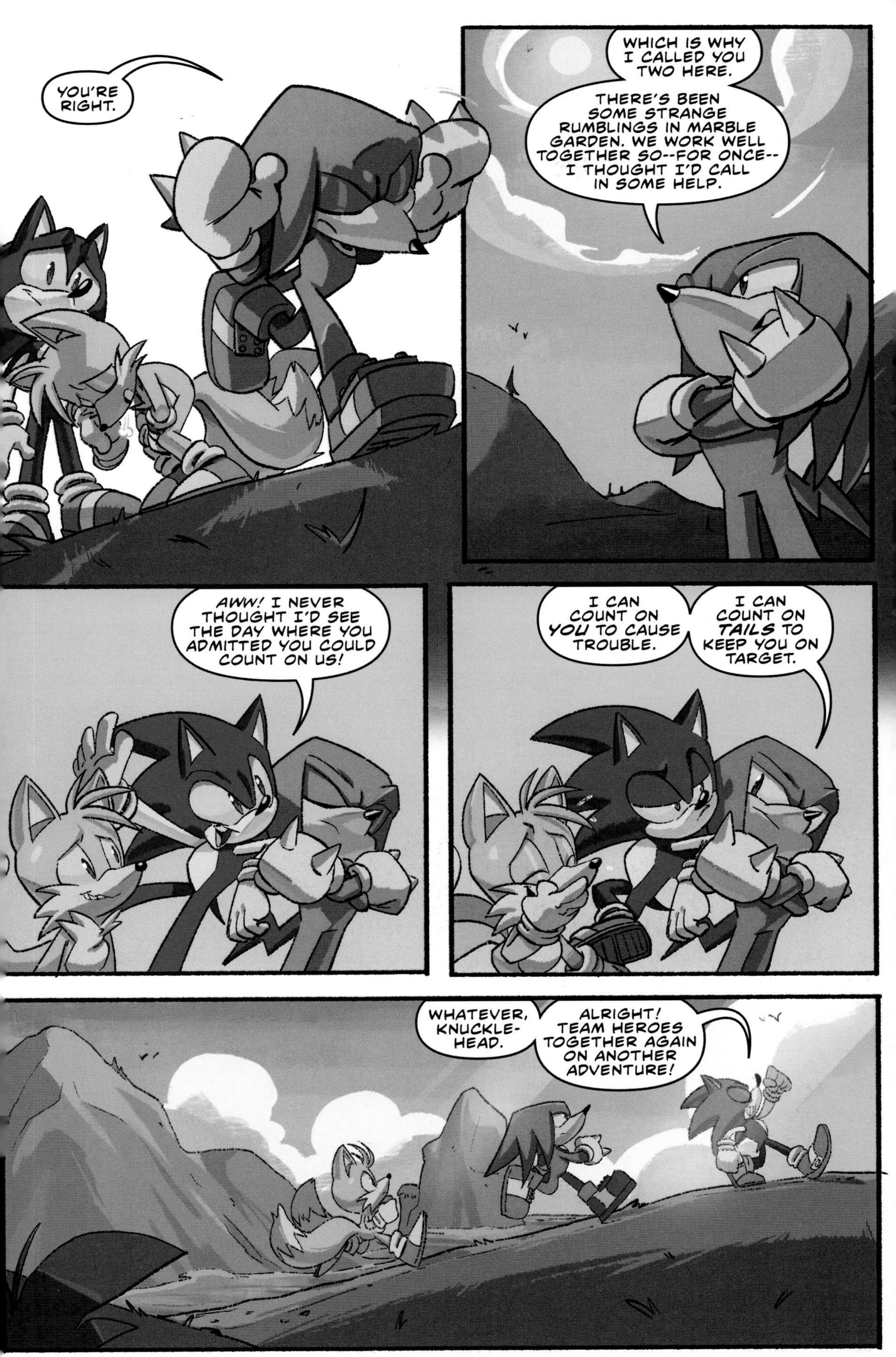
YOU'RE RIGHT.
WHICH IS WHY I CALLED YOU TWO HERE.
THERE'S BEEN SOME STRANGE RUMBLINGS IN MARBLE GARDEN. WE WORK WELL TOGETHER SO--FOR ONCE-- I THOUGHT I'D CALL IN SOME HELP.
AWW! I NEVER THOUGHT I'D SEE THE DAY WHERE YOU ADMITTED YOU COULD COUNT ON US!
I CAN COUNT ON YOU TO CAUSE TROUBLE.
I CAN COUNT ON TAILS TO KEEP YOU ON TARGET.
WHATEVER, KNUCKLE-HEAD.
ALRIGHT! TEAM HEROES TOGETHER AGAIN ON ANOTHER ADVENTURE!

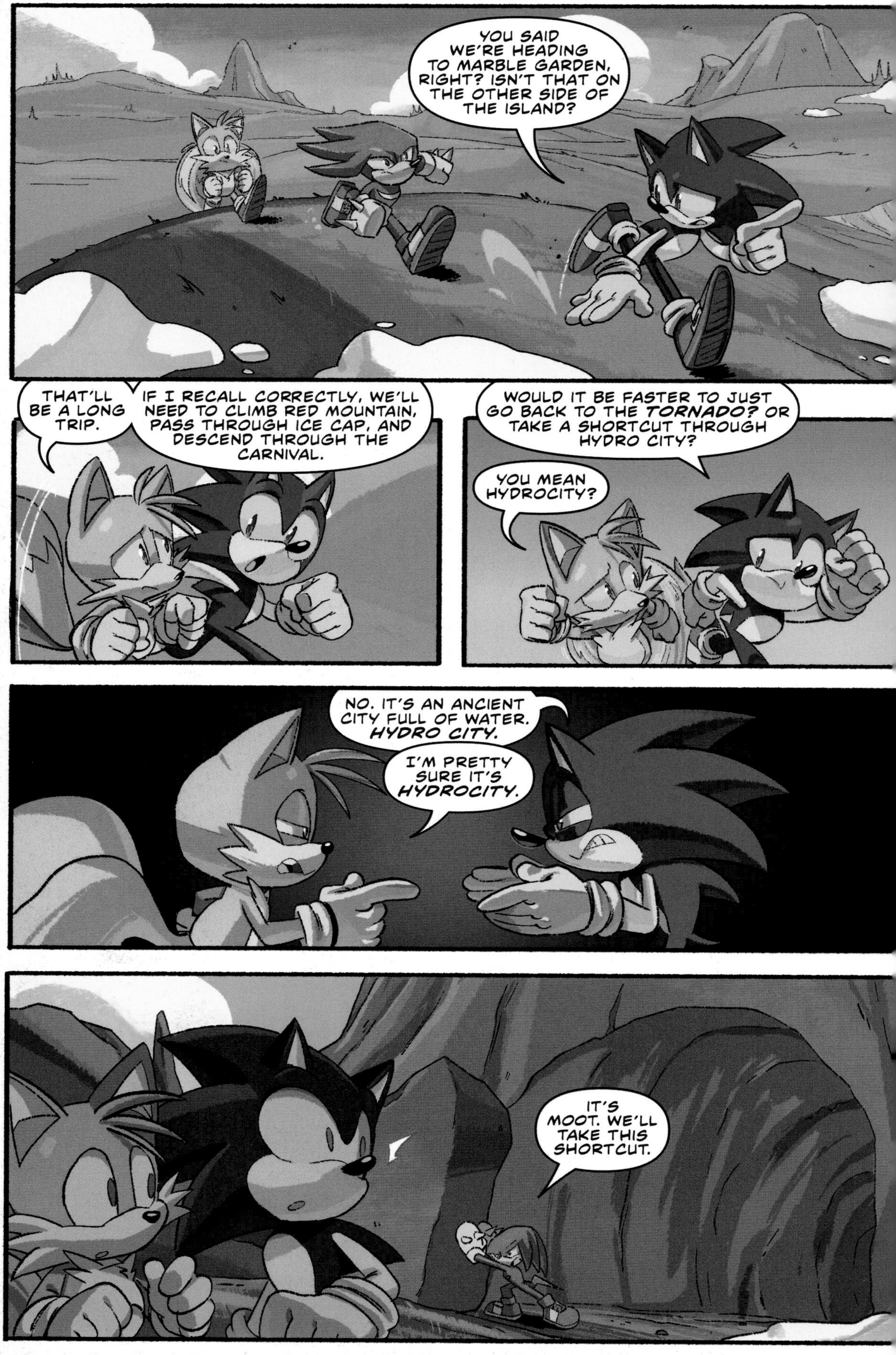
YOU SAID WE'RE HEADING TO MARBLE GARDEN, RIGHT? ISN'T THAT ON THE OTHER SIDE OF THE ISLAND?
THAT'LL BE A LONG TRIP.
IF I RECALL CORRECTLY, WE'LL NEED TO CLIMB RED MOUNTAIN, PASS THROUGH ICE CAP, AND DESCEND THROUGH THE CARNIVAL.
WOULD IT BE FASTER TO JUST GO BACK TO THE *TORNADO?* OR TAKE A SHORTCUT THROUGH HYDRO CITY?
YOU MEAN HYDROCITY?
NO. IT'S AN ANCIENT CITY FULL OF WATER. ***HYDRO CITY.***
I'M PRETTY SURE IT'S ***HYDROCITY.***
IT'S MOOT. WE'LL TAKE THIS SHORTCUT.

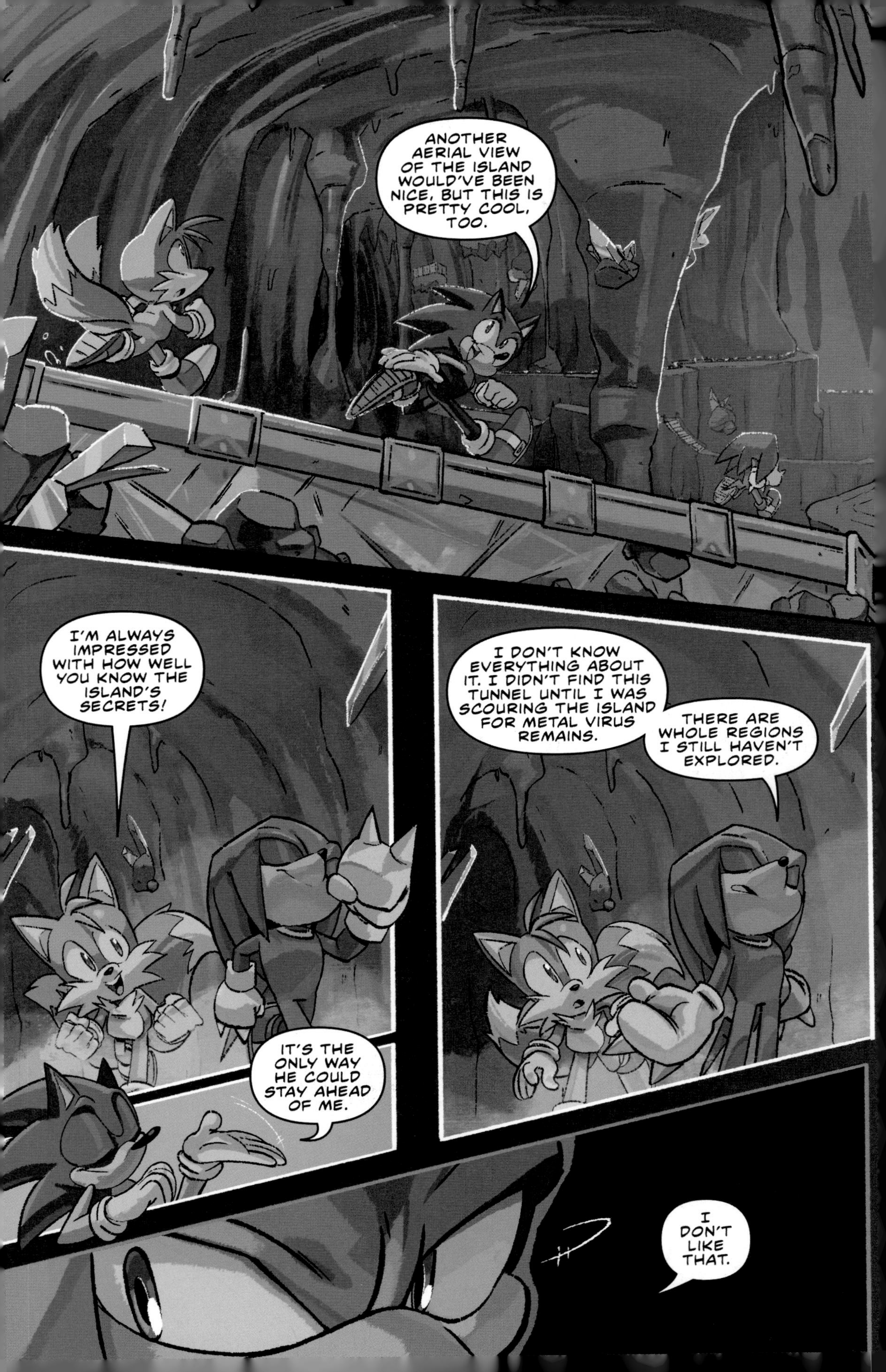
ANOTHER AERIAL VIEW OF THE ISLAND WOULD'VE BEEN NICE, BUT THIS IS PRETTY COOL, TOO.
I'M ALWAYS IMPRESSED WITH HOW WELL YOU KNOW THE ISLAND'S SECRETS!
IT'S THE ONLY WAY HE COULD STAY AHEAD OF ME.
I DON'T KNOW EVERYTHING ABOUT IT. I DIDN'T FIND THIS TUNNEL UNTIL I WAS SCOURING THE ISLAND FOR METAL VIRUS REMAINS.
THERE ARE WHOLE REGIONS I STILL HAVEN'T EXPLORED.
I DON'T LIKE THAT.

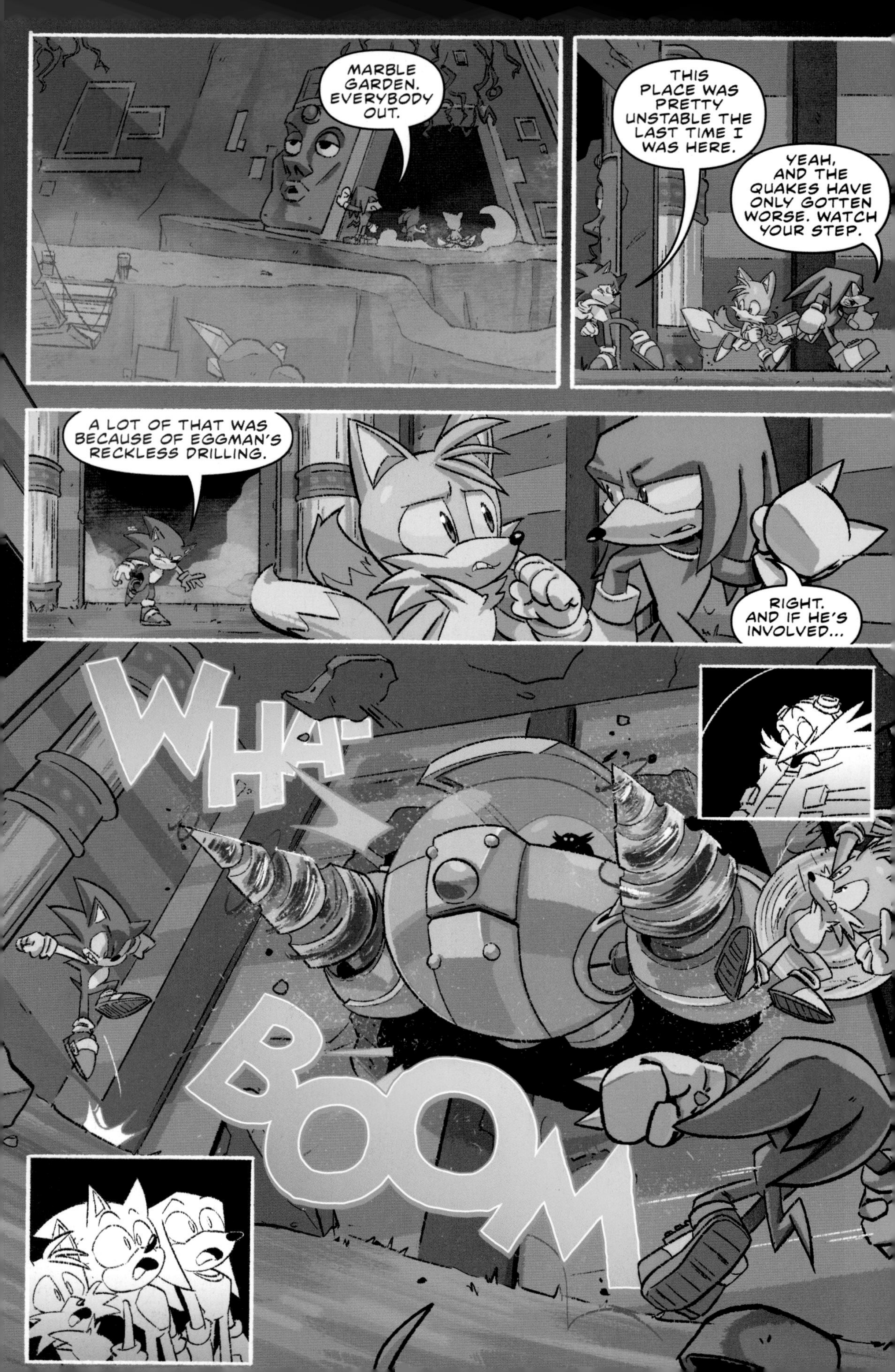
MARBLE GARDEN. EVERYBODY OUT.
THIS PLACE WAS PRETTY UNSTABLE THE LAST TIME I WAS HERE.
YEAH, AND THE QUAKES HAVE ONLY GOTTEN WORSE. WATCH YOUR STEP.
A LOT OF THAT WAS BECAUSE OF EGGMAN'S RECKLESS DRILLING.
RIGHT. AND IF HE'S INVOLVED...
WHA-
BOOM

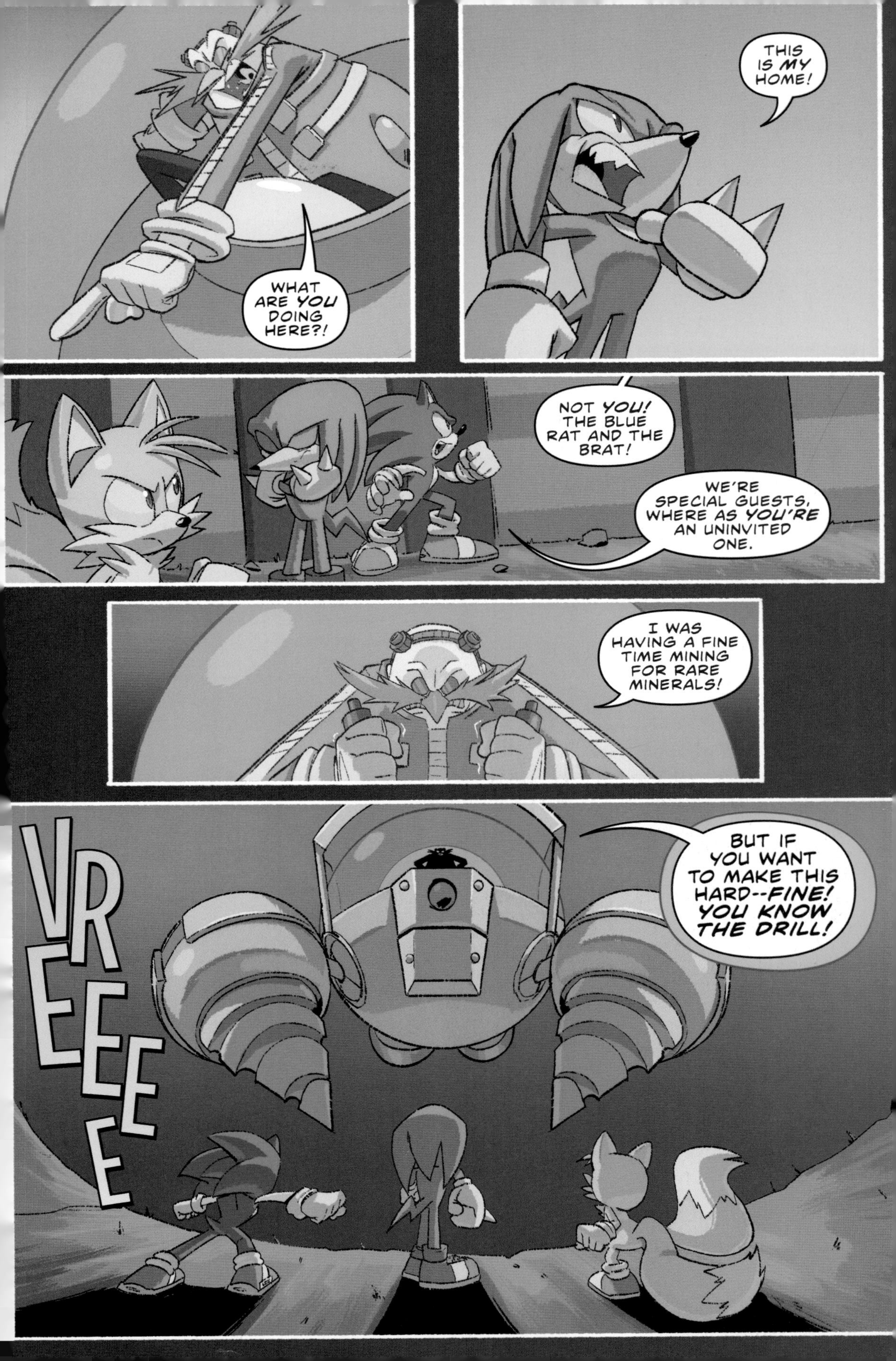
WHAT ARE YOU DOING HERE?!
THIS IS MY HOME!
NOT YOU! THE BLUE RAT AND THE BRAT!
WE'RE SPECIAL GUESTS, WHERE AS YOU'RE AN UNINVITED ONE.
I WAS HAVING A FINE TIME MINING FOR RARE MINERALS!
VREEEEE
BUT IF YOU WANT TO MAKE THIS HARD--FINE! YOU KNOW THE DRILL!

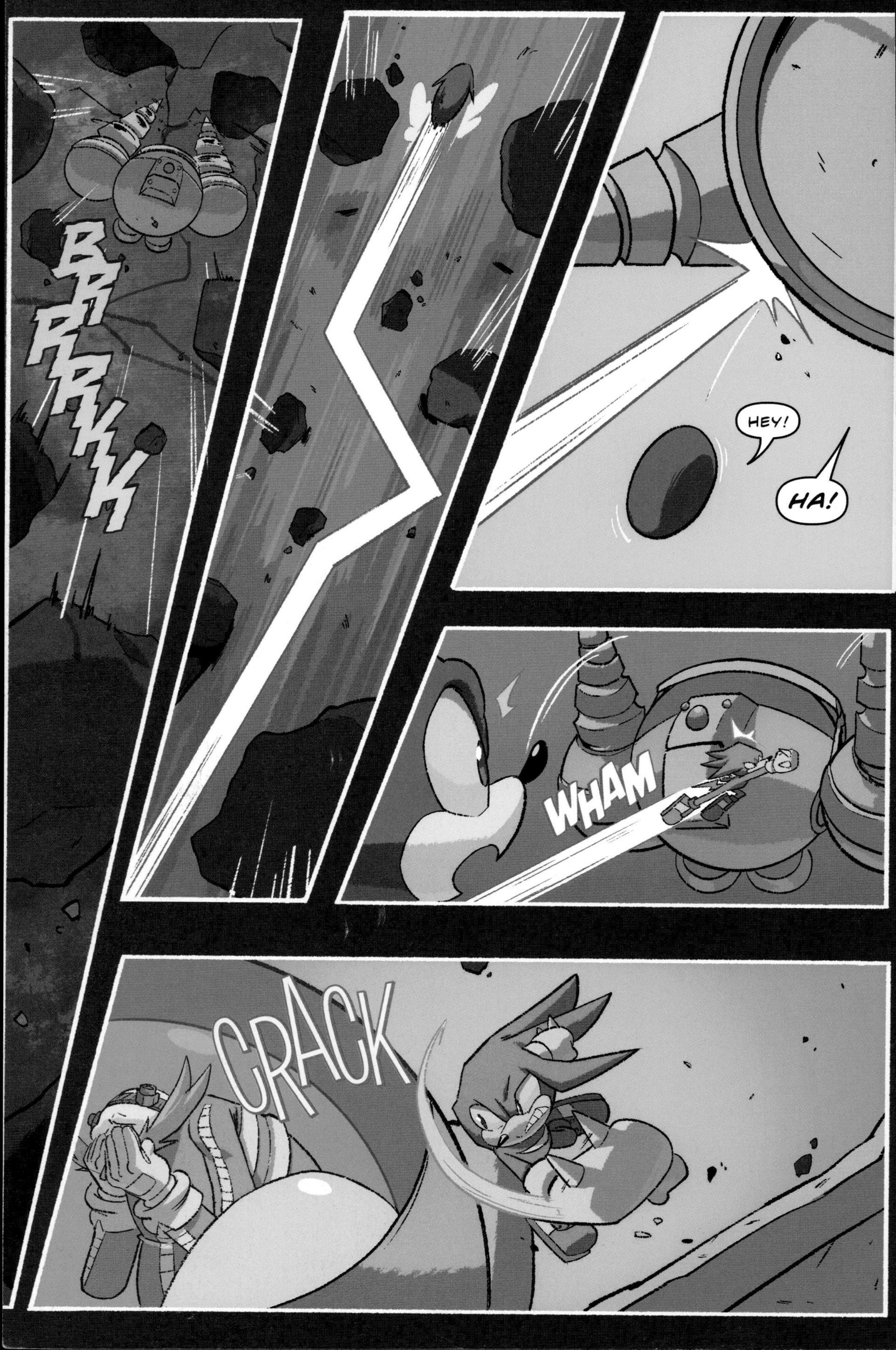
BRRRKK
HEY!
HA!
WHAM
CRACK

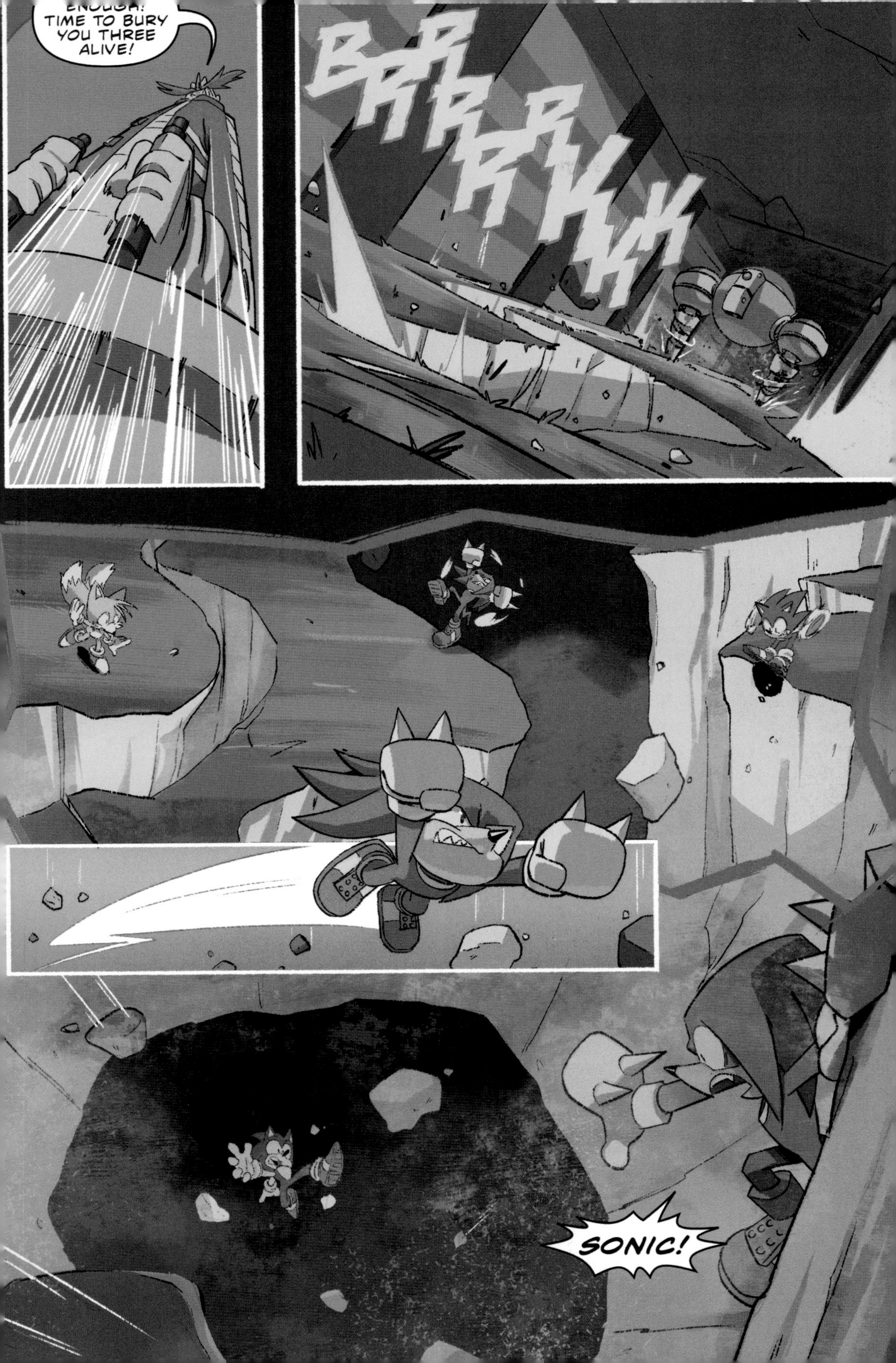
TIME TO BURY YOU THREE ALIVE!
BRRRRRKKK
SONIC!

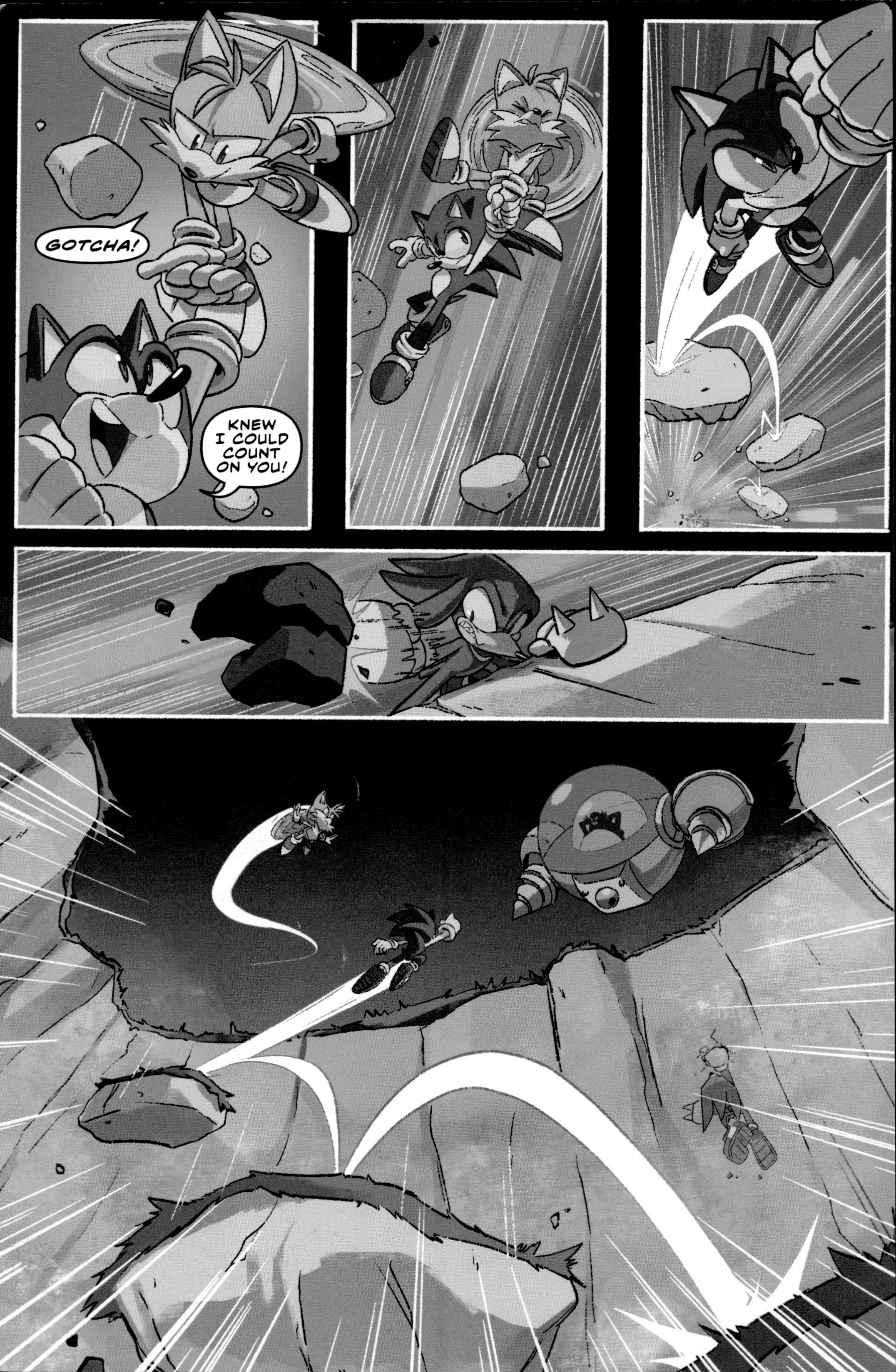
GOTCHA!
KNEW I COULD COUNT ON YOU!

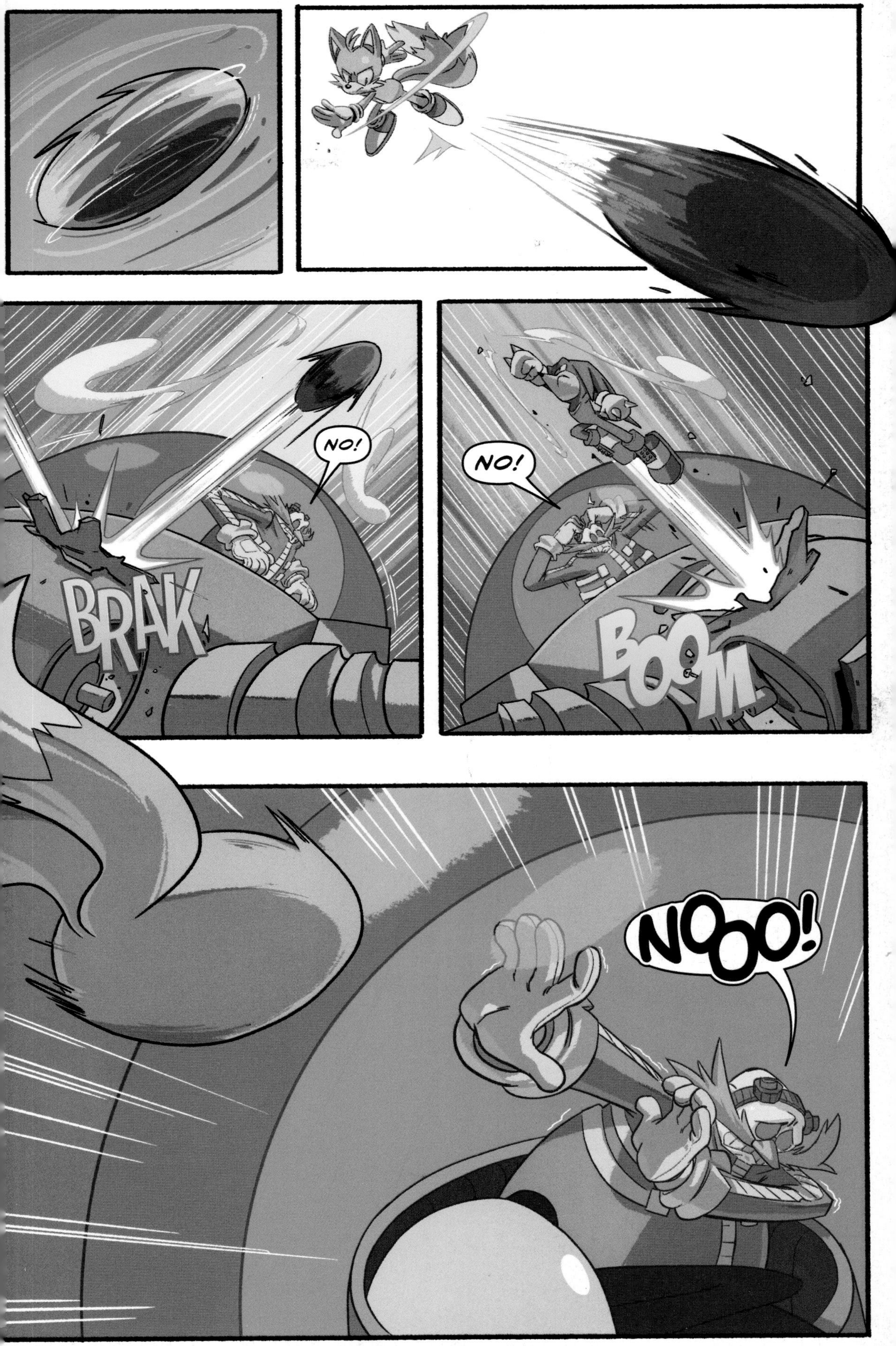
NO!
BRAK
NO!
BOOM
NOOO!

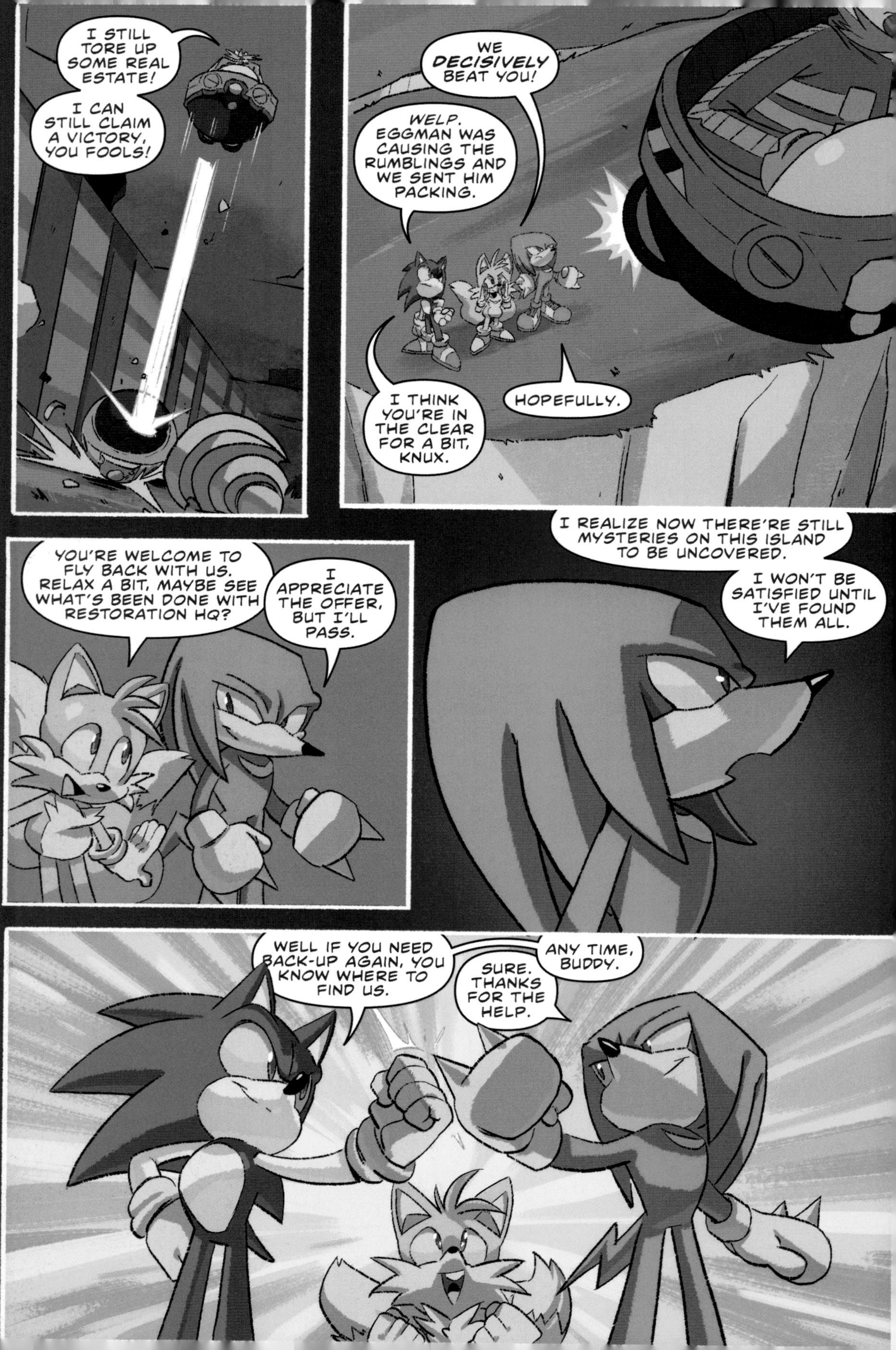
I STILL TORE UP SOME REAL ESTATE!
I CAN STILL CLAIM A VICTORY, YOU FOOLS!
WE *DECISIVELY* BEAT YOU!
WELP. EGGMAN WAS CAUSING THE RUMBLINGS AND WE SENT HIM PACKING.
I THINK YOU'RE IN THE CLEAR FOR A BIT, KNUX.
HOPEFULLY.
YOU'RE WELCOME TO FLY BACK WITH US. RELAX A BIT, MAYBE SEE WHAT'S BEEN DONE WITH RESTORATION HQ?
I APPRECIATE THE OFFER, BUT I'LL PASS.
I REALIZE NOW THERE'RE STILL MYSTERIES ON THIS ISLAND TO BE UNCOVERED.
I WON'T BE SATISFIED UNTIL I'VE FOUND THEM ALL.
WELL IF YOU NEED BACK-UP AGAIN, YOU KNOW WHERE TO FIND US.
SURE. THANKS FOR THE HELP.
ANY TIME, BUDDY.

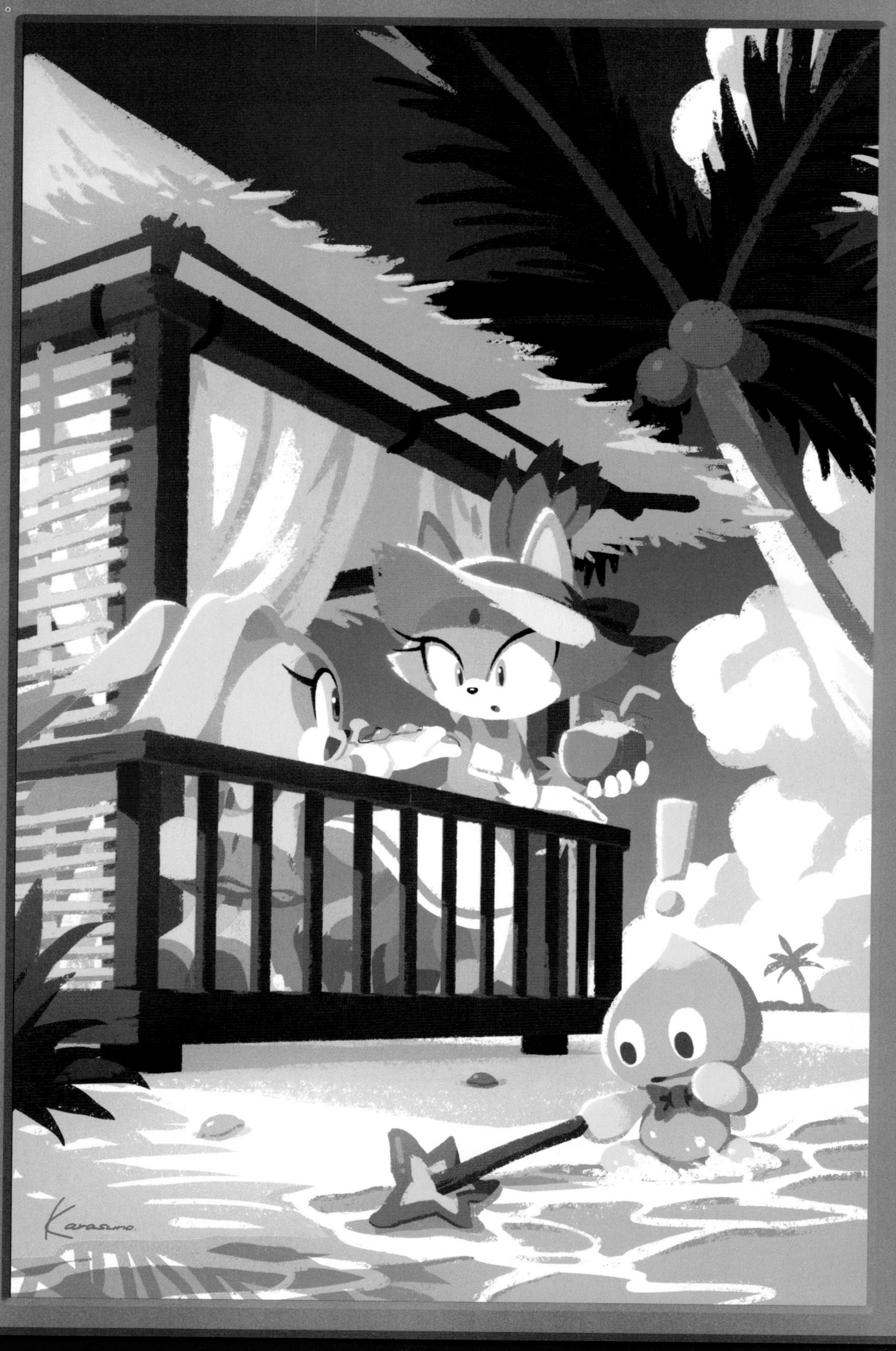
Karasuno.

ART BY **YUI KARASUNO** OF SONIC TEAM

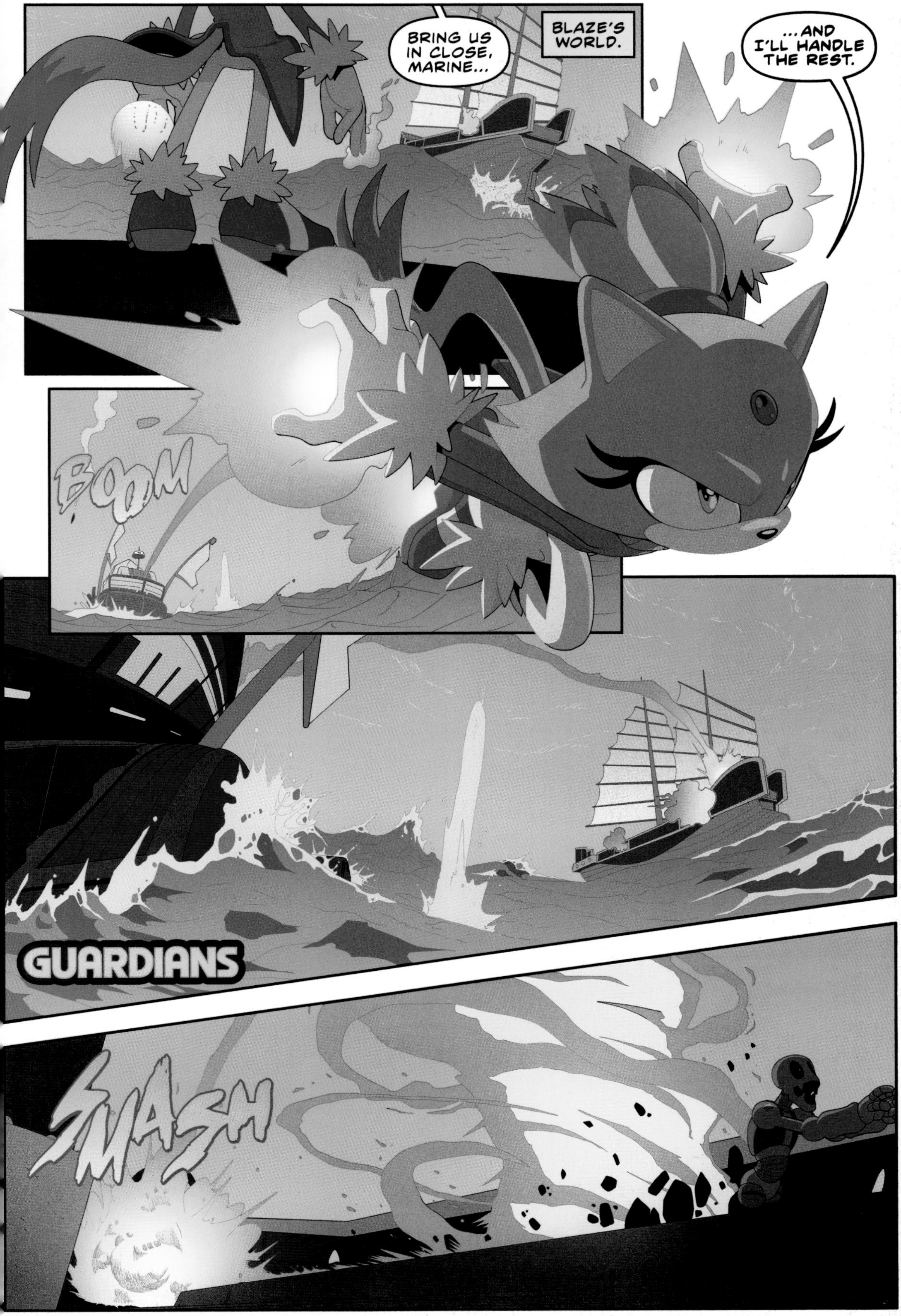
BRING US IN CLOSE, MARINE...
BLAZE'S WORLD.
...AND I'LL HANDLE THE REST.
BOOM
GUARDIANS
SMASH

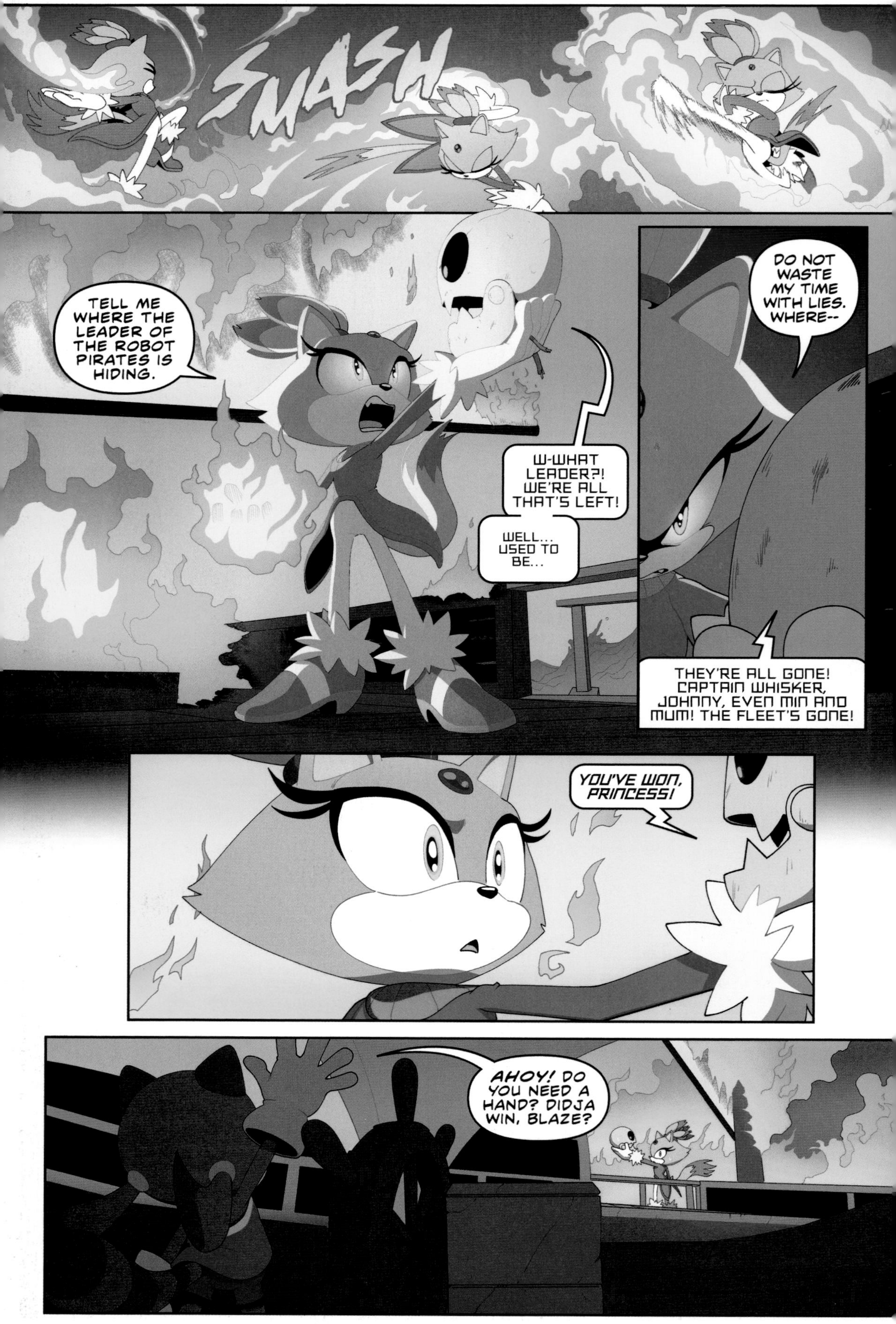
SMASH
TELL ME WHERE THE LEADER OF THE ROBOT PIRATES IS HIDING.
W-WHAT LEADER?! WE'RE ALL THAT'S LEFT!
WELL... USED TO BE...
DO NOT WASTE MY TIME WITH LIES. WHERE--
THEY'RE ALL GONE! CAPTAIN WHISKER, JOHNNY, EVEN MIN AND MUM! THE FLEET'S GONE!
YOU'VE WON, PRINCESS!
AHOY! DO YOU NEED A HAND? DIDJA WIN, BLAZE?

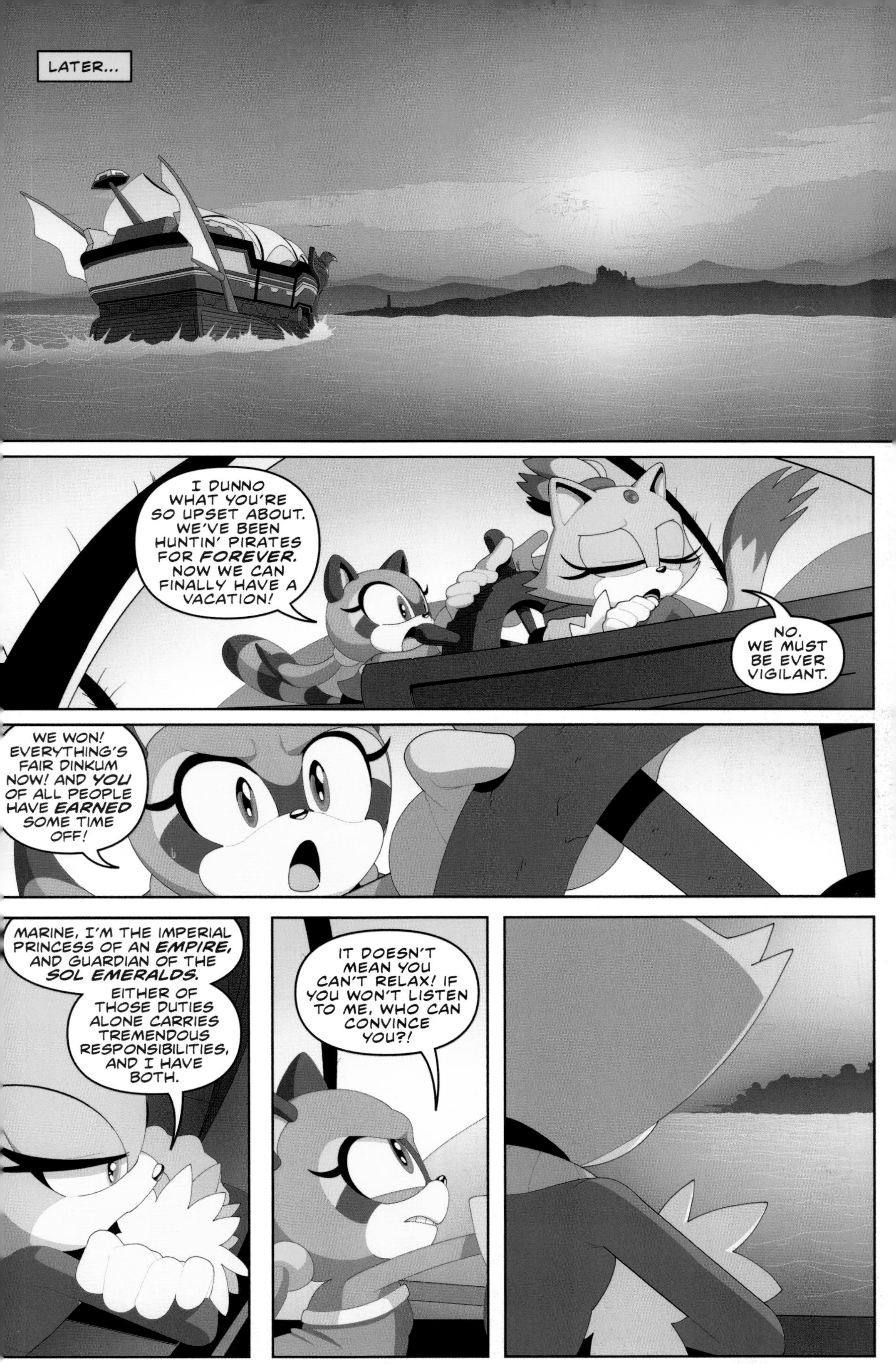
LATER...
I DUNNO WHAT YOU'RE SO UPSET ABOUT. WE'VE BEEN HUNTIN' PIRATES FOR FOREVER. NOW WE CAN FINALLY HAVE A VACATION!
NO. WE MUST BE EVER VIGILANT.
WE WON! EVERYTHING'S FAIR DINKUM NOW! AND YOU OF ALL PEOPLE HAVE EARNED SOME TIME OFF!
MARINE, I'M THE IMPERIAL PRINCESS OF AN EMPIRE, AND GUARDIAN OF THE SOL EMERALDS.
EITHER OF THOSE DUTIES ALONE CARRIES TREMENDOUS RESPONSIBILITIES, AND I HAVE BOTH.
IT DOESN'T MEAN YOU CAN'T RELAX! IF YOU WON'T LISTEN TO ME, WHO CAN CONVINCE YOU?!

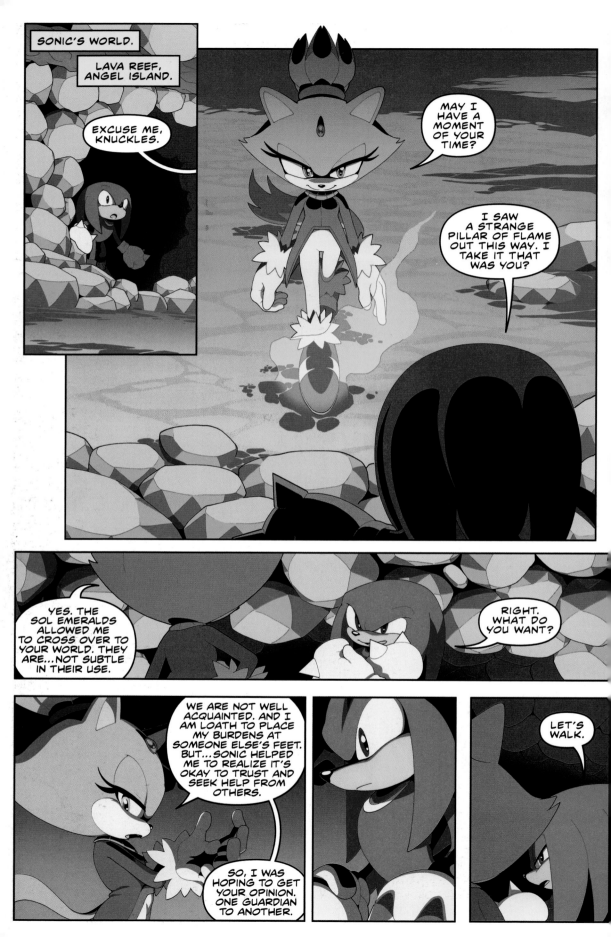

SONIC'S WORLD.

LAVA REEF, ANGEL ISLAND.

EXCUSE ME, KNUCKLES.

MAY I HAVE A MOMENT OF YOUR TIME?

I SAW A STRANGE PILLAR OF FLAME OUT THIS WAY. I TAKE IT THAT WAS YOU?

YES. THE SOL EMERALDS ALLOWED ME TO CROSS OVER TO YOUR WORLD. THEY ARE...NOT SUBTLE IN THEIR USE.

RIGHT. WHAT DO YOU WANT?

WE ARE NOT WELL ACQUAINTED. AND I AM LOATH TO PLACE MY BURDENS AT SOMEONE ELSE'S FEET. BUT...SONIC HELPED ME TO REALIZE IT'S OKAY TO TRUST AND SEEK HELP FROM OTHERS.

SO, I WAS HOPING TO GET YOUR OPINION. ONE GUARDIAN TO ANOTHER.

LET'S WALK.

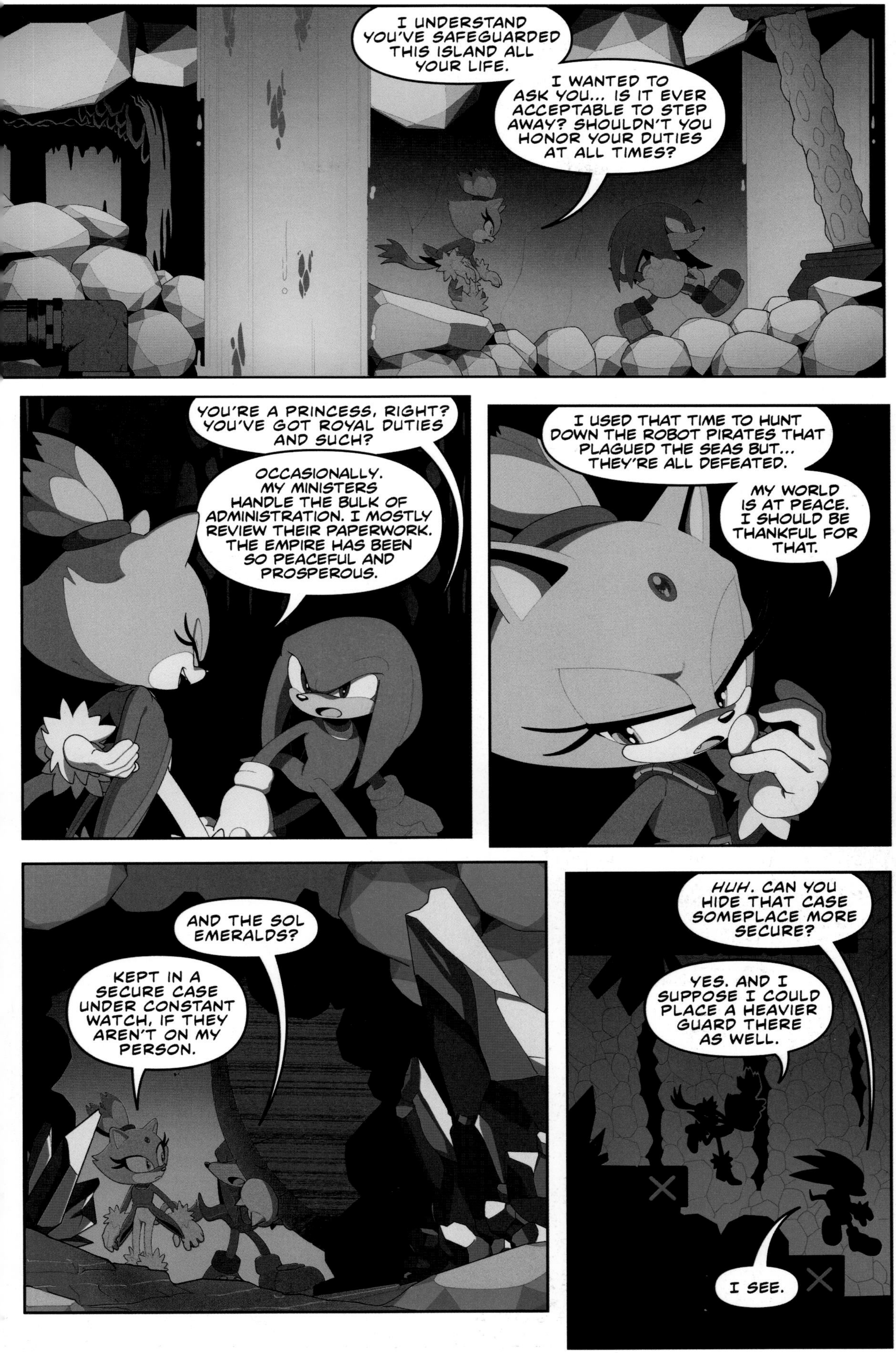
I UNDERSTAND YOU'VE SAFEGUARDED THIS ISLAND ALL YOUR LIFE.
I WANTED TO ASK YOU... IS IT EVER ACCEPTABLE TO STEP AWAY? SHOULDN'T YOU HONOR YOUR DUTIES AT ALL TIMES?
YOU'RE A PRINCESS, RIGHT? YOU'VE GOT ROYAL DUTIES AND SUCH?
OCCASIONALLY. MY MINISTERS HANDLE THE BULK OF ADMINISTRATION. I MOSTLY REVIEW THEIR PAPERWORK. THE EMPIRE HAS BEEN SO PEACEFUL AND PROSPEROUS.
I USED THAT TIME TO HUNT DOWN THE ROBOT PIRATES THAT PLAGUED THE SEAS BUT... THEY'RE ALL DEFEATED.
MY WORLD IS AT PEACE. I SHOULD BE THANKFUL FOR THAT.
AND THE SOL EMERALDS?
KEPT IN A SECURE CASE UNDER CONSTANT WATCH, IF THEY AREN'T ON MY PERSON.
HUH. CAN YOU HIDE THAT CASE SOMEPLACE MORE SECURE?
YES. AND I SUPPOSE I COULD PLACE A HEAVIER GUARD THERE AS WELL.
I SEE.

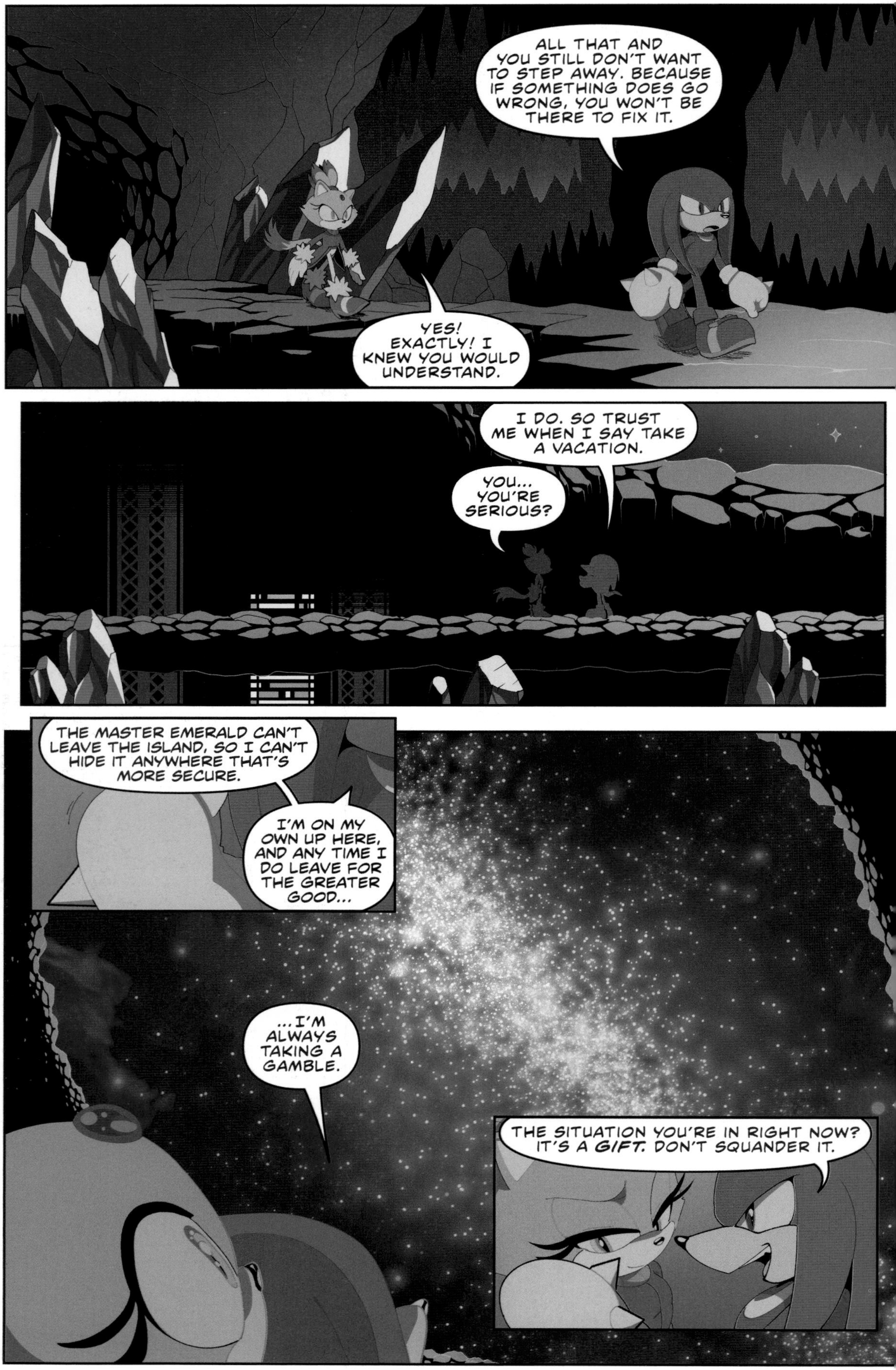
ALL THAT AND YOU STILL DON'T WANT TO STEP AWAY. BECAUSE IF SOMETHING DOES GO WRONG, YOU WON'T BE THERE TO FIX IT.
YES! EXACTLY! I KNEW YOU WOULD UNDERSTAND.
I DO. SO TRUST ME WHEN I SAY TAKE A VACATION.
YOU... YOU'RE SERIOUS?
THE MASTER EMERALD CAN'T LEAVE THE ISLAND, SO I CAN'T HIDE IT ANYWHERE THAT'S MORE SECURE.
I'M ON MY OWN UP HERE, AND ANY TIME I DO LEAVE FOR THE GREATER GOOD...
...I'M ALWAYS TAKING A GAMBLE.
THE SITUATION YOU'RE IN RIGHT NOW? IT'S A *GIFT.* DON'T SQUANDER IT.

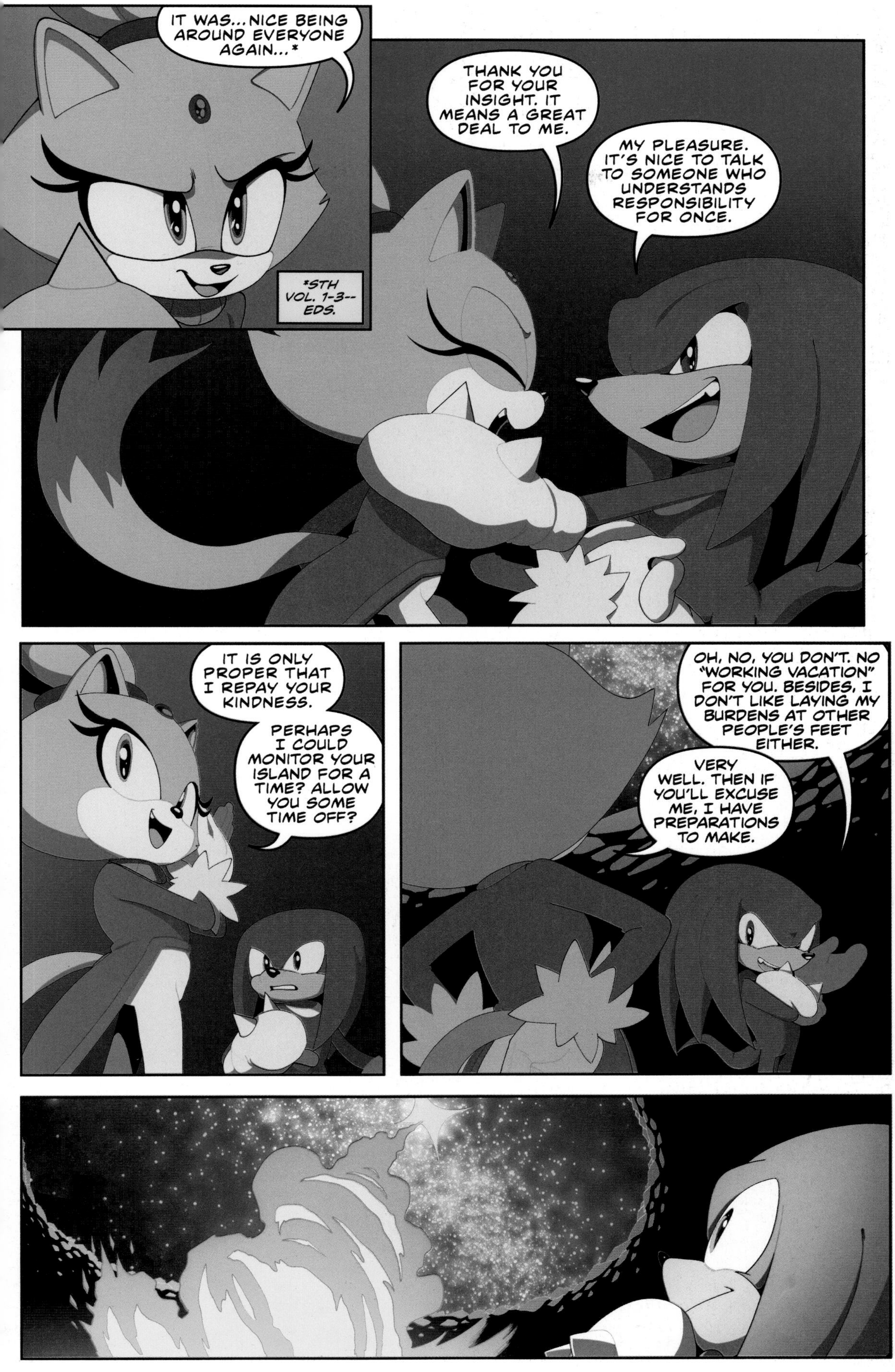

IT WAS...NICE BEING AROUND EVERYONE AGAIN...*
*STH VOL. 1-3--EDS.
THANK YOU FOR YOUR INSIGHT. IT MEANS A GREAT DEAL TO ME.
MY PLEASURE. IT'S NICE TO TALK TO SOMEONE WHO UNDERSTANDS RESPONSIBILITY FOR ONCE.
IT IS ONLY PROPER THAT I REPAY YOUR KINDNESS.
PERHAPS I COULD MONITOR YOUR ISLAND FOR A TIME? ALLOW YOU SOME TIME OFF?
OH, NO, YOU DON'T. NO "WORKING VACATION" FOR YOU. BESIDES, I DON'T LIKE LAYING MY BURDENS AT OTHER PEOPLE'S FEET EITHER.
VERY WELL. THEN IF YOU'LL EXCUSE ME, I HAVE PREPARATIONS TO MAKE.

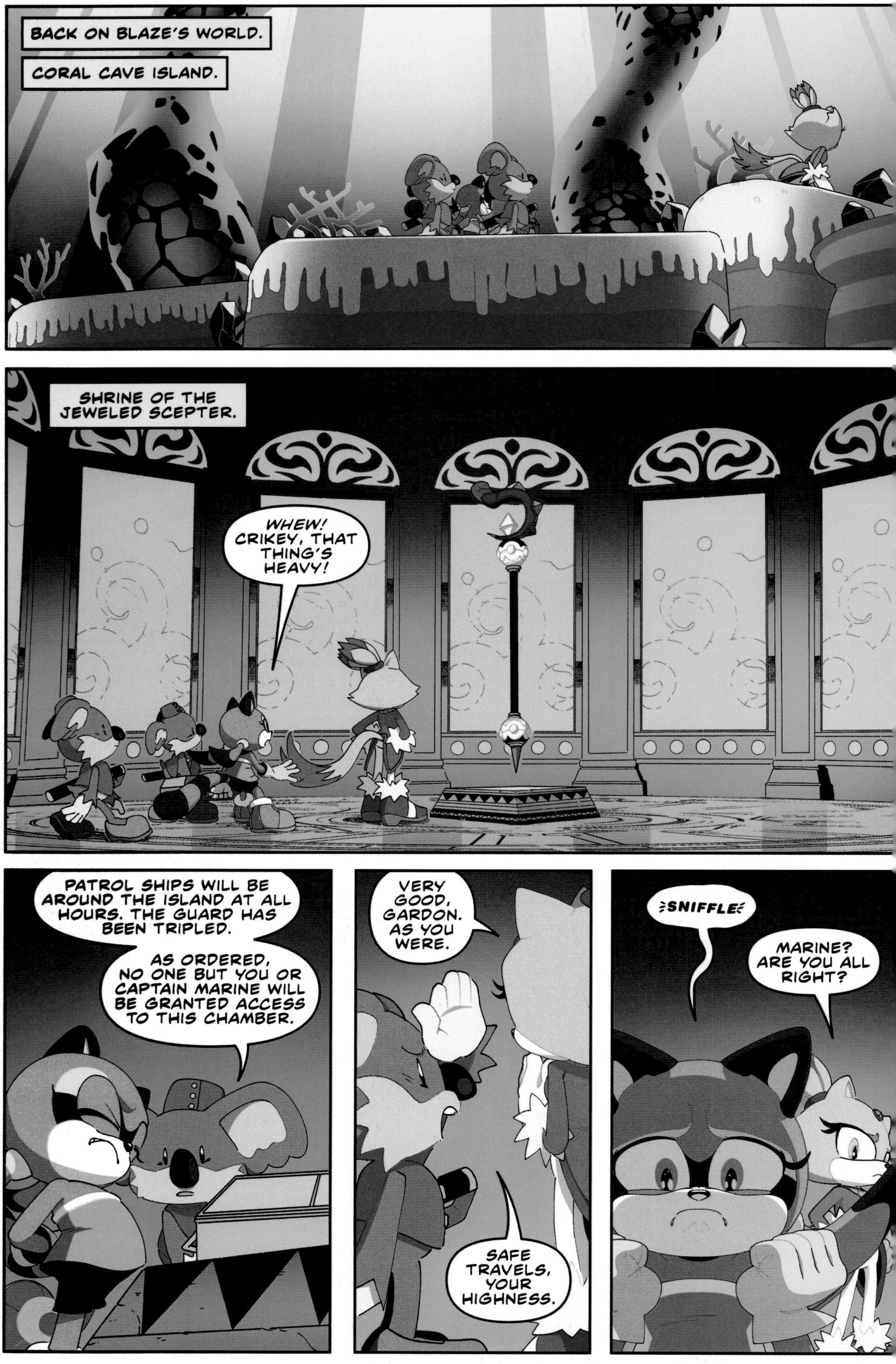
BACK ON BLAZE'S WORLD.
CORAL CAVE ISLAND.
SHRINE OF THE JEWELED SCEPTER.
WHEW! CRIKEY, THAT THING'S HEAVY!
PATROL SHIPS WILL BE AROUND THE ISLAND AT ALL HOURS. THE GUARD HAS BEEN TRIPLED.
AS ORDERED, NO ONE BUT YOU OR CAPTAIN MARINE WILL BE GRANTED ACCESS TO THIS CHAMBER.
VERY GOOD, GARDON. AS YOU WERE.
SAFE TRAVELS, YOUR HIGHNESS.
SNIFFLE
MARINE? ARE YOU ALL RIGHT?

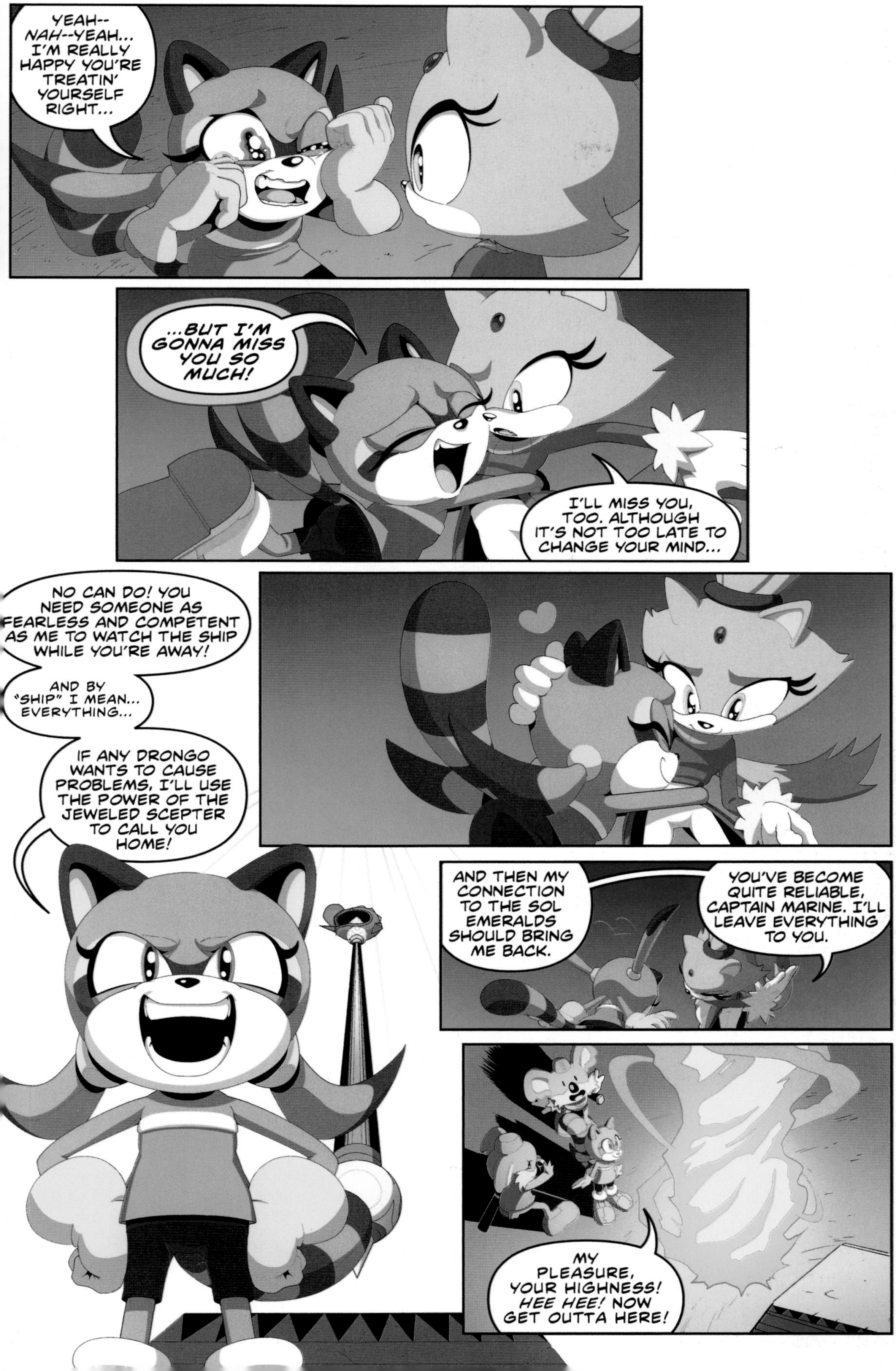
YEAH-- NAH--YEAH... I'M REALLY HAPPY YOU'RE TREATIN' YOURSELF RIGHT...
...BUT I'M GONNA MISS YOU SO MUCH!
I'LL MISS YOU, TOO. ALTHOUGH IT'S NOT TOO LATE TO CHANGE YOUR MIND...
NO CAN DO! YOU NEED SOMEONE AS FEARLESS AND COMPETENT AS ME TO WATCH THE SHIP WHILE YOU'RE AWAY!
AND BY "SHIP" I MEAN... EVERYTHING...
IF ANY DRONGO WANTS TO CAUSE PROBLEMS, I'LL USE THE POWER OF THE JEWELED SCEPTER TO CALL YOU HOME!
AND THEN MY CONNECTION TO THE SOL EMERALDS SHOULD BRING ME BACK.
YOU'VE BECOME QUITE RELIABLE, CAPTAIN MARINE. I'LL LEAVE EVERYTHING TO YOU.
MY PLEASURE, YOUR HIGHNESS! HEE HEE! NOW GET OUTTA HERE!

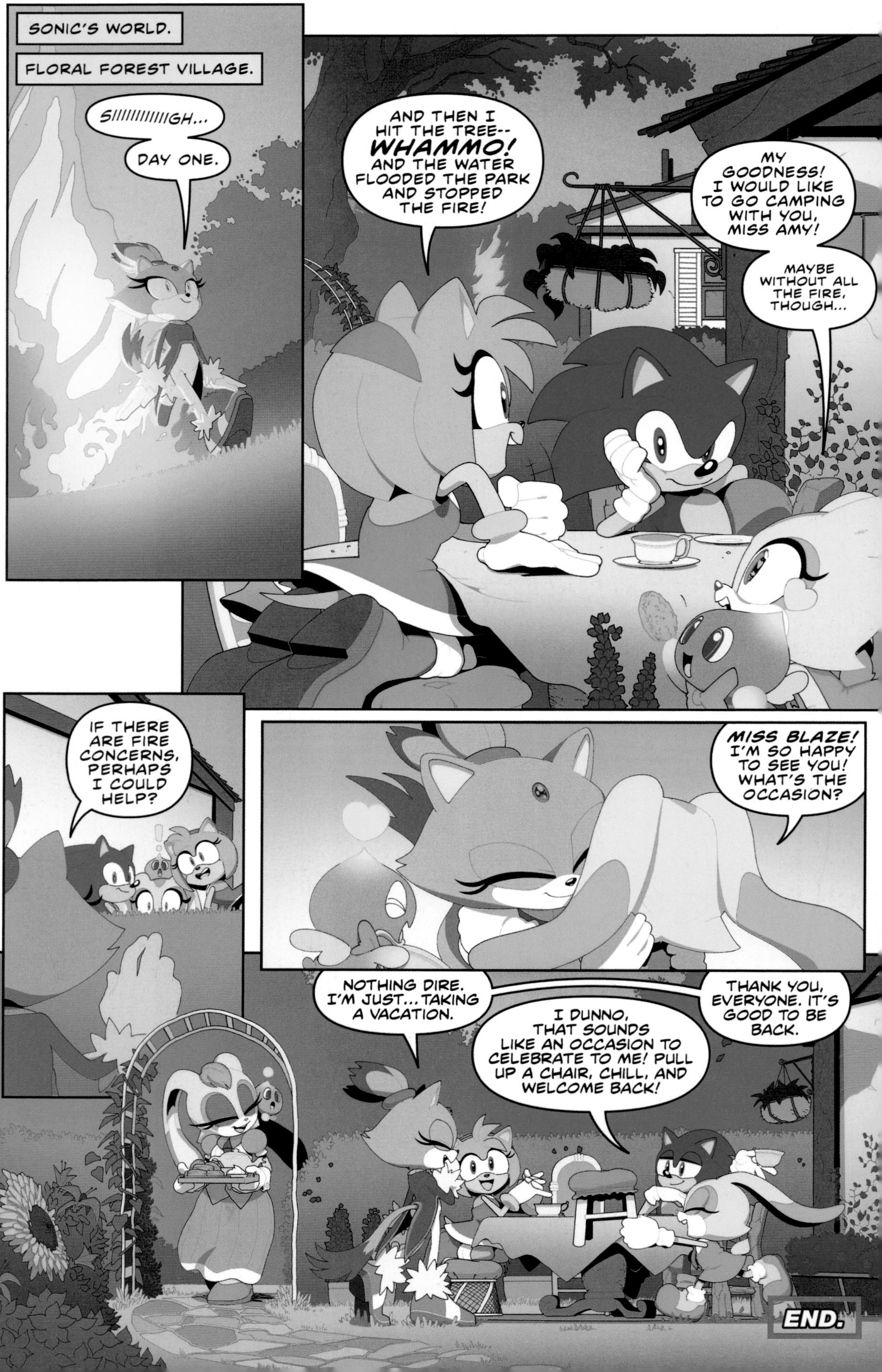
SONIC'S WORLD.
FLORAL FOREST VILLAGE.
SIIIIIIIIIIIIGH...
DAY ONE.
AND THEN I HIT THE TREE-- WHAMMO! AND THE WATER FLOODED THE PARK AND STOPPED THE FIRE!
MY GOODNESS! I WOULD LIKE TO GO CAMPING WITH YOU, MISS AMY!
MAYBE WITHOUT ALL THE FIRE, THOUGH...
IF THERE ARE FIRE CONCERNS, PERHAPS I COULD HELP?
MISS BLAZE! I'M SO HAPPY TO SEE YOU! WHAT'S THE OCCASION?
NOTHING DIRE. I'M JUST... TAKING A VACATION.
I DUNNO, THAT SOUNDS LIKE AN OCCASION TO CELEBRATE TO ME! PULL UP A CHAIR, CHILL, AND WELCOME BACK!
THANK YOU, EVERYONE. IT'S GOOD TO BE BACK.
END.

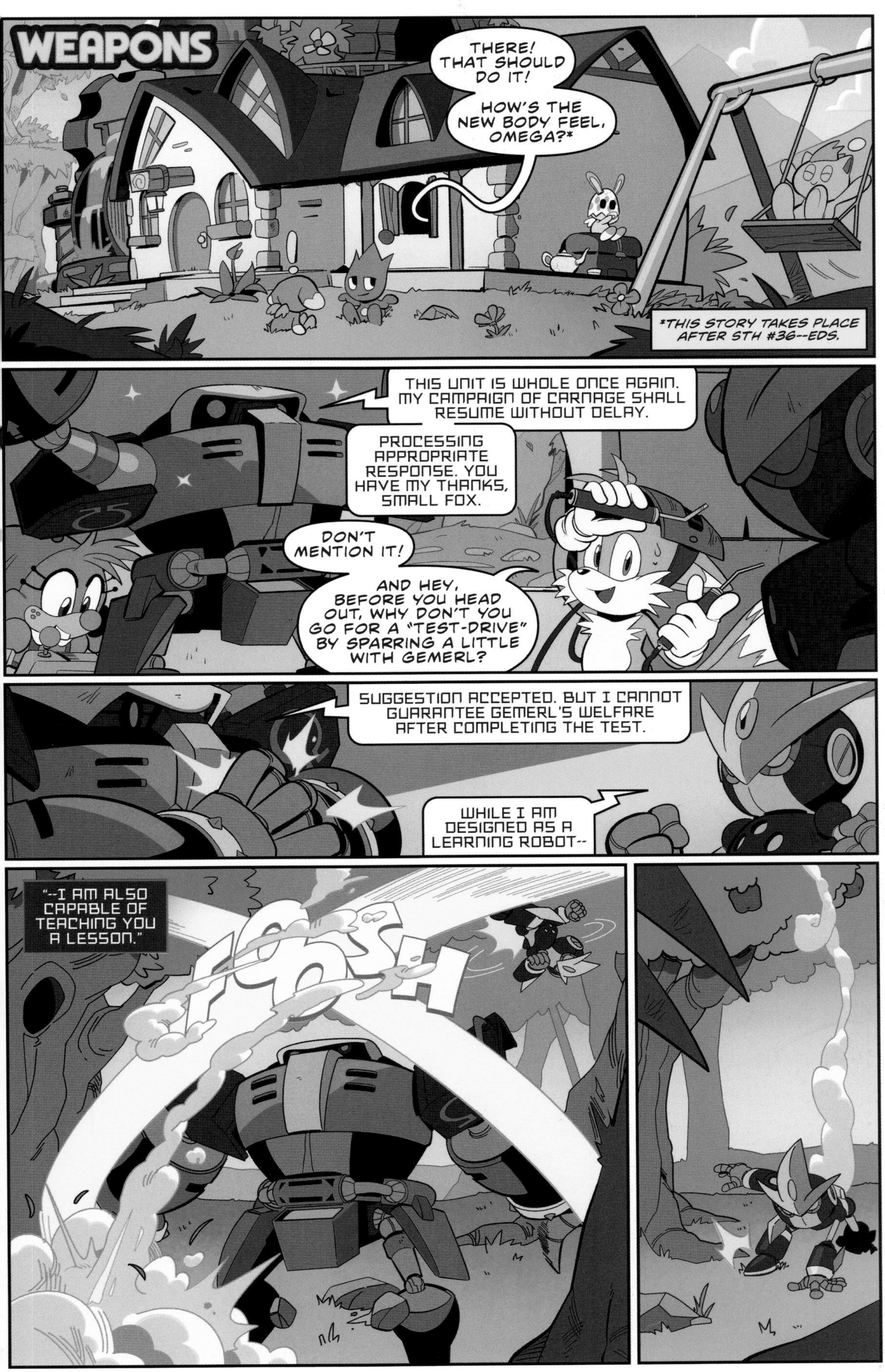
WEAPONS
THERE! THAT SHOULD DO IT!
HOW'S THE NEW BODY FEEL, OMEGA?*
*THIS STORY TAKES PLACE AFTER STH #36--EDS.
THIS UNIT IS WHOLE ONCE AGAIN. MY CAMPAIGN OF CARNAGE SHALL RESUME WITHOUT DELAY.
PROCESSING APPROPRIATE RESPONSE. YOU HAVE MY THANKS, SMALL FOX.
DON'T MENTION IT!
AND HEY, BEFORE YOU HEAD OUT, WHY DON'T YOU GO FOR A "TEST-DRIVE" BY SPARRING A LITTLE WITH GEMERL?
SUGGESTION ACCEPTED. BUT I CANNOT GUARANTEE GEMERL'S WELFARE AFTER COMPLETING THE TEST.
WHILE I AM DESIGNED AS A LEARNING ROBOT--
"--I AM ALSO CAPABLE OF TEACHING YOU A LESSON."
FOOSH

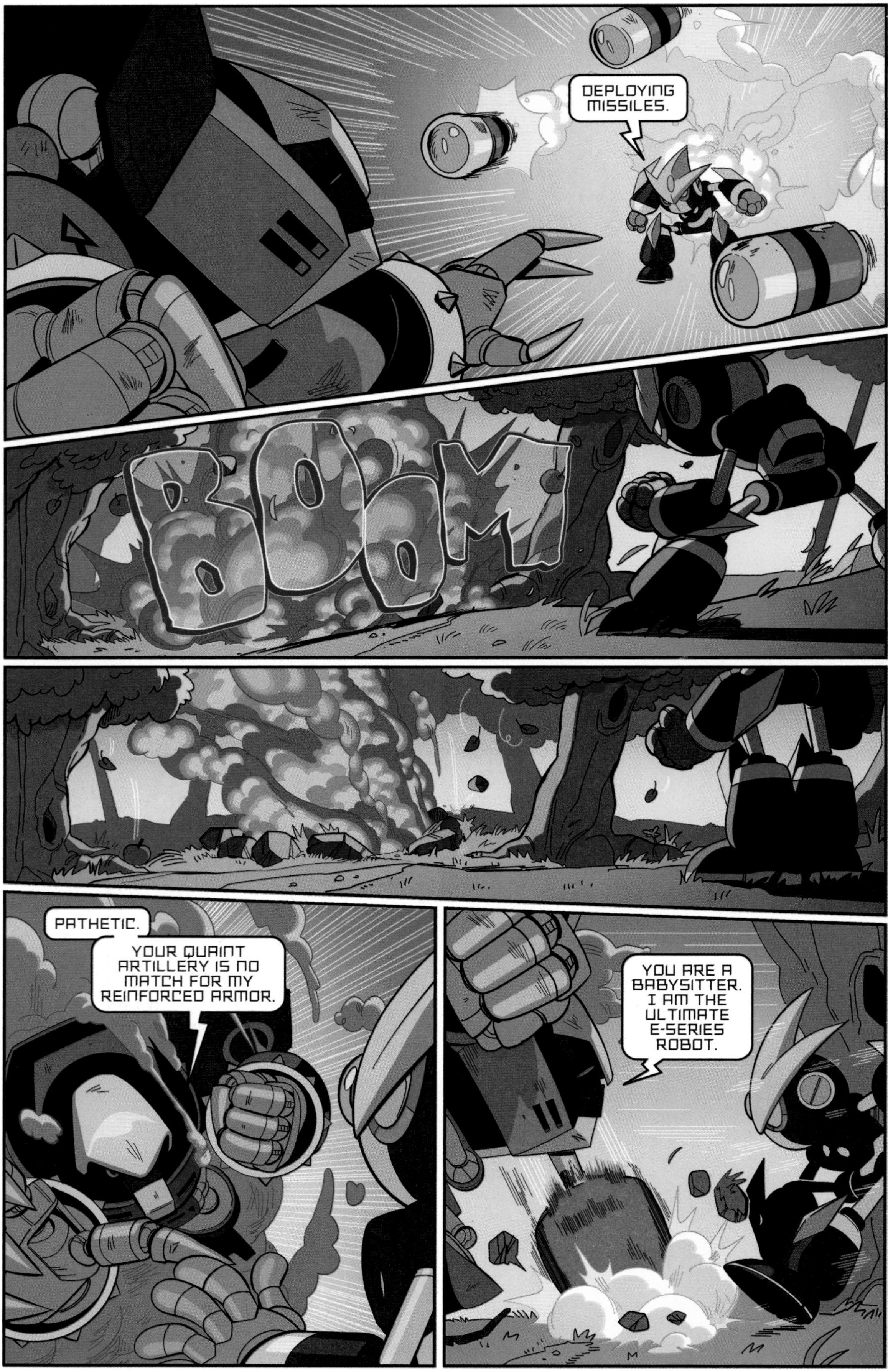

DEPLOYING MISSILES.
BOOM
PATHETIC.
YOUR QUAINT ARTILLERY IS NO MATCH FOR MY REINFORCED ARMOR.
YOU ARE A BABYSITTER. I AM THE ULTIMATE E-SERIES ROBOT.

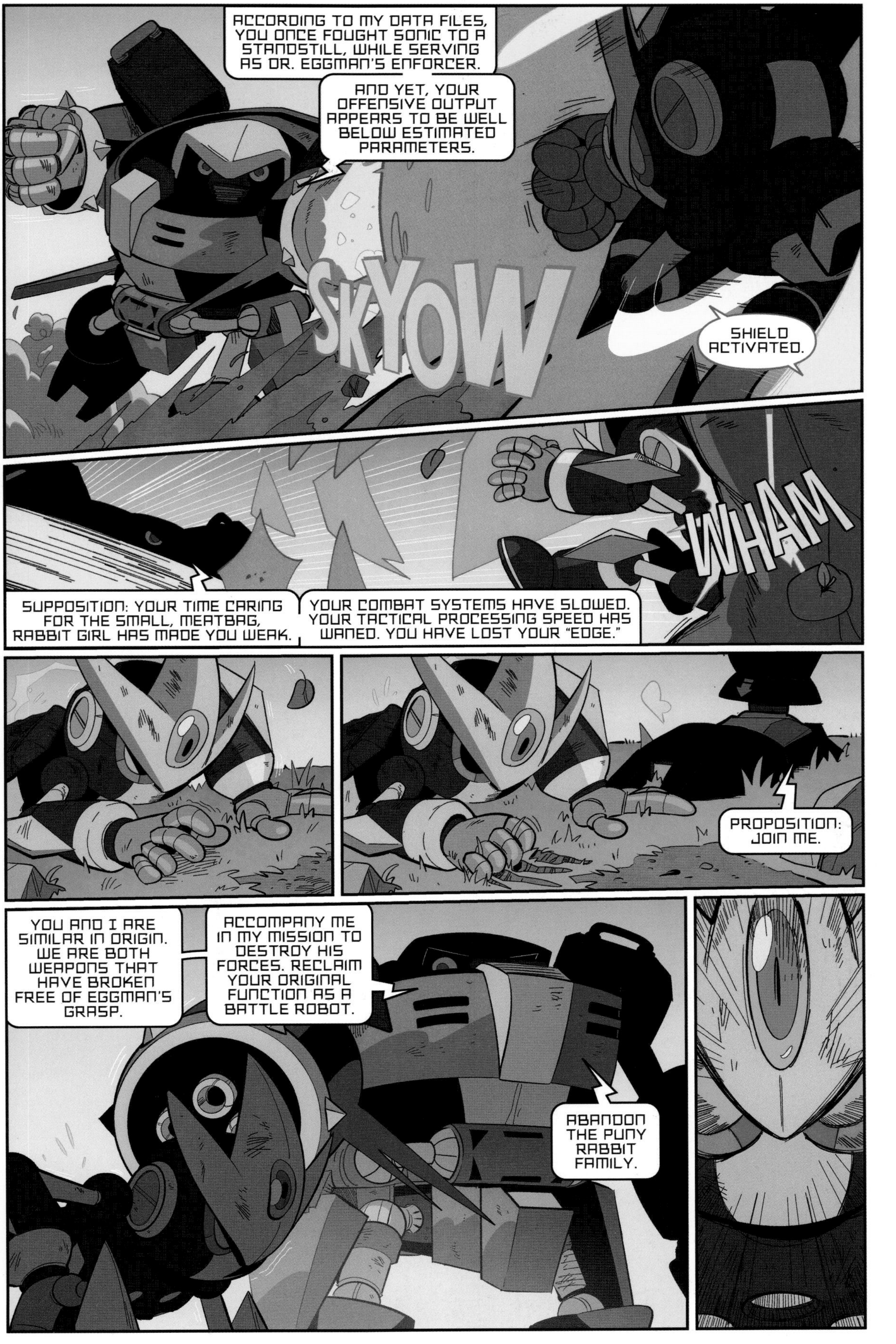

ACCORDING TO MY DATA FILES, YOU ONCE FOUGHT SONIC TO A STANDSTILL, WHILE SERVING AS DR. EGGMAN'S ENFORCER.
AND YET, YOUR OFFENSIVE OUTPUT APPEARS TO BE WELL BELOW ESTIMATED PARAMETERS.
SKYOW
SHIELD ACTIVATED.
WHAM
SUPPOSITION: YOUR TIME CARING FOR THE SMALL, MEATBAG, RABBIT GIRL HAS MADE YOU WEAK.
YOUR COMBAT SYSTEMS HAVE SLOWED. YOUR TACTICAL PROCESSING SPEED HAS WANED. YOU HAVE LOST YOUR "EDGE."
PROPOSITION: JOIN ME.
YOU AND I ARE SIMILAR IN ORIGIN. WE ARE BOTH WEAPONS THAT HAVE BROKEN FREE OF EGGMAN'S GRASP.
ACCOMPANY ME IN MY MISSION TO DESTROY HIS FORCES. RECLAIM YOUR ORIGINAL FUNCTION AS A BATTLE ROBOT.
ABANDON THE PUNY RABBIT FAMILY.

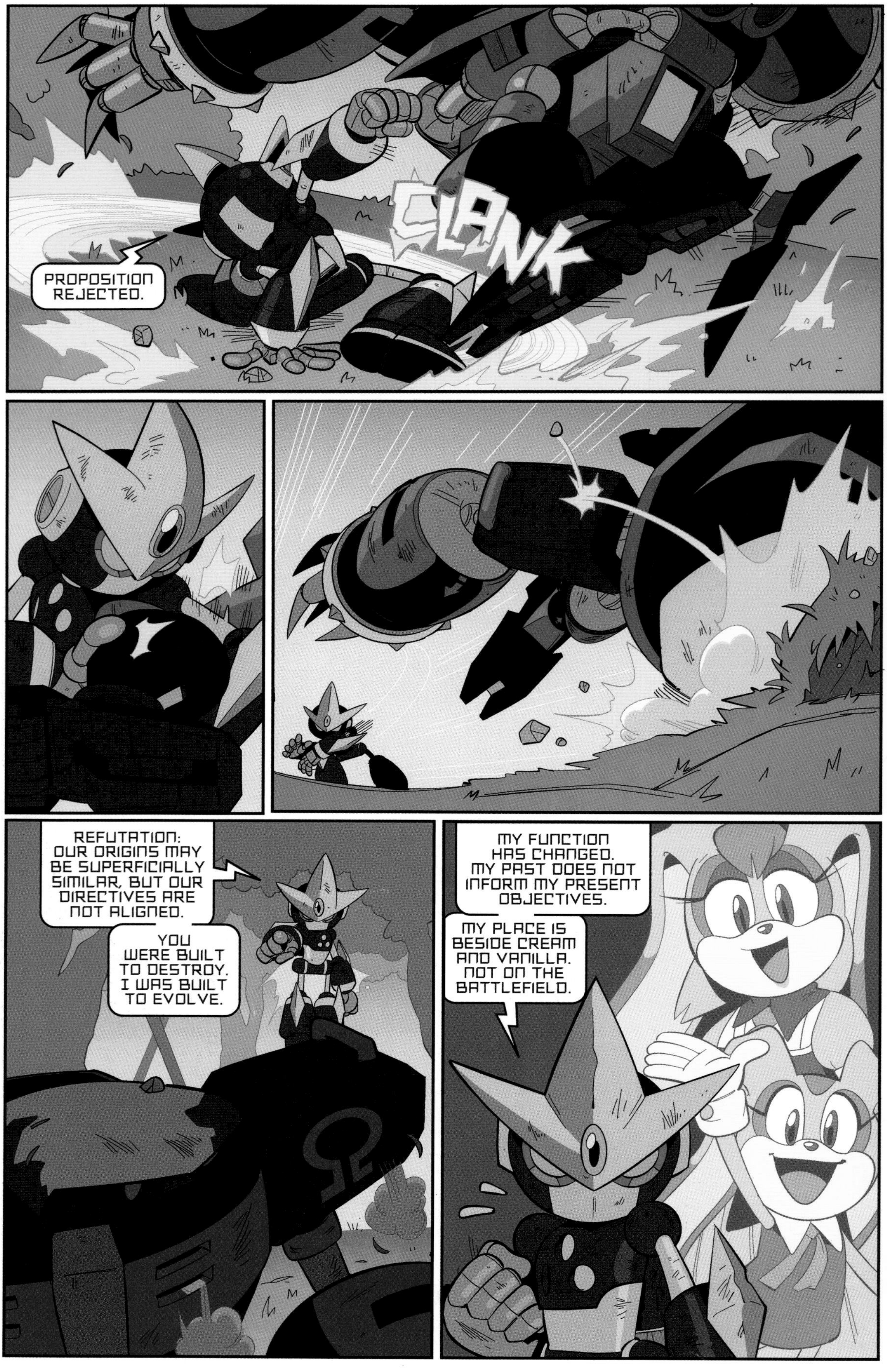
CLANK
PROPOSITION REJECTED.
REFUTATION: OUR ORIGINS MAY BE SUPERFICIALLY SIMILAR, BUT OUR DIRECTIVES ARE NOT ALIGNED.
YOU WERE BUILT TO DESTROY. I WAS BUILT TO EVOLVE.
MY FUNCTION HAS CHANGED. MY PAST DOES NOT INFORM MY PRESENT OBJECTIVES.
MY PLACE IS BESIDE CREAM AND VANILLA. NOT ON THE BATTLEFIELD.

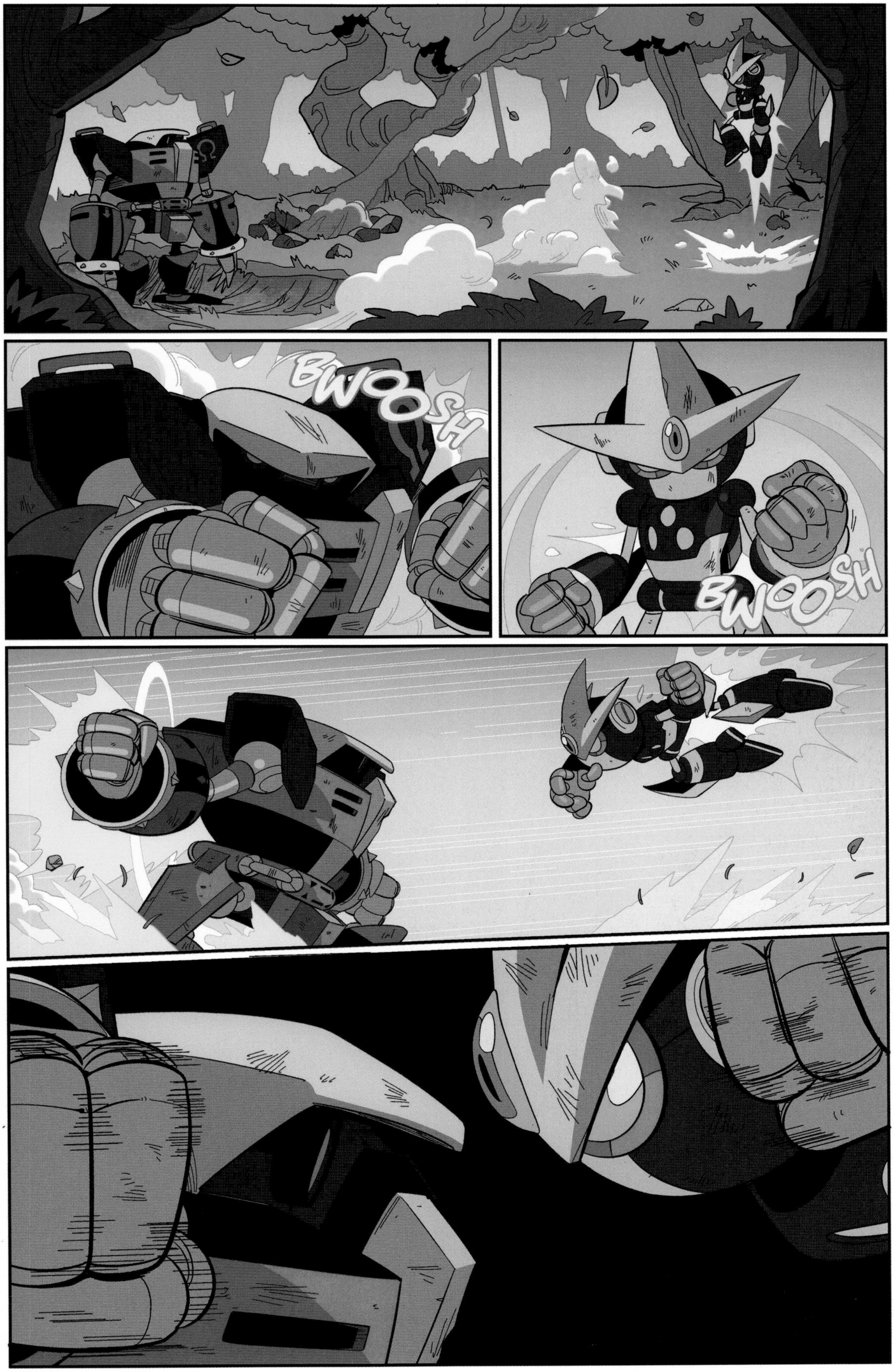
BWOOSH
BWOOSH

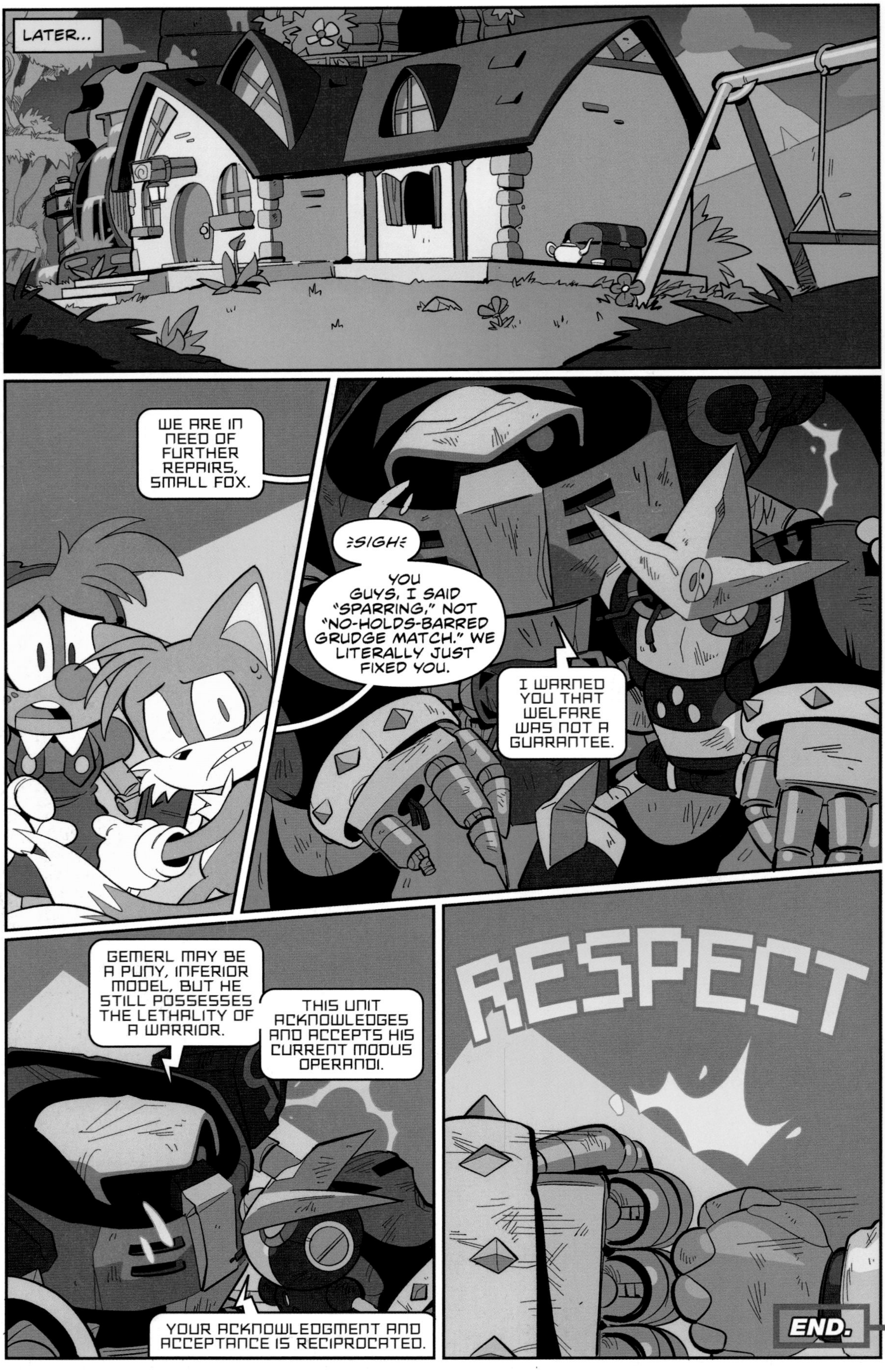
LATER...
WE ARE IN NEED OF FURTHER REPAIRS, SMALL FOX.
SIGH
YOU GUYS, I SAID "SPARRING," NOT "NO-HOLDS-BARRED GRUDGE MATCH." WE LITERALLY JUST FIXED YOU.
I WARNED YOU THAT WELFARE WAS NOT A GUARANTEE.
GEMERL MAY BE A PUNY, INFERIOR MODEL, BUT HE STILL POSSESSES THE LETHALITY OF A WARRIOR.
THIS UNIT ACKNOWLEDGES AND ACCEPTS HIS CURRENT MODUS OPERANDI.
YOUR ACKNOWLEDGMENT AND ACCEPTANCE IS RECIPROCATED.
RESPECT
END.

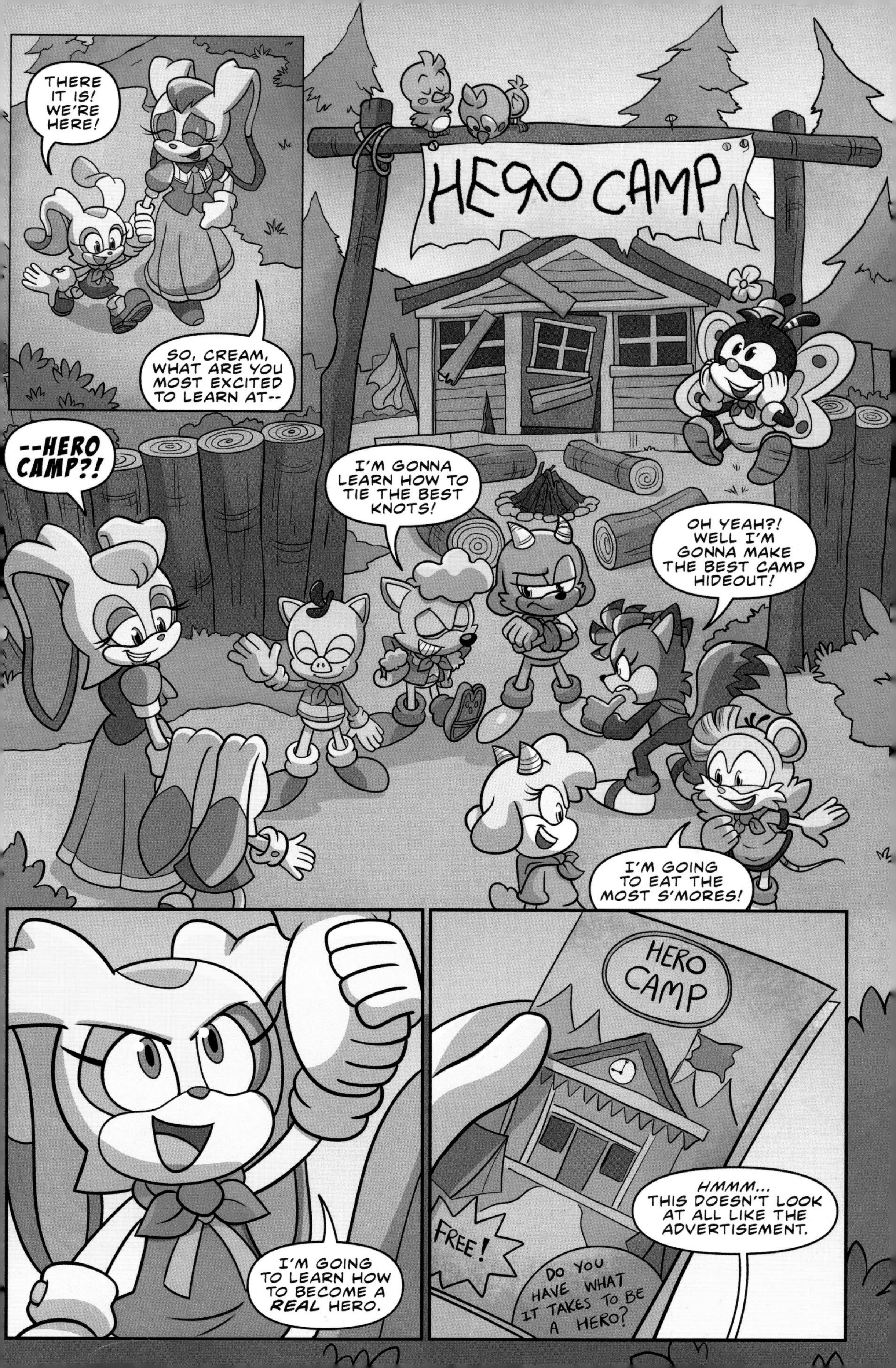

HERO CAMP
THERE IT IS! WE'RE HERE!
SO, CREAM, WHAT ARE YOU MOST EXCITED TO LEARN AT--
--HERO CAMP?!
I'M GONNA LEARN HOW TO TIE THE BEST KNOTS!
OH YEAH?! WELL I'M GONNA MAKE THE BEST CAMP HIDEOUT!
I'M GOING TO EAT THE MOST S'MORES!
I'M GOING TO LEARN HOW TO BECOME A REAL HERO.
HERO CAMP
FREE!
DO YOU HAVE WHAT IT TAKES TO BE A HERO?
HMMM... THIS DOESN'T LOOK AT ALL LIKE THE ADVERTISEMENT.

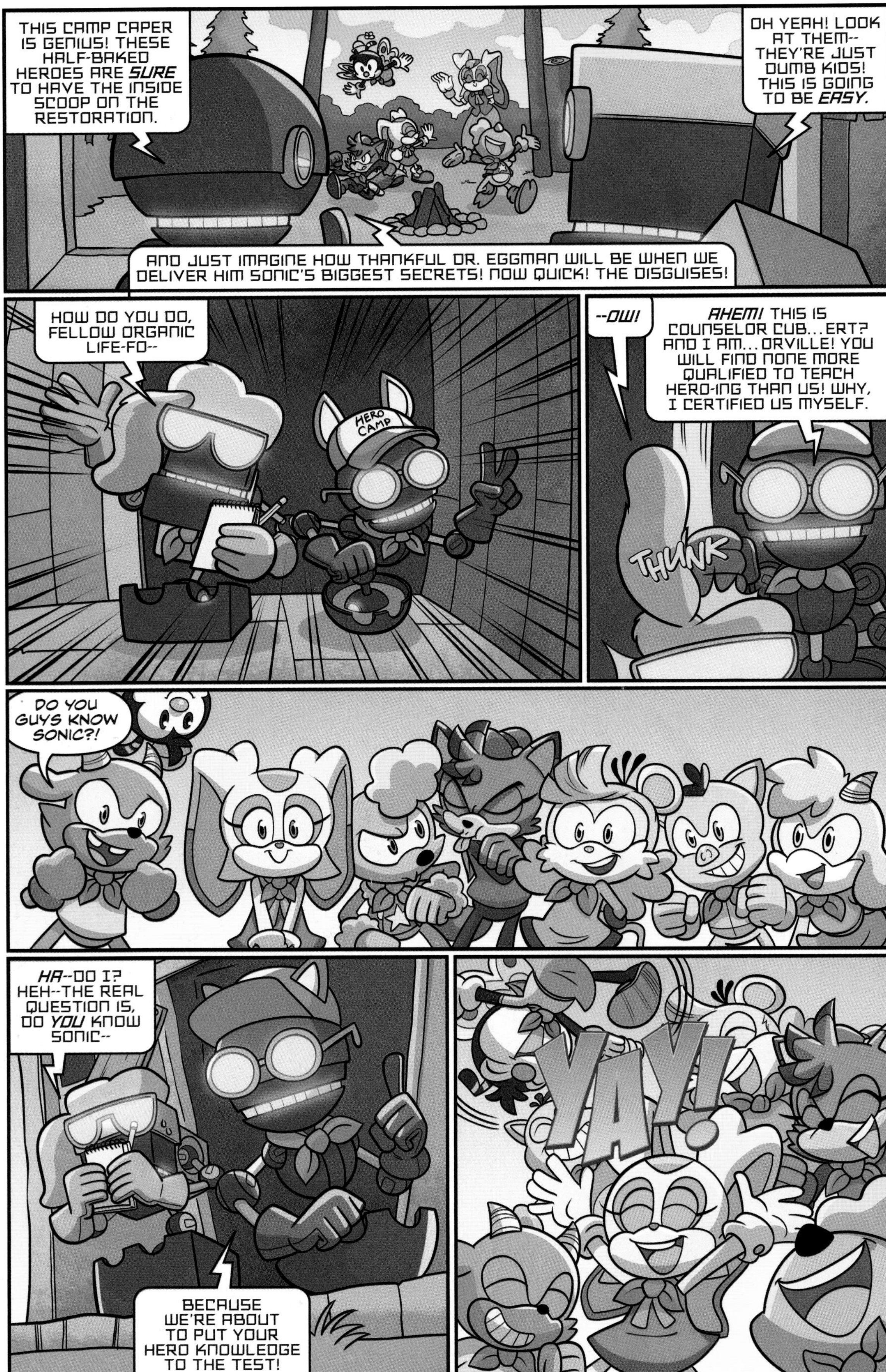
THIS CAMP CAPER IS GENIUS! THESE HALF-BAKED HEROES ARE *SURE* TO HAVE THE INSIDE SCOOP ON THE RESTORATION.
OH YEAH! LOOK AT THEM--THEY'RE JUST DUMB KIDS! THIS IS GOING TO BE *EASY.*
AND JUST IMAGINE HOW THANKFUL DR. EGGMAN WILL BE WHEN WE DELIVER HIM SONIC'S BIGGEST SECRETS! NOW QUICK! THE DISGUISES!
HOW DO YOU DO, FELLOW ORGANIC LIFE-FO--
HERO CAMP
--OW!
AHEM! THIS IS COUNSELOR CUB...ERT? AND I AM...ORVILLE! YOU WILL FIND NONE MORE QUALIFIED TO TEACH HERO-ING THAN US! WHY, I CERTIFIED US MYSELF.
THUNK
DO YOU GUYS KNOW SONIC?!
HA--DO I? HEH--THE REAL QUESTION IS, DO *YOU* KNOW SONIC--
BECAUSE WE'RE ABOUT TO PUT YOUR HERO KNOWLEDGE TO THE TEST!
YAY!

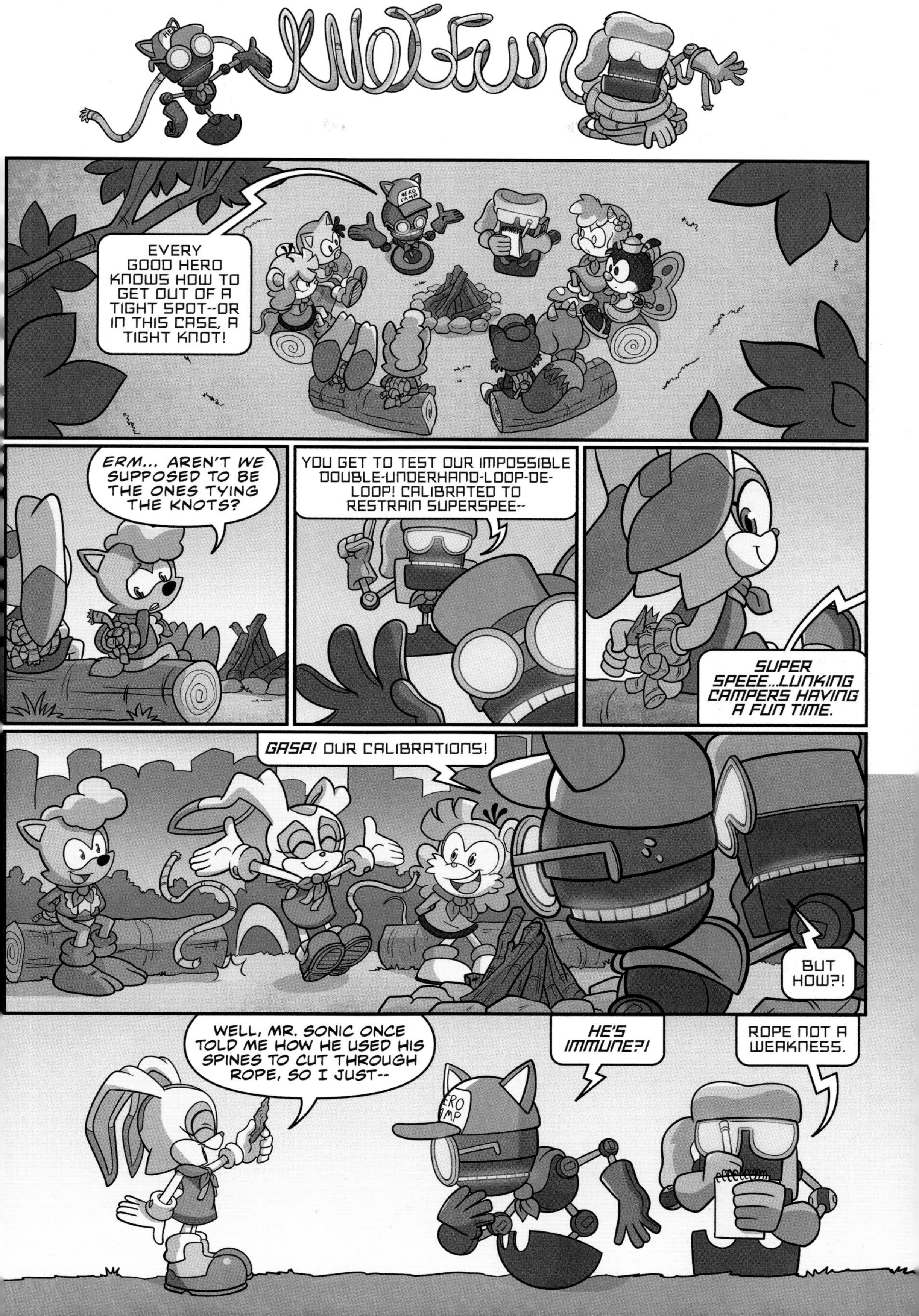
KNOT FUN
EVERY GOOD HERO KNOWS HOW TO GET OUT OF A TIGHT SPOT--OR IN THIS CASE, A TIGHT KNOT!
HERO CAMP
ERM... AREN'T WE SUPPOSED TO BE THE ONES TYING THE KNOTS?
YOU GET TO TEST OUR IMPOSSIBLE DOUBLE-UNDERHAND-LOOP-DE-LOOP! CALIBRATED TO RESTRAIN SUPERSPEE--
SUPER SPEEE...LUNKING CAMPERS HAVING A FUN TIME.
GASP! OUR CALIBRATIONS!
BUT HOW?!
WELL, MR. SONIC ONCE TOLD ME HOW HE USED HIS SPINES TO CUT THROUGH ROPE, SO I JUST--
HE'S IMMUNE?!
ROPE NOT A WEAKNESS.

BUILDING A HIDEOUT

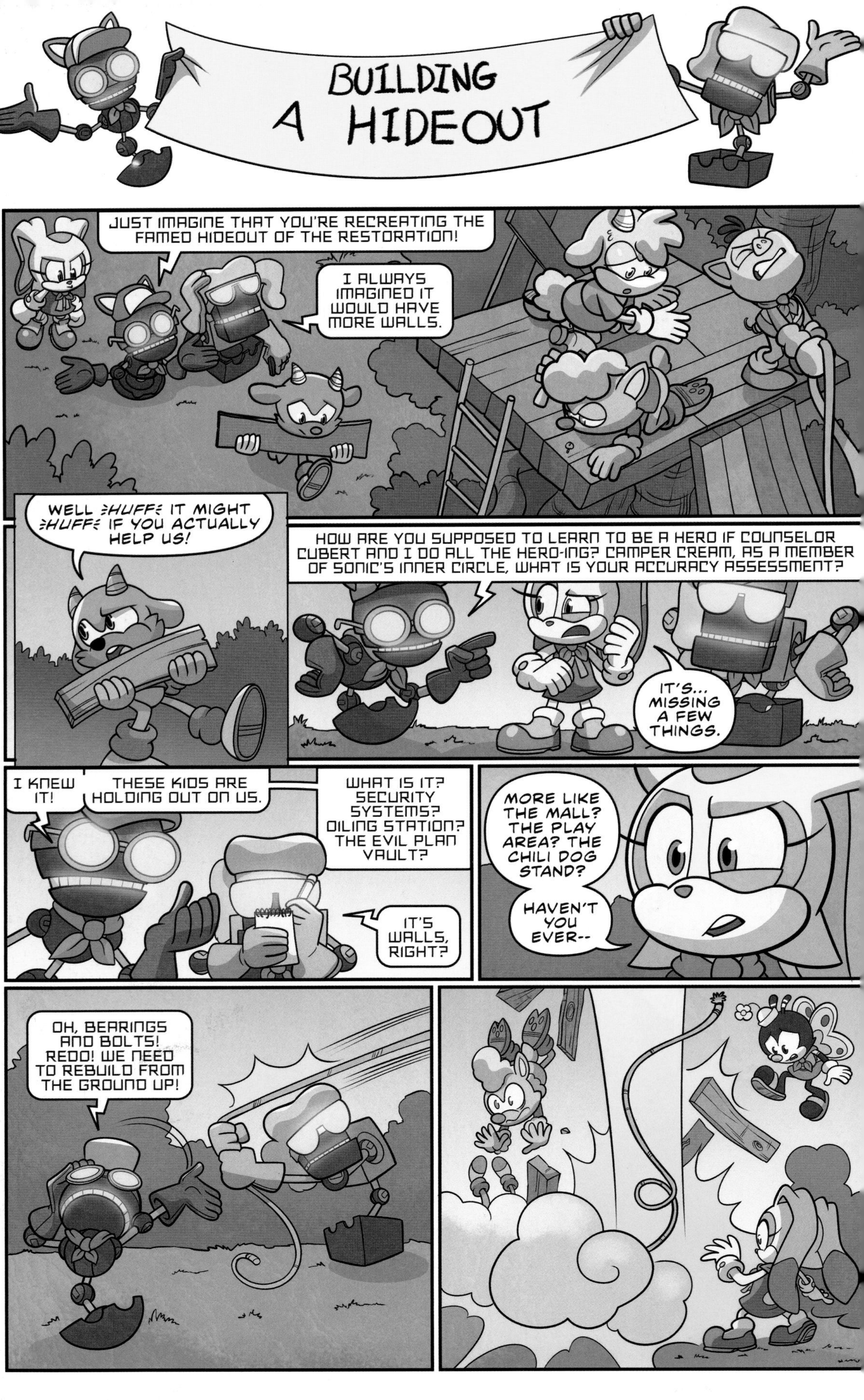
JUST IMAGINE THAT YOU'RE RECREATING THE FAMED HIDEOUT OF THE RESTORATION!
I ALWAYS IMAGINED IT WOULD HAVE MORE WALLS.
WELL *HUFF* IT MIGHT *HUFF* IF YOU ACTUALLY HELP US!
HOW ARE YOU SUPPOSED TO LEARN TO BE A HERO IF COUNSELOR CUBERT AND I DO ALL THE HERO-ING? CAMPER CREAM, AS A MEMBER OF SONIC'S INNER CIRCLE, WHAT IS YOUR ACCURACY ASSESSMENT?
IT'S... MISSING A FEW THINGS.
I KNEW IT!
THESE KIDS ARE HOLDING OUT ON US.
WHAT IS IT? SECURITY SYSTEMS? OILING STATION? THE EVIL PLAN VAULT?
IT'S WALLS, RIGHT?
MORE LIKE THE MALL? THE PLAY AREA? THE CHILI DOG STAND?
HAVEN'T YOU EVER--
OH, BEARINGS AND BOLTS! REDO! WE NEED TO REBUILD FROM THE GROUND UP!

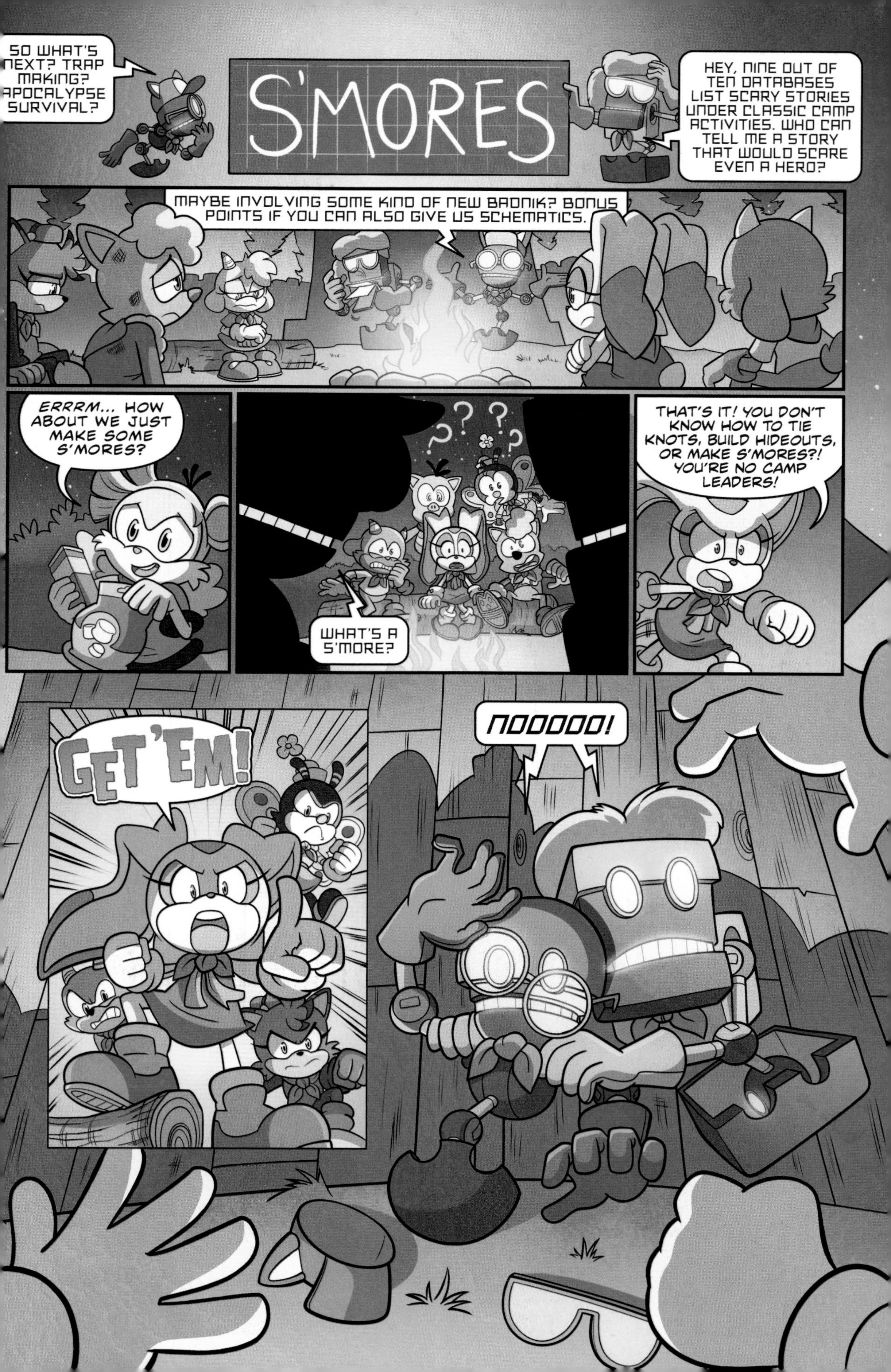
SO WHAT'S NEXT? TRAP MAKING? APOCALYPSE SURVIVAL?
S'MORES
HEY, NINE OUT OF TEN DATABASES LIST SCARY STORIES UNDER CLASSIC CAMP ACTIVITIES. WHO CAN TELL ME A STORY THAT WOULD SCARE EVEN A HERO?
MAYBE INVOLVING SOME KIND OF NEW BADNIK? BONUS POINTS IF YOU CAN ALSO GIVE US SCHEMATICS.
ERRRM... HOW ABOUT WE JUST MAKE SOME S'MORES?
WHAT'S A S'MORE?
THAT'S IT! YOU DON'T KNOW HOW TO TIE KNOTS, BUILD HIDEOUTS, OR MAKE S'MORES?! YOU'RE NO CAMP LEADERS!
GET 'EM!
NOOOOO!

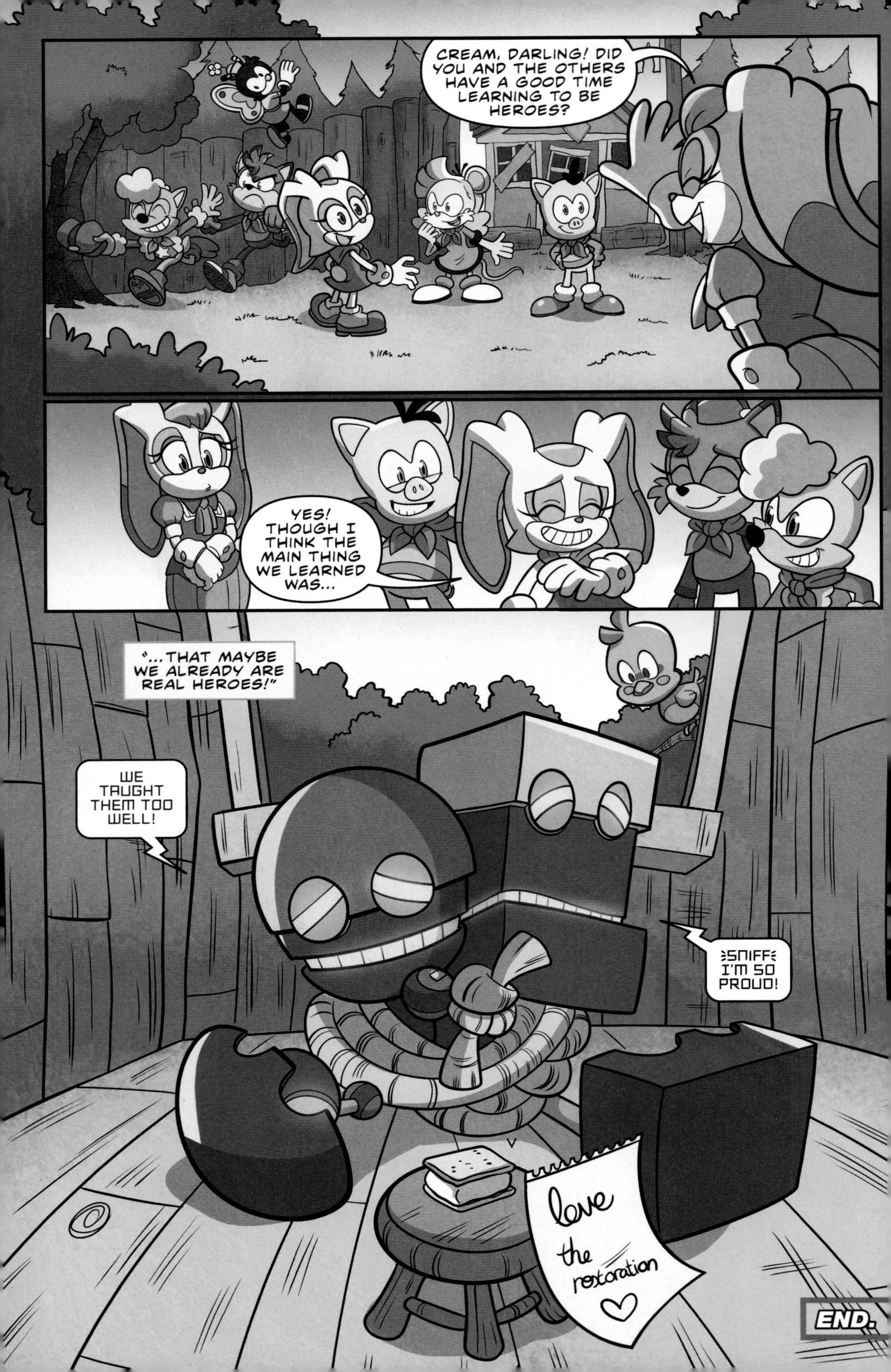
CREAM, DARLING! DID YOU AND THE OTHERS HAVE A GOOD TIME LEARNING TO BE HEROES?
YES! THOUGH I THINK THE MAIN THING WE LEARNED WAS...
"...THAT MAYBE WE ALREADY ARE REAL HEROES!"
WE TAUGHT THEM TOO WELL!
SNIFF I'M SO PROUD!
love the restoration
END.

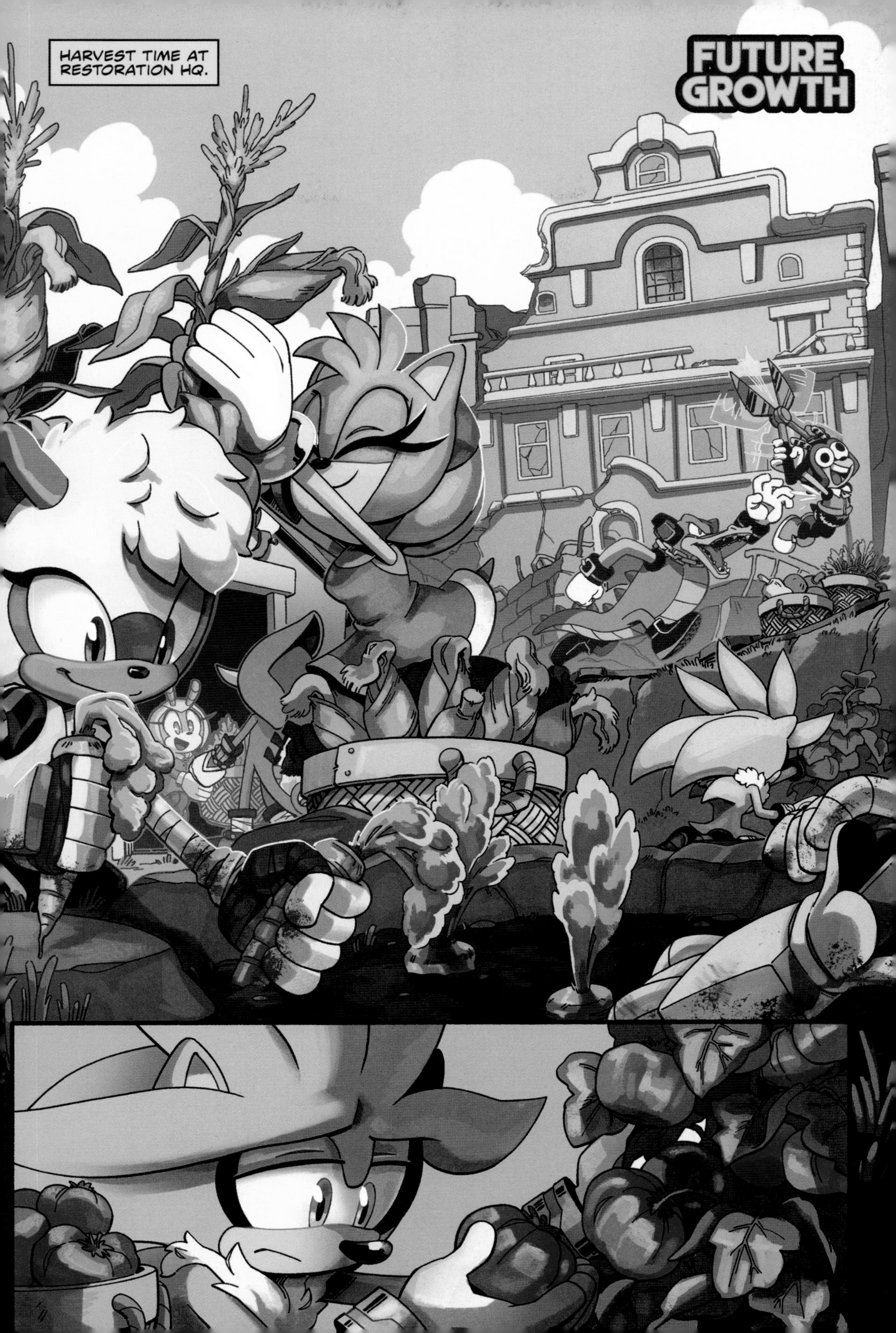
HARVEST TIME AT RESTORATION HQ.
FUTURE GROWTH

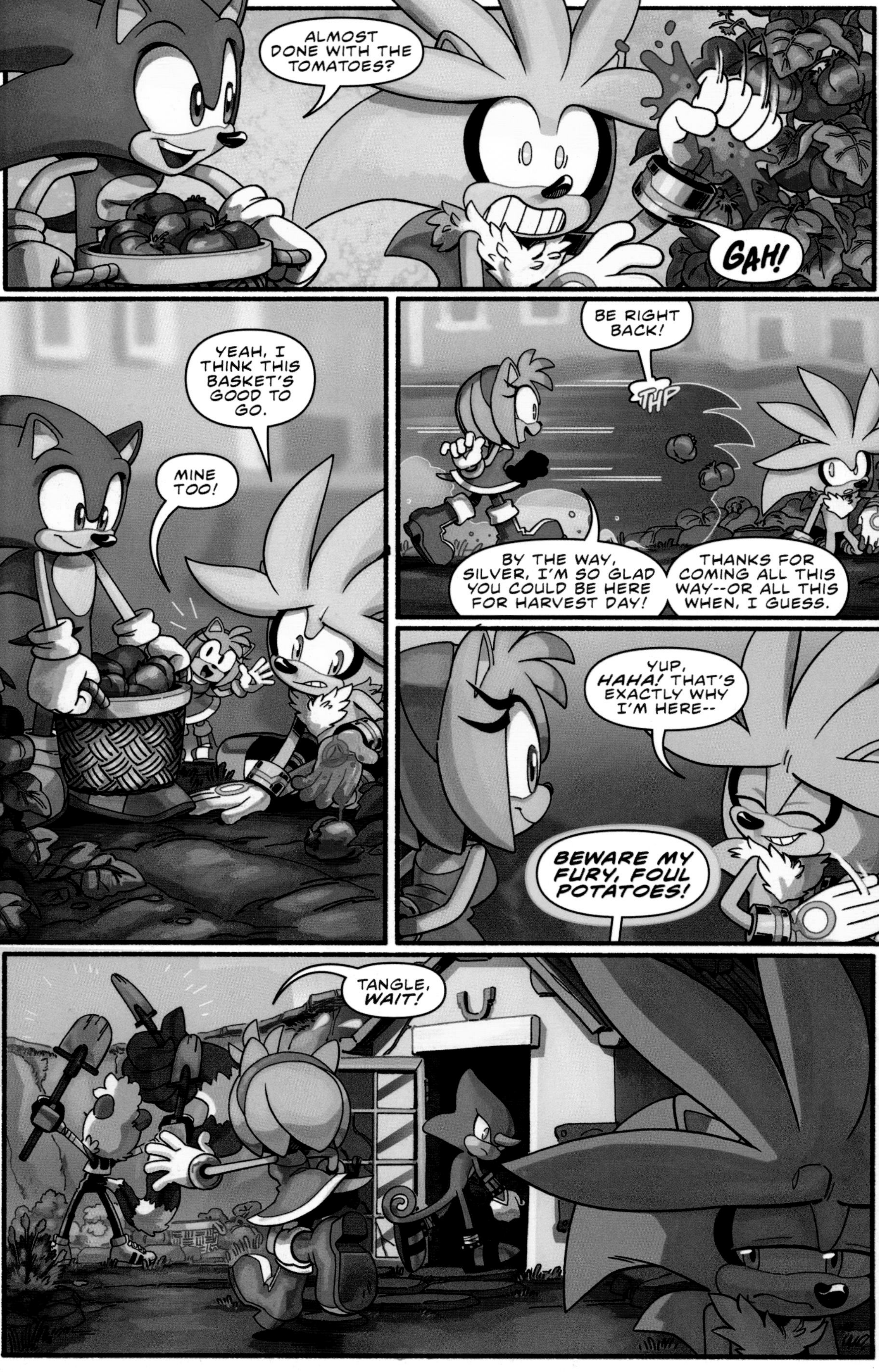
ALMOST DONE WITH THE TOMATOES?
GAH!
YEAH, I THINK THIS BASKET'S GOOD TO GO.
MINE TOO!
BE RIGHT BACK!
THP
BY THE WAY, SILVER, I'M SO GLAD YOU COULD BE HERE FOR HARVEST DAY!
THANKS FOR COMING ALL THIS WAY--OR ALL THIS WHEN, I GUESS.
YUP, HAHA! THAT'S EXACTLY WHY I'M HERE--
BEWARE MY FURY, FOUL POTATOES!
TANGLE, WAIT!

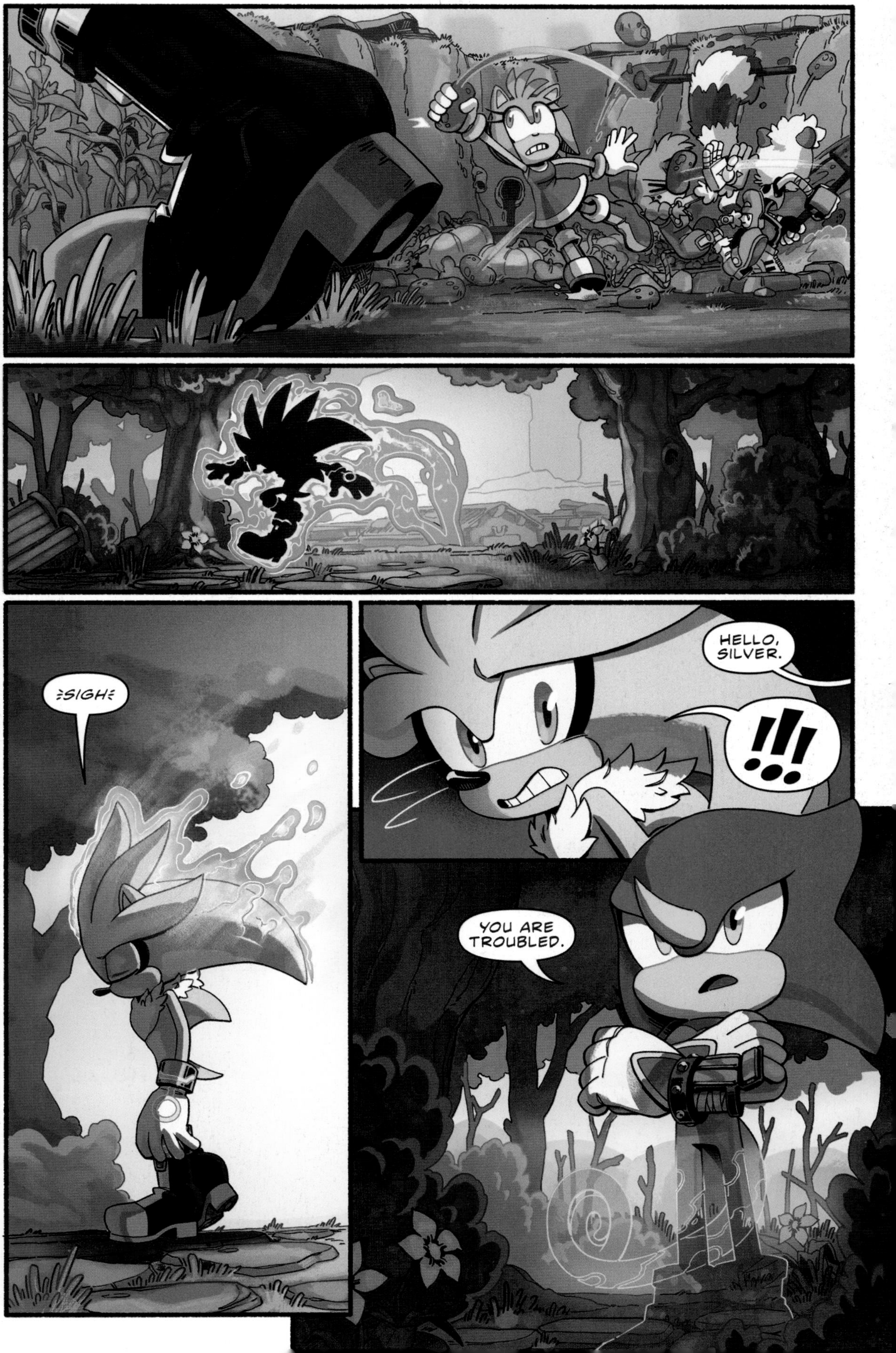

≈SIGH≈
HELLO, SILVER.
!!!
YOU ARE TROUBLED.

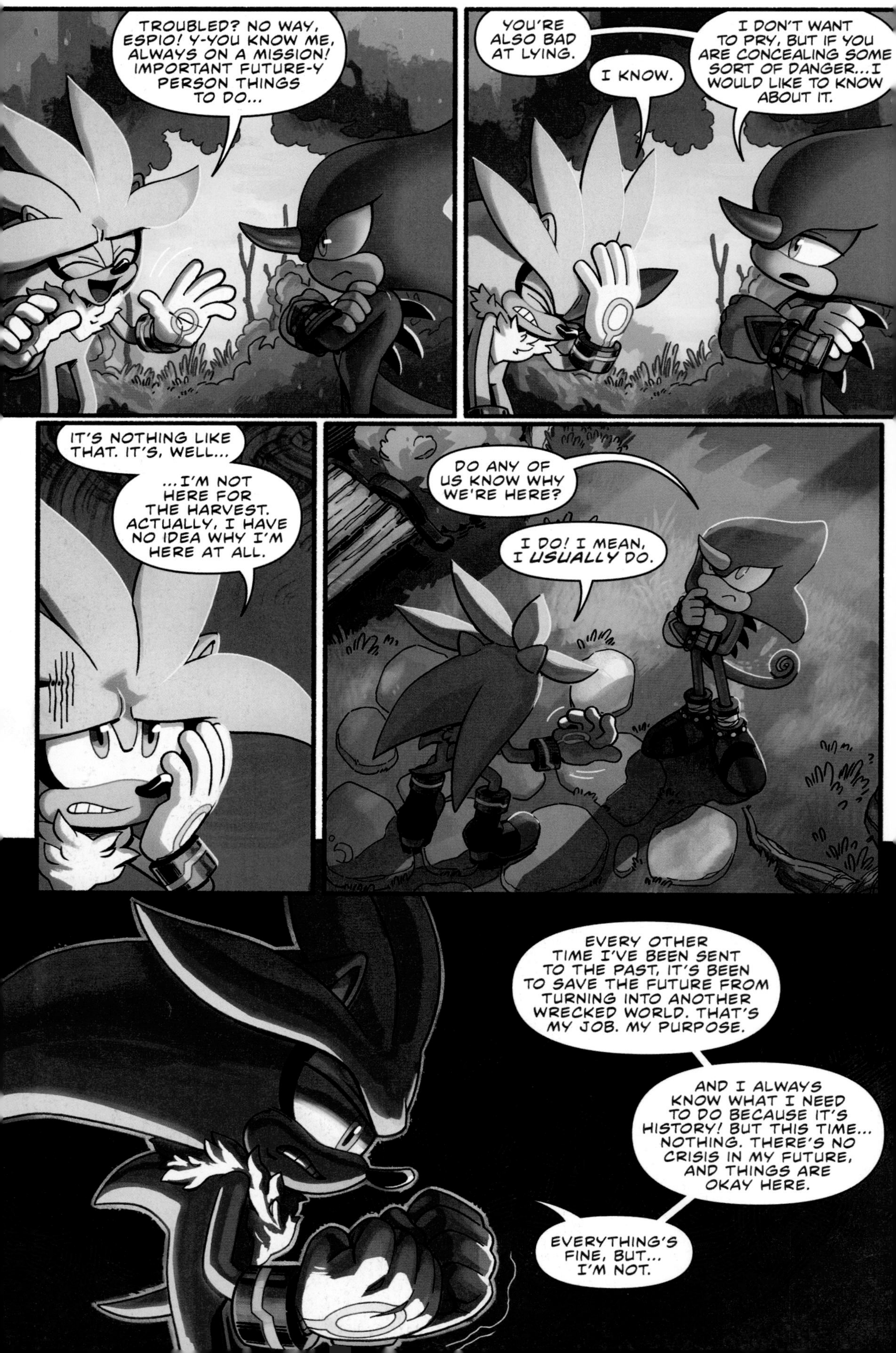
TROUBLED? NO WAY, ESPIO! Y-YOU KNOW ME, ALWAYS ON A MISSION! IMPORTANT FUTURE-Y PERSON THINGS TO DO...
YOU'RE ALSO BAD AT LYING.
I KNOW.
I DON'T WANT TO PRY, BUT IF YOU ARE CONCEALING SOME SORT OF DANGER... I WOULD LIKE TO KNOW ABOUT IT.
IT'S NOTHING LIKE THAT. IT'S, WELL...
...I'M NOT HERE FOR THE HARVEST. ACTUALLY, I HAVE NO IDEA WHY I'M HERE AT ALL.
DO ANY OF US KNOW WHY WE'RE HERE?
I DO! I MEAN, I *USUALLY* DO.
EVERY OTHER TIME I'VE BEEN SENT TO THE PAST, IT'S BEEN TO SAVE THE FUTURE FROM TURNING INTO ANOTHER WRECKED WORLD. THAT'S MY JOB. MY PURPOSE.
AND I ALWAYS KNOW WHAT I NEED TO DO BECAUSE IT'S HISTORY! BUT THIS TIME... NOTHING. THERE'S NO CRISIS IN MY FUTURE, AND THINGS ARE OKAY HERE.
EVERYTHING'S FINE, BUT... I'M NOT.

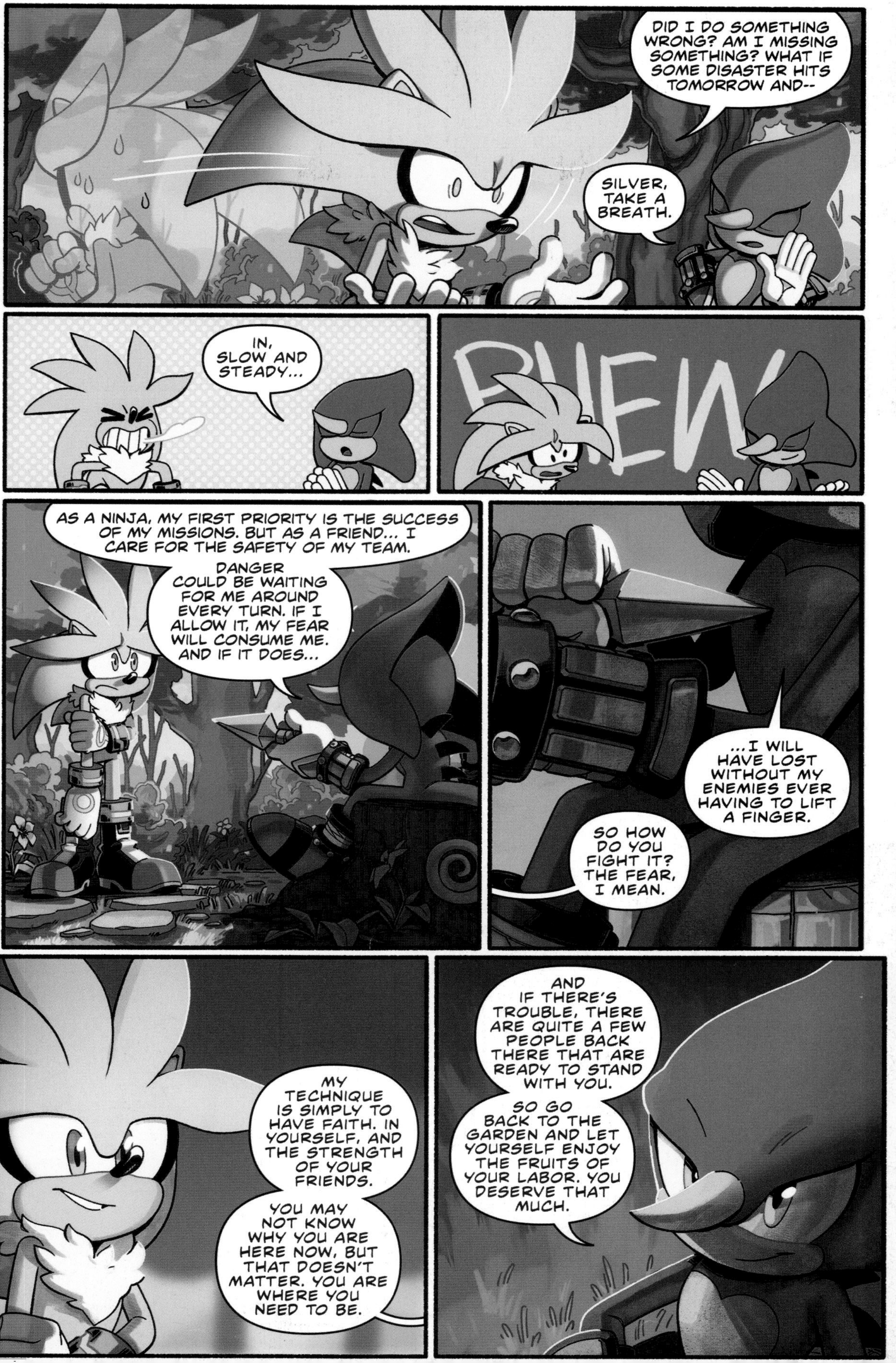
DID I DO SOMETHING WRONG? AM I MISSING SOMETHING? WHAT IF SOME DISASTER HITS TOMORROW AND--
SILVER, TAKE A BREATH.
IN, SLOW AND STEADY...
PHEW
AS A NINJA, MY FIRST PRIORITY IS THE SUCCESS OF MY MISSIONS. BUT AS A FRIEND... I CARE FOR THE SAFETY OF MY TEAM.
DANGER COULD BE WAITING FOR ME AROUND EVERY TURN. IF I ALLOW IT, MY FEAR WILL CONSUME ME. AND IF IT DOES...
...I WILL HAVE LOST WITHOUT MY ENEMIES EVER HAVING TO LIFT A FINGER.
SO HOW DO YOU FIGHT IT? THE FEAR, I MEAN.
MY TECHNIQUE IS SIMPLY TO HAVE FAITH. IN YOURSELF, AND THE STRENGTH OF YOUR FRIENDS.
YOU MAY NOT KNOW WHY YOU ARE HERE NOW, BUT THAT DOESN'T MATTER. YOU ARE WHERE YOU NEED TO BE.
AND IF THERE'S TROUBLE, THERE ARE QUITE A FEW PEOPLE BACK THERE THAT ARE READY TO STAND WITH YOU.
SO GO BACK TO THE GARDEN AND LET YOURSELF ENJOY THE FRUITS OF YOUR LABOR. YOU DESERVE THAT MUCH.

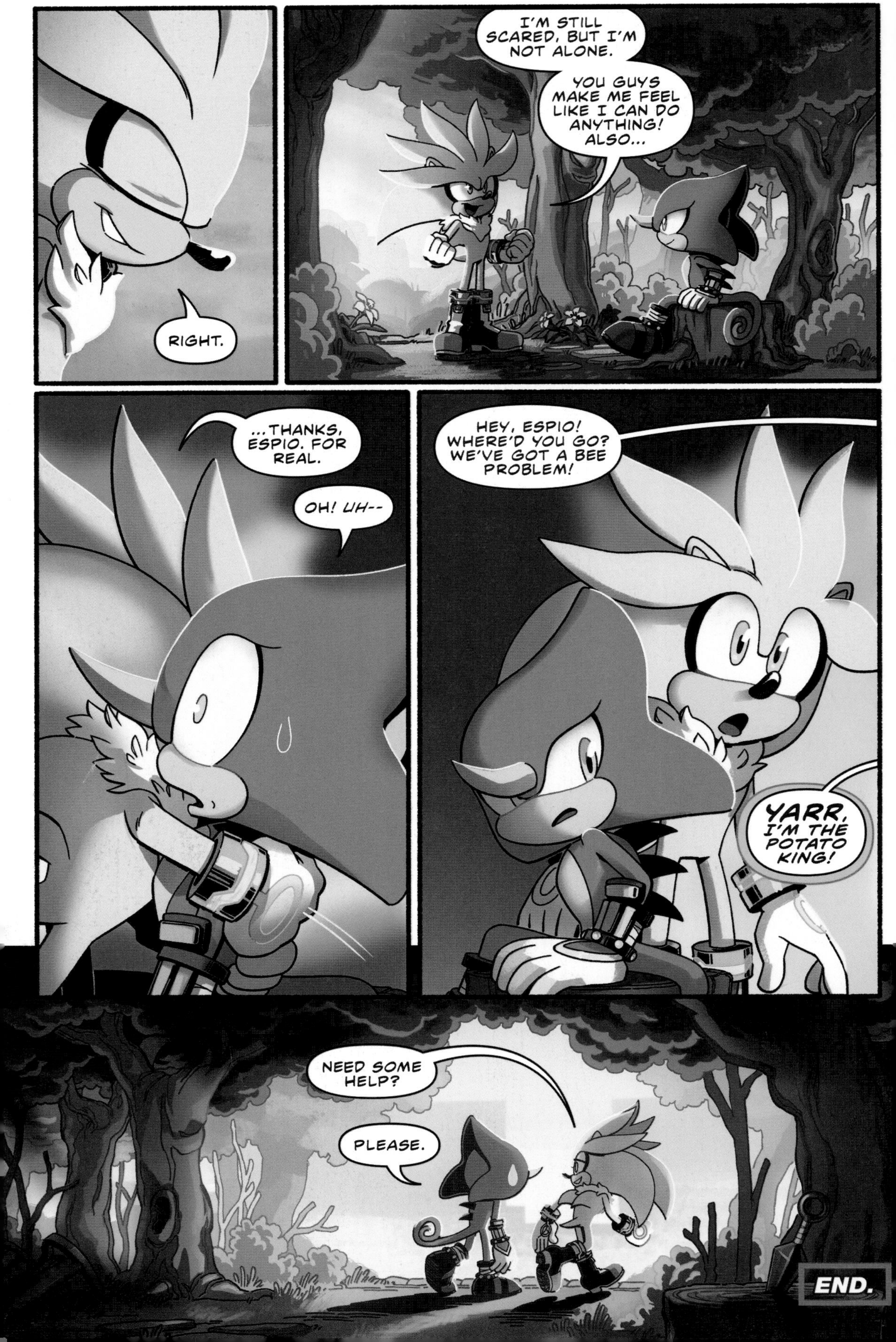
RIGHT.
I'M STILL SCARED, BUT I'M NOT ALONE.
YOU GUYS MAKE ME FEEL LIKE I CAN DO ANYTHING! ALSO...
...THANKS, ESPIO. FOR REAL.
OH! UH--
HEY, ESPIO! WHERE'D YOU GO? WE'VE GOT A BEE PROBLEM!
YARR, I'M THE POTATO KING!
NEED SOME HELP?
PLEASE.
END.

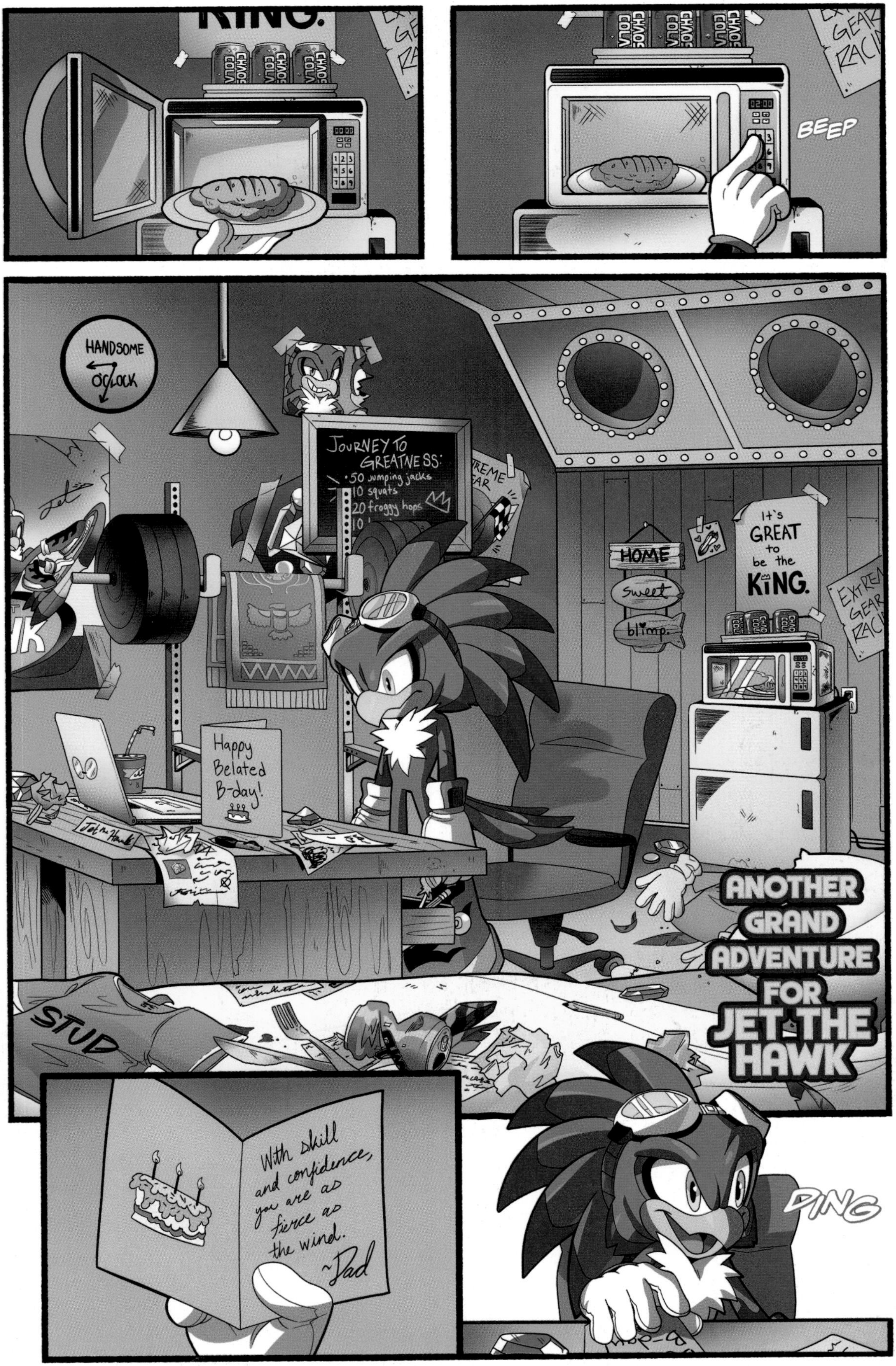
KING.
BEEP
HANDSOME O'CLOCK
JOURNEY TO GREATNESS:
•50 jumping jacks
10 squats
20 froggy hops
HOME
sweet
blimp.
It's GREAT to be the KING.
Happy Belated B-day!
STUD
ANOTHER GRAND ADVENTURE FOR JET THE HAWK
With skill and confidence, you are as fierce as the wind. ~Dad
DING

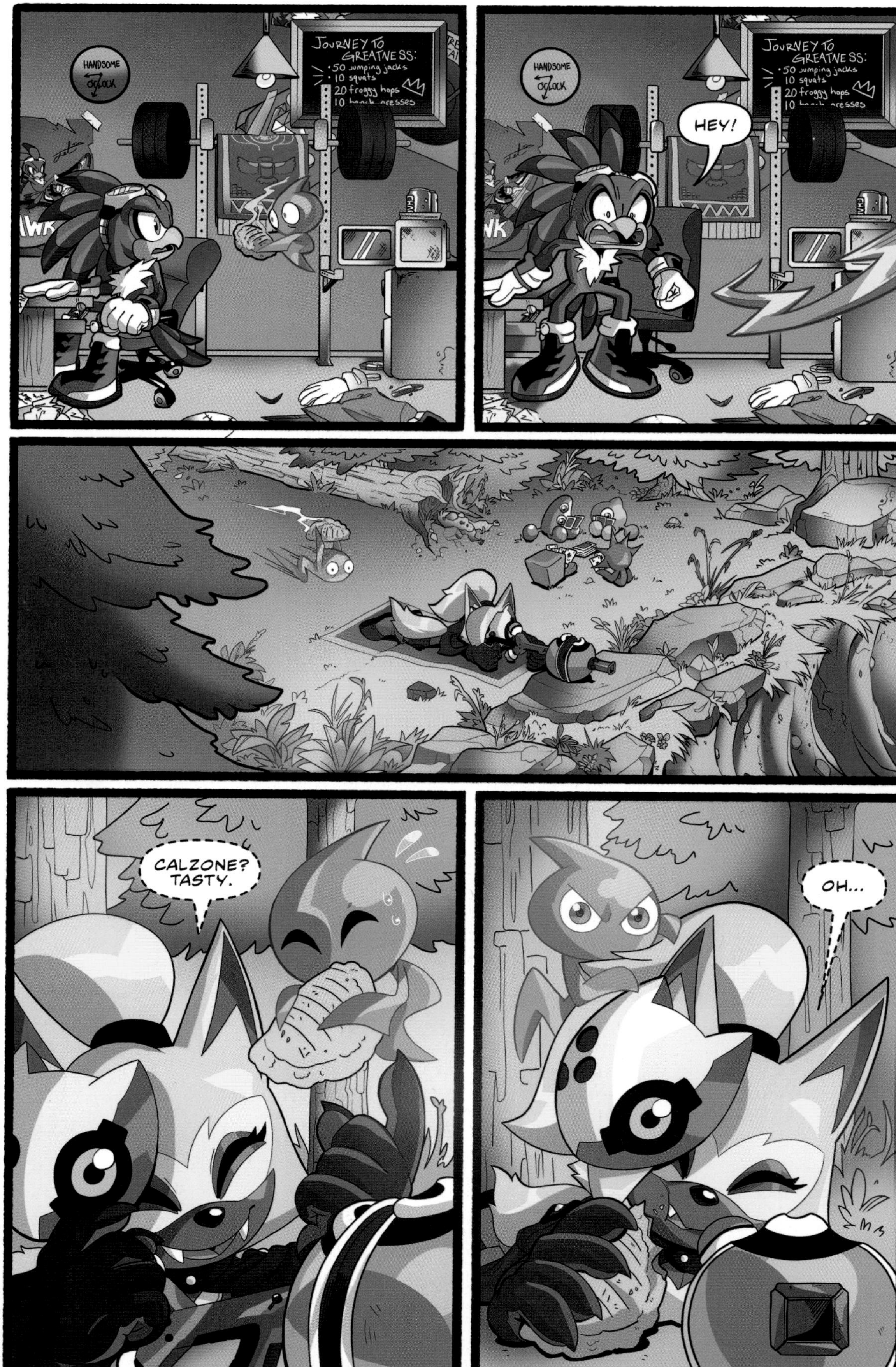
HANDSOME O'CLOCK
JOURNEY TO GREATNESS:
•50 jumping jacks
•10 squats
20 froggy hops
10 bench presses
HEY!
CALZONE? TASTY.
OH...

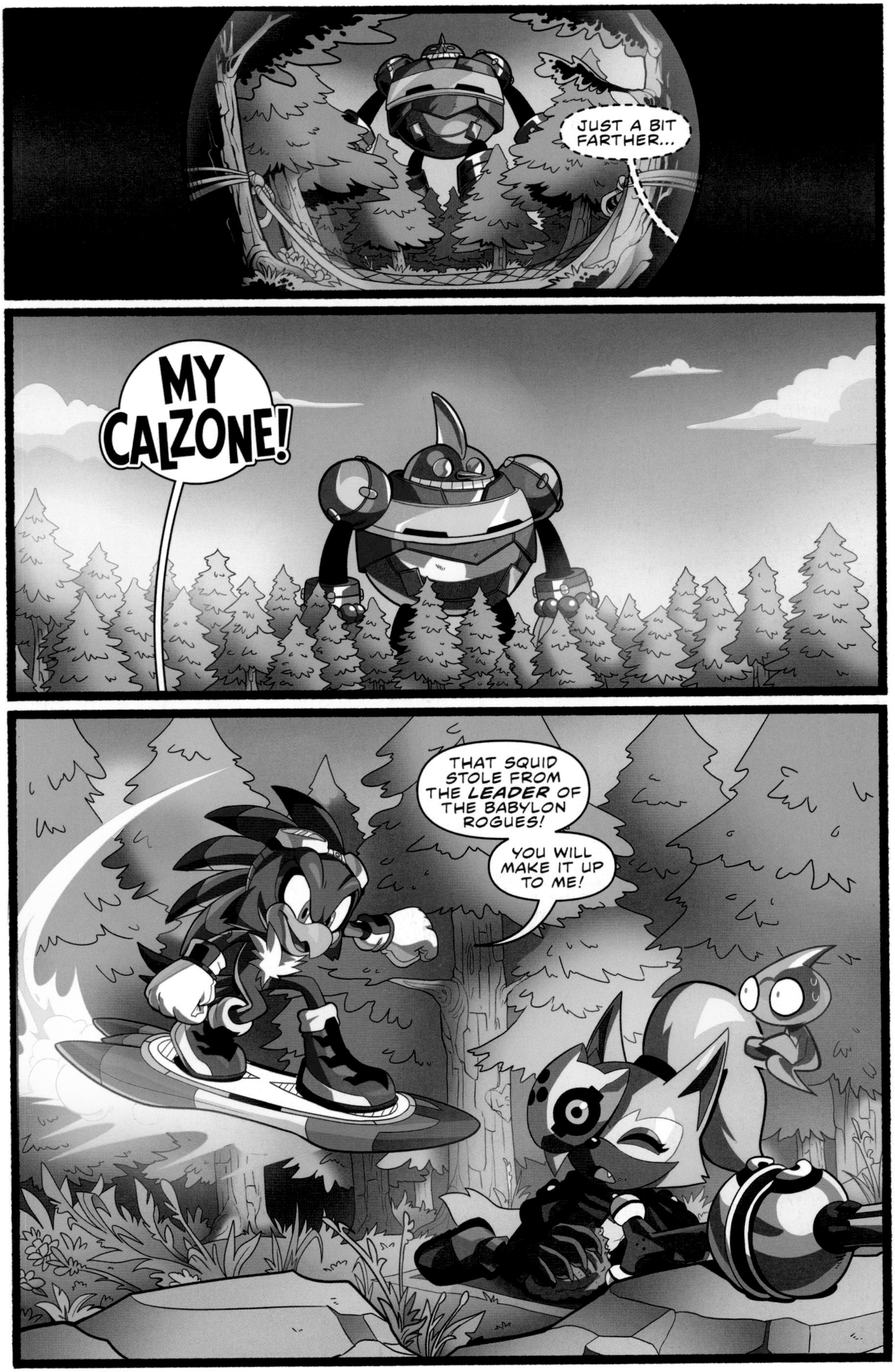
JUST A BIT FARTHER...
MY CALZONE!
THAT SQUID STOLE FROM THE *LEADER* OF THE BABYLON ROGUES!
YOU WILL MAKE IT UP TO ME!

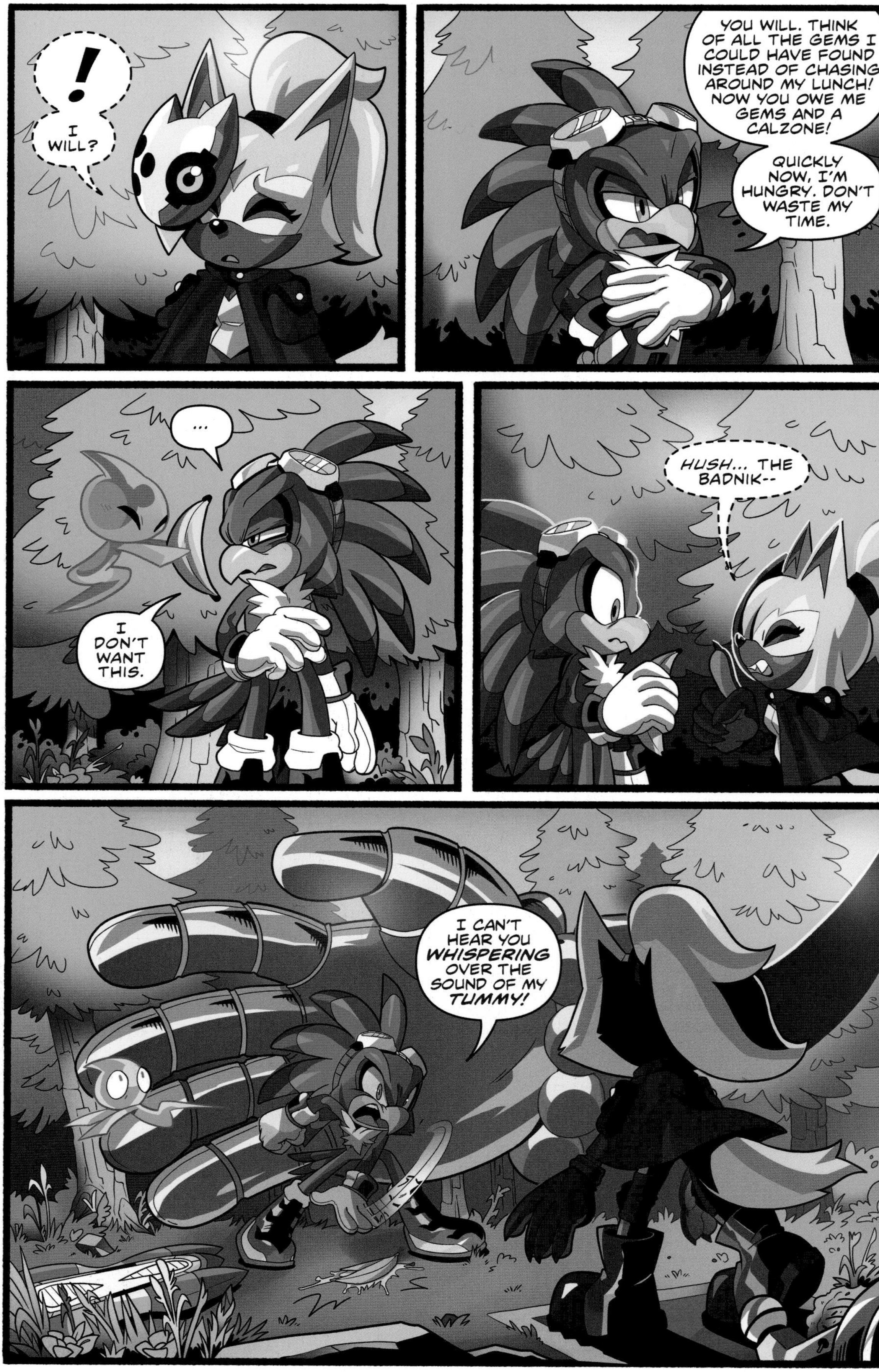
!
I WILL?
YOU WILL. THINK OF ALL THE GEMS I COULD HAVE FOUND INSTEAD OF CHASING AROUND MY LUNCH! NOW YOU OWE ME GEMS AND A CALZONE!
QUICKLY NOW, I'M HUNGRY. DON'T WASTE MY TIME.
...
I DON'T WANT THIS.
HUSH... THE BADNIK--
I CAN'T HEAR YOU WHISPERING OVER THE SOUND OF MY TUMMY!

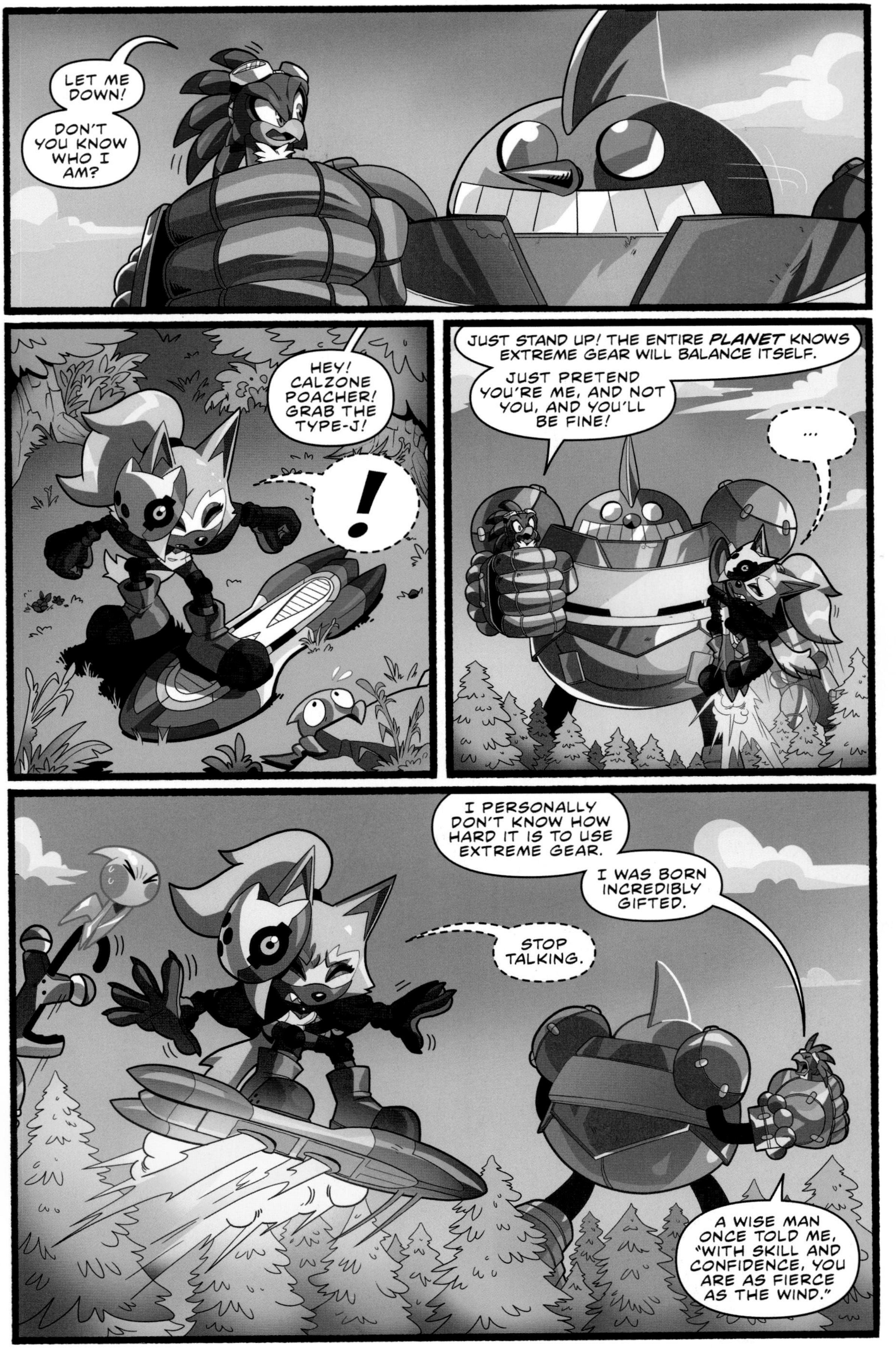
LET ME DOWN!
DON'T YOU KNOW WHO I AM?
HEY! CALZONE POACHER! GRAB THE TYPE-J!
!
JUST STAND UP! THE ENTIRE PLANET KNOWS EXTREME GEAR WILL BALANCE ITSELF.
JUST PRETEND YOU'RE ME, AND NOT YOU, AND YOU'LL BE FINE!
...
I PERSONALLY DON'T KNOW HOW HARD IT IS TO USE EXTREME GEAR.
I WAS BORN INCREDIBLY GIFTED.
STOP TALKING.
A WISE MAN ONCE TOLD ME, "WITH SKILL AND CONFIDENCE, YOU ARE AS FIERCE AS THE WIND."

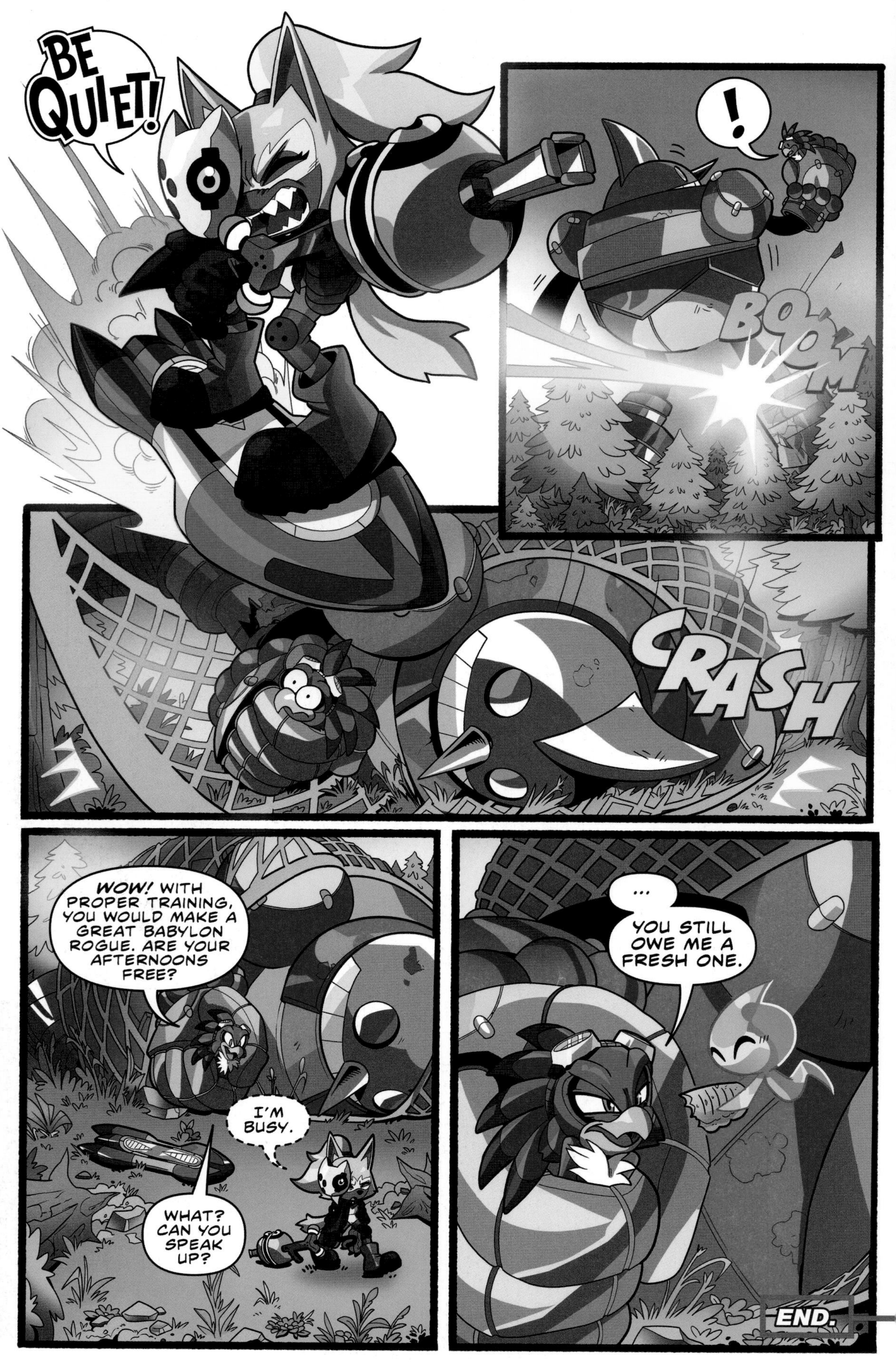
BE QUIET!
!
BOOM
CRASH
WOW! WITH PROPER TRAINING, YOU WOULD MAKE A GREAT BABYLON ROGUE. ARE YOUR AFTERNOONS FREE?
I'M BUSY.
WHAT? CAN YOU SPEAK UP?
...
YOU STILL OWE ME A FRESH ONE.
END.

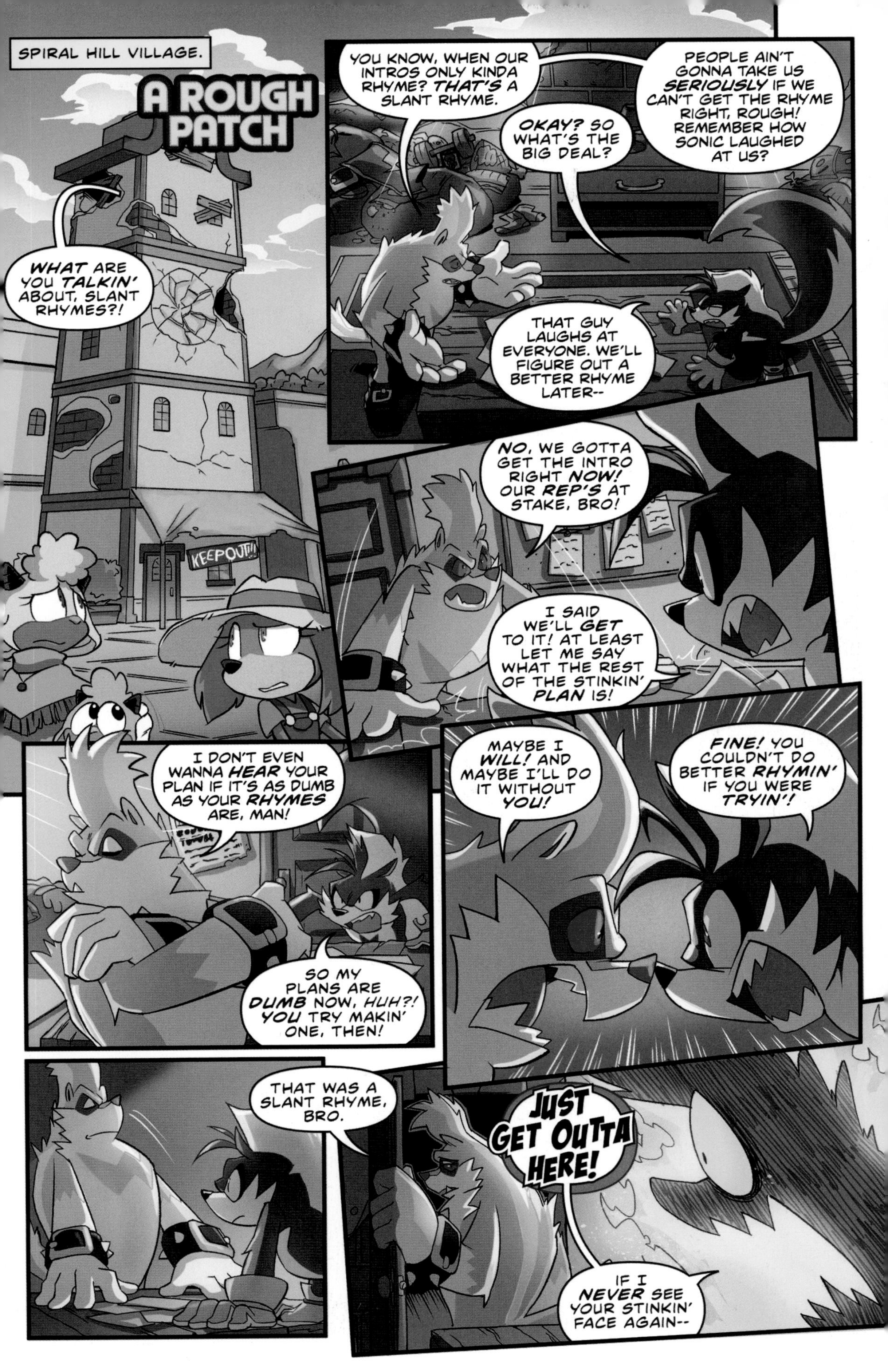

SPIRAL HILL VILLAGE.
A ROUGH PATCH
WHAT ARE YOU TALKIN' ABOUT, SLANT RHYMES?!
KEEPOUT!!!
YOU KNOW, WHEN OUR INTROS ONLY KINDA RHYME? THAT'S A SLANT RHYME.
OKAY? SO WHAT'S THE BIG DEAL?
PEOPLE AIN'T GONNA TAKE US SERIOUSLY IF WE CAN'T GET THE RHYME RIGHT, ROUGH! REMEMBER HOW SONIC LAUGHED AT US?
THAT GUY LAUGHS AT EVERYONE. WE'LL FIGURE OUT A BETTER RHYME LATER--
NO, WE GOTTA GET THE INTRO RIGHT NOW! OUR REP'S AT STAKE, BRO!
I SAID WE'LL GET TO IT! AT LEAST LET ME SAY WHAT THE REST OF THE STINKIN' PLAN IS!
I DON'T EVEN WANNA HEAR YOUR PLAN IF IT'S AS DUMB AS YOUR RHYMES ARE, MAN!
SO MY PLANS ARE DUMB NOW, HUH?! YOU TRY MAKIN' ONE, THEN!
MAYBE I WILL! AND MAYBE I'LL DO IT WITHOUT YOU!
FINE! YOU COULDN'T DO BETTER RHYMIN' IF YOU WERE TRYIN'!
THAT WAS A SLANT RHYME, BRO.
JUST GET OUTTA HERE!
IF I NEVER SEE YOUR STINKIN' FACE AGAIN--

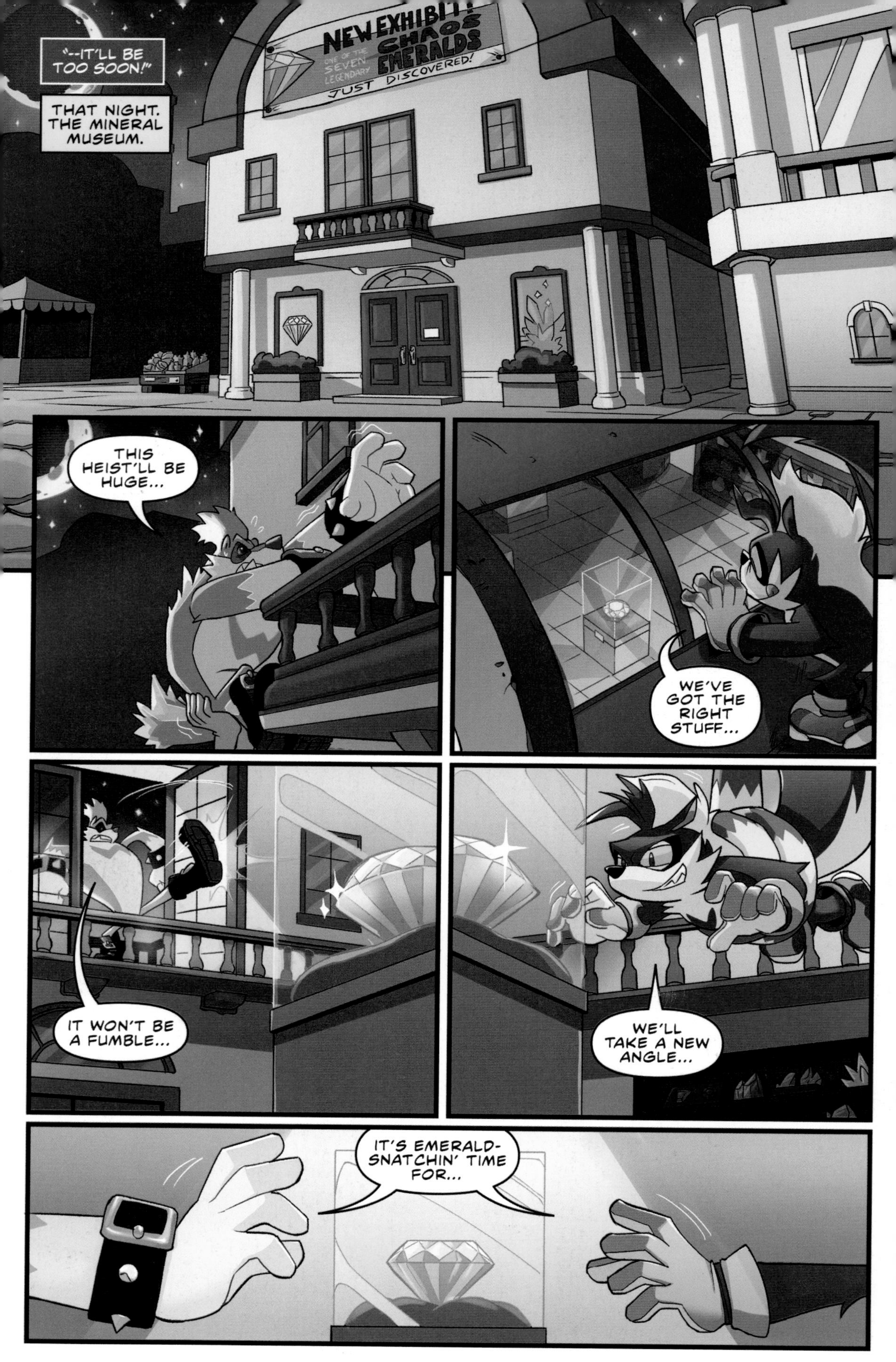
"--IT'LL BE TOO SOON!"
THAT NIGHT. THE MINERAL MUSEUM.
NEW EXHIBIT! ONE OF THE SEVEN LEGENDARY CHAOS EMERALDS JUST DISCOVERED!
THIS HEIST'LL BE HUGE...
WE'VE GOT THE RIGHT STUFF...
IT WON'T BE A FUMBLE...
WE'LL TAKE A NEW ANGLE...
IT'S EMERALD-SNATCHIN' TIME FOR...

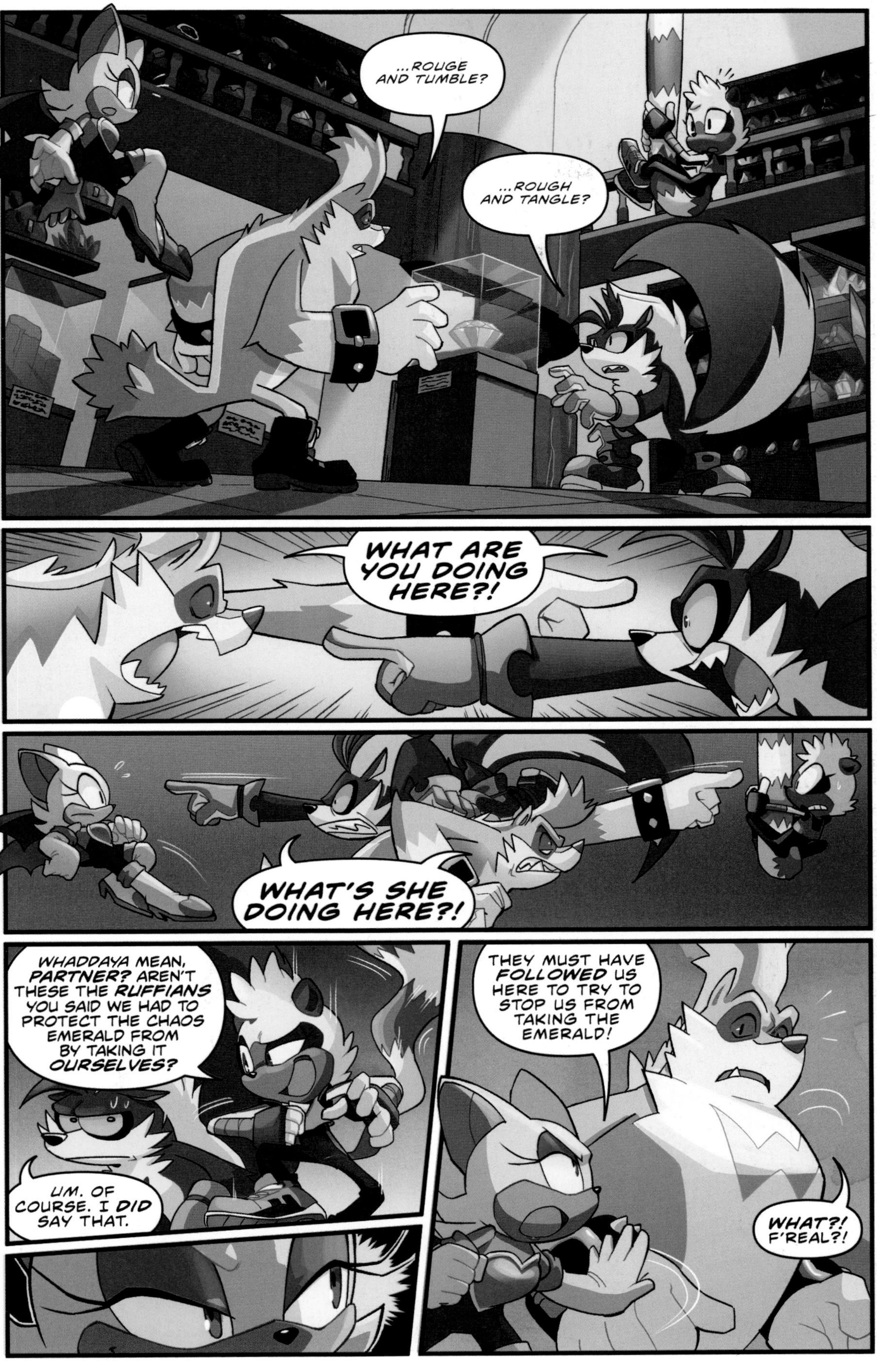
...ROUGE AND TUMBLE?
...ROUGH AND TANGLE?
WHAT ARE YOU DOING HERE?!
WHAT'S SHE DOING HERE?!
WHADDAYA MEAN, PARTNER? AREN'T THESE THE RUFFIANS YOU SAID WE HAD TO PROTECT THE CHAOS EMERALD FROM BY TAKING IT OURSELVES?
UM. OF COURSE. I DID SAY THAT.
THEY MUST HAVE FOLLOWED US HERE TO TRY TO STOP US FROM TAKING THE EMERALD!
WHAT?! F'REAL?!

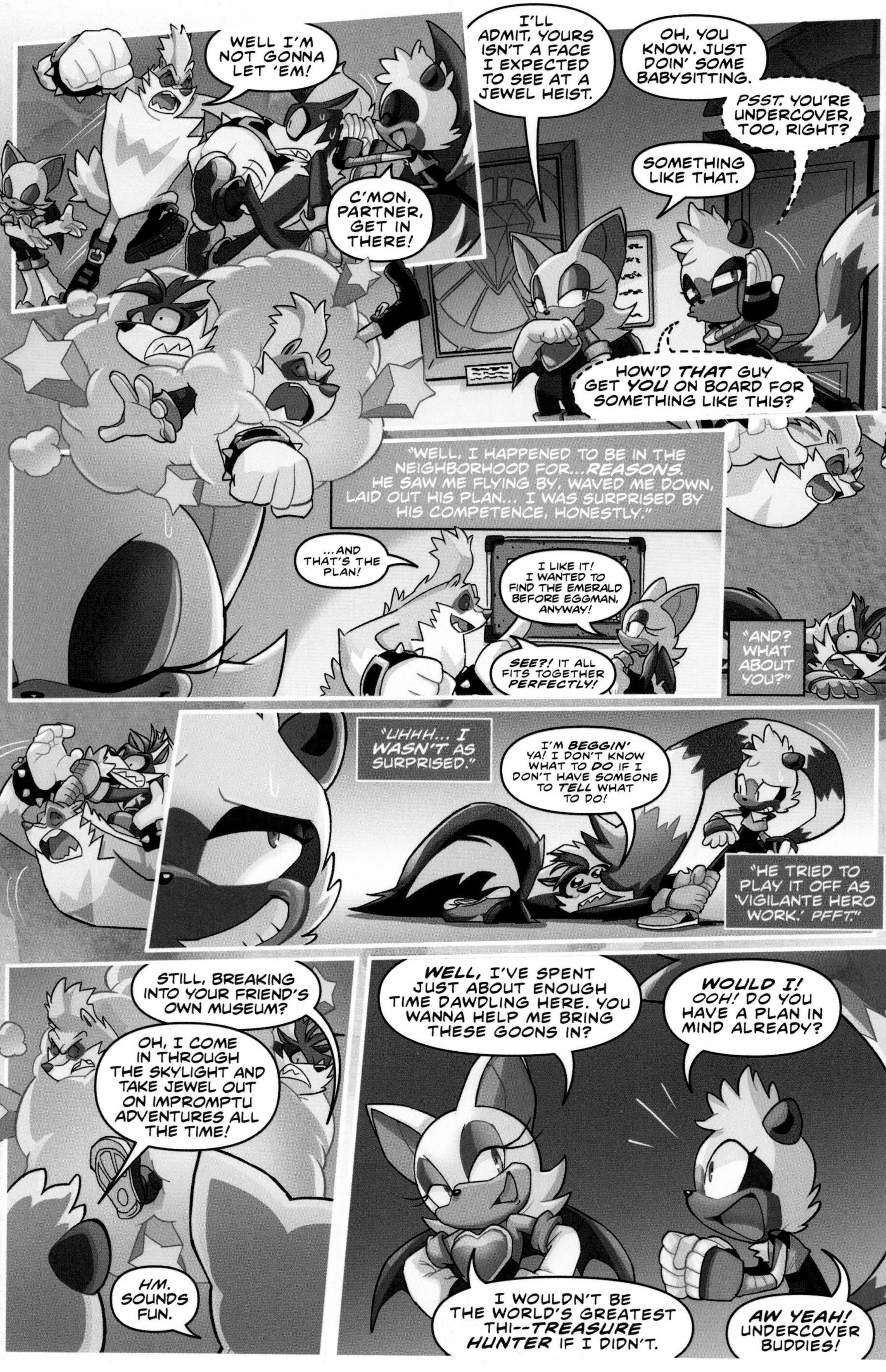
WELL I'M NOT GONNA LET 'EM!
C'MON, PARTNER, GET IN THERE!
I'LL ADMIT, YOURS ISN'T A FACE I EXPECTED TO SEE AT A JEWEL HEIST.
OH, YOU KNOW. JUST DOIN' SOME BABYSITTING.
PSST. YOU'RE UNDERCOVER, TOO, RIGHT?
SOMETHING LIKE THAT.
HOW'D THAT GUY GET YOU ON BOARD FOR SOMETHING LIKE THIS?
"WELL, I HAPPENED TO BE IN THE NEIGHBORHOOD FOR...REASONS. HE SAW ME FLYING BY, WAVED ME DOWN, LAID OUT HIS PLAN... I WAS SURPRISED BY HIS COMPETENCE, HONESTLY."
...AND THAT'S THE PLAN!
I LIKE IT! I WANTED TO FIND THE EMERALD BEFORE EGGMAN, ANYWAY!
SEE?! IT ALL FITS TOGETHER PERFECTLY!
"AND? WHAT ABOUT YOU?"
"UHHH... I WASN'T AS SURPRISED."
I'M BEGGIN' YA! I DON'T KNOW WHAT TO DO IF I DON'T HAVE SOMEONE TO TELL WHAT TO DO!
"HE TRIED TO PLAY IT OFF AS 'VIGILANTE HERO WORK.' PFFT."
STILL, BREAKING INTO YOUR FRIEND'S OWN MUSEUM?
OH, I COME IN THROUGH THE SKYLIGHT AND TAKE JEWEL OUT ON IMPROMPTU ADVENTURES ALL THE TIME!
HM. SOUNDS FUN.
WELL, I'VE SPENT JUST ABOUT ENOUGH TIME DAWDLING HERE. YOU WANNA HELP ME BRING THESE GOONS IN?
WOULD I! OOH! DO YOU HAVE A PLAN IN MIND ALREADY?
I WOULDN'T BE THE WORLD'S GREATEST THI--TREASURE HUNTER IF I DIDN'T.
AW YEAH! UNDERCOVER BUDDIES!

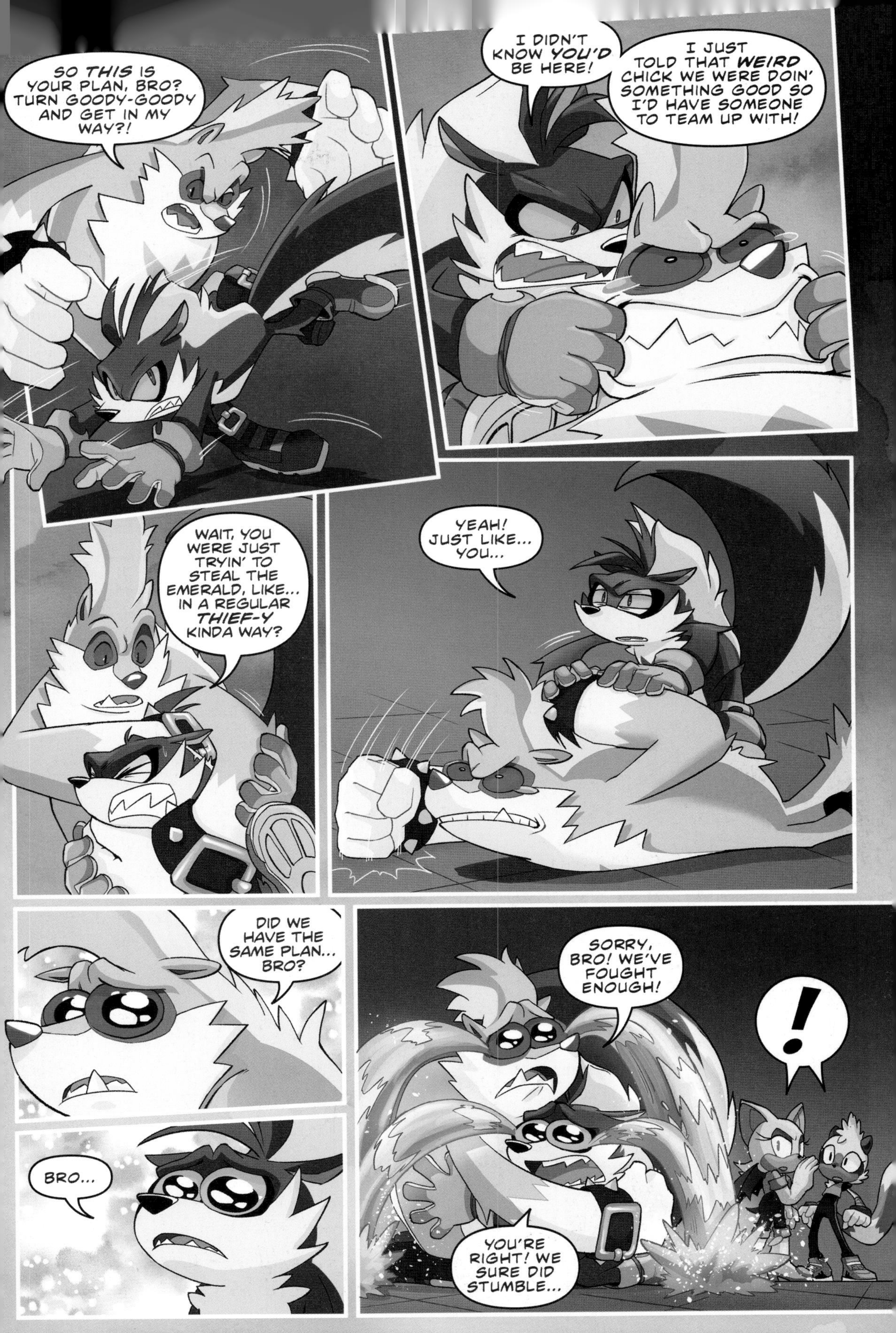
SO THIS IS YOUR PLAN, BRO? TURN GOODY-GOODY AND GET IN MY WAY?!
I DIDN'T KNOW YOU'D BE HERE!
I JUST TOLD THAT WEIRD CHICK WE WERE DOIN' SOMETHING GOOD SO I'D HAVE SOMEONE TO TEAM UP WITH!
WAIT, YOU WERE JUST TRYIN' TO STEAL THE EMERALD, LIKE... IN A REGULAR THIEF-Y KINDA WAY?
YEAH! JUST LIKE... YOU...
DID WE HAVE THE SAME PLAN... BRO?
BRO...
SORRY, BRO! WE'VE FOUGHT ENOUGH!
!
YOU'RE RIGHT! WE SURE DID STUMBLE...

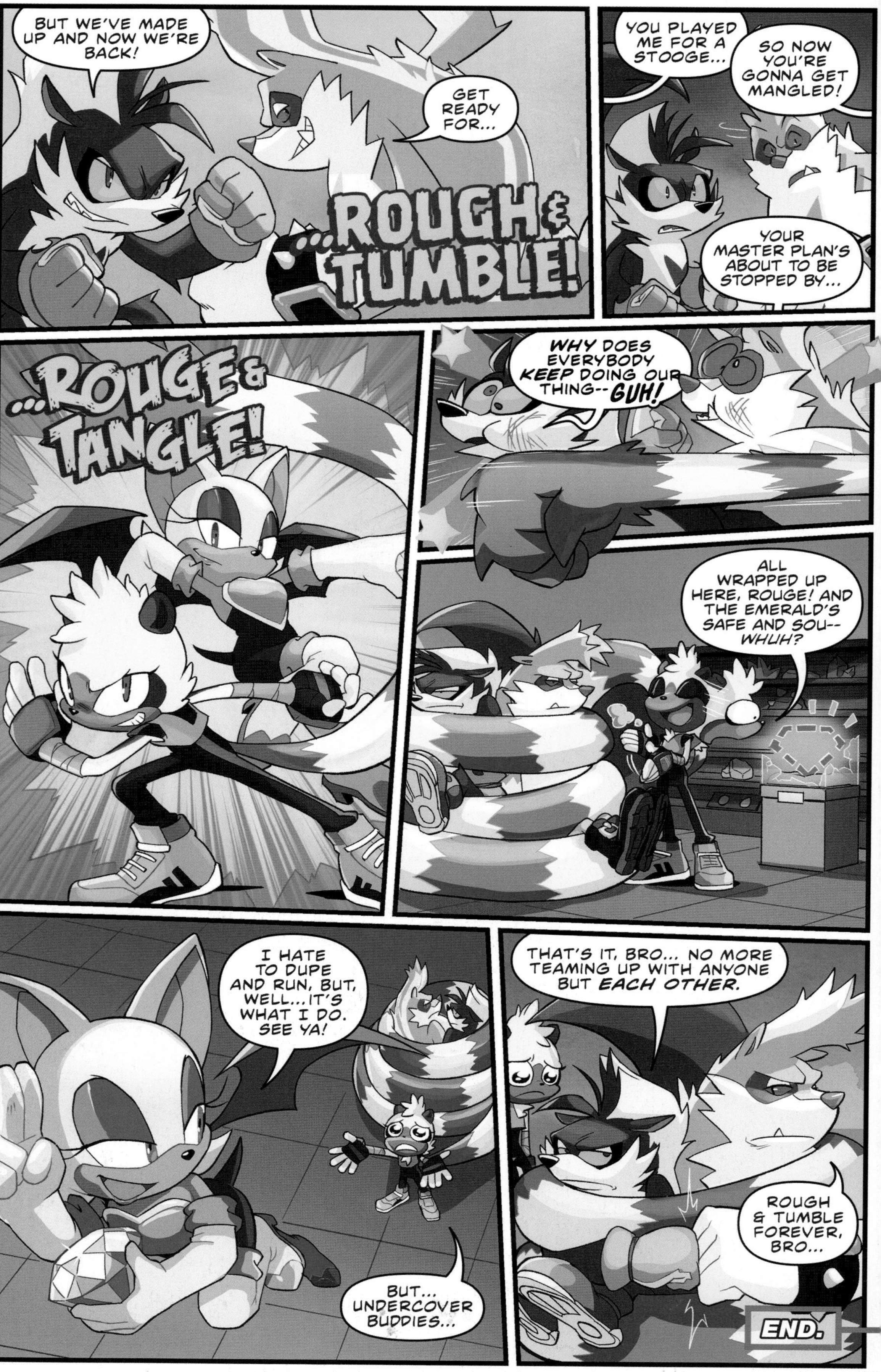
BUT WE'VE MADE UP AND NOW WE'RE BACK!
GET READY FOR...
...ROUGH & TUMBLE!
YOU PLAYED ME FOR A STOOGE...
SO NOW YOU'RE GONNA GET MANGLED!
YOUR MASTER PLAN'S ABOUT TO BE STOPPED BY...
...ROUGE & TANGLE!
WHY DOES EVERYBODY KEEP DOING OUR THING--GUH!
ALL WRAPPED UP HERE, ROUGE! AND THE EMERALD'S SAFE AND SOU-- WHUH?
I HATE TO DUPE AND RUN, BUT, WELL...IT'S WHAT I DO. SEE YA!
BUT... UNDERCOVER BUDDIES...
THAT'S IT, BRO... NO MORE TEAMING UP WITH ANYONE BUT EACH OTHER.
ROUGH & TUMBLE FOREVER, BRO...
END.

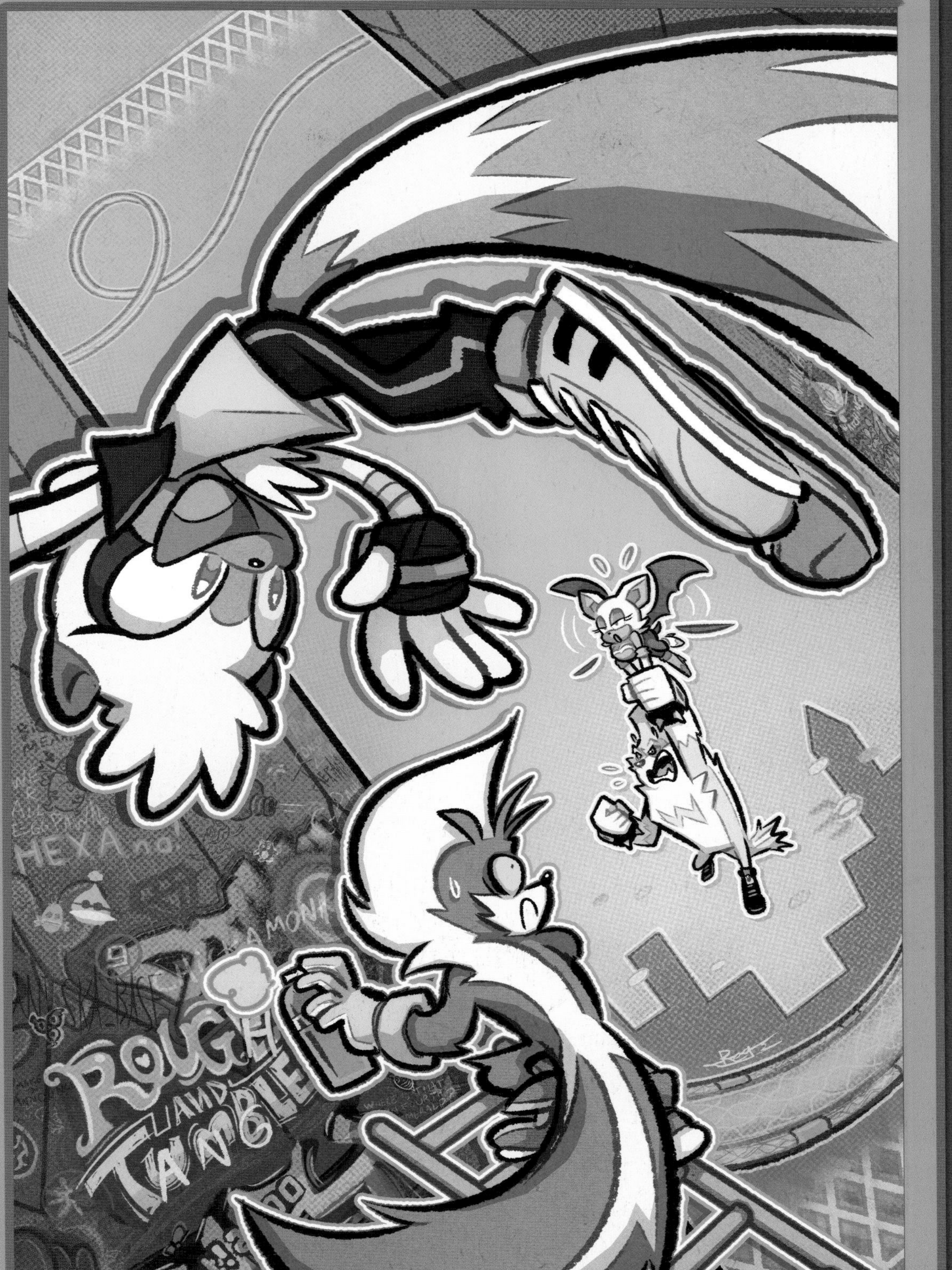
ROUGH AND TUMBLE

ART BY **REGGIE GRAHAM**

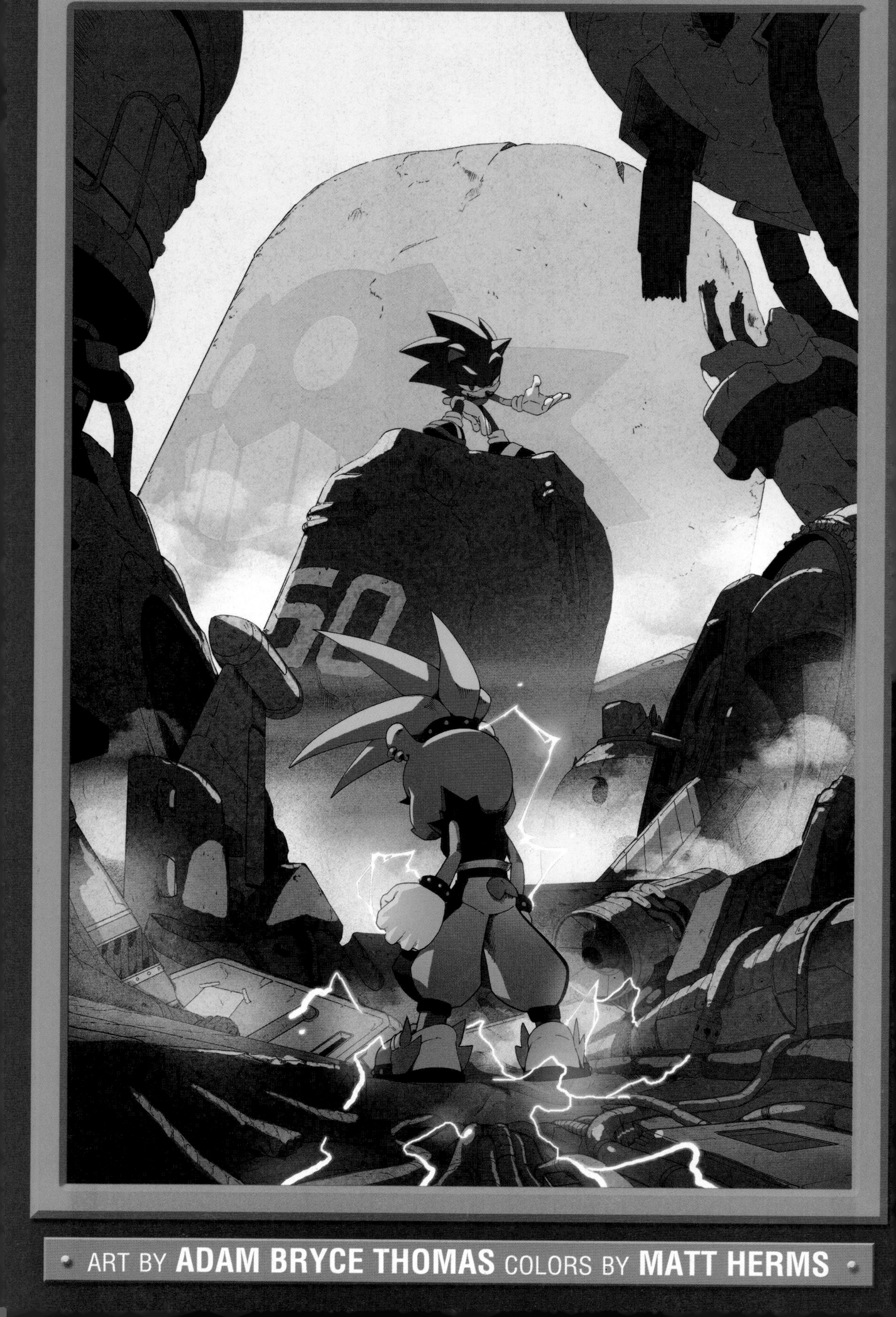
50

ART BY **ADAM BRYCE THOMAS** COLORS BY **MATT HERMS**

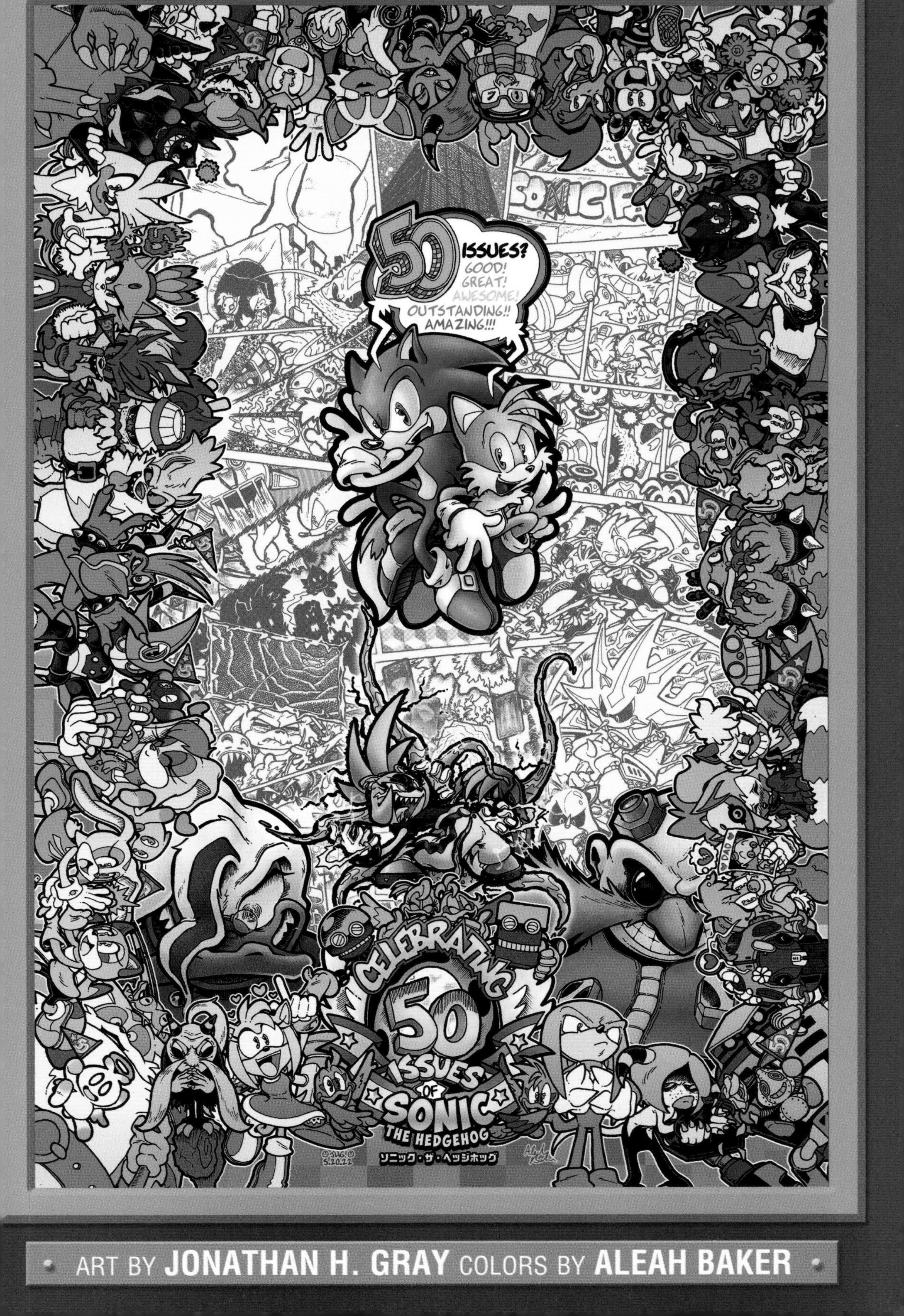
50
ISSUES?
GOOD!
GREAT!
AWESOME!
OUTSTANDING!!
AMAZING!!!
CELEBRATING
50
ISSUES
OF
SONIC
THE HEDGEHOG
ソニック・ザ・ヘッジホッグ

ART BY **JONATHAN H. GRAY** COLORS BY **ALEAH BAKER**

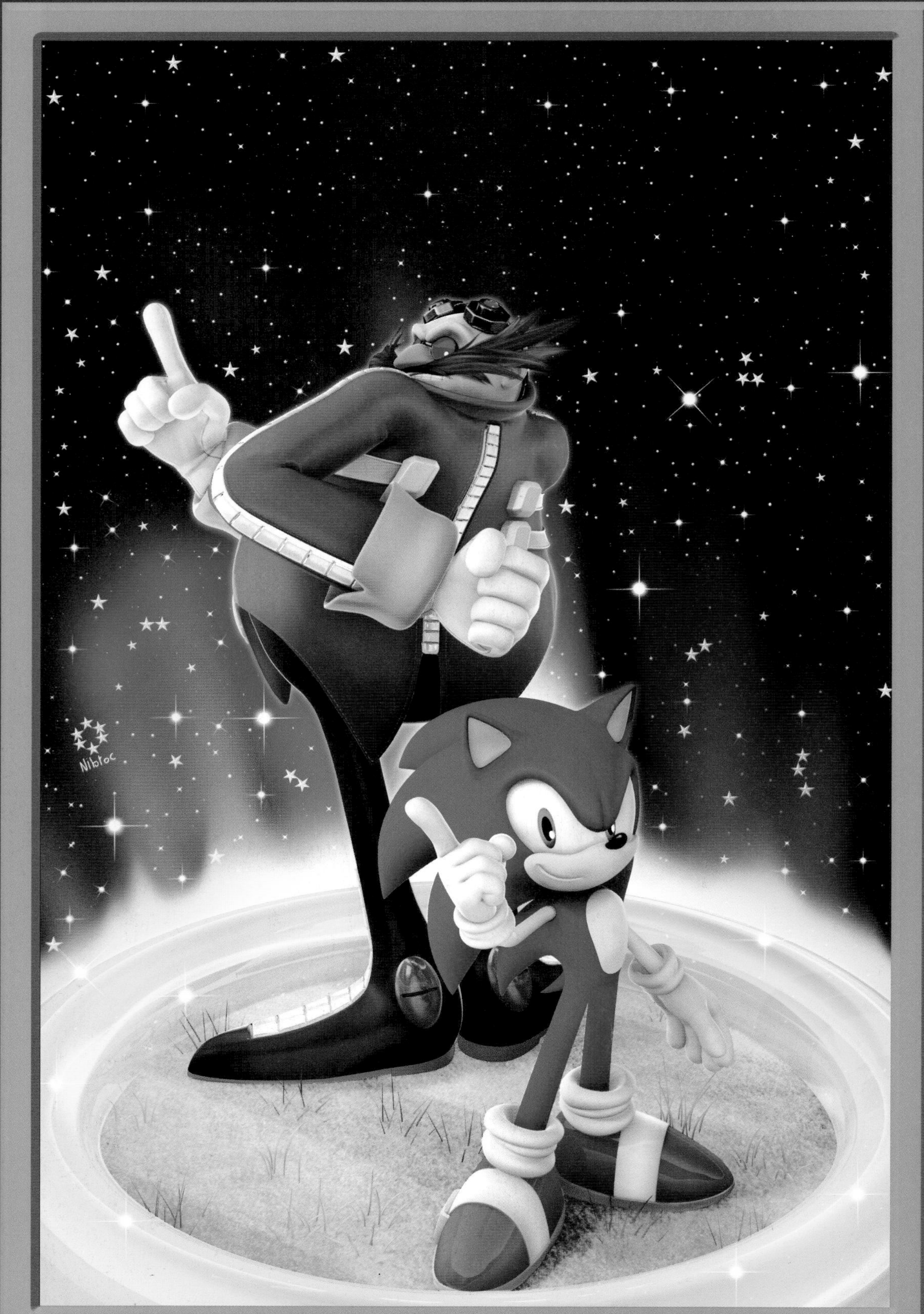
Nibroc

ART BY **NIBROC SARKARIA**

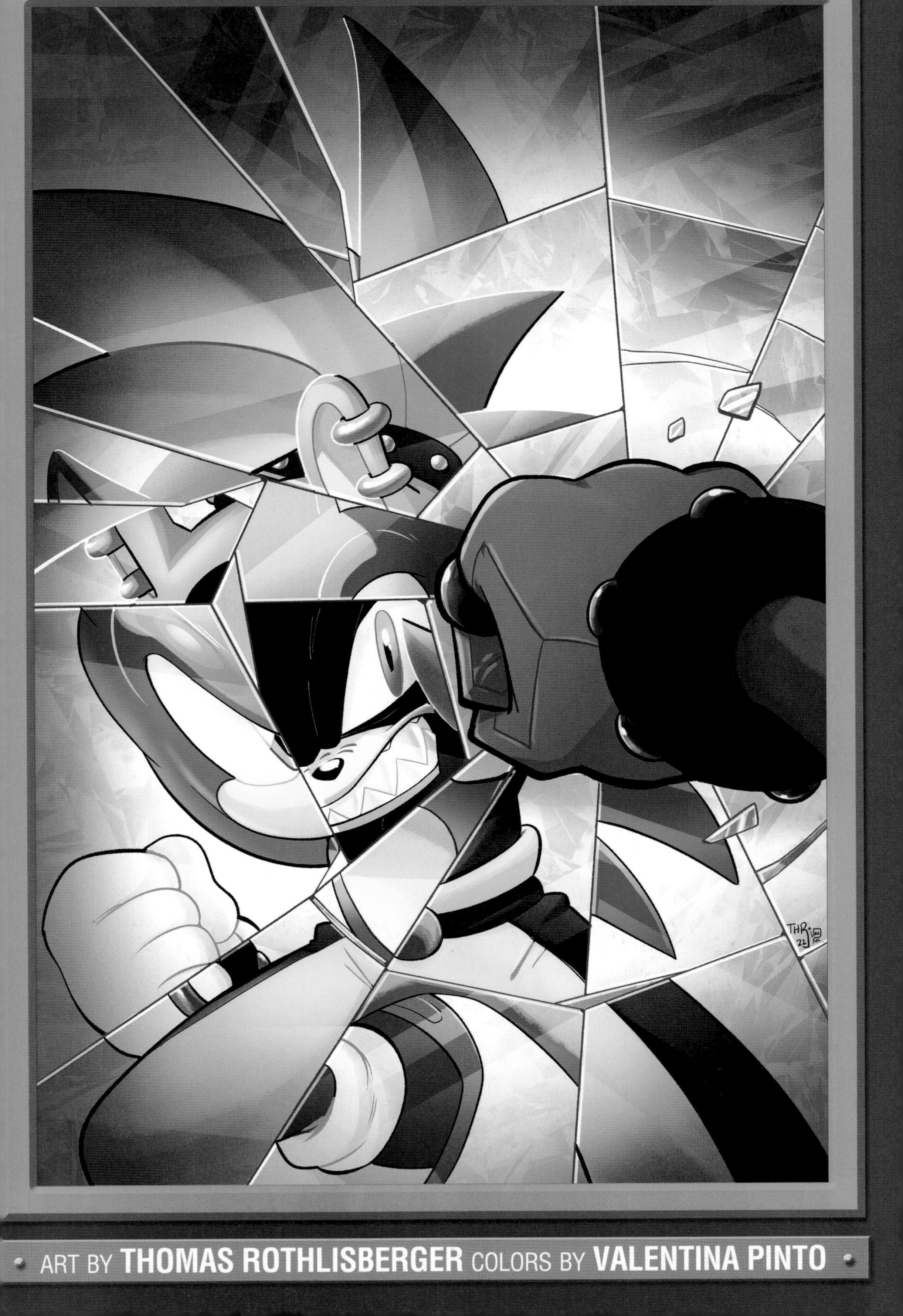

ART BY **THOMAS ROTHLISBERGER** COLORS BY **VALENTINA PINTO**

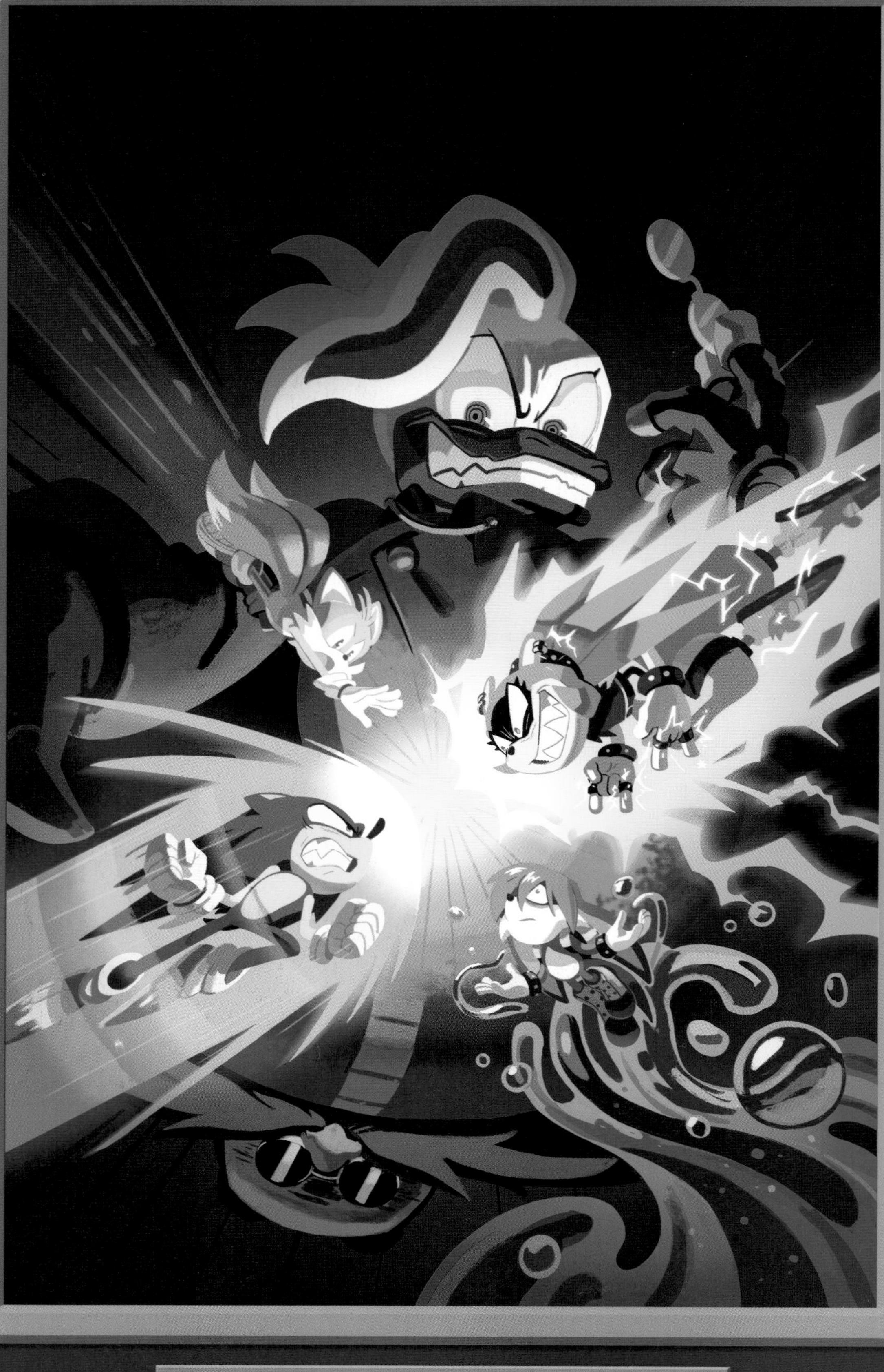

ART BY **NATHALIE FOURDRAINE**

50

ART BY **TYSON HESSE**

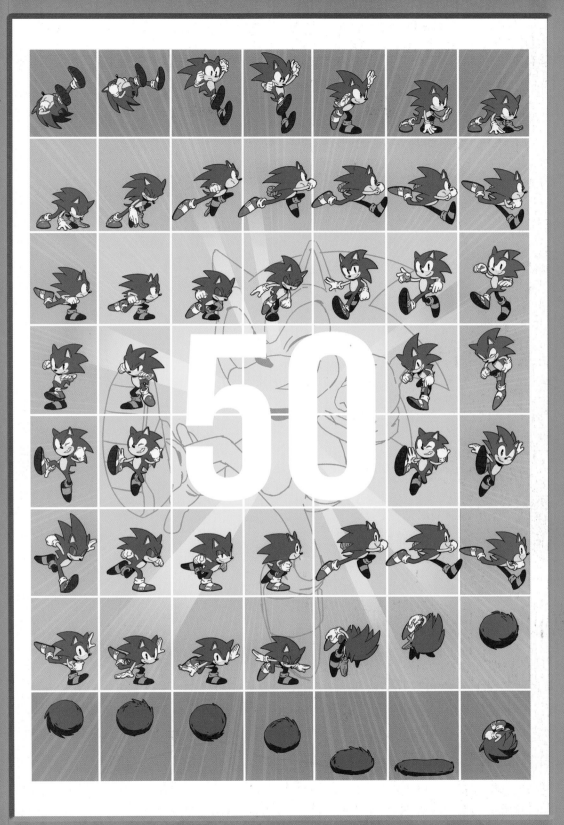

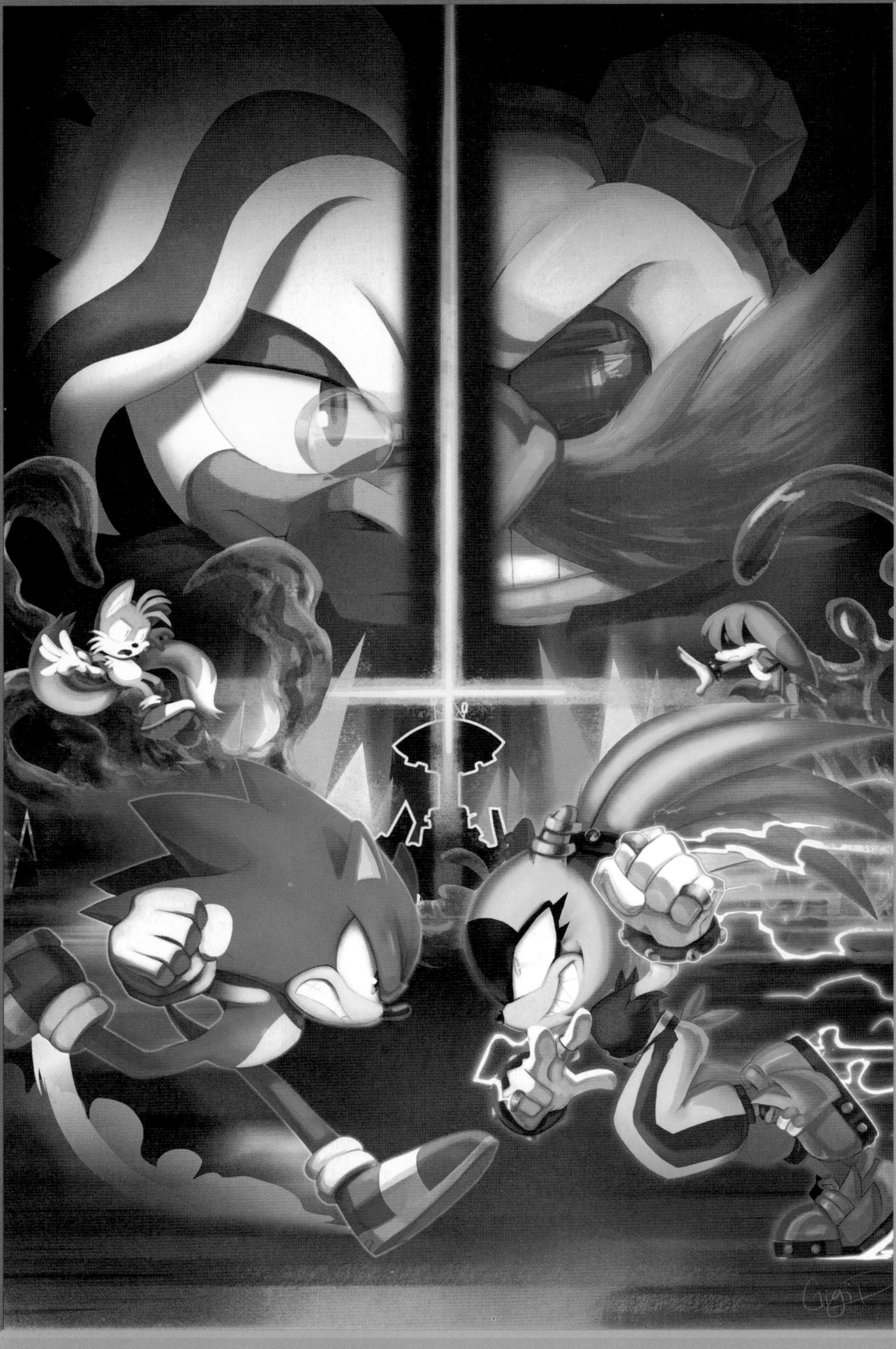

ART BY **GIGI DUTREIX**

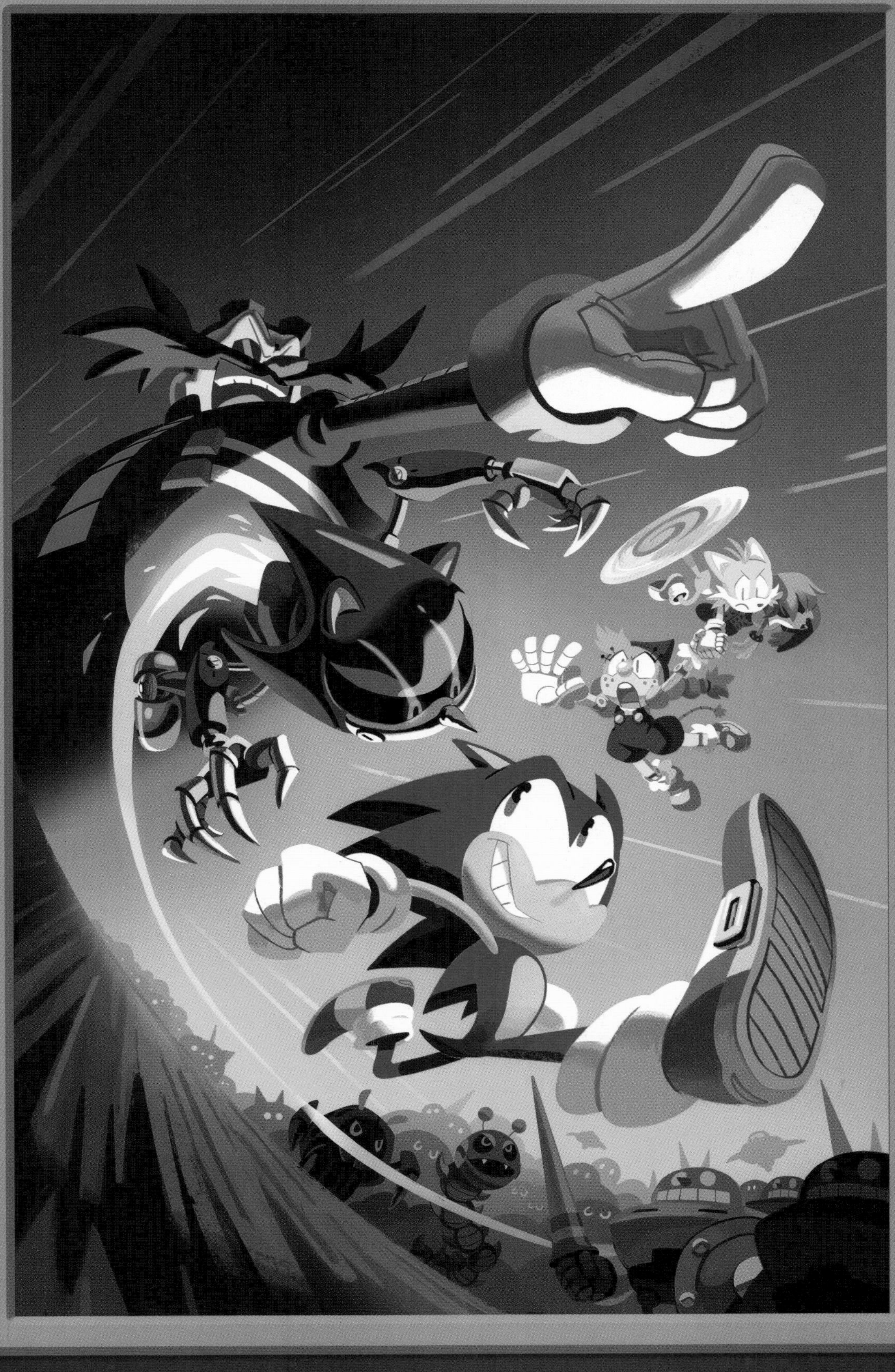

ART BY **NATHALIE FOURDRAINE**

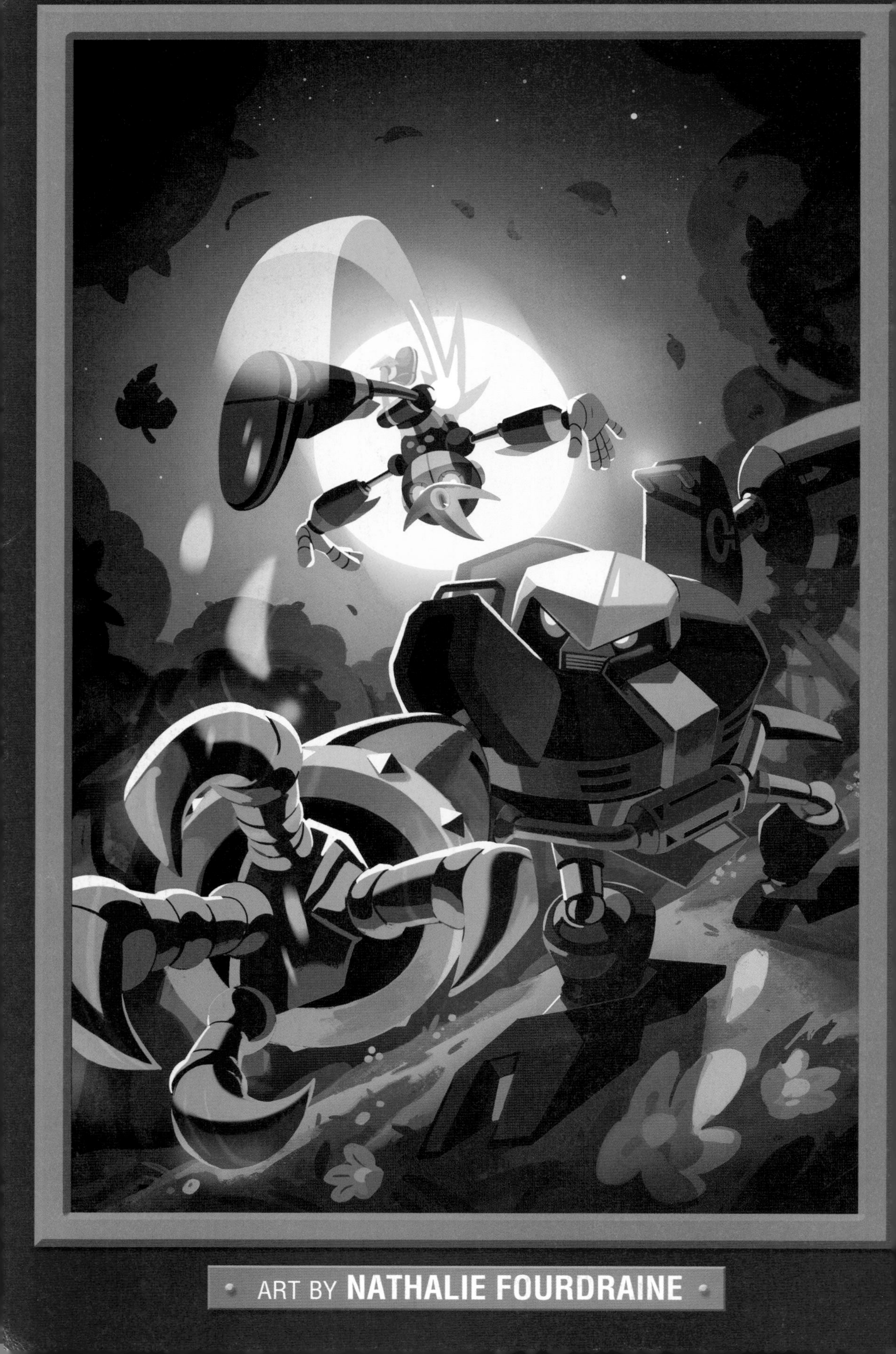

ART BY **NATHALIE FOURDRAINE**

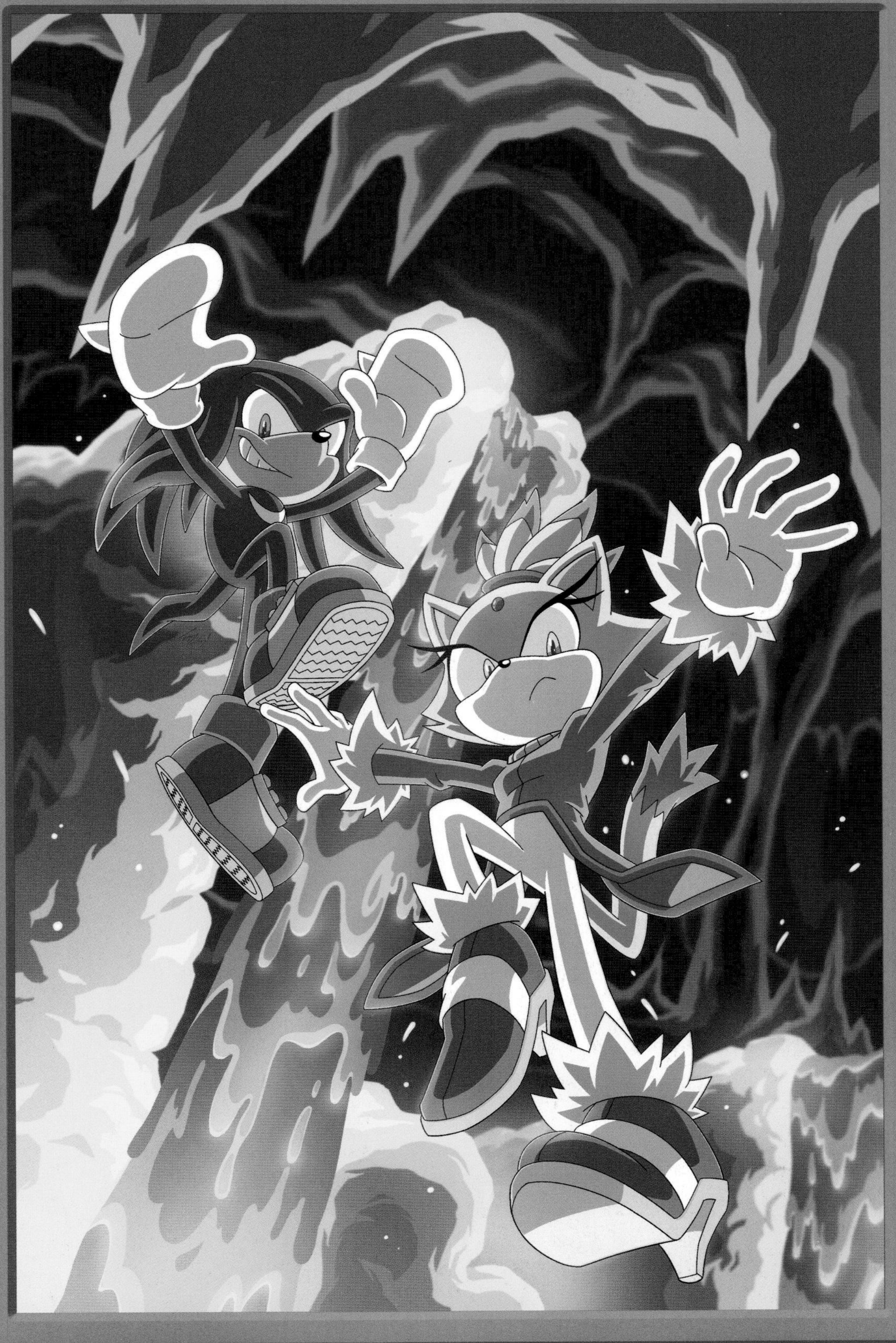

ART BY **TRACY YARDLEY**

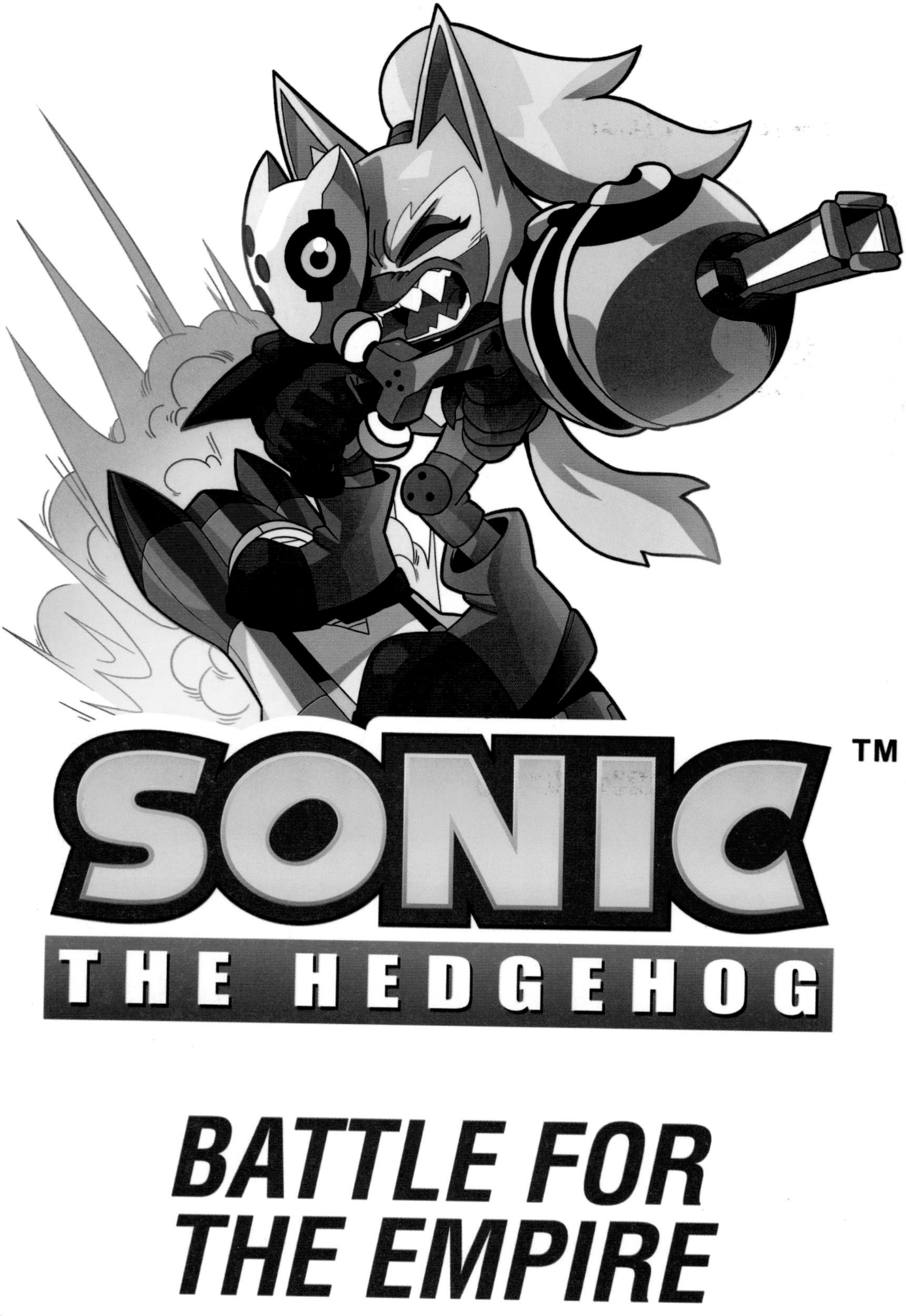

SONIC™ THE HEDGEHOG

BATTLE FOR THE EMPIRE

SEGA®